# Season of the Runer
## Book V
## A Cure for Fate

---◆---

# Abigail Linhardt

A SpaceDragon Creations book. First publication date November 8th, 2024 by SpaceDragon Creations.

Edited by J.H. Flemming. Cover art and design by Andrei Bat.

Also available in audiobook and ebook.

Paperback ISBN: 978-1-957175-22-5

Hardback ISBN: 978-1-957175-23-2

Ebook ISBN: 978-1-957175-21-8

# SEASON OF THE RUNER
# BOOK V: A CURE FOR FATE

## ABIGAIL LINHARDT

# ACKNOWLEDGMENTS

One last time I'd like to thank K.N. Nguyen for reading the early draft of this story. I could not put these books out without you and your invaluable insight.

Thanks to my brother Luke, too, for letting me bounce ideas off him and ask him about some hard hitting situations that I was too scared to write about on my own.

Big thank you to J.H. Flemming, my editor, who asked the hard hitting questions and made me tackle some major fixes. Thanks for reading these books and for diving in with me all those years ago.

Special thanks to my narrator Aaron, as well. I remember the first conversation we ever had when I was begging for a talented narrator and didn't know what I was doing. And I'm grateful every day that you auditioned for this series all those years ago and stuck with me through the whole thing. Once again, thank you for giving my words a voice.

*To the person I was before I wrote this series. I've come a long way and I know you'd be proud of me. Thank you for not giving up.*

# CONTENTS

# Chapter 1
## Conquest

Smoke wafted up from the burning thatched roofs, obscuring the carnage of the battle. Bodies littered the streets of Gypsu and blood ran in the gutter. Fire took the structures, heating the night.

Tarkan stepped over a dead priest as he entered the golden throne hall of the pharaoh of Gypsu. The ruler knelt on the floor, Acenoth looming over him with his weapon drawn. The pharaoh, a black-haired cat-like Masahk, glared up at Tarkan as he entered, flanked by his Apostles. He held his great bloody blade in his left hand and commanded a host of risen with his right as he entered the throne hall.

"Heretic," the pharaoh spat, his black fur standing on end down the back of his neck. His feline ears pressed down hard into his black hair. "Blood fiend. Foreigner."

"Are these to be your last words?" Tarkan asked, coming to a stop before the pharaoh. Outside, the crash of a building succumbing to the flames echoed into the open hall. Tarkan looked around at the slaughtered royal guard. "I am glad you put up a valiant fight, your majesty. I would hate to take Gypsu more easily."

"The others will come for you, Necro'Khan," the pharaoh hissed. "You will not take all of Alika."

Tarkan offered the bound pharaoh a condescending smile. "It's not

Alika I want. But I already have it. Sokar'Xenoteph is my prisoner, and the ruby throne is mine. Your stubbornness and bravery are wasted, my king." Tarkan looked up to Acenoth and nodded. He had no more words for the conquered pharaoh.

Acenoth raised his scythe and brought it down with a powerful swing, severing the pharaoh's head from his neck. The feline's head spun and rolled down the steps to the side of the throne room. Tarkan watched it, bored with the bloodshed. He turned to his Apostles.

"A portion of the One Thousand and One will stay with you," he said. He turned to an Apostle at his side. "Kalmar, you shall sit upon the vacant throne and the rest of you will answer to him."

The other Apostles all bowed and nodded to Kalmar, who smiled darkly.

"Keep your risen close," Tarkan advised. "Do not let your guard down. Make the city submit. If they do not, kill them. We are not to show mercy even once."

"Yes, my Khan," Kalmar said with a deep bow.

"We will leave three hundred of the undead behind," Tarkan went on. "Acenoth, return to Mysir and tell Ashkan and Faraji that I will return once I have Gypsu under control."

Acenoth bowed and turned, leaving the throne room.

Tarkan knelt and picked up the head of the pharaoh. "We must show the people," he said. He handed the head to Kalmar. "Put it on a stake in the city square so they understand what has happened. Slaughter any who speak. Once you have finished in the square, go to the temple and offer the Kehann their lives for their service. Any who refuse, kill them."

Tarkan turned on his heel and marched out of the throne hall into the palace to inspect his work. He stepped over bodies and splashed through puddles of blood on his way out. He almost coughed on the smoke, but pushed the urge away as he exited the palace and looked over the city from a partially destroyed balcony. Below, Gypsu burned. He watched as best he could as his soldiers finished the job, milling through the streets slowly. They slaughtered any who stood up to run. The once white sands were splashed with red. He watched until his mind wandered, leaving the streets of Gypsu.

In his mind's eye, he saw Porsh, still and glassy. He remembered his brother and Ishmael. Thinking of his family made him tighten his grip on the sword where his father's heart pulsed with power. Before he could stop it, he thought of Zeva and the battle he'd won for her. His chest twinged in slight pain as his dead heart ached for her.

He stopped as he was about to step over one more body on the balcony. It was a young cat-like Masahk girl. She wore the gold and white of the royal family and had no shoes on her little feet. Her long black hair was bloodied from a wound on her head. A twisted expression of worry and fear warped her young face. Tarkan looked down at her and inspected her more closely. She had to be the pharaoh's daughter.

*So young,* he thought to himself. She, no doubt, was innocent. Like Zeva.

He shoved those thoughts aside. It had become easier and easier to put those feelings aside, and he was glad of it.

"Sira," Kalmar whispered from behind him.

Tarkan inhaled in slight shock, unaware of the Apostle sneaking up behind him. He didn't turn to face Kalmar as he approached, instead locking his eyes on the young girl.

"The palace is secured and the temple is locked down," Kalmar reported.

Tarkan blinked. How long had he been standing, taking in the violence? Time seemed to pass differently since he'd gained his immortality. He glanced to the east. The sky began to purple, showing the sun would rise soon. He blinked away the shock and inclined his head to Kalmar.

"And the Kehann?" he asked.

"Those who sided with us have been spared," Kalmar informed him. "Those who stood up to us now line the streets on pikes as a warning to others. As does the head of their pharaoh."

Tarkan gripped the alabaster rail of the balcony and took in a deep, satisfied breath. "You have done well. All of you have. I am pleased."

Kalmar bowed deeply, a slight smirk on his face. "I am honored to have pleased you. What is your next step, my Khan? What can I do for you?"

In truth, Tarkan wanted to be left alone with his thoughts. Yes, the conquest was necessary, but it tired him, not just in his body, but in his power as well. Sustaining the magic that kept the undead alive had been taxing over the last several weeks. He wanted to fight his own battles, but had been relegated to the sidelines once again because of the magic. He could not partake in the slaughter, and that frustrated him. He wanted to rest, but there was so much more to do.

"I will return to Mysir," he said with a heavy sigh. "I will take a small host with me."

"You will not travel through the God Deep?" Kalmar asked.

Tarkan shook his head. "Not this time. I want to see the devastation we have wrought upon Alika. And I want them to see me."

The return journey to Mysir only took a few days since he traveled slowly down the river, taking in the ravaged land. Exhausted from the battle for Gypsu and the travel, Tarkan went to the Dynast Palace to rest. When he arrived, Ashkan met him at the gate and followed him inside. The Apostle saw the dark circles around Tarkan's eyes.

"Acenoth told us little of the battle," Ashkan said as they trudged through the halls of the palace toward the throne room. "Was it a success?"

"We are unkillable, Ashkan," Tarkan said with a small smile. "We slaughtered the pharaoh and took his palace. Soon the city will fall, and we can move on."

"Where to next, my Khan?" The Apostle didn't sound eager, but Tarkan knew Ashkan only followed him out of fear for his own life. He had no loyalty outside his survival.

Tarkan thought about his answer before he spoke. "Xia. With the north under our control, I doubt any on Alika will stand up to us. And we have the most precious thing to Alika: the Dynast Pharaoh."

They entered the throne room. It had changed since Tarkan had taken over. The gold seemed dimmer and the moats had dried up. The plants wilted, and some had even turned to ash. It was as if Tarkan's very presence brought a blight to the palace.

Lying on the floor before the throne was Sokar, chained by a metal collar around his neck to the foot of the throne. Nearby, standing watch over him and also shackled, was Nasor. The Vizier had a limp from a wound in one leg, and injury he'd sustained during the initial battle for the palace that hadn't healed properly. He stood, favoring his good leg as he watched over Sokar. When Tarkan entered, Nasor's ears pressed back into his black hair and a small snarl curved his canine lips. Sokar raised his head. Spotting Tarkan, he cowered against the side of the throne, keeping his head bowed low. His long, feathery ears drooped in fear and apprehension. Nearby, a jailor armed with a whip and the keys stood waiting for orders. Sometimes Tarkan put the pair in the prison below the palace. Other times, he liked to have them where he could see them, reminding him of all he'd accomplished.

Tarkan marched up to the ruby throne, knowing his Apostles would want an audience with him, and sat down. He sighed heavily, weary and tired, resting his arms on the throne. He glared down at Sokar. The pharaoh gulped when he made eye contact and shivered in fright. Tarkan imagined finishing the boy off, stabbing him with his blood blade and soaking up that precious, golden blood of his. He idly wondered what the boy's Masahk gift was as he finished out the bloody image in his mind.

Sokar gasped and looked away, shaking.

"My Khan," Ashkan said, looking up at Tarkan from the lower floor. "The Apostles wish to have an audience with you."

"As I suspected," Tarkan said, waving his bone-thin hand. "But first, I need sustenance." His eyes flitted to Nasor, then to Sokar briefly. The pharaoh remained curled at his feet.

Ashkan nodded and motioned to Faraji, who stood nearby. The taller, more savage Apostle left to do Tarkan's bidding. Ashkan then said, "We have two men, sheikhs from the south, in our custody."

Tarkan frowned. "And?"

"They were trying to stir an uprising, my Khan," Ashkan informed him. "We caught them and put down their followers. But we thought you'd want to handle them." He motioned to the grand doors. "Shall I have them brought before you?"

Wan and feeling sick, an audience with rebels was the last thing Tarkan wanted. But there was no time like the present. Besides, he was still bloody and dirty from the battle in Gypsu. It might lend credence to his position. He waved his hand, motioning Ashkan to bring in the sheikhs. Ashkan turned and snapped his fingers at the guards near the doors. They opened them and a small host of kehann from the temple entered. Between them were two shackled men in what had once been royal robes. They looked just as tired and dirty as Tarkan felt.

No sooner had they been marched to the foot of the stairs that ascended to the ruby throne than one spat at Tarkan's feet. Tarkan blanched and stood up. He gripped his blood blade and descended the stairs to face the men.

"You will fall, Necro'Khan," one of them, clearly older, said from behind barred teeth. "Alika will not stand for a usurper risen from the slaves."

Tarkan almost laughed. "I was no slave, sira. I was born and raised on Porsh. I care not for my brothers and sisters in chains here on Alika. Those who did not convert and submit to being Scriven have been executed. I am no risen slave."

The sheikh looked confused then. "No matter," he said after a moment. "Alika will not let a Necro'Khan walk free. You will be stopped."

"Will I?" Tarkan raised his blade and shoved it through the older man's middle with a single thrust.

The man's eyes went wide and his mouth popped open in shock. He groaned and leaned over the blade as his blood seeped out and dribbled onto the stone floor.

With a mighty pull, Tarkan removed the sword and stepped back as the man fell.

"Father!" the younger man shouted, straining against his captors.

Tarkan turned to him. "I will give you a chance to pledge yourself and your people to me. Fight for me in the south when the time comes and you shall be spared."

The young man glared at Tarkan through tears of rage. "Never," he spat.

Tarkan sighed and turned, his eyes landing on Sokar. When they did, the young pharaoh gasped and tried to make himself as small as he could. Tarkan reached toward Sokar and merely had to think of what he wanted to do. No spells, no words. Just intent.

Sokar yelped in pain and writhed on the floor as Tarkan pulled blood from his very veins with a wave of his hand.

"Necromancer, don't," Nasor begged, pulling on his own chains.

The pharaoh's body bent backward from the torment of having his blood pulled from his body and out his pores. He moaned and soon wailed in agony until Tarkan held a small orb of his Masahk blood. The orb floated above his palm. Sokar panted, lying prone as blood trickled from his eyes and ears.

Tarkan turned back to the young lord, holding the orb of immortal blood. He thought about his intent again and the blood began to dissipate into mist in the air. As it did, the sheikh on the floor jerked and moaned, coming back to life. The risen corpse rose to its feet and faced the other man.

"Father?" the young man gasped. "What—?"

The risen man drew his blade and swung it, stopping just before cutting the younger man's neck. The younger man winced, closing his eyes.

"Pledge your people and your swords to me," Tarkan said, almost bored with the interaction. He held the risen still while the young lord opened his eyes again. "You must understand," Tarkan went on, "you have no hope of standing up to me. I have my hands around the throat of more than just Alika. You cannot comprehend what is going on beyond the borders of your country."

The man swallowed hard, eyeing Tarkan. "And if I don't bend my knee to you?"

The Necro'Khan smiled, hoping he would deny him. He wanted to see more blood. "Then I send my undead army to the south and conquer the lands there as easily as I did Gypsu. You weren't there. You didn't see how the great city fell before me. Look into your father's eyes and know the truth."

7

The man glanced at his risen father and finally nodded. "As you command, my Khan."

Disappointed, Tarkan let the risen fall. He snapped his fingers and had the kehann see the man out and remove the corpse. He turned back to Sokar and Nasor where they waited, shackled. Sokar pushed himself up to sitting and attempted a defiant glare. Tarkan briefly thought about seizing the whip from his jailor and flogging the boy within an inch of his life. Imagined his golden-red immortal blood flowing freely from his smooth, bronze flesh.

Sokar shuddered. "Alika will rebel against you, necromancer," he spat as boldly as he could.

Tarkan took up his blade and gently pressed the tip into the underside of Sokar's chin, forcing him to look up and meet his eyes. He imagined pushing the blade forward, shoving it into the pharaoh's neck.

Sokar gulped and tried to pull away, but the chain around his neck went taut, holding him in place. "No, please," he whispered.

At this, Tarkan paused. He tilted his head curiously. The boy was reacting as if he could read Tarkan's mind. Like he knew his thoughts, had seen the image he'd conjured in the privacy of his own mind.

*Your Masahk magic,* he thought. *You can hear what is inside my mind?*

The pharaoh sobbed softly, tears filling his eyes, having been found out. "I'm sorry," he whispered, pleading. "I can't control it when I'm afraid. I can't hear everything. Just parts. It's too loud. It makes me afraid."

Sudden rage ignited in Tarkan. His every emotion, thought, plan— it was all laid bare to this boy he'd kept at his side for the last several weeks. Making him bleed would hardly be justice enough for his spying. Tarkan spun and dropped his blade. He grabbed the whip from the jailer's belt, raised his arm, and brought the tail down across Sokar's chest. The Masahk screamed and rolled over, arms over his head as Tarkan brought the whip down again and again on his bare back. Nasor roared beside him, but couldn't pull free of his own shackles.

Tarkan put his entire body into swinging the whip, watching as Sokar's blood splattered out. He smiled when flecks of it hit his face.

Sokar tried to pull his one wing over his back to shield himself from the lashing, but the damage had already been done. Tarkan stopped, gasping for air and looked down on his work. Sokar sobbed and moaned where he lay in a puddle of his own blood.

Tarkan laid his right hand on the pharaoh's flayed back and ran it down his spine. When he lifted his hand, it was covered in the golden-red blood of the Masahk. Tarkan lifted his fingers to his mouth and slowly licked the blood away. Once he swallowed it, noise, voices, breath, the beating of hearts—all converged in his mind. It was as Sokar had described: loud.

The thoughts bombarded his brain, coming from the jailer, Nasor, Sokar, and the guards in the hall. He couldn't distinguish who the individual thoughts belonged to, and they reverberated in his skull. He tried to focus on Sokar and finally heard the boy's voice alone. He was weeping in his own mind, praying for the pain to stop. He was afraid.

As quick as it came, it went. Tarkan winced and rubbed at his temples, a dull ache left behind in the blood power's wake.

"That is why I cannot abide court," Sokar said weakly. "I can hear their thoughts. Their pleas and prayers. Everything they want from me. I know how they see me." His arms shook as he tried to push himself up. Too weakened from the beating, he fell back to the ground with a moan.

"Sokar," Nasor said, worry creasing his canine brow. "Are you all right?"

The boy didn't reply; he just lay in a heap upon the floor, breathing hard.

"You must control yourself in my presence," Tarkan growled. "Enter my mind again and..." He imagined flaying Sokar's flesh from his bones while he screamed. Imagined plucking his beautiful green and gold feathering from his soft body. He glanced down at the pharaoh.

Sokar gave no sign that he had read Tarkan's mind then.

"Did you never read Sharar's mind?" Tarkan asked. He dropped the whip with a clatter and lowered himself onto the ruby throne.

Sokar shook his head weakly. "I never had need. He told me everything. I promised him on the day Father died to trust him. To never read his mind. I never feared him, so it was easy."

Annoyed, Tarkan balled his hands into fists. The boy was just as useless as he'd guessed on day one. There was no point in keeping him, except to put him on display to Alika should he need to.

"Faraji," Tarkan called.

The necromancer entered, looking attentive.

"Get Ashkan. We sail for Xia soon. We will take three hundred of the undead with us. Acenoth will stay in Alika."

Faraji nodded, but frowned. "Is it wise to weaken our hold here? Do you trust the kehann and the others to fight for you?"

Tarkan weakly smiled. "Once they are in the heat of battle, they will fight for themselves, to preserve their own lives. Yes, they will fight for me. And we need not leave many behind on Xia. Once I am finished with Xia, they will be fighting among themselves." His smile spread.

# Chapter 2
# A Sorcerer's Diplomacy

The pages of the Mahit'Onomicon were thick and stiff in Sharar's hand as he turned yet another page. His eyes ran over the strange text as it danced before him, coming into focus one word at a time. Or at least, that's how it felt to him. The script was not simply words, but more like ideas and understanding. Each time he read a page, something new came to him. He stood in his study in his wing of the sultana's palace, leaning over the desk while he read the book. The opulent room was gilded in every touch of finery he could have asked for, but he didn't care about that so much. Soft gauzy curtains blew in the gentle desert breeze, a grand balcony waited to the room's left, a large mirror reflected almost the entire room back, and a bed covered in silks waited to the right of him.

The clinking of chains was the only sound that broke his concentration from time to time. Vicdan lay on the floor near the balcony, chained and bridled. Sharar had forced him to wear black robes to stave off any haunts that might be drawn to such a creature as a necromancer, and Vicdan had hated it. His pale hands and bare feet stuck out against the dark swaths around his body. He'd gotten paler and thinner than before, refusing to eat what Sharar supplied for him:

blood and flesh. If the necromancer didn't eat soon, he'd be useless to him.

He'd thought about torturing Vicdan the way he had Tarkan. That seemed to make the necromancer more pliable. But he didn't have the means. Yes, the sultana's palace had a dungeon and even a few tempting devices for bringing pain. But none of them satisfied his need. So he turned to the book instead.

Sharar looked up as Vicdan shifted on the floor in a shallow sleep. Despite knowing the necromancer was his prisoner, he enjoyed conversation with the once-singer. Vicdan was educated, didn't need history explained to him at every turn, and—despite the occasional jibe—often had intelligent things to say. It was a pity he had to be bridled more often than not.

Frustrated with the book, Sharar moved around the desk to Vicdan and gave his face a swift kick to wake him up. The necromancer moaned in pain and blood dribbled out from between his lips. He glared up at Sharar. The sun had not yet risen, so the room was dark save for a few oil lamps.

"The sun will rise soon," Sharar said in a soft whisper. "We must be ready to meet our guests."

Vicdan coughed and spat out blood in reply. He weakly pushed himself up into a sitting position and looked out the exit to the balcony to look for the sun. He sighed and shook his head to dislodge the pain. His arms were shackled behind his back.

"This book angers me more than it enlightens me," Sharar said, turning back to the desk and marching to the book. "It's like each new page is a riddle to be solved."

Vicdan gave a half-hearted groan at this.

"Yes," Sharar mused, touching the pages and once again reading the script there. "It is a book written by the gods. I suppose it's not meant to be understood as I imagined. But there's more." He turned and looked Vicdan in his green eyes. "I have been reading about sorcerers in these pages, and I don't like what I have learned."

Vicdan swallowed nervously.

Sharar flipped to the next page, his eyes dancing over the script. "Two spells," he said. "I can only sustain two spells at once because I made two wishes on the djinn. The damned thing. It knew. I was afraid to make too many wishes since each one empowers a djinn, you see. I didn't want to give the demon more power than I had to. Enough to break free, perhaps. That's always a risk. So I have done this to myself."

He looked up when Vicdan didn't say anything and sighed. Then he marched back across the room and roughly unlocked the bridle, tossing it aside.

"Speak," he commanded.

Vicdan waited a moment, savoring the sensation of having the sharp metal removed from his mouth. Then he said, "Fear keeps us all in check, I suppose."

Sharar half nodded and went back to his desk to bend over the book again. He flipped another page. "I am master of the elements. I can move things with my mind. I can heal. The storms bend their knees to me, and yet..." He stopped, dolefully looking down at the book.

"You are not satisfied?" Vicdan tried.

"I am not satisfied," Sharar parroted softly. "I sense there must be more. Something I am missing. Something I don't understand." He ran a finger over the page and sighed with longing. "There must be more. Like the gods are taunting me. Daring me to speak with them. To ask them."

"What more can you want?" Vicdan asked.

Outside, thunder rolled over the sky. Sharar turned his head to glance at Vicdan over his shoulder. "I want the power of life and death in my hands. To be able to speak the words and take a man's spirit from his body. To raise the dead and bring back a life stolen too soon. I want to guide the stars across the sky. I want the map to fear my absolute power. I want ultimate understanding, to have nothing be a mystery to me ever again."

Vicdan frowned slightly. "Your ambition outreaches the boundaries of this world, Sharar. You don't want to be a sorcerer; you want to be a god." He clicked his tongue in mock resignation. "You'll have to settle for sorcerer, I'm afraid."

Sharar glared at Vicdan, not appreciating his audacity.

Before he could retaliate, a knock sounded on the door. Sharar called for the doors to be opened. A manservant stood there, looking slightly nervous.

"The sultana wanted me to fetch you," the servant said through his shaking. "The royals from Bahratt have arrived. You told me to let you know when they arrived. They will be on their way to court within a few hours."

Sharar's glare softened. "Ah, yes." He looked at Vicdan. "Can I trust you to not do anything foolish if I bring you along?"

Vicdan wilted a little. "I couldn't if I wanted to. I'm too weak."

Sharar smiled darkly. "Tell the sultana we are on our way down."

The sun rose and Sharar waited. He donned his best robes, combed his hair, and administered to his beard while he waited to be summoned. Once the servant arrived to lead them to the throne room, the day was already warm and the sun shone brightly. Sharar let it. If he needed to, he'd show the visitors from Bahratt his power.

Sharar and Vicdan made their way through the palace, led by the servant from before. The palace buzzed cautiously these days with him inside. Everyone bowed to him as he passed and moved out of his way. They treated him as they treated the sultana herself.

The golden doors to the palace's throne room opened as they approached and Sharar marched in, head held high. He scanned the room and found the sultana on her throne. It was made of gold and shaped in the likeness of a lion. Pink gauzy curtains lined the sides between the sand-colored pillars. Kalil stood beside her and tried his best to hide his look of apprehension as Sharar entered. There was a gilded chair set beside the sultana just for him.

"Sabi," Sharar said in greeting to the sultana. He bowed before taking a seat beside her. Vicdan stood behind him, hands hanging limp at his sides.

"So you have heard the prince from Bahratt has come to see me," the sultana said, sighing. Her hand went to her overly large belly, rubbing it gently. She was due any day.

"I have my eyes and ears," Sharar replied with a grin. "I am curious why you didn't tell me yourself."

"Are you, sorcerer?" she shot back at him, glaring boldly. Kalil put his delicate hand on her shoulder. She withdrew her malice from her eyes and nodded. "Of course you are. This is what you wanted, after all. Me, on the throne. You, behind it."

"A mere means to an end, sabi," he replied. "Just as you shall see today."

Curious, she frowned at him. Keeping eye contact with him, she called to the guards to let the visitors in. The double doors opened again and only two figures stood in the archway now. Sharar recognized one: the magi ambassador who had pestered Sokar not three months ago. She stood tall and beautiful in her red and gold, veiled mysteriously. Beside her was a young handsome man decorated in all the trappings of Bahratt royalty. Sharar watched the young man as they marched together toward the throne. He walked with a slightly unsure air about him, but held his head high like a proper royal. His hand rested on a decorative scimitar at his side. The turban around his head glittered with tiny gems.

The pair stopped just below the stairs that rose to the throne. The magi spoke first.

"Your majesty," she said to the sultana with an elegant and beautiful bow. Her black-lined eyes lifted as she did and landed on Sharar. They widened in stunned but quiet shock. Her body didn't even betray her shock as she stood next to the gilded young man. "May I present," she went on in a strong and unfazed tone, "the adopted heir to maharaja Saksham's throne and the prince of Bahratt: Prince Rhaji."

The younger man, a boy to Sharar's eyes, stepped forward and bowed, bending at the waist, hand still on his sword pommel. "Your majesty," he said to the sultana, "it is a great honor to meet you and discuss our countries' treaty this day."

The sultana nodded, her hands still clasped over her large belly. "So you are Saksham's adopted heir." Her tone was even, neither judgmental nor disappointed. "I was sorry to hear of Prince Rahul's murder at the hands of the death fiend that day. And who were you prior to your adoption by Saksham?"

Rhaji held himself tall, chest puffed out. "I was the only son of a raja from New Gypsu. Our estate supplied the wine to the palace and the maharaja knew me well. My father died that day as well in the palace, and Saksham took me in as his own. I may yet be displaced as the rani—his wife—is with child, as you are. Should she bear a son, it will be my duty to mentor him and raise him to be the ruler after Saksham."

Sharar listened with great interest. Bahratt was in a volatile state and no doubt would play any game of diplomacy safely. Just like the sultana. Both countries had no heirs and were on the cusp of getting one.

"And should the child be a girl?" the sultana asked.

"Then I remain heir to the throne," Rhaji answered.

The sultana hummed in thought at this. "My father did not see things the same way."

"No, your majesty," Rhaji said. "But Bahratt still hopes for a male heir."

"And you?" Sharar asked. "How do you feel about being replaced?"

"Honored," Rhaji said quickly. Beside him, the magi smiled under her silken veil. "It was never my lot in life to rule Bahratt. Should it happen, praise Krishvu. Should I be the one instead who watches over the throne as steward as the child grows, I would be most honored."

Sharar shifted in the chair at this. Rhaji was righteous and good. He'd not be tempted by anything Sharar could offer him, he saw that. So instead, he'd have to be removed, should the maharaja not be as pliable as he hoped he was.

"We have come to offer gifts," Rhaji said, changing the subject. "We've brought wine, emeralds from our mines, oil, and wool. Saksham wanted to send a host of slaves as well, but I advised him against it, knowing Al'Myrah's laws."

"Wise," the sultana remarked pertly. "Are you bringing such gifts to all in the eastern alliance?"

Rhaji nodded. "Alika is our next stop."

Sharar stood up at this. "Do not go to Alika, my boy."

At this, Rhaji glanced sideways at the magi. Sharar remembered her name to be Nefiri. He let his eyes float to her in turn. She cleared her throat and swallowed, but remained quiet.

"Yes, the magi was telling me something about that," Rhaji said. "I don't quite understand."

"What did you tell the prince?" Sharar asked Nefiri.

"That a Necro'Khan has risen," she started. "That he overtook Alika and holds the Dynast Pharaoh captive."

"The same Necro'Khan that killed Prince Rahul," Sharar added. "Does the maharaja know?"

"No," Nefiri answered. "I met Prince Rhaji on the road in Hatal. I have not been back to Bahratt yet."

Rhaji faced the sultana then. "As the hub of the civilized world and our greatest ally, you must be thinking of doing something to stop this monster."

"We will," Sharar answered in her stead. "What I want to know is if we can count on Bahratt to support us. We have, after all, a long-standing alliance. And Bahratt's fleet is the strongest in the eastern triangle."

Nefiri glared at Sharar now. She understood what he wanted before Rhaji did. She asked, "How do you intend to take down a Necro'Khan, especially one as powerful as this? I witnessed some of his power as I fled Bahratt. My prince, he is strong and ruthless. We cannot hope to stand against him."

"Not alone," the sultana put in before Sharar could answer. "But together, we may stand a chance. We must stop him before his darkness spreads."

"Is that your wish or your sorcerer's?" Nefiri spat.

The sultana glared at the magi. "You speak boldly to me in my own home."

Nefiri narrowed her eyes and raised her brows. "I do not fear you."

Rhaji raised his hands, trying to defuse the rising tension. His brows slightly bent in a frown at this. "I will take the information back to the maharaja, see what Saksham will advise. Nefiri, will you come with me? Your testimony is vital."

Nefiri bowed to the prince, but kept her eyes on Sharar.

Sharar imagined smiting her. Calling upon the powers of the gods themselves and striking her down where she stood. She'd not be as easily swayed as the young prince.

ༀ

Later that night, Sharar returned to his study to find Amir waiting there. The Runer stood over his desk, absentmindedly flipping through the pages of the Mahit'Onomicon. Sharar forced Vicdan back to the pile of chains that waited in the corner.

"Amir, so good to see you," he said. He motioned to Vicdan, ordering Amir to re-shackle the singer. The Runer didn't argue and moved, easily wrestling Vicdan back into his chains. "Any news?" Sharar asked once the necromancer was bound again.

Amir moved to the desk and lit a lamp, knowing Sharar could not see in the dark like he could. "I've been all over Al'Myrah in the last several weeks and haven't found Tzarik," he said, sounding weary and parched. "I have other Runers on the lookout as well."

Sharar pressed his palms into the table and growled softly. "How can one man hide so well that—" He gasped as a sudden, biting pain ripped through his side. He immediately crumpled onto the floor from the pain and pressed his hand into his side. Quickly, he unfastened his sash and pulled his robes off to inspect the ignited wound. Black blood leaked steadily from the malignant wound and black veins spread over his ribs from the spot where he'd been stabbed all those years ago.

Moaning in agony, he pressed his hand into it and wished he could use his magic for himself. Amir appeared by his side and pried his hand off the wound. He quickly drew the healing rune, which didn't mend the wound, but took some of the pain away. Sharar panted, doubling over.

"You need a healer," Amir said.

"Don't you think I know that?" Sharar barked, sweat beading on his brow from the pain. "I've searched for one who might know something about malignant wounds, but each one is as stupid as the next."

Amir braced Sharar against himself as another wave of pain wracked his body. Sharar gripped Amir's arms to hold himself up in a sitting position, but couldn't stop the moan that tore from his lips.

"It's spreading," Amir noted. "Getting stronger. You may be running out of time."

Sharar nodded, teeth clenched. "It ignites more and more often now."

"A Xian might know how to treat it," Amir offered. "But it will take time to find one."

"I may not have that time!" Sharar blurted in desperation. He waited a moment more and the pain subsided. He flicked his head up, motioning to Amir to help him stand again.

Once he stood, he bent over the Mahit'Onomicon and began to flip the pages. "There must be something in here about the Xian sigils," he mumbled. "Something that tells us what they are. But it takes time to read the pages, for the understanding to come to me."

"I have another piece of information," Amir said as Sharar pored over the book. He hummed, showing he was listening. Amir said, "Sokar is still alive. Tarkan keeps him chained nearby at all times, but he's alive."

Something in Sharar lightened at the Runer's words. "Alive?" he asked. He could barely believe it. "Why would Tarkan keep him alive?"

But he was glad. His heart grew lighter upon hearing the news. Curious about why, he delved into the sensation. It was a pleasant one, but he wasn't sure what it meant. It would require further study.

"How strange," he murmured.

"What?" Amir asked.

"Something in me has eased, knowing the boy is alive."

Amir kept his lips shut, but Sharar could tell he wanted to say something. He was glad Amir didn't.

"I wonder," Sharar mused, "if there is a way to get back to Alika and perhaps spy on Tarkan's court. I am going mad, not knowing what he's up to. And nothing has come to Al'Myrah's shores from the south yet."

"Did you expect him to attack?"

"I did." Sharar pushed off the table and stood tall, slipping his arms back into his robe. "He must have something else planned, and I need to know what it is."

# Chapter 3
# Kazamar

T zarik looked out the window, but did not see the sunrise. The dark red sky glowed as the orange orb rose slowly, bringing with it the smell of morning over the desert. A light breeze disturbed the gauzy white curtains and stirred the scent of the city waking up. The smell of fresh bread mingled with the aroma of incense burning in the temple. Somewhere, a rooster crowed and the noise of the city began to rise. But his mind was a million realms away, not taking in the sight before him.

Behind Tzarik, the soft snoring of Signar drew his attention back inside. Signar had still not become accustomed to sleeping alone and came to Tzarik's room almost every night. Tzarik never stopped him, even if Sybal had already joined him in bed. She slept silently, too, unaware that he'd left her side.

He listened to their breathing, knowing they had perhaps all the time in the world. They weren't sure where Sharar was and didn't know if Tarkan had sent men after him. There were a million possibilities, and they couldn't track any of them. Tzarik never knew when a moment might be his last. What if Tarkan captured Sharar and killed him? Would he? Or would he keep the sorcerer and drink his blood whenever the whim suited him? Not knowing drove Tzarik mad and stole his sleep. They waited on word from Amir, but waiting had never been a virtue of his, either. The agony of not knowing twisted in his chest.

Behind him, Signar yelped lightly in his sleep and whined. Tzarik turned and sat on the edge of the bed, gently pressing his hand onto Signar's forehead. The boy still had nightmares about his mother. He often told Tzarik about them after waking, terrified. His other hand gently clasped the boy's bare shoulder in a firm grip. Signar was shuddering, but when Tzarik touched him, the shaking receded just enough.

"It's just a dream, Signar," Tzarik whispered close to his ear. "She's not here. She can't hurt you anymore."

A single tear leaked out from under Signar's pale lashes and ran down his nose. Tzarik's heart ached for the boy and he wiped it away. He waited a few more moments and soon Signar's breathing evened out and he didn't shake anymore. Tzarik stood and wandered back to the window, looking out into the city.

A moment later, a pretty, lithe hand slithered around his middle, pulling him back into a tall, warm body. Sybal buried her face in his hair and kissed him. Her hand glided over his chest and stomach, pressing him into her. He gave in and leaned his head back, offering her his neck. She lightly kissed him, making her way down to his collarbone.

"I can see your tension," she whispered, sliding her hands under his nightshirt to touch his skin. "I see your worry in the way you stand. In how your eyes are not seeing the beauty before you."

"We've waited long enough," he whispered, his voice hoarse from her touches. "I cannot sit by and wait to take my last breath."

"We've not been idle," Sybal replied.

"Scouring libraries, haunting temples, questioning a priest," Tzarik spat a little more aggressively than he meant to. "Perhaps there is no answer."

"I won't accept that," Sybal said. "I know it's hard. We cannot let Tarkan get his hands on Sharar, but we cannot simply stop Sharar by killing him. We will find a way."

"We need to find the sorcerer first," Tzarik reminded her. "When did Amir leave?"

"Two days ago."

He took her hand from his middle, where she'd been caressing him, and kissed her palm. "If we cannot control Tarkan and Sharar, the only thing left to do is find a cure for this fate binding."

"I've thought of someone else to ask," Sybal said. Tzarik waited. She went on, "There is a warlock in Hatal who is rumored to be well-traveled and seasoned in the magic arts. He might know something."

"Crystals, moon water, and herbs surely could not be my salvation," he said.

"No," Sybal said, smiling and giving him another kiss. "But he might know where to look. Might know something we don't."

Tzarik doubted it, but it was better than any of the ideas he'd had recently in the privacy of his own mind. He'd had one idea, but didn't dare mention it, especially to Sybal. She'd want to try it and Tzarik wasn't willing to risk Signar like that.

"Very well," he sighed, resigned to her suggestion. "This morning we will visit the warlock."

Hatal boasted many warlocks and witches, but the one Sybal had heard of lived on the outskirts of the grand city near a smaller village called Unemar. They rode out alone, leaving Signar behind, since they didn't know what might come from the meeting with the strange magic-wielder. The village of Unemar was small and had a population that was equal parts sheep and sentient kind. The warlock was not hard to find in the small village. His home, made of golden sandstone with a thatched roof, stood out by the ample and overflowing garden of herbs and other fragrant plants. Crystals and glimmering stones hung in glittering bouquets from the arbor around certain parts of the garden. A soft tinkling and ringing came from the perimeter of the land as well.

Sybal tapped Tzarik's shin with her foot to get his attention and pointed up with a nod of her head. "Bells," she said quietly. "They're all around the garden and hanging from the roof outside."

Tzarik looked and beheld a myriad of bells of various sizes and makes hanging from thin rope. "Protection," he mumbled. "Several kinds of monsters are held at bay by the ringing of bells."

He glanced around and saw the other homes in the village did not boast the same protection. He hummed in thought. Something must be coming after the warlock specifically. He sighed.

"We'll most likely have to bargain," he informed Sybal as they dismounted and looked for the front entrance to the small home.

"What makes you say that?" she asked.

Tzarik took the lead, heading into the garden and following the winding path up to the front wooden door. "This is the only home with the protection of bells. Some monsters mark their prey, or focus on one sentient at a time, hunting them." He frowned, thinking, going through the bestiary he held in his mind. "A shamaka," he said at length. "They tend to fixate on prey and not stop until they've killed them."

"What's that?" Sybal asked.

Before he replied, Tzarik hammered on the door and called out to the warlock inside. He doubted this glorified gardener would have any new ideas for them, but he wanted to placate Sybal. He didn't want to admit that he had no idea where to begin looking for a cure for his fate-binding. Didn't want to admit that he worked every day to accept his fate. Besides, his demise would help save the map from a terror none of them had ever seen before.

No, he couldn't think like that.

"Runers?" a voice from within said with some relief. The door swung open to reveal a tall, older Al'Myrahn with long, tangled white hair. He had a long, matching white beard that had grown down to his belt. "Thank the lion," the old warlock crowed. "I have been on the verge of looking for Runers for nearly a fortnight now. I couldn't bring myself to reach out to your lot. No offense," he added quickly. He rubbed his old, wrinkled hands together and inspected them. "A woman Runer?" he asked.

Sybal didn't smile or give any indication that she'd heard him. "We are in need of information, warlock," she said stiffly.

"Alamur," the warlock said, introducing himself. "Come in, have something to drink." He stood back as they entered. "Though I must admit, I never thought Runers would seek me out." He smiled nervously.

Alamur went to his open fireplace and pulled an old brass kettle off and poured the hot water over tea leaves in small, simple cups. He took one for himself and offered the Runers the others.

Tzarik shook his head. "We need information and we were told you might have the knowledge we seek."

The warlock took a drink of the tea and blanched at the flavor. "Not quite right," he sighed, placing the cup down. "Cheese?" He hurried back to a small cabinet on the wall and took out a cloth wrapped around a large chunk of white goat cheese.

"No." Sybal sighed. "We need to know if you've ever come across a fate-binding before."

Alamur froze before turning around. He set the cheese down. His hand went to his long beard. He stroked it in deep thought for only a moment before he smiled. "That is djinn magic." He stopped before going on, holding his breath. "Runers, I do know a little something about that. Very little indeed, but more than my fellow witches and warlocks."

Tzarik sensed the ultimatum coming long before the warlock was ready to mention it. He crossed his arms and glared at the warlock. "We'll dispatch your shamaka if you can tell us all you know, little though it may be."

Alamur smiled and tapped the side of his nose. "Perceptive, Runer. I've heard your lot are. It's almost like you can read minds."

Tzarik felt Sybal smile at him from where she stood behind him.

"Just observant," Tzarik said, waving the compliment off. "Does that sound like a deal we can make?"

Alamur rubbed his hands together eagerly. "Absolutely. Bring me the thing's head—its brains have some light magical properties—and I will tell you all I know about fate-bindings."

Tzarik nodded, dropping his arms. "Tell us where it beds down and we'll have it to you by sundown."

Tzarik eyed the opening to the cave beneath the sandy dunes. The shamaka would be sleeping during the day, so they had the advantage. Sybal shifted in her saddle next to him. He knew she waited for his instructions, his oration on how they were going to take the monster down. But he also sensed her other questions, the ones she'd not asked for weeks now. She wanted to know his thoughts, but he had cut her off from their once deep, probing conversations. She knew it, and he tried to ignore her silent prodding. Sybal always liked talking while they scouted a monster, but now he craved the silence.

"What exactly is this creature?" she asked, narrowing her eyes as she, too, looked into the cave. She pulled her runes to the outside of her armor and touched them lightly, as if counting to make sure all five were still there.

"A shamaka is a lion-like creature," Tzarik said. That was mostly correct. "They have wings like a dragon, breathe fire, and have a tendency to fixate on prey."

Sybal screwed up her face, trying to imagine the creature. "Sounds like they're related to chimeras," she tried.

"Perhaps," Tzarik agreed. He'd never thought much about the genus of monsters before. Now, he didn't have time to learn and cared even less about it. "Come on. Follow me."

He dismounted and slowly walked to the cave entrance. He drew atan for light and looked into the cave. The sudden stink of rotting flesh hit him hard, deep in his nostrils. He grimaced, but didn't gag. Sybal wretched and coughed, turning away, her hand over her nose.

"They collect their prey," Tzarik informed her. He carefully walked deeper into the cave. She followed, her own slowly-drawn light held in her hand.

Skeletons of all kinds of sentients lined the cave floor the deeper they got into the tunnels. Sybal drew closer to him, holding her light aloft.

Tzarik stopped suddenly when his ears picked up the sound he'd been searching for. The soft, rumbling breathing of the monster greeted him. He held up his hand, stopping Sybal mid-step.

"I hear it," she whispered. "Can we kill it while it's sleeping?"

"We can wound it," Tzarik said. "But it will wake and it will breathe fire. Be ready to defend yourself." He reached to his thigh and pulled the small crossbow out from where it hung and prepared an arrow. He'd aim for its eye. That would be a soft target that would partially cripple the beast. It would make it angry, but he was ready for that. "Get halat," he instructed her. "Be ready to block the fire."

"And you?" she asked, following him deeper into the grotto.

"I'll be fine," he replied curtly. He felt Sybal give him a look, but ignored it. He wasn't being reckless. He would hide behind a rock or a bend in the tunnel. He was ready.

They came around one final corner and he stopped, holding his hand up to stop Sybal. He pressed his finger to his lips, signaling to be quiet. She thankfully did. He pointed ahead, snuffing his light. There, amidst a pile of bones and scattered limbs, slept the shamaka. Its fur was red with dried blood and its mane was long and tangled. Its leathery wings were pulled in tight against its sides.

Sybal broke from Tzarik and moved to a small, overhanging ledge to get a better shot at the beast. She unsheathed her small crossbow as well and drew her scimitar in her left hand where her runes hung. She nodded to Tzarik when he glanced back.

Tzarik skirted around the mountain of bones and knelt behind a short stalagmite. He looked up, judging the height of the cave ceiling. It wasn't very tall. The beast would have a hard time flying. It would be trapped for just a few moments before it retreated either deeper into the network of caves or ran for the exit. Craning his neck around, he noted Sybal's location near the entrance where she was perched on a tall outcropping. Good, she could deter its escape.

He pulled back the string, raised the bow, and aimed. The thing's great head made an easy target. The closed eye was harder to hit, but he knew he could do it. Aiming carefully, holding his breath, he fired the single shot. The arrow thudded hard into the shamaka's skull, bursting the eye. The monster roared and reared up, clawing at the air. No sooner had its massive forepaws landed on the ground than it spewed a jet of flames, fanning its wings in an arch over its head. He heard Sybal gasp, but saw the flames splatter against the runic shield she'd drawn.

Focusing, his pupils constricting, he looked into the now darker cave. The shamaka roared and pawed at its eye as the hiss and thud of another arrow lodged into its shoulder. He heard Sybal curse and move. He moved at the same time. They surrounded the beast and dived at it with their scimitars out. Tzarik slashed at its hind legs, drawing a thick stream of blood. The monster mewled and tucked its hindquarters, trying to hide from the attack.

With a screech, it swiped at Sybal and caught her arm just as she drew halat. The blow still rocked her and sent her flying onto her back. Tzarik took the opportunity to slash at the monster again, but missed as it leapt out of the way. The thing turned and belched another stream of fire from its maw. Tzarik didn't move fast enough and felt the flames lick his skin before he rolled out of the way.

Sybal managed to nock another arrow to her crossbow and fired, hitting the thing in its ribs. This made it angrier, and it bore down on her, heavy footfalls vibrating the floor under Tzarik's feet as it ran. With it distracted, Tzarik also reloaded his crossbow and aimed. Sybal drew buhkar and vanished into mist. The monster stopped and looked around, confused.

Tzarik shouted, getting its attention back on him. The monster turned, roaring. He fired the bolt and it lodged with a thud into the thing's other eye. Screaming now, the shamaka reeled and spat fire in every direction. Sybal rematerialized and caught a face-full of flames before rolling out of the way. Her scream spurred Tzarik into action.

He dashed up behind the monster and shoved his scimitar between its ribs. The monster flung its head around and clamped its jaws over his arm. Sensing it had its prey, it ripped its head back and forth, flinging Tzarik easily with it. He couldn't see through the sudden tears that sprang to his eyes or hear over his screams and the roar of the shamaka, but he felt blood smatter over his face before his arm was suddenly released. He fell to the ground with a thud and looked up.

Sybal, giving a shrill war cry, hacked at the shamaka's neck with her scimitar. She brought the blade down again and again until the head finally split from the neck and tumbled down. It rolled and came to a stop at Tzarik's feet. He clutched his wounded arm to his middle and looked up in awe. Through the blood on her face, he saw a burn on her left cheek. She panted, looking down at him.

"Are you all right?" she gasped, offering him her hand. He took it.

"Yes," he panted, still cradling his wounded arm. He looked around for his sword and bow, spotting them not too far off. "Well done," he said.

Sybal smiled, still winded, and picked up the monster's head. "Heavier than I thought," she mused. She pulled the arrows from its eyes and handed the bolts back to Tzarik. "Hope we didn't ruin anything the warlock wanted."

◈

Alamur screamed as Tzarik plunked the shamaka's head down onto his table. The blood still leaked from it and spread over the wooden surface, tainting the plants he had lain out there.

After taking a moment to compose himself, the warlock stammered, "Thank you, Runers. Really, this is... Well, I'm not sure. A relief, perhaps." An awkward moment of silence passed before Alamur clapped his hands together, rubbing them excitedly. "So, a fate-binding is it?"

"Have you come across anything like it before?" Sybal asked.

The warlock stroked his long beard. "That is djinn magic, lady Runer. Djinns are rare at the best of times."

"We know," Tzarik said, a little agitated.

Alamur nodded and turned to poke at his fire. "I met a man once, long ago, who owned a djinn. Had it enslaved for some years, I believe. He never made a wish upon it and died bound to it."

Curious, Tzarik asked, "What happens when a mortal bound to a djinn dies?"

"The binding is broken," Alamur replied. "The gods have no need of dead mortals. Nor do their servants, the demons. A djinn may wish that their dead master had wished them free before death. But once that happens, they must simply hope the artifact falls into the hands of another who is willing to be bound to a demon in exchange for a few wishes."

Tzarik scoffed at this. "Mortals are eager for such magic. Fools."

Alamur raised his bristling white brows. "On the contrary, Runer. I have lived ninety-five years on this map and have seen men turn down the powers of a djinn. They fear the demons too much."

"Did this man have a fate-binding?" Sybal asked.

The warlock swallowed and frowned before answering. "He did," he sighed. "I don't know to whom or how it came about. I think that's why he never made a wish on his djinn. He was afraid of the power." He shrugged. "The only one who will know how to remove a fate-binding, or stop such a curse, is a djinn themselves."

"What?" Tzarik barked. He straightened up from where he'd been leaning against a support beam. "You don't know? You led us to believe you had an answer." His temper rose.

Alamur backed away slowly, raising his hands. "I told you no such thing. I said I had information. And better still, I might know where a djinn you can ask is."

Sensing Sybal was about to burst out and speak, Tzarik turned and glared at her. She shut her mouth, realizing what she was about to say. No one needed to know a djinn had entered Hatal's province and was bound to a boy from Caerwren.

Tzarik growled in frustration. "Is there anything else you can tell us? Anything. Please."

Alamur looked at them sadly. "I understand. I do. And I am sorry, Runer. There are others you can ask who are of a magical persuasion."

"Who?" Sybal snapped.

"There is a magi with the prince of Bahratt," he offered. "Perhaps other Runers might know."

"May as well ask the Dohkma himself," Sybal said sarcastically.

At this, Alamur raised his brows and pressed his lips together. "Perhaps," he said haltingly. "Though none make it back from the Frozen Nation."

Sybal glared at the warlock.

He shrugged again in reply. "Speak to the magi," he reasoned. "Seek out other Runers if you don't want to hunt down the djinn. And I will be happy to aid you in any way I can."

"That was an ungodly waste of time!" Sybal roared as they rode back to her estate. "We learned nothing."

Tzarik glared ahead in silence for a moment. "I didn't want to ask the djinn as I didn't want to risk any more bargains," he began. "But I had thought about it. Signar needs to be released from the djinn and it no doubt wants freedom. There may be something we can arrange."

"More oaths and promises," Sybal sneered. "I will not bargain Signar like that."

"Nor will I," Tzarik agreed. "It will answer to us from now on. Signar promised it one wish, and he's been granted that wish."

Sybal didn't reply.

"We need to unbind Signar and get rid of the djinn," Tzarik finished. "But first, we can promise it its freedom if it aids us. I'd be willing to release the djinn in exchange for an answer."

Sybal looked sidelong at him, but didn't say anything.

They rode back in silence the rest of the way. Once they were inside her manor, they called for Signar. He came running down the stairs and greeted them with wide eyes.

"You're safe," he said with great relief. "I wasn't sure what the hunt would be like." He reached up and touched the fresh burn on Sybal's face. She smiled into his touch and took his hand.

"We need the djinn," Tzarik said sternly.

Signar reached under his tunic and pulled the artifact out. "I carry it with me always."

"Call it out," Sybal instructed.

Signar touched the crest and must have called out with his mind. In a mist of frost of ashen clouds, the djinn appeared. It looked from Tzarik to Sybal, then to Signar. It crossed its arms and raised one white brow.

"Have you called me forth to release me, pale man?" it said to Signar. "Our deal has been done."

Before Tzarik could reply, Signar said, "We bargained for one wish.

I cannot wish you free. I am sorry." He glanced at Tzarik as if waiting for him to ask the djinn whatever he wanted.

Tzarik forced a small smile down at Signar's cleverness, though he saw the rage on the djinn's face. The monster's brows furrowed and his lips turned down fiercely. The sound of frost crackling accompanied the rage.

"You western bastard," the djinn growled softly. Then its face broke into a devious smile. "You are perhaps more cunning than your years imply." The djinn shrugged. "I care not. Make more wishes upon me. Sooner or later, I will either become strong enough to break free or you will grow tired of your power and set me free to rid yourself of all I have given you. I can wait out your meager lifetime if it comes to that. You will only live so long, while I have eternity. You may have won the battle, little man, but not the war."

"Will you wait out every sentient's life?" Tzarik asked. "You will still be bound to the amulet."

"No thanks to you, Runer," the djinn retorted. Then it eyed Tzarik. "You want something. Ready to make another bargain, are you?"

Sybal stepped forward. "Tell us how to remove a fate-binding."

"Ah," the djinn mused, eyes going wide as it looked at Tzarik. "I knew I smelled another binding on you when you first found me. So that's what it was. How unfortunate." His eyes shifted to Sybal. "And you are god-touched. You will soon join me. I saw that from the start. But what is the harm of a fate-binding? Unless..." He gestured to Signar.

"No, demon," Tzarik said. "I am bound to a sorcerer, one who is in danger of being captured by the first Necro'Khan to rise up in a thousand years."

The djinn's face fell at this. It floated a short distance away and contemplated, crossing its arms again. "We made a deal once. My freedom in exchange for my silence and complacence."

"Yes," Tzarik said, getting restless. "Are you willing to bargain again, demon?"

"Kazamar," the djinn replied. "My name in life was Kazamar."

Sybal said, "No tricks this time."

"You are desperate," Kazamar mused. "A fate binding to a sorcerer might prove useful, if one is willing to sacrifice."

"No," Sybal cut in fiercely.

Tzarik felt a pang of guilt and fear hit him at her sharp tone. Should he be willing to give up his life to save the map from the terror of the Necro'Khan and the sorcerer? It would be so simple.

As if reading his mind, Sybal took his hand and squeezed hard. She glared sidelong at him, warning him against the thoughts he'd just been having.

Kazamar considered the pair of Runers before him. "Have no fear," he began. "This is the first time I have been bound. If you make three wishes upon me, it will not empower me enough to break free."

The fact that the djinn admitted this told Tzarik he was ready to bargain. If this was the monster's first time being bound, it must crave freedom fiercely.

"I will keep my end of the bargain," Kazamar offered, "if you set me free after you make your wishes."

"No wishes," Tzarik cut in. "We want information."

"We shall see." Kazamar nodded. "The fate-binding. I am sorry, mortals, but there is no way to undo what another djinn has done. You could perhaps beg the god who made the djinn to revoke the curse, but the gods are petty and fickle beings."

"And cruel," Sybal sighed.

"The Dohkma," Tzarik added. "The Pale God. The one who resides hidden in the Frozen Nation. They say he is the cruelest god, perhaps even the first god who made all other gods and monsters."

"The god of Runers," Kazamar added. "A journey to the Frozen Nation would be perilous, but informative." A moment of silence passed before Kazamar said, "I am sorry, Runers. But I can still grant your wishes. I cannot deny you that."

Tzarik knew the djinn was more sorry that there was no bargain to be made. Its freedom was not negotiable any longer. But Tzarik still wanted to unbind Signar.

"We will find a way," the boy said, breaking into Tzarik's thoughts. "If I have to climb every mountain on the map and swim every sea— we will find a way."

# Chapter 4
## Runers and the Magi

Sybal slinked out of her home in the dead of night. The moon above painted the golden sands of Al'Myrah into white mounds around the city. She had double-checked the letter from Amir that had arrived by a falcon that night. It had said to meet in a public house she knew well on the outskirts of the city. She felt a small amount of guilt for sneaking out and leaving Tzarik behind, but she wanted to do her part to find a cure for him. And she wanted to have news of Sharar when he woke in the morning.

She stopped at a street corner under a large brass oil lamp and looked around the sandstone building. Not three doors down, the public house lit up the street with music and light. The smell of mint tea, fruity tobacco, and roasting meat wafted up the street to her. A drunk couple stumbled out the front door, giggling and holding on to one another. Sybal watched them with some jealousy as they meandered down the street, holding each other's hands. If only her life could be that simple.

Waiting only a moment more, she whipped around the corner, pulling a mask over her face and her hood over her head. She ducked into the house and looked around with her keen blue eyes. They spotted Amir easily. The tall man sat in a corner near the fire where a bard was playing a soft tune on a lute. She sashayed around the softly talking patrons and slid onto the bench opposite Amir, keeping her eye on the door behind.

When she sat down, his eyes lit up, and he almost smiled. "Nervous?" he asked, motioning to her hood and mask.

She pinned him with her eyes, half smiling. "Sharar's spies are everywhere. I cannot take any chances."

"Fair point." Amir smiled back. He shoved a tankard over to her and motioned a servant to bring another cup. "Fresh mead," he said to entice her.

Her nerves were bunched under her skin. The sweet drink might help her relax. Caving in, she took the second cup from the servant. She pulled her mask down and took a quick drink. Amir watched her intently as she drank. The mead went down smooth and sweet, instantly calming her.

"Tell me what Sharar is up to," she said, licking her lips and pouring another glass. "Everything has been silent. I expected him to clamber for a position of power."

"He has," Amir said, his face turning serious. "He stands behind the sultana and dictates her every move with threats. They are in talks with Bahratt even now to order an army and a fleet to attack Alika."

"A fool's mission," she said, her brows furrowing. "Tarkan will not fall to a simple mortal army."

"Of course not," Amir agreed. "But Sharar is desperate and afraid."

A sudden thought struck Sybal. "And Vicdan? How is he?"

Amir tilted his head in thought. "Beaten, but brave. He holds out against Sharar's orders as best he can."

Sybal sighed in awe and placed her hand on Amir's wrist, squeezing gently. "You both are so brave."

Amir's eyes sparkled at the praise. His cheeks flushed slightly pale with the rush of his sulfates. "We are simply doing what is required," he said after a moment. "But I'm not sure how to stop Bahratt. There is a magi with the adopted prince who I think will try to stop the invasion if she can."

Sybal sat up, withdrawing her hand from his wrist. "Is her name Nefiri?"

Amir nodded. "You know her?"

"In a fashion," Sybal replied. "Where is she?"

"In a contingent outside the city limits with the prince."

"The prince," Sybal repeated softly. She'd not thought about how Rahul had died in some time. Emotion filled her. She'd been engaged to the prince of Bahratt at one time in her life. That life seemed an eternity ago. She would have been queen of an entire nation.

"Sybal?" Amir reached out and touched her hand gently.

She blinked and a tear fell. She wiped at it fiercely and cleared her throat. "We haven't found a cure yet," she said, sharing her own news now. "We spoke to a djinn we bound some time ago. We even went to see a warlock, and he had no advice for us other than to speak to the djinn."

Amir watched her, interested in how she spoke about simply conversing with the djinn. She caught the interested light in his eyes as he watched her intently.

"Tzarik has a way with monsters," she said, deflecting any incoming praise. "Has a way of taming them, making them obey him. Or in this case, converse with him."

"A rare talent," Amir agreed.

She nodded and looked down into her mead, the tears coming back. "I don't know what else to do," she whispered, afraid her voice would crack if she spoke too loud. "I'm scared to lose him. Afraid he'll take his own life." She took a quick drink and allowed the sweet alcohol to settle in her stomach, warming her limbs and calming her. "When I met him, he was searching for a way to end it all. He wanted to die. Tired of the hunt, I suppose."

"Or the loneliness," Amir offered, taking a deep drink from his own tankard. "If it hadn't been for my last apprentice, Ashar, I would have no doubt followed a similar path."

Another thought struck Sybal. "And if death isn't an option? What then?" What about her? If Tzarik died, she'd be alone. The same mentality might take her, but for her, there was no escape. She clenched her jaw, willing the sadness to not well up inside her.

Seeing her so distraught, Amir stood up and moved to sit next to her. He put one arm around her and waited. Sybal leaned into him and eventually turned and embraced him entirely. She buried her face in his shoulder and sniffled as the tears came.

"I feel so trapped," she whispered between soft sobs.

Amir hugged her tight, his left hand coming to the back of her head, where he held her gently. He didn't say anything, and she was grateful for that. His arms were longer and thicker than Tzarik's, engulfing her entirely. She felt small and fragile in his strong embrace. His chest was broad and firm with muscle. She almost melted into him then, desperate to feel wrapped in his arms, safe and secure.

"I've never told him that I love him," she said with a sigh. "He's never said it to me, either."

"He knows," Amir said with assurance, but softly.

"But I want to hear it," she retorted. "I need him to say it. *I* should say it. We have to tell one another before it's too late."

Sybal sighed and sat up, running her hand under her nose. She quickly wiped at her tears and cleared her throat before taking another drink. Her cheeks burned in embarrassment. She almost apologized, but realized that would just make it worse.

"We cannot stay in Hatal," she said with a slight shudder to her voice. "We have to move, to find a cure. We have to look everywhere we can. I'm afraid we have to leave you two."

Amir nodded mutely at first. He fiddled with the tankard of mead before saying, "I understand. Don't worry, I'll protect Vicdan."

Sybal relaxed in relief. Amir and Vicdan were in a dangerous position, and she appreciated that. Leaving them would be risky. "I wish I had some sort of heading. Knew where to start."

At this, Amir perked up a little. "Speak with the magi. I know where she has set up camp."

Sybal almost rolled her eyes and growled.

"You may not admire her," he went on, "but she is wise and well-traveled. And she might be a good ally. She sees through Sharar and is trying to convince the prince to not lend the Bahratt fleet to the sultana and her lost cause."

Sybal chewed her bottom lip, tapping her thumb against the side of her tankard. Her dislike of Nefiri shouldn't stop her from speaking to the magi. She had helped them, had warned them of the danger and saved them on Alika.

She grumbled and shook her head. "Fine. Take me to her."

The night was cool and a light wind stirred the sandy dunes as Sybal and Amir rode over them under the moon. Dotted around the outskirts of Hatal's city walls were many small camps. Nomadic tribes stopped outside, travelers and refugees from other cities made camp there as well. Nefiri's contingent was easy to spot among them. Her large red and gold tent and many white horses nearly glowed in the evening light. Several kehann stood guard around the tents and stopped them as they drew closer.

"Why is she not staying in the sultana's palace?" Sybal asked. "Especially with the prince with her?"

"Sharar's presence no doubt has her on edge," Amir offered.

Sybal hummed in agreement.

"Tell Nefiri my name," Sybal said after some back and forth between her and the guard. "She'll see us then."

The kehann eyed her carefully and turned to bring Nefiri the message. Sybal understood their caution and didn't fault them for it. She looked around, curious which tent held the adopted prince of Jarabu. She wondered what he was like. Would he be a good ruler once Saksham was gone? She prayed he'd chosen an heir wisely. But of course, news of his wife's pregnancy had traveled to Al'Myrah and even Sybal had heard it. She hoped, though she wasn't sure why, that the rani bore a son and that a legitimate heir would take the throne after Saksham moved on. Somehow, it seemed the better option, even if the child became maharaja at a young age. It had happened more often than not and wasn't that unheard of on Bahratt.

"Lady Sybal?" the kehann said, breaking into her thoughts. "The magi will see you."

Sybal and Amir slid off their horses and let the kehann lead them through the small camp of tents to the larger one in the center, where a great fire burned outside. A few servants, horsemen, and others stood silently around the fire. When she passed by, their eyes followed her. By now, she was used to the shock and awe her status as a lady Runer brought her.

The smell of incense filled her nostrils as they passed under the thick curtain that stood for a front door of the tent. The inside was littered with colorful cushions and ornate rugs to cover the sand. A golden table hovered just inches above the ground where a tea set waited with mint leaves and hot water.

"I never thought I'd see you again," the smooth, deeply feminine voice of Nefiri said from Sybal's right. The magi appeared in an archway made of silks and red adornments. She wore a gold and red robe so sheer Sybal could see her body's every detail through it. Her hair was long and unbraided down her back, and the markings on her skin were more visible now than ever. She had removed all the golden rings and chains that normally adorned her face.

Beside Sybal, Amir flushed pale at the sight of the magi's near nakedness. She saw him turn his face away and heard him swallow before she spoke. She hated that Nefiri had no doubt chosen to be seen in such a state to shock them and muddle their minds. Sybal didn't care and locked eyes with the magi.

"What brings you to Hatal?" she asked. "Did you ever make it back to Bahratt?"

Nefiri poured some hot water into a golden tea pot, her hands delicately picking the carafe up. She gently plucked some mint leaves up and dropped them into the pot. "I have not," she confessed. "I miss home greatly. I met Rhaji on the road. He is doing well, meeting with allies, talking, getting to know them."

"The prince of Jarabu?" Sybal asked. She shook her head, frowning. That's not why she was here. She couldn't get distracted. "Magi, I need your...help. Your advice."

Nefiri looked up, raising her perfectly manicured black brows. "And who is this by your side? Where is Tzarik?" She said it like a jibe. Sybal felt the ulterior motives behind the question immediately.

"Amir," Sybal replied. "A friend and colleague."

Nefiri narrowed her brows. "Have I seen you before?" She studied

Amir hard, looking him up and down. The frown never left her face as she hummed in thought.

"Magi," Sybal started again. "We need your help."

Nefiri poured the tea. "With what?" She offered a cup to Sybal, who took it out of habit.

"Tzarik," Sybal said. "You know."

The magi went stiff, holding a hot cup of tea. Her eyes became dull and unfocused. "I do. I didn't think you'd come to me for help, though. What can I do?"

Sybal's heart fell a little. "I was hoping for counsel."

Nefiri motioned for the Runers to sit and she floated down onto the cushions around the golden table. "I told you what to do when we first discovered the fate-binding," she said.

"I refuse to kill him," Sybal said sternly. "You are a woman of magic. You must know something."

"Must I?" Nefiri cut back harshly. Her face softened and she looked apologetic. She looked away from Sybal and let her lustful gaze fall on Amir. Sybal watched her examine the tall, strong Runer for some time before cutting in, knowing exactly what Nefiri was imagining. It somehow made Sybal angry.

"We've been told about the Frozen Nation," Sybal said. "Is there any credence to that?"

Nefiri snapped her eyes from Amir to Sybal. "So it is to be the Dohkma," she sighed. Nefiri tilted her head in thought. "Not many return from the Frozen Nation when they journey there. But you might have a better chance than most."

Sybal frowned. "What do you mean?"

Nefiri sat up and adjusted her hair to cascade over one shoulder. "I read the stars, Runer. I divine from the most mundane things. I saw some time ago that an immortal had been born. I read it in the stars in the constellation Amaranthine, the warrior queen. When I met you, I understood, though it was some time later." She took a sip of her tea, her eyes never leaving Sybal's. "I am curious to know how it happened."

"Your curiosity will have to go unsated for a time," Sybal replied. "For now, help me. Please. For him."

The magi blinked. "He's not here. He doesn't know you've come to see me. Why are you skulking about at night without him?"

When Sybal didn't answer, Nefiri nodded.

"He wants death," the magi deduced quickly. "He is noble like that."

"And I won't allow it," Sybal snapped.

Nefiri studied Sybal for some time before she sat up, placing her tea cup down. "There might be someone you can ask. Someone older than I, with more magic than I."

Eager, Sybal leaned forward. "Who?"

"More like what," Nefiri said. She frowned. "Don't you know? All Runers know."

"Know what?" Sybal snapped, not willing to let Nefiri play her cryptic games. "Tell me now."

"Of course," Amir said, speaking for the first time since entering the tent. "The mori."

Nefiri smiled and nodded.

"The what?" Sybal asked.

Amir said, "The mori are strange monsters. Sentient monsters. They are bloodsucking creatures that live in hiding. Some live in caves, others in abandoned structures. I've even run into one living in a crypt in a graveyard. But some," he almost smiled, "live in plane sight, masquerading as rich lords or magistrates, even."

Sybal held her breath, trying to wrap her head around what Amir was saying. "And Runers know this?"

"Because of the sulfates," Nefiri answered. Amir shot her a glare. "I know how the sulfates are made," she said, as if to calm him. "I am one of the few who is not a Runer who knows."

"I'm confused," Sybal said. "What does the mori have to do with the sulfates?"

"Aside from the poisons we use to make them," Amir said, "the blood of a mori is one of the ingredients. I'm surprised you don't know."

Sybal blinked, looking into the middle distance. "So am I." Her mind reeled then. She'd never asked Tzarik how to make the sulfates that gave her life now, let alone what they were made of. There was so much she didn't know. She needed him. He couldn't die yet. She'd be lost without him.

Her heart suddenly ached and tears sprang to her eyes. She looked away, swallowing her sorrow and blinking it away.

"I see," Nefiri sighed. "That aside, there must be a mori in the city. There are those Runers within the city walls who sell the sulfates almost exclusively."

"Some Runers make it their job in life to only sell sulfates," Amir concurred. "They hunt the nolrieth and the mori and make sulfates to sell to other Runers."

"The what?" Sybal asked, not knowing the other monster Amir had mentioned.

"Another ingredient," he said with a half smile. "I'll show you sometime."

"Yes," Nefiri said. She sat up from where she had been lounging. "There are such Runers in the city. You should find one and ask them where the mori is hiding."

"And the mori will know what we can do to save Tzarik?" Sybal asked, wiping at the tears that refused to leave her eyes.

"It might have some ideas," Nefiri offered. "They are old, have magic of their own—if anyone might know, it would be him. But, Sybal..." She almost reached a hand out to take Sybal's, but stopped herself. "Promise me one thing."

Sybal frowned, curious what the magi might have her swear.

"I have seen Sharar in the palace of the sultana," she went on. "He controls our sultana even now. I don't know what his endgame is, but he must be stopped. He already has the ear of Prince Rhaji and is tempting Bahratt to attack Alika to try to stop the Necro'Khan. If Bahratt attacks, Al'Myrah will be drawn into the conflict whether it wants to be or not. You know the Necro'Khan. You've seen a fraction of his power and know that it will be a slaughter."

"Tarkan must be stopped," Sybal cut in. "We will find a way. We made him what he is."

Nefiri nervously licked her lips, keeping eye contact with Sybal. "If nothing can be done, promise me you will kill Tzarik to rid the world of the sorcerer and to remove him from Tarkan's grasp."

Sybal gasped.

"Please!" Nefiri begged. "I beseech you. We cannot fight this battle on two fronts. We know we can remove Sharar."

"I won't do it," Sybal shouted, leaping to her feet. "We will find a way to break the fate-binding. I swear I will. If I have to journey to the Frozen Nation myself and beg the Pale God on my hands and knees, I will find a way."

Amir gently touched her shoulder, reminding her to stay calm. "I have to return," he said. "The sun will rise soon and I cannot draw suspicion."

Sybal faced him. "Thank you, Amir." She gave him a quick embrace before he turned and left the tent.

Nefiri watched him go. "He has feelings for you."

"Don't try to confuse me," Sybal snapped. "Amir is a friend and ally. A brave one at that. You won't distract me from saving Tzarik."

Enraged, Sybal turned on her booted heel and marched out of the magi's tent.

# Chapter 5
## The Fall of Xia

Xia gleamed like a spike of emerald as the ship neared the shore. A circlet of white clouds topped the mountains miles above. Beside Tarkan on the ship, Ashkan also looked up at the mountainous land before them.

"We have a long way to travel," Ashkan mused, a little despondently.

"We have the time," Tarkan reminded him. "There is no rush, no reason to hurry."

They unloaded their single wagon and three horses. One they hitched to the wagon to pull it along; the other two they mounted and started their long journey. Xia was a beautiful country and Tarkan was almost sad to think about what he had planned for the place. A few people watched them pass, curious eyes latching on to the men in black and the black-painted wagon behind them, but no one stopped them as they journeyed away from the docks and into the province of Wu-Tang. His advisors had told him Wu-Tang was the birthplace of Wushito and closest to the road that led to the Royal City.

Tarkan, being Necro'Khan and drawing his strength from the blood in his blade, pushed through the day and wanted to walk through the night, but Ashkan needed rest. Sleeping at night on Xia was peaceful.

The waterfalls, rivers, and the night creatures sang such a lovely song that Tarkan found himself drifting off to sleep easily, though he had expected not to.

The next day, they passed a small village along a river where every able bodied citizen fished over the sides of little docks. A few farmers surveyed their rice fields on the terraced hills and watched as the mysterious men in black passed. No one tried to stop them; no one approached them.

On the third day, Ashkan finally broke the silence. "What is your plan, my Khan?" he asked.

Tarkan had been taking in the Xian sun and felt his spirits fall when Ashkan spoke. "The ships are not far behind us. My fleet will soon arrive and take Wu-Tang under control. The risen and the undead alike will hold that position and stop any who attempt to climb the roads to the Royal City. Once Wu-Tang is taken, the three hundred undead will follow and decimate the Royal City after I have all ready completed my task."

"What do you intend to do?" Ashkan asked. Tarkan was glad to hear some nervousness in his voice.

"Kill the Di-Huan," he replied easily. "Remove the steward and take control of Xia from the top."

Ashkan frowned. "The Di-Huan is a child. He can't be a threat."

"His very existence gives the Xians hope," Tarkan replied. "I need them broken, hopeless. People without hope are far more easily controlled."

He said it with finality, hoping Ashkan wouldn't speak again for some time. And he was right. The necromancer remained silent for the next day and night. His true goal was, of course, the Crypt. But he needed Wushito to enter the Crypt. Once he had control of the Royal City, the Hallow City would no doubt bend to his will. Or so he hoped. Even if they didn't, it mattered little. He could slaughter any who stood up against him once his fleet arrived.

The farther up the continent they traveled, the cooler the winds got. Tarkan kept his eyes on the clouds above. Somehow, it felt like there were eyes in those clouds and that they watched him. He'd read much about Xia's White Dragon and how it balanced the country in its claws, but he wasn't sure if he believed it or not. After their experiences on Caerwren, he was almost willing to believe those clouds were indeed the White Dragon himself.

The silver mountains gave way to pink peaks as they neared the Royal City. Trees covered in white and pink flowers blossomed along the roads and from the silver rocks that lined the blue rivers. Green grass grew long along the rivers and waved in the breeze. The smell of the rivers filled the air with a clean, cool scent and mingled with the flowery aroma of the trees.

Another settlement came into view, a cluster of scholars in white and blue robes leaving just as Tarkan and Ashkan arrived. The man in the lead pulled up on his red reins to stop his white steed as they neared. He eyed them carefully.

"Travelers," the scholar called out to them. "How fairs Al'Myrah?"

Being mistaken for an Al'Myrahn suited Tarkan just fine. He looked up at the Wushito scholar and said, "How do you know we hail from Al'Myrah?"

"Are you not Runers?" the scholar asked. "Your blue eyes give you away. We heard that the Runers who instigated the end of the civil war had blue eyes and came to us from Al'Myrah. They are still honored every year on the anniversary of the end of the war."

Interested, Tarkan tilted his head. "No doubt two Runers. One was a woman?"

The scholar beamed. "Have you not heard the story of the Runers who saved Xia? They tell it like a legend these days. The lady Runer saved our princess and thus our Di-Huan, who even now waits to sit on the golden throne. You should be proud of your people, Al'Myrahn."

Tarkan nodded. "I am. We are on our way to the Royal City. How close are we?"

The scholar craned his body around in his saddle and pointed up the mountain path. "Perhaps a day's journey." He turned back to face them. "Tell the guards at the gate who you are and they will let you pass, no doubt. What news do you bring from Al'Myrah?"

Tarkan shook his head. "We bring news from the sultana herself. A message for the steward alone."

"Nothing dark, I pray."

"Nothing of the sort." Tarkan smiled.

"Then we are well met, Al'Myrahns," the scholar said with a jovial smile. "And may your journey be easy and blessed." He gave them a slight bow and then clicked his tongue to get his horse to move.

Tarkan and Ashkan moved aside to let them pass and waited until they were gone to speak.

"We will be invited into the royal palace," Tarkan said with a devious grin. "Perhaps this will be easier than I thought."

"We could be brought right to the throne room," Ashkan agreed.

"We need to wait," Tarkan said. "Once the Royal City is surrounded, we will make our move. Until then, we wait. The kehann will be here soon and then we will have our escort."

Two days later, a dozen of Tarkan's loyal kehann met them outside the Royal City's walls. They had arrived on a separate ship and took a different path to avoid suspicion, but now he needed them. Tarkan stood atop a hill, taking in the Royal City. It was magnificent. Small villages dotted the rolling prairies and little mountains that made up the highlands of Xia. The city itself nestled amongst powerful peaks. A jade-colored river ran around the city for protection. Golden and red arched bridges spanned the river here and there, each one guarded by a gate house. Stone lion-like creatures stood on the walls and the gate-houses, roaring to the north. The air this high up felt thin to breathe, but Tarkan didn't mind. Neither Ashkan nor the kehann beside him showed any discomfort, either.

He admired the city as they drew closer to a single gatehouse. It was almost a pity he was going to destroy it. Xia was old and strong. Taking it down would be an honor. Beside him on his horse, Ashkan took out a brass glass and scanned the hills below them.

"The others are near," he whispered. "I see them on the perimeter."

"They will fight the guards at the gatehouses," Tarkan said. "Once we have the border, the people inside will be at our mercy. The three hundred will move in to stop any palace guards who are feeling brave."

"The city is smaller than I imagined," Ashkan mused. "This will be a slaughter."

"It will." Tarkan smiled. "Once we have the steward and the child in our grasp, Wushito won't have a choice but to obey. We will have the Crypt by sunset."

As they neared the guard house on the bridge, a few men exited and approached them, weapons drawn. Tarkan raised his wrapped hands in peace and slid off his horse to meet the men.

In Xian he said, "Peace, soldiers. We bring news from Al'Myrah for the steward. We were sent by Runers."

The man in the front eyed Tarkan and his kehann. "Who sent you?" he asked.

"A man called Tzarik," Tarkan said simply. "Tell the steward I have come on his orders."

"The Al'Myrahn," the man gasped. He leaned back and whispered to his men before one mounted a white horse and sped off toward the palace.

"You will wait," the lead man said.

Tarkan bowed his head and went back to Ashkan.

"How will the others pass?" he asked softly once Tarkan was close.

"The same way we will," Tarkan whispered in reply. "And if not, they will fight their way in. These Xians don't know we're not of Al'Myrah. And all we need is one gatehouse under our control to let in the three hundred. They cannot be killed. The Royal City has no chance against us, Ashkan. Have some faith in me."

The necromancer didn't reply, but looked ahead instead. "I trust you, Tarkan."

They waited only a few minutes before the runner came back, saying Hiro would see the travelers in the audience chamber.

"Just you," the commander said to Tarkan. "The others stay."

"I insist I bring at least three of my guards," Tarkan said stoutly.

The commander eyed the kehann, but then nodded. "I will escort you to the palace."

Tarkan bowed in thanks and nodded to Ashkan. The necromancer bowed and turned to walk back to the wagon and the remaining kehann.

"Lead on," Tarkan said to the commander.

The man gave Tarkan a look that said he was still suspicious of him, but led him through the gate nonetheless. The royal city was small, as Ashkan had pointed out. It would take them no time at all to follow a gray stone path through the small city where no doubt the servants and others who worked the land lived. The path led right to the great golden doors of the palace. The commander spoke to the guard at the gate, who gave the order to have it opened.

The expansive courtyard inside almost took Tarkan's breath away. Little pavilions lined the outside, and a fountain and a small stream ran through the gardens there. The place was strangely empty, though. He imagined at one point it had been bursting with concubines and children, but now it loomed empty and silent.

The commander led him across the courtyard to a set of red doors. "The steward waits within," he said. He shoved open one door and stood aside to let Tarkan in. "I will be right on the outside of this door should anything happen."

Tarkan marched through the door and into the audience chamber. The room was wide open and empty save for a dais where a golden table stood. Two elaborate chairs waited behind the table. One was empty; the other was occupied by a young man in jade-colored silks. He stood when Tarkan entered. His long black hair hung to his middle and was so smooth and shiny it almost looked to be made of the same silk. His brow furrowed a little when he took in Tarkan.

"Who are you?" the man asked in Al'Myrahn. His hand instinctually went to his side where a sword might hang, but there was none there now, so his hand fell limp. A muscle in his jaw twitched.

"I am a friend," Tarkan said gently. Relief at getting into the city flooded him. This was all he needed. The others would fight their way in, and soon he'd have everything within his grasp. "I know Tzarik and Sybal. They have sent me to you with a message."

Hiro's face didn't lose its cautious furrow. "The Runers? Why couldn't they come themselves?"

"Because they are occupied." Tarkan moved closer to Hiro. He looked around the room and saw no guards. The kehann waited for his signal. "They seek a remedy to a dire situation they have found themselves in. They asked I come and seek council from Xia as the magic runs deep here."

Hiro's keen eyes roamed up and down Tarkan, taking in the great sword at his side. Then they clipped from the kehann back to Tarkan. The Necro'Khan got the feeling Hiro might call for a guard, so he spoke quickly.

"There is something of a curse upon Tzarik," he said. "He mentioned that Wushito hunts and studies the same kind of creature that placed the curse on him."

"A curse?" Hiro asked, his face finally showing some of his guard slipping. He dropped his other hand to his side. "What has happened? How can Xia help?"

Tarkan listened, but didn't hear any clatter yet. Soon, his men would be within the palace walls if all went according to plan.

"A djinn," Tarkan said, deciding to divulge the story. It didn't matter, anyway. Hiro would be dead soon. "Do you know what a fate-binding is?" He repeated the phrase in Xian. When he said it, Hiro's eyes widened.

"Like a genie or a yokai," Hiro offered. "That is deep, strong magic indeed. And you are correct, Wushito would know. But I must warn you, even I do not know all their secrets. But I can have the master of Wushito brought to the palace for you to speak with. If you'd—"

A sudden crash cut off Hiro's words. Then the unmistakable yowling cry of a young child broke the second of silence.

"Yoshi?" Hiro said. He spun, sharp eyes glaring at Tarkan. He turned like lightning and took one dashing step for the door when the kehann behind Tarkan released a shot from a crossbow.

Hiro grunted in pain and fell as the bolt thudded hard into his left thigh. Tarkan ran to him and aimed a swift kick at his face, stunning the man. Hiro valiantly pushed himself up and prepared to run.

"Subdue him," Tarkan ordered the kehann, taking a step back to look out the doors behind the table.

The kehann rushed Hiro and started to beat him. The steward fought back, but couldn't throw off three of them. Somewhere out in the halls, a woman screamed. Tarkan ran to the doors and hauled them open, looking out.

"Here!" he called, seeing one of his Apostles followed by a small horde of risen. The risen already had bloodied blades. The Apostle turned and shouted back down the hall for the others to follow him.

Ashkan appeared a moment later, a host of guards and the commander from before following as prisoners. In Ashkan's arms was a small Xian child with shocking white hair. The child looked as though he'd been bawling only moments ago, but now held his tongue as if he understood. Tears streaked down his ruddy face and his lips pouted. But he was silent.

"On their knees," Tarkan ordered.

The other Apostles and their risen forced the prisoners onto their knees. Tarkan went back to Hiro, bloodied and gasping now. He reached down and gripped Hiro by his long hair and dragged him forward to face his people.

"My prince!" the commander sputtered.

"Silence," Tarkan hissed. With a grunt, he tossed Hiro onto the ground. Hiro landed in a heap, blood speckling the golden floor before him. Tarkan unsheathed his bloody blade and set the tip at the nape of Hiro's skull. He pushed down, making Hiro lower himself to the floor completely in subjugation.

"Is that the child?" Tarkan asked.

"It was the only child in the palace," Ashkan replied. "His room was guarded and there was only a woman inside with him."

"What do you want?" Hiro spat bravely, despite his subdued position. "Who are you?"

Tarkan smiled and twisted his blade, drawing a little blood. Hiro quivered, but Tarkan couldn't tell if it was from rage or fear. "I am Necro'Khan. And I am here for the Crypt."

"Death fiend!" Hiro snarled. "Only Wushito can open the Crypt. And our Wushito master will never do it."

Tarkan reached down and grabbed a handful of Hiro's hair, pulling his head back painfully far. He leaned closed to his face and whispered, "Are you sure about that? Ashkan."

The Apostle unsheathed a ruby blade and poised it over the young Di-Huan's soft skull.

"Don't!" Hiro begged. He reached out one bloodied hand toward

Ashkan as if he could stop him. "Wushito won't submit to you, death fiend," he said, "even if I ordered them to."

"I expect you to cooperate, prince," Tarkan snarled back. "Bring forth the master of Wushito and let him see the situation. I am sure his mind will be made up quite quickly."

"We will never submit to—" Hiro started.

Tarkan roared, raised his blade, and plunged it into the ground just inches from Hiro's face. The prince winced and cringed away, but didn't make a noise. In that moment, Tarkan made up his mind.

No matter what Hiro did, he'd kill the child.

Even if the prince submitted to his every whim, obeyed without question. Even if the Wushito master put up no fight. Xia needed to know he would stop at nothing to get what he wanted.

Tarkan jerked his blade free and rested the tip once again at the base of Hiro's skull. He pushed down until the prince was completely pressed against the floor in submission once again.

"Call for Wushito," he ordered. "And do not even think about betraying my trust now and calling for the city guards. I will not hesitate to kill the child."

At this, the young Di-Huan yowled once again, crying piteously in Ashkan's arms.

Hiro swallowed hard and nodded. "Commander," he ordered from where he lay. "Bring Wushito master Wu-Ji-lin and Wu-Yasuke to the palace. Don't tell them why."

"Of course, my prince." The commander looked to Tarkan, waiting to be released. Tarkan nodded and the man ran out the great doors.

# Chapter 6
## Alliance

Sharar stood on his balcony, the book floating before him. He twisted his hand as a small orb of light flitted and danced around his long fingers. He faced south toward Alika, thinking of what Tarkan might be doing right at that moment. He felt too idle, like he was waiting for something, but didn't know what. He turned his palm facing up and let the light stop and hover there in his hand. He looked into it, almost making his eyes water in the darkness. Sighing, he snuffed the light. The silence annoyed him, so he turned to face the dark corner where Vicdan was chained. The necromancer watched him with sad eyes.

"Don't pout, my boy," Sharar said as jovially as he could, despite his own anxious spirit. "You bring this suffering on yourself." He walked back inside the room and stood before Vicdan, examining the younger man for a moment. "I could remove the bridle, I suppose."

Sharar lifted a set of small keys from his belt and unlocked the metal device clamped around Vicdan's jaw. As it fell away, Vicdan moaned in pain. He spat a large glob of blood onto the golden floor and opened his mouth wide like he might yawn.

"There's no call for such barbarity," Vicdan said around his pained tongue. "Shackling my arms is good enough, you know. Why so paranoid?"

"Because you won't eat," Sharar said simply.

"I'm starving," Vicdan countered with a light glare. "I haven't eaten or drunk anything in days, no thanks to that damned bridle."

Sharar scoffed lightly through his nose. "I offered you blood and flesh."

Vicdan turned slightly green at the mention of the cannibalistic ways of his people. "I won't consume."

"I know," Sharar said. "And so you will starve."

"What good am I to you weak?"

"What good are you at all?" Sharar quipped back. "If you are to cast, you must consume. Your refusal makes me reconsider keeping you alive. You understand that, yes?"

Vicdan gulped and nodded silently.

Sharar turned on his heel and went to his cabinet. He flung the doors open to reveal many oddities and scientific equipment. Scanning the inside, he quickly found what he sought. He pulled a water skin from a hook on the door and turned back to Vicdan. Then he marched over, pulling the cork out.

"I won't," Vicdan began.

Sharar ignore him and forced the flask between his lips. He gripped Vickan's head with one arm and held the skin to his face, forcing him to drink. Vicdan coughed and sputtered, but eventually gave in, drinking ravenously. Satisfied, Sharar backed away. Vicdan choked, but had swallowed a good amount. Some spilled down his chin and onto the black robes Sharar had forced him into earlier.

The necromancer panted, but color quickly came back to his cheeks and his eyes brightened.

"You see?" Sharar said, wiping some of the blood from his hand onto his robe. "You feel stronger already, don't you?"

Vicdan didn't reply. He winced and hung his head in shame.

"Finish it and I will call for food to be brought to you," Sharar bargained.

Vicdan looked up, his eyes glimmering with unshed tears. He gagged, but nodded. Sharar knelt and, gently this time, pressed the flask to Vicdan's lips. The necromancer drank until all the blood was gone. Vicdan looked away once he was finished, looking like he might vomit.

"Good boy," Sharar whispered. He turned and walked to the door, flinging it open. The servant on the outside jumped then bowed. "Bring food," Sharar ordered. "Something savory."

The servant nodded, bowed again, and scampered off down the hall. Sharar turned back to his room and walked toward Vicdan. "Don't even think about raising anything," he warned. Then he bent over and produced the ring of keys. Quickly, he unlocked Vicdan's hands. Eyeing him carefully, he turned back to his desk. Holding his hand out, he summoned the book to himself and caught it deftly.

"There are many spells in this book," he began, as if giving a lecture at the seminary. "But I am afraid to use them. Each one would open a new door for me, a new show of power. There are spells to master the elements, to control things with my mind, to make animals bend to my will. I should be ruling Al'Myrah and yet..."

"And yet you are afraid," Vicdan offered. "Why?"

"Power corrupts, my boy," Sharar said simply. "I have the most power of any creature on the map. I don't want it to overtake me. Not yet. I want to be master of it, not for it to have mastery over me."

Vicdan frowned. "How prudent of you. I am shocked, to say the least."

"The same goes for this alliance with Bahratt," the sorcerer went on. "I need it, but I don't want them to think we are desperate for their fleet."

"Aren't you?" Vicdan asked. He pushed himself up onto his knees. "Al'Myrah's military is a thing of beauty to be sure, but you cannot hope to stand up to Tarkan's undead army. We've seen what that blade of his can do. Any red bloods you march to his doorstep are fodder for his undead horde. And he has to have many Apostles by now. I don't see how—"

Vicdan's words abruptly cut off as he screamed, doubling over.

Sharar flexed his long fingers, envisioning wrapping them around the necromancer's heart. He felt the pulsating muscle in his palm and squeezed. Vicdan gasped, but couldn't take in a deep breath. He winced and tears fell from his green eyes as he writhed in agony on the floor. Sharar held his heart there in his grasp and squeezed once more, knowing the immortal wouldn't die. But the pain was enough to satisfy him.

He let go.

Vicdan gasped and pressed his hands to his chest, groaning. "Let it never be said you are not a heart-stopper, sorcerer," he moaned.

Sharar shook his head and gently placed the book down on the table. "Ever the jokester. Tell me, what will it take to make you cease?"

Vicdan pushed himself back up, still rubbing his aching chest. "I thought you removed the bridle so I could converse with you, scholar. Was I wrong? You seem so lonely while I'm incapacitated. I wanted to soothe that ache in you."

Before Sharar could answer, the door opened and two servants came in, bearing a carafe of wine and a plate of food. He pointed to Vicdan and they set the things down near him before bowing and quickly rushing out.

Vicdan tore into the food, using his hands. He closed his eyes and moaned as he swallowed his first bite. "I could sing a ballad about this lamb right now," he said through his full mouth.

"Don't," Sharar warned him. He turned a moment and watched as the once-jongleur drown himself in water and wine. Then he looked back down into the Mahit'Onomicon and flipped a page lazily. Yes, the book terrified him. Somehow he didn't feel like he commanded the magic, but that it commanded him. Because of that, using the spells had made him wary. But he didn't have time to be worried. He needed to master it, and soon.

"Acenoth IV used the Mahit'Onomicon when he fought off the last sorcerer," Sharar mused out loud to Vicdan as he ate. "They say the gods let him read the book and he raised his army back from the dead. But it wasn't the pharaoh who read the book. No, a slave called Ishmael did."

"Tarkan's father?" Vicdan asked.

Sharar nodded. "Ishmael wrote the scriptures onto his flesh and took them back to Porsh, where he destroyed his entire county for the sake of wielding the sacred texts. He was powerful then, even as a

Scriven. Porsh couldn't stand up to him. For nearly a thousand years, he ruled. He made Apostles in that time, but never broke his own covenant scar. Not until he had an heir."

Vicdan swallowed. "They must have defeated the sorcerer. The story goes that it was an Al'Myrahn man. The map may start to believe we in Al'Myrah have an unhealthy desire for our outlawed magic."

Sharar hummed, but he hardly heard Vicdan. His eyes scanned the book. "But there is nothing about the undead in the Mahit'Onomicon," he went on. "It's gone. Like Ishmael took it the moment he carved the scriptures into his own flesh."

Vicdan frowned in thought. "Maybe Nephron removed them when he stole them? The book was penned by the gods, after all. They could alter it."

"Or during the battle, they decided the power was too much for one sentient and thus divided it."

"Maybe Nephron wrote the scriptures on Ishmael," Vicdan suggested, clearly loving the weaving of the tale. "Perhaps they were never in the Mahit'Onomicon?"

This idea gave Sharar pause. He rubbed his groomed beard in thought. This was why he wanted a necromancer. Only they knew what the necrotic scriptures said. "We can never know. Ishmael is dead. All we know is that the necrotic scriptures are not inside the book."

"Yes, he is dead," Vicdan mused. "I was there. Or rather, Tzarik and I found him after Tarkan got to him."

Sharar looked up from the book. "You've been to Porsh?"

"Do not recommend it," Vicdan said quickly. "Everything is dead and blighted. The necromancy has seeped into the very soil, killing it with unlife."

The sorcerer paced now. "What does Tarkan want, then?"

"Freedom," Vicdan said, wiping his mouth with the back of his hand. "You tortured him. Made him do terrible things. I saw him on Caerwren, too. He doesn't want anyone to have power over him ever again. He thinks if he's the most powerful being on the map, then he will never need to fear again. He wants to be free from fear. From pain." Vicdan shook his head. "He'll destroy everything to make that happen. The world cannot harm you if it's all dead."

Sharar didn't answer. He took in what Vicdan had said and looked out onto the balcony where the night grew old.

"And you, sorcerer?" Vicdan asked gently. "What do you want?"

Sharar thought about it. He wanted the power over the dead, the only power he didn't possess. He wanted to be able to bring back those who had gone. Yes, the jongleur would like that story. "I had a son, once. He was taken from me. Runed, but he was innocent. He died from the cursed sulfates." He faced Vicdan. "I want him back. He didn't deserve that fate. Tarkan raised him once for me, but it didn't last. The runes took him again. Tzarik is an innocent Runer. I think he is the key to saving my son."

Vicdan's green eyes rounded. "Tzarik cannot help you. He won't know why the runes spared him any more than you do. Trust me, he's frightfully ignorant."

"I don't intend for him to know. I intend to cut him open. To find why the gods spared him and not my son."

"The hubris of scholars," Vicdan scoffed. "The gods do not answer to sentient kind. You cannot make them, let alone the Dohkma and his white blood."

Sharar smirked. "I am a man of science. The gods do not frighten me."

"They should," Vicdan quipped back. "Go spend a winter on Caerwren and then tell me how you feel about the gods."

Sharar sighed, tired of the conversation. "If the gods are so powerful, why has Nephron not smitten Tarkan? He defies his god by making his own spells, writing his own scriptures in the alphabet of the Mahit'Onomicon."

"Unlike you, scholar, I don't deign to know the gods' wills. I cannot say why the terrifying god of death has not put a stop to Tarkan. Perhaps he likes the heresy. Perhaps in the life of a god, Tarkan is a mere smudge on the grand design. Just as you are."

Sharar bristled at the insult. "Do I need to remind you of my power?" He called up a storm then, making the sky go dark and lightning crackle overhead. His fingers tingled with the electricity of the storm. He imagined sending a bolt of lighting down onto Vicdan like he'd done before. He remembered the scream that was torn from Vicdan's throat then and smiled.

Vicdan shockingly didn't wince or cringe away. He stood his ground. "No," he replied softly. "And I don't believe you."

Sharar glared at Vicdan. "What do you mean?"

"It's not about your son. You just want power. You want to be second only to the gods. The knowledge is too much for you, though. But you want it. You cannot stand not having it."

Lightning snapped between his fingers. Vicdan was right, of course. Sharar seethed for only a moment before he wrangled control of himself again.

He let the spell go, the clouds dissipating and the lightning between his fingers vanishing. "We must go see our sultana now. We must discuss our Bahratt allies before it's too late."

"It's the middle of the night," Vicdan said.

"And they leave in a few days' time. We cannot miss the chance."

Sharar marched through the darkened palace, Vicdan in tow. A few oil lamps burned on the pillars here and there, lighting the way down the golden halls. A servant moved silently between the shadows, but didn't stop them as they approached the great double doors that led to the sultana's bedroom. Guards on the outside of the door stepped forward.

"Step aside," Sharar growled. "This is urgent."

"Sira, we cannot allow—"

Sharar raised his arms and whipped them wide apart. The guards flew to the sides, crashing into the hallway. They moaned, shocked more than hurt, then rolled onto their feet, weapons poised. Sharar ignored them and shoved the bedroom doors open. A soft gasp came from inside. He marched through the grand bedroom to the large bed draped in sheer veils.

Inside, the sultana rushed to grab a robe to cover her nakedness. Kalil was next to her and moved just as quickly.

"What is the meaning of this?" the sultana barked, tying a sash around her pregnant middle. She shuffled to the edge of the bed and threw the curtains open, glaring at Sharar.

He heard the guards rush in after him, babbling apologies to the sultana. Kalil slid off the bed and marched up to Sharar.

"Don't," the sorcerer warned the young man. "I am here to speak to the sultana on a matter of utmost importance. Time is of the essence." He turned to look at the guards behind him. He pointed easily to Kalil. "Take him back to the harem and make sure he stays."

The guards didn't move, looking to their sultana for orders or confirmation.

"Do as he says," she whispered sadly.

"No!" Kalil shouted, shoving past the guards. "I won't leave you with this man."

"Brave imbecile," Sharar said. He was getting tired of people defying him. "Do you want to risk my wrath at this moment?"

"Kalil, go," the sultana said gently. She climbed off the bed, went to him, and kissed him passionately. "I'll be fine. We both will." Her hands went to her belly.

Kalil glared at Sharar, but did as his wife instructed him. The guards marched him out and finally the three of them were alone. The sultana sniffled and blinked. A single tear ran down her honey-colored cheek.

"What do you want, sorcerer?" she asked.

Sharar squared up to her. "You must meet with the prince of Jarabu before he leaves and ask him for allies. We simply must move on Alika before it's too late."

The sultana's eyes flitted to Vicdan, who stood behind Sharar, and then back to him. He held her gaze. "The blight hasn't reached Al'Myrah yet," she tried. "And to march on Alika—our allies—would require a vote from the nobles and the court."

"Alika has been overtaken," Sharar pressed. "Sokar'Xenoteph is no longer ruling over the land." He stopped. A sudden great sadness rose up in him. A lump formed in his throat that he had to swallow down. He'd left Sokar that day. Was the boy even still alive?

*Gods, let him live,* he thought suddenly. If he was still alive, what would Tarkan do to him? Perhaps it was better the boy died rather than endure whatever horrors Tarkan would bring upon him.

"Scholar?" the sultana asked, her face twisting in confusion.

"Apologies," Sharar said quickly, shrugging off his emotions. "You are not attacking your allies, you are coming to their aid," he reasoned. "I was there, sabi. I swear to you that the Necro'Khan has taken Alika and will come to Al'Myrah."

"Sabi," Vicdan said gently, stepping out from behind Sharar. "You know I am but a prisoner here. I promise you, what he says is true."

The sultana's brows went up even as more tears filled her eyes. "You would urge me to send Al'Myrahns to their deaths alongside our Bahratt brothers?"

Vicdan shuffled his feet. "I cannot speak for Sharar, but I can for Al'Myrah. I saw the battle in Mysir. The Necro'Khan has an undead army. It will take as many warriors as we can muster to overtake Alika and save it. And... I know the Necro'Khan. I know he will move on Al'Myrah. We won't have a choice but to fight."

"Bring the fight to him," Sharar counseled. "You don't want this fight on Al'Myrahn land where your people will be the casualties of war."

The sultana frowned, raising her chin as she thought. "You care for Al'Myrah?" she asked Sharar.

The truth was he wanted Tarkan either dead or once again subjugated to him. He imagined having the Necro'Khan under his thumb once more, chained in his dungeon, bleeding and weak. He wanted that power to submit to him.

"Of course," he lied easily. "It is my home." He felt Vicdan's eyes boring into the back of his head as he said it. "Sabi," he said more gently. "You don't have a choice in this matter. There is too much at stake."

She glared at him. "How dare you threaten me," she growled.

Sharar flexed his fingers and reached out to the sultana with his mind. He probed and prodded over her body until he found what he sought. Then he squeezed. The woman gasped and doubled over, holding her belly.

"No, please!" she cried. "My son!"

Sharar twisted his hand, bringing the woman to her knees as she wailed in pain and fear.

"Stop!" she yowled. "I'll do it. I'll speak to the prince. I'll do whatever you want. Just let him go."

Sharar released his fingers. The sultana gasped and fell onto her side against the cool ground. "You will tell the prince to bring this message to the maharaja and demand a fleet to join ours in the Black Sea. We will sail to Alika and dock in Gypsu. Then we march on Mysir. Simple, really. Do you understand?"

Tears rolling down her face, the sultana nodded. "I will do as you say, sorcerer."

# Chapter 7
## The Mori

Tzarik tightened the girth on Alvakar and double-checked his saddlebags. They wouldn't be gone but a day or two at the most, but he still wanted to make sure they had everything they might need. There was no telling what kind of quest they might be sent on while looking for a Runer who knew where a mori was hiding. He sighed and pet Alvakar's mane. Behind him, Sybal hummed as she sifted through her own black box. Something clinked in her hands. Tzarik turned to see her eyeing the sulfates.

"I'm sorry I never told you," he said. The night she'd come back, she'd asked him about them and told him about meeting Nefiri and Amir. Guilt had filled him so much that he'd not been able to speak much to her. And his mind reeled with the thoughts of everything else he'd never taught her. She wasn't ready for him to leave her. Not yet. He'd not trained her to be an independent Runer.

"I know now," she said kindly. "That's all that matters. And you'll have time to teach me anyway." She avoided looking into his eyes, choosing instead to count her crossbow bolts.

He swallowed. Would he have the time? "We don't know that," he said at length. He laid his hands on Alvakar's neck, then looked up at Sybal to find her blue eyes fixed on him.

"Please stop," she said sternly. "We're on our way. We'll find a way to cure this."

"Before Tarkan kills Sharar?" He moved around his horse to be closer to her. "We can't know what the Necro'Khan is planning. Or where he is."

"We have eyes on Sharar," she said back. "I trust Amir. And I doubt Tarkan would come to Al'Myrah." She blinked. "Yet, anyway. I don't know that's his plan. And we know he doesn't want Sharar dead. He wants his blood."

Tzarik waited, hoping she'd come to him. But she didn't. "You don't think he'd kill Sharar just to stop him? You think his lust for the blood of a sorcerer is stronger than his fight for dominance?"

This gave Sybal pause. She froze in her work and frowned. "I hope so. We know Tarkan. We know he is afraid."

"That's what I mean," Tzarik pointed out. "He may be scared enough to put a stop to Sharar rather than risk holding him hostage."

"Tzarik, please!" Sybal snapped. She balled her fists and closed her eyes tightly. She breathed a moment, then opened her eyes again.

He waited, seeing she wanted to say something. She shook her head.

"Never mind," she grumbled. "Let's go into the city and find a Runer."

"Wait!"

They both turned to see Signar trotting to them, slinging a cloak around his shoulders. His long yellow hair flowed like a silk flag behind him in the desert wind. He smiled when he caught up to them.

"I'm coming with you," he announced. He clapped Tzarik on the shoulder and then moved around to his horse, which he mounted bare-back and with no bridle.

"Signar," Sybal started, but didn't go on. They both knew it was useless to try to make him stay.

Tzarik smiled weakly. He didn't mind towing the boy along with them.

"I'll follow you if you leave me behind," Signar said to Sybal when she spied Tzarik's smile. "I want to help in any way I can."

Tzarik met Sybal's eyes over the horses and he shrugged lightly. She rolled her eyes and mounted, clicking her tongue to take the lead. The men followed her out into the city limits to find a Runer.

⤙❧⤚

"Runers are few on Al'Myrah," Signar noted as his keen green eyes scanned the city streets. "I've not seen one since being here."

"We are a rare breed," Tzarik agreed. "The people of Al'Myrah do not fear Runers like they do on Caerwren. Here, we are treated as less than. As an other. What you did on Caerwren, putting a Runer on your throne, would be met with rebellion here on Al'Myrah."

Signar hummed in thought as he nodded. "I hope Tage is well. I have dreams about Altevine almost every night."

Tzarik looked sideways at Sybal, who looked just as concerned. They'd spoken many times about taking Signar back to Caerwren, but knew the boy would put up a fight. He'd tell them Dain and Tage would be fine, that they could handle anything the malignation threw at them. Tzarik wasn't so sure, though. The blight Tarkan had brought to Caerwren was unlike any curse the map had ever seen.

"Let's go to the graveyard," Sybal suggested. "There's one not too far from here. They're always haunted. And I bet a Runer has been through recently."

Tzarik nodded and let her take the lead again as they wound their way through the city and out toward the temple on the outskirts. It didn't take long to find the groundskeeper and learn that a Runer had indeed been through.

"His name was Nadim," the groundskeeper said as he leaned on a shovel over an open grave. "Came through from Yenka and dispatched a ghoul for me. Said he was going to stay in the city one more night before sailing to Bahratt."

Tzarik understood this life. He'd hunted on Bahratt almost as much as on Al'Myrah and had often traveled between the two countries to find enough hunts. Runers were not as hated on Bahratt as they were on Al'Myrah thanks to their ties to the Tashid temple and the magi there. Bahratt didn't outlaw magic like Al'Myrah did.

They thanked the groundskeeper and immediately started to check public houses around the area.

"How far have you gone for a hunt?" Signar asked. "You'd never been to Caerwren. Have you never gone so far north?"

Tzarik scoffed lightly and smiled. "I've been to Rhostrana many times. They are a rich country and pay well."

"You speak Rhostranan?" Sybal asked.

Tzarik nodded. "Haven't we discussed this before?"

Sybal shrugged. "I'm happy to be surprised again, if that's the case."

Signar smiled, looking between the two of them. Then he pulled up on his horse and pointed. "Look," he whispered. "There, going into that public house."

Tzarik looked up and spotted the Runer easily. His black garb stuck out among the colorful street performers and rich people who mingled there in the middle of the afternoon. He had the black skin of a man from Yenka and long hair down to his shoulders. He slipped into the public house and vanished from sight. Tzarik slid off his horse, threw the reins over a hitching post, and ducked inside. Sybal and Signar were on his heels.

Once inside, Tzarik growled. His stature didn't let him see around the midday crowd that filled the house. Farmers on breaks, traveling merchants, pirates, and all kinds of other people filled the space.

"Where is he?" he asked Signar beside him.

The tall boy narrowed his eyes and looked around. "Ah, by the back door. He's sitting alone."

Tzarik began to push his way through the crowd.

"Won't he be wary of strangers?" Signar asked.

"Hopefully not of fellow Runers," Sybal supplied quickly. "And my presence tends to make them take a moment before turning us away."

Signar smiled at her and Tzarik was glad to see her reciprocate the grin.

"Nadim?" Tzarik asked as he broke through the crowd.

The Runer looked up from the table, where he'd been staring into the middle distance. "Brother?" he said casually. "And..." His blue eyes, which stood out more shockingly in his face than in any other Tzarik had ever seen, locked onto Sybal. "Are you a sister of the runes?" he asked. A small, amused smile tugged at his face.

"I am," Sybal said, swinging her legs around the bench and sitting down across from Nadim. She motioned for Tzarik and Signar to join her.

"And a pale man." Nadim's eyes widened when they took in Signar and his sheer size. "To what do I owe this great pleasure?" He folded his hands on the table, but Tzarik noticed a hidden blade on his wrist.

With a quick scan, Tzarik noticed a hidden blade on the other wrist as well. The gauntlets appeared to be a sort of contraption that would eject the blade somehow. They were well-hidden, though, so he doubted Sybal had picked up on them. The man had a scimitar at his side as well as a sling. A small bag hung near it where Tzarik assumed some sort of stone with magical properties was kept.

"We need information," Tzarik said as evenly as he could.

Nadim frowned. "What can I tell you that you don't already know?"

"We're looking for Runers who deal in trade of the sulfates," Tzarik said.

"Ah," Nadim said, nodding. "I know a little about that. But most Runers from Hatal do."

Tzarik tilted his head, preemptively preparing to play the game of riddles folk often did when wary of strangers.

"We're not from Hatal," Sybal said quickly.

"Clearly." Nadim nodded to Signar. "What would you give in exchange for the information you seek?"

"We have money," Tzarik offered.

"Gems," Sybal said quickly. She reached into her hip satchel and pulled out a small sapphire. She plunked it onto the table and eyed the man.

Nadim's blue eyes sparkled. "I am a simple Runer, sabi," he said with a grin. He tapped the table near the gem. "But this speaks of desperation. Hatal is my city, and I deserve to know what you are so desperate for."

"You're not from Yenka?" Sybal asked.

"I was," Nadim replied curtly. "But I've lived in Hatal most of my life. Now, tell me. What have you brought to my city?"

Sybal frowned, but Tzarik understood. The Runer was sharp.

"A curse?" Nadim asked. "You want to know about Runers who deal in the sulfates, the white blood, sabi," he said to Sybal when he saw her confused face. "But you don't want the sulfates, do you? You want the creature they come from." He leaned back and tapped the table again. "Why do you want to find a mori?"

Sybal's mouth popped open in shock at the man's deduction. Tzarik, however, was not as surprised. He'd played the same kind of trick many times before. One day, Sybal would be just as observant. Some day soon, he hoped.

"If we tell you," Tzarik said, "will you direct us to the mori?"

Nadim raised his brows and half shrugged. "Do I have to kill you to stop whatever blackness you have brought to my city?"

Tzarik shook his head. "Only I will suffer. We seek a cure for a fate-binding."

Now Nadim's face turned from one of guarded suspicion to something softer. "I am sorry, Runer. That is djinn magic. Hard to undo." He pointed to the brand on Signar's shoulder. "You have a djinn. But not the one who cursed you?"

"Yes," Tzarik said, realizing now the man had been eyeing Signar for some time. "But we're not using it. We're planning on getting rid of it as soon as we can."

"Good." Nadim took in a deep breath and sighed heavily. "I will not abide a djinn in my city. Let alone one tied to a boy."

"I'm no fool," Signar spat.

"It's not you I don't trust," Nadim said seriously. "It's the demon you carry with you. Listen to me, Runers." He leaned onto the table and lowered his voice. "Take your demon and leave Hatal, and I will tell you what you need to know." He reached over, scooped up the gem, and pocketed it as well.

"We have no intention of staying longer than we need to," Tzarik promised him. "Where is the mori?"

Nadim sat up and rubbed his unshaven chin. "There is Bahratt nobility in the east quarter. A kumari from Jarabu has lived there for decades."

"So?" Sybal spat. "We don't care for the foreign nobility."

The other Runer smiled. "You have a lot to learn, sabi. This kumari is known throughout the city. He throws massive gatherings of debauchery and hedonism. One such gathering is happening tonight. You should go to his estate." He reached into his satchel then, pulled out a bit of parchment, and wrote down an address in the eastern quarter.

Tzarik frowned. "Why? Will the mori be at this gathering?"

Nadim smiled and nodded. "I've been to one of these nighttime events with fellow Runers who deal in the white blood trade. You will find what you seek there. And not to worry, you will not be out of place. Runers are common at the kumari's gatherings. He is called Khali. Find him, and you will learn all you want to know."

Doing as Nadim instructed, they waited until nightfall. The city came alive at night with a different crowd than what normally walked about during the day. The men and women who walked the streets of the night for money seemed to grow in number the closer they got to the address. A bold young man approached the three of them and brazenly solicited sex from all of them. Tzarik had to threaten him before he left them alone.

It was Signar who picked out the home first. His nose twitched, and he pointed ahead a few blocks. "That smell," he whispered in a mix of shock and awe.

"What is it?" Tzarik asked.

Signar waited a moment before answering. "It's like a battlefield: blood, sweat, bodies, fire. But the music."

"You can hear music?" Sybal asked.

Signar nodded. "And so many voices." He stalled in the street then. "It's so loud."

Tzarik took a hold of Signar's upper arm and forced him forward gently. "You can control your wolf now. You have no reason to fear the noise."

But Signar's face still twisted slightly in concern as they moved down the street to the house at the end. There was no land attached to the grand manor. The gate and facade loomed right on the street of Hatal. Tzarik saw everything Signar had described when they stood just on the other side of the gate. Looking in, he spotted bodies hanging out windows. Loud music echoed in the air, and shouting and singing came from inside. Fires brightened the place and multicolored silks blew in every window. And the smell was just as Signar had described it: hot, fleshy, and humid. The slightest tang of red blood could be smelled as well.

"Stay close," Tzarik warned Sybal. "Do not leave one another's sights."

She looked down at him meaningfully. She and Signar would be spotted just fine, being taller than most Al'Myrahns. He, on the other hand, could be swept away without them knowing.

"Runers?" a man at the gate asked. He had no weapons, only stood on the other side of the locked iron bars.

"We're here to see Khali," Tzarik said easily. There was no reason to lie. He had to shout to be heard over the din of the gathering.

"Of course you are," the man laughed, his corpulent belly jiggling with the effort. "Many Runers are here tonight. But he will see you. He likes your lot." The man pulled a great ring of keys from his belt and unlocked the bars. "Go on," he instructed.

Tzarik led them up the path, past a great fountain in the courtyard where several drunk party-goers were splashing about. Two men in ornate, decorated garments at the front opened the double doors for them.

The party hit them hard in the face when the doors opened. The sound deafened them and the smell overcame them. Bright light blazed from a great fire pit in the center of the room. Topless dancers moved on the rails of the upper level and Masahk slaves in chains slipped between the crowd serving food and liquor. The massive drums spread over the room rocked the walls around them and the chattering filled Tzarik's ears to bursting. He gripped Signar's hand

and marched into the cacophony of people. Sybal followed close behind.

Intoxicated guests stumbled over the golden steps leading to the upper levels, and others danced shamelessly with the performers around the hall. Couples were strewn across the furniture, kissing passionately, running their hands over one another, and some even went further despite the crowd around them. Sybal quickly pulled Signar away from a rather amorous couple. Tzarik followed, but then stopped when she did.

"What is it?" he asked.

"I found him," she whispered close to his ear. She pointed over the crowd and Tzarik looked between the patrons.

Across the room was a huge fountain surrounded by a blue pool. A set of water-type Masahk danced with fire around it. Beyond this a platform with a grand throne atop it rose into the air. Sweating bodies were piled around the throne. Tzarik hoped they were alive and not a stack of sacrifices given to the mori. Sitting on the throne, a black cobra draped around his neck, was Khali. He wore the traditional red and gold of the nobles and royals of Bahratt. He dripped in gold decor: a gold ring in his nose and a golden, ornamental chain around his head, with a single ruby hanging down between his immaculate dark brows. His hair was the shiniest Tzarik had ever seen, long and feathery down to his shoulders. Behind him were four statues of the many-armed Bahratt gods made of onyx.

Khali's eyes were a bright, blood-red.

As they made their way to the mori, a woman threw herself over Khali's lap and gripped his face. She kissed him passionately and giggled when he returned the gesture, biting her lip. The woman was almost entirely naked. She sat up and straddled Khali's lap, kissing his angular face as they approached. When they neared, his red eye snapped up to them over the woman's bare shoulder.

Tzarik then noticed several Runers among those lounging nearest Khali. He spotted four before he stopped counting. He'd never seen so many Runers in one place on Al'Myrah. He guessed they were all here for Khali's blood. But they didn't hunt him. No, they were patiently waiting. But he understood. It was hard for most Runers, whose crime was murder, to hunt a mori, since they were sentient. They couldn't kill the monster without the runes taking them. So more diplomatic means were required.

Khali shoved the naked woman off and she squealed as she fell from the throne and rolled down the stairs. He stood up. "More Runers," he said in a melodious voice that held a strange attraction. "Come for my blood, have you? I've never seen you here before. I know most of my Runers. But Nadim did say I'd have fresh company this evening." As he spoke, he seductively ran his hand up and down his cobra's hood.

"We're not here for your blood, monster," Tzarik said as evenly as he could.

"I only deal in blood, Runer," Khali replied curtly. The woman at his feet whimpered and touched his legs, pleading with her eyes for him to come back to her. He kicked her aside and flicked his finger for the three to follow him.

They pushed through the river of bodies and followed Khali out behind the statues of gods. He led them through a garden where far fewer guests lingered and then into a room off the side, which he opened with a ruby key from his own belt. Once inside the room, where there were no patrons, Signar visibly relaxed. He took a quick breath and let it out, closing his eyes.

More statues of the Bahratt gods loomed in the library they now found themselves in. A few lounges flanked another, smaller throne and a desk waited at the head of the room. A few astral instruments lingered in the darker corners, and Tzarik recognized some of them as being ones only magi used.

Khali moved to a golden carafe on a table near a set of bookshelves and poured himself what Tzarik realized was blood. The mori brought it to his nose and inhaled.

"It's getting old," he sighed after a quick sip. "No matter." He smiled and looked at them sideways.

Signar quelled a little, no doubt picking up on the scent from the goblet. He moved one step closer to Tzarik. "How does a mori become a noble of Bahratt?" he asked shyly.

Khali dabbed at his lips after taking a light sip from the goblet. "I was a noble before I was a mori. It's a long story, my pale boy. One that is steeped in tears and fermented in the sorrow of two hundred years of slavery to another mori. But that's not what you're here for. Nadim mentioned your problem to me. Said you were fate-bound."

"I am," Tzarik said, glad to have the basics out of the way. "He said you might be able to counsel us."

Khali boldly stepped closer to them. He sniffed the air like he was testing a delicate wine. "You reek of white blood, Runers. But this one," he pointed to Signar and raised his hand like he might stroke the boy. "He smells of fire and amber."

"Leave him be," Tzarik snapped quickly. "Your discussion is with us."

Quick as lightning, the mori moved around Tzarik and Sybal and grabbed Signar's arm. The Vaeson panicked, but couldn't pull himself free of the undead's grip. Khali pulled Signar's arm to his nose and took a long, deep breath. "You have good veins," he added, tracing one up Signar's arm.

Tzarik's hand flew to his sword hilt and he took one menacing step toward Khali before the mori's red eyes flashed to him in warning.

"Stand your ground, Runer," Khali warned even as Signar struggled to be released. "I am three hundred years old. I didn't get to live so long by letting Runer scum like you hunt me down."

He released Signar and the boy backed away. Tzarik placed himself between the mori and Signar. Sybal's hand still gripped her scimitar's hilt, though.

Khali straightened. He tapped his glassy nails together deviously as he smiled. "Here is my proposition, Runer. And it's quite simple. Don't make it more complicated than it needs to be."

Tzarik glared, knowing exactly what the mori was going to ask for. "No," he growled.

Khali smiled, his handsome face turning predatorial. "I deal only in blood, Runer. Take it or leave it."

Tzarik looked at Signar. The boy tilted his head in confusion.

"Let me taste him," Khali said, licking his lips, "and all I know shall be yours."

"Hells," Sybal swore. "We'll never let you touch him."

"Wait," Signar said, pushing them both aside. "If it helps, I'd be glad to give a little blood."

Khali smiled maniacally.

"No," Sybal said to Signar. "I won't let you get hurt."

"Please," Khali said, gesturing with his hands. "You don't get to be my age by killing indiscriminately. Just a little bite on his neck, nothing more."

"I'll do it," Signar said quickly. He stepped toward the mori.

"Signar," Tzarik pled.

"It's our only option," the boy shot back. "And I'm not afraid."

Khali tapped his long, glass-like nails together harder in anticipation. "Then we have an understanding?"

Tzarik glared. "I'm warning you—"

"Yes, yes, I understand," the mori said, waving his hand like he were swatting away a fly. "Come here, boy." He held his hand out to Signar.

Tzarik's mouth went dry, watching Signar approach the monster. He laid his hand on his sword hilt once again, just in case. Khali gave him a warning look before turning his attention back to Signar.

Khali reached up and gripped the back of Signar's head. With a swift motion, he pulled, bending the boy over backward and exposing his neck. Signar gasped, but his breath was cut off when the sharp fangs of the mori broke the surface of his flesh. Tzarik swore he heard the bite. Signar moaned and gripped Khali's shoulders as he took his first swallow. Tzarik's heart pounded in his ears as he watched. The mori swallowed again and then again, each time pulling a moan from the Vaeson. His moans became softer and softer.

Signar's eyes rolled in his head and his hands dropped, hanging limp at his sides.

"Enough!" Tzarik roared, unsheathing his blade and marching forward.

Khali pulled away, dropping the boy to the ground with a thud. Red blood dribbled down his chin. He wiped at it and licked his lips clean of Signar's blood. "I am so sorry," Khali panted. "I almost lost myself in his blood. Notes of fire and snow in every drop. Delicious."

Sybal ran to Signar's side and knelt beside him. She sat him up, bracing his unconscious body against her chest. "He's alive," she said, eyes shining. She gripped him tightly and embraced him, gently petting his long hair. "Monster," she hissed at the mori.

"Of course." Khali smiled. "Now, what can I tell you about djinn and fate-bindings?" He wiped once more at his mouth and sauntered away from the three of them. His lack of fear enraged Tzarik.

The mori turned and met Tzarik's eyes.

Tzarik quickly looked away, knowing a mori could read his thoughts if he let them in through intense eye contact. Khali smiled again when Tzarik turned his face away.

The mori moved to the throne and sat down. Once comfortable, he said, "Have you heard of a yokai, Runers?"

Tzarik shook his head.

"Demons from Xia," Khali explained. "They are the most like our djinns here on Al'Myrah, Alika, and Bahratt. But perhaps they are more powerful as they cannot be bound. But they have an affinity for sentients and have physical bodies, unlike our djinn. If a mortal lays with a yokai, they produce what is called gini."

Sybal looked up. "We knew one once. She sacrificed her one wish to help us."

Khali raised his brows. "That is a precious gift. The yokai are similar to our djinn in that they hold the most powerful of magics, but are not restrained by the tethers our gods have put on their demons. I suppose the gods on Xia trust their demons more."

"Wushito can bind them," Tzarik put in. "They think their powers come from the gods, though."

"Perhaps they do," Khali agreed. "You could seek out a yokai on Xia and make a deal with one to wish away your fate-binding."

"Could it be that easy?" Sybal asked. "Are yokai stronger than djinn?"

"They are different from djinn," the mori corrected, "and perhaps stronger. They are not unlike the mogwai. But again, different. But, no, lady Runer, it is not simple. Finding one will be difficult. Trapping one, even more so. Bargaining with one? Dangerous. You could be trading one curse for another."

Tzarik thought about that for a moment. Would he be willing to forgo one curse in lieu of another? He'd had enough of curses and bindings for one lifetime.

"What else might we try?" he asked.

Khali steepled his fingers and a dark, mischievous smile overtook his handsome face. "You might speak to your god. Unlike the other gods, the Dohkma does not reside in the God Deep. He is among us. The Pale God."

"Go to the Frozen Nation?" Sybal asked. "No one comes back from that."

"You're not the first to tell us to do that, either," Tzarik said.

Khali opened his hands wide. "Perhaps you should heed the suggestion? The Dohkma is eager to see his people. That's why he does not live in the God Deep like the others. He stays in the north as a test. Only those worthy to see him make it there and back."

"Or immortals," Sybal mused. She looked up, her eyes suddenly bright. "I could go. I could make it there and back."

"Oh?" Khali asked, suddenly interested.

"Sybal, no," Tzarik tried. But he knew she was far too stubborn.

"We can go to Xia," she suggested. "We'll split up. You hunt down a yokai and I'll go north."

"And Signar?" Tzarik asked.

"Take him with you," Sybal said. "I'll go alone, or..." She frowned in thought.

Unsure what she was thinking, Tzarik looked back at the mori. "Any advice on how to trap a yokai?"

"They are not always malevolent," Khali said. "Perhaps treating one with kindness will be a good start. Assuming you find one. I hear the Wushito keep Xia fairly clear of monsters. I wish you good luck on finding one."

Sybal hugged Signar's unconscious body more tightly. "To Xia, then."

# Chapter 8
# The Crypt

"Stand up," Tarkan ordered Hiro. He stepped back, removing the sword from the nape of his neck where it had been resting it for the last several moments. "Strip your armor."

Hiro hesitated for only a moment before pushing himself up to standing. He locked eyes with Tarkan as he unlaced his light Xian armor. He tossed it aside one piece at a time until he stood in only his thin robes. "What is happening now, death fiend?" he asked, completely defenseless now.

"The Royal City's perimeter is overrun by my risen," Tarkan said. "Soon the undead will flood Wushito's stronghold and overtake them. With the two powers of Xia toppled and under my command, I will take the country. Your trust of the Al'Myrahn Runers has ruined you."

Bravery and defiance welled up in Hiro's dark eyes. Before the young prince could fight back, Tarkan ordered him to kneel before him once again. Hiro's eyes flitted to Yoshi—he cried softly now in Ashkan's arms—before he submitted himself once again to Tarkan's orders. He knelt slowly, one knee at a time, until he was under Tarkan's blade once more.

The doors behind them opened again and the commander of the royal guard returned. The commander was sniveling, eyes red-rimmed, and his hands shook. He carried a silver platter with something on it. Tarkan watched, curious, as the commander approached. Once he drew close enough, Tarkan saw what the platter held: the head of an old Xian, the long hair caked in blood. The head's eyes were rolled back into its sockets, the mouth hung open, and the tongue lolled out. Tarkan blanched, but felt a bit of pride in Faraji. This was no doubt his doing.

"Wushito Master Wu-Ji-lin," the Xian commander stammered. "They've killed him. He was in the palace, waiting for..." But the man couldn't go on. He gasped and his hands shook even more as he looked down at the gruesome sight.

Hiro snarled and leapt up. He shoved past a distracted Tarkan and charged at Ashkan. The kehann lunged and stopped him before he could get far and threw him back onto the floor before Tarkan. They drew their swords and pointed them down at Hiro.

"Don't be foolish," Tarkan said, glaring at Hiro. He turned back to the commander to ask where the other Wushito Hiro had mentioned was when the doors opened again. This time, four of the undead soldiers appeared. Tarkan's heart rose at seeing them. That meant they'd been successful as well. Between them, arms pinned behind him, came a fox-like Masahk. His face shone with defiance as well, and his ears, sticking out from his red hair, were pinned back. He had the tiny fangs of a fox as well and they were barred in a feral snarl. The Masahk wore the white robes of a Reaver, but all his weapons had been removed.

"You," the Masahk snarled. "I've heard of you. The Necro'Khan." He struggled once against his captors, but stopped when he spotted Hiro and Yoshi.

"My reputation precedes me?" Tarkan asked. "How flattering."

"Yasuke," Hiro said from where he knelt, "what happened? Wu-Ji-lin is dead."

Yasuke's eyes flitted to the severed head in the commander's hands. "They came to us in our wing of the palace," he said. "We were overcome, and they had the element of surprise. We tried to fight back, but it was just the two of us."

Hiro's face fell.

"Yasuke, is it?" Tarkan asked. He motioned to the undead soldiers and then forced Yasuke to kneel as well. "We're going to the Crypt and you're going to open it for me. Do you understand?"

Yasuke's sharp yellow eyes took in the situation around him. Tarkan saw him calculating before he nodded mutely. "It will take us a day of travel even on the well-worn paths to make it to the Hallow City," he said.

"I don't care," Tarkan replied. "But you will open it."

"I can," Yasuke replied. "We'll need Wu-Ji-lin's blade."

"We have it," one of the undead soldiers said from behind them.

Tarkan sheathed his blood blade. "Then we start now. Ashkan, bring the child."

Just over a day later, Tarkan examined the mouth of the stone arch above him. It was made from what looked like a hollowed-out mountain. He saw nothing but hills through it.

"Is this a joke, Wushito?" he asked Yasuke as his men unshackled him and Hiro.

"No," Yasuke said easily. "This is the entryway to the Hallow City. All you must do is walk through."

Tarkan carefully approached the titanic archway and looked beyond. The more he looked, the more he thought he saw wavering lines glittering in the sun, just visible to his eye. He reached out and tried to touch them. When he did, his hand vanished. Gasping, he stepped back.

"Some sort of veil," he mused. "Strong magic." He turned to his kehann, Faraji, Ashkan, and the few undead with him. "Let them walk without shackles. We need not draw more attention than necessary. You two." He faced Hiro and Yasuke. "If you so much as run, the child dies. I will not hesitate."

Hiro gave Yasuke a stern look and the Masahk bowed his head. "We will obey," Hiro promised.

Tarkan took the lead again and walked under the mountainous

archway. When he did, he gasped. Once he passed underneath, a small fortress on a hill rose before him. A wall surrounded the fortress and a single drawbridge led the way to it.

"You will get us inside," Tarkan ordered Yasuke.

The Masahk bowed and pushed his way to the front of the strange caravan. When the guards in the towers saw him, they let the bridge down without question. Once inside, Tarkan spotted only a few Wushito warriors, scholars, and apprentices. They glanced once, but seeing Hiro and Yasuke, none stopped them as they journeyed up the mountain to the top of the fortress. Yasuke led them to a large red and gold temple with jade statues around it.

"For years, Sharar and I studied the Wushito and their temples," Tarkan said. "So very little outside Xia is known. Is this the place?"

Yasuke nodded, his face full of hard obstinance. "It takes two to open the door to the Crypt." He touched a medallion around his neck. "This and the sword of the Wushito master are needed."

"Then let us open it together," Tarkan said, taking the sword from one of his kehann. "Lead the way."

Yasuke took them through the rooms of the temple until they went out the back and came upon a large set of stairs. They traversed up the steps and by the time they reached the top, the sun was high in the sky. A huge circular building with the common sloping roofs of Xia waited atop it. Tarkan noted stone seals around the outside of the building. He counted six and realized there must be twelve on the entire thing. Each bore a Xian sigil.

Yasuke led Tarkan around to the front, where a great set of double wooden doors waited. A beam ran across them and was locked on either side. The locks were too far apart for one person to handle both at the same time. Tarkan understood. He moved to the narrower lock and slid the sword inside like a key.

"Don't do this," Hiro begged.

"Silence, prince," Tarkan snapped. He glared at Yasuke.

The Masahk approached the other lock and slid the medallion in. He made eye contact with Tarkan and nodded. They both turned their respective items and the doors clicked and groaned. The beam retracted back, unlocking the doors. Yasuke stumbled back quickly, looking up at them. Tarkan held his ground, unafraid of whatever lurked beyond. He gripped one of the doors and heaved it open. Behind him, the undead soldiers took Yasuke in their grip and pulled him back.

Inside the Crypt was almost total darkness. Except for one thing: like a storm cloud, something crackled and snapped within. Tarkan entered and beheld a great rift like he'd seen on Caerwren. Only this one shot up into the air around him and thin tendrils of darkness and lightning crackled out from it. From within, he heard the cries of those inside the God Deep. The monsters growled, and the souls screamed. Looking at the massive rift brought joy to his heart.

He reached out and touched it. A shock of power jolted through him, bringing him to his knees. He groaned as the power coursed through his body, acknowledging him as Necro'Khan. As quick as it had come, it vanished. He looked up through the sliver of the rift and beheld the God Deep beyond. Ghosts, spirits, lost souls—all whirled about within the rift, kept stagnant by the Crypt. Satisfied, he stood and backed out. Once outside again, he shut the door and twisted the locks back into place.

"Faraji, Ashkan," he said. He held out the medallion to Faraji and the sword to Ashkan. "You will guard the Crypt until I give word for it to be opened. Then you will destroy the sigils and open the doors."

Hiro looked up at this, terror filling his eyes. "Release the rift onto Xia?"

Tarkan smiled. "It will be magnificent."

"Our county will be consumed by a blight," Yasuke said, "a malignation the likes of which Wushito will not be able to stop."

"Yes," Tarkan said, nodding. "Now..." He approached Ashkan and took the child from him. Then he turned and faced the space behind the Crypt. A huge waterfall roared there, dumping into a river that flowed out and down the mountainous province. Tarkan tracked the river with his eyes and saw it flowed into a city below them. He wasn't sure what city it was, but it hardly mattered.

"What are you doing?" Hiro asked, trying to throw off the hold of the kehann who had him.

Tarkan approached the waterfall and looked over the edge. Behind him, Hiro screamed and begged. It was just noise over the rushing of the waterfall. Yoshi cringed away from the sound of the roar and clung tightly to Tarkan's robes. The child fussed silently and buried his face in Tarkan's chest.

A sudden memory hit Tarkan. The little hands clinging to him brought up an image of Zeva when she was just a child. Her small hands had often clung to him. Everything had terrified her but him. She should have feared him, too, but something in her had known he'd care for her.

Cautiously, Tarkan touched Yoshi's white hair, remembering little Zeva in his arms. How had she died? Alone?

He closed his eyes against the thought. The Runers had killed her, he reminded himself. And then they'd taken her. He hadn't even been able to say goodbye, to bury her properly.

Yoshi cried louder now, bringing him back to the present. He took a deep breath, shoving his emotions and memories away.

"Please!" Hiro screamed over the roar of the waterfall. But Tarkan didn't hear anything else.

Holding Yoshi out at arm's length over the river, he looked into the child's round face. The boy cried loudly, kicking his legs. He didn't understand. He just knew he was afraid. The child had no idea what Tarkan was about to do. Behind him, he heard a ruckus as no doubt Hiro and Yasuke were both fighting for freedom now. He had very little time.

Realizing that, he pried the child's hands from his sleeves and let go.

The crying vanished almost instantly. Everything went silent. The sun shone down on the river, making a rainbow appear.

The child vanished into the mist, disappearing from view before his small frame even hit the water hundreds of feet below.

Tarkan felt nothing.

A terrifying scream made him whirl around. Hiro charged him, a blade in his hand. The prince's body collided with Tarkan's and he felt the sword pierce his side and come out his back. The pain it shot through him wasn't lessened by knowing it wouldn't kill him. Tarkan groaned and shoved at Hiro, tossing him off. Hiro stumbled back, looking at the blade piercing through Tarkan's middle.

Behind them, Ashkan grabbed a crossbow from one of the kehann and fired it. It hit Hiro in his side, forcing him to his knees. The prince clutched at the bolt and wept.

Tarkan gripped the handle of the blade and pulled it out. He glared down at Hiro. "Don't wound an animal you cannot kill," he whispered. He raised his bloody hand and backhanded Hiro hard across his face. The prince fell to the ground in a heap.

Yasuke ran to Hiro and knelt beside him, hands pressing into the bleeding wound. "Why, Necro'Khan?" he roared. "We did as you asked."

Tarkan dropped the sword Hiro had stabbed him with and drew his own. He contemplated a moment. He could run them both through, but what if he needed them again? He'd hate to give up two fine assets.

Deciding against it, he said, "I want the child's body to wash up on shore. I want his corpse found."

Hiro let out a soft sob.

Tarkan went on, "They will know their prince, the heir to the throne, is dead. Each house will vie for the throne. Things will escalate as they so often do. Xia will be plunged into madness even as the rift opens upon your land. By the time the people realize a malignation is spreading, it will be too late. The Di-Huan is dead, and Wushito will be leaderless.

"The Royal City is mine; my Apostles will have taken it by now. And soon, ships carrying three hundred of my undead warriors will land upon these shores and take the provinces. You see, prince, you do not stand a chance."

Hiro swallowed hard, body shaking from rage and pain. "Are you going to kill me?"

Tarkan shook his head. "I do not fear you."

He turned and walked away from the edge, head held high.

"Yasuke, don't!" Hiro cried.

Tarkan whirled at the same time one of his kehann moved, blade held above his head. Yasuke blinked in a haze of fire from where he had been kneeling with Hiro, appearing just in front of Tarkan, where the kehann crossed blades with him. The fiery Masahk's yellow eyes blazed with a kind of rage Tarkan had not seen in a man in some time. He stepped back as the kehann shoved Yasuke off and they entered combat. Tarkan watched, almost bored, and moved around them with three quick steps. He waited for his opportunity to strike.

The kehann quickly fell behind the Wushito's fast-paced attacks and Tarkan saw he was going to lose. So he stepped in. When they maneuvered around one another and Yasuke's back was to Tarkan, he stepped forward and made a quick stab at Yasuke. His blood blade pierced the Masahk's side from behind. Seeing he'd hit his mark, he shoved harder, running his blade up to the hilt through Yasuke's middle. The Wushito warrior stopped moving instantly and dropped his blade.

Behind Tarkan, Hiro screamed a string of unintelligible words.

Tarkan ripped his blade back out and watched as the Wushito warrior fell before him. Yasuke landed on his back and his once bright, fiery yellow eyes stared up into nothingness, empty and hallow. Tarkan watched his golden-red blood pool underneath him. He sighed in frustration. It was a waste of perfectly good immortal blood.

Tarkan turned back to Hiro. "Don't be as foolish and you will live," he warned. Then he flicked his head to his men and signaled for them to follow him. The kehann went to Hiro and lifted him, following Tarkan out.

"Ashkan, Faraji," he said as he marched away from the wounded and weeping prince, "we will go to the Royal City. That is where you will make our stand. Have the other Apostles defend the walls and do not venture out beyond until the undead come to the gates. That's when it will be safe. We will establish ourselves in the Royal City and take down Wushito as we can. Understood?"

"Yes, my Khan," Faraji said as Ashkan said, "Of course."

"And then?" Faraji asked, keeping pace with Tarkan.

"Then we find the sorcerer and that damned Runer," Tarkan said.

# Chapter 9
## The Maharaja

Sybal caught her breath, panting hard as sweat dripped down her naked body. Tzarik rolled off her in a tangle of limbs and came to rest beside her. She was glad to hear him fighting for breath, too. She stared up at the ceiling of the room, letting the cool desert night air wash over her for just a moment before she turned to face him once again. The room was dim and she could just make out his face in profile next to her.

Her desire still burned hot, so she ran her hand over his chest and drew herself close to him. She pressed her body against his and kissed his neck. He tilted his head up, inviting her to keep going, so she did. She gripped his chin in her hands and roughly turned his face to give her better access to his throat. She swung herself up on top of him and gently started to sway her hips once again. Diving onto him, she nipped at his chest as his hands roamed up and down her scarred torso.

When his hand touched the bite mark of the snake god, he stopped and his fingers lightly traced the wound. She shivered at his delicate touch and moaned as she kissed him. Overcome with need again, she repositioned herself over his hips and prepared to start again. But his touches stopped and his brows furrowed.

"What is it?" she whispered. She listened, wondering if Signar had walked into their room again. The young man still came to Tzarik's room in the night and often slept on the floor near his bed.

Tzarik's hand traveled around her side once again, finding every contour of the god-touched scar. "Tell me," he whispered hoarsely. "Tell me what it was like when you died."

A freezing wave washed over Sybal, taking every amorous feeling with it. Her body turned from hot love to cold sorrow so quickly, she shivered in the night air. She rolled off Tzarik and sat next to him. He propped himself up on his elbow and looked her in the eye.

"Please," he said, touching her leg lovingly.

"Don't you remember?" she asked. "The Vorlamir killed you, too."

His hand didn't leave her thigh where he ran the back of his hand over her skin. "I hardly remember it," he confessed. "It was just blackness. Emptiness. Nothing. I remember feeling cold. Lost." A strange sorrow, or perhaps worry, pinched his brows.

"That's what it feels like," she said. "Like you've gone somewhere no one else can follow and you're alone. But that was just one kind of death. In the Deep. Here, it will be different."

"Is that what the scriptures tell you?" he asked, slight sarcasm coming back into his voice. But he said it with a smile.

"Yes," she whispered seriously. "Layth'asad is the lion of Al'Myrah. Our god. He will take your spirit to Janna or to Nah'jaha. I pray he takes you to Janna so we may meet again in the afterlife."

Tzarik didn't reply, but she saw his face turn serious. He took a quick breath, craned his neck, and kissed her leg before turning to lie on his back again. She knew they were done with the conversation and was glad. She didn't want to discuss death with him. They'd find a way to save him, and he'd have many more decades left to live on the map.

"We should split up," she said after a moment. "To the Frozen Nation and to Xia. That way, we cover more ground."

Tzarik's face almost broke at the mention of splitting up. "I want to be by your side until the curse is lifted. I cannot bear the thought of you facing the Pale God alone."

"We talked about this," she said. "You didn't object then."

Tzarik's eyes went dark. "I was hoping to think of another solution."

"And?" Sybal asked, raising her brows. Tzarik shook his head. "I have to go to the Frozen Nation," she went on. "No matter what happens to me, I won't perish. We don't know how perilous the trail may be. It will be dangerous for you."

Tzarik turned to face her. His hand went to her face and stroked her cheek as he tried to find more words to argue with.

"I've faced many gods," she put in quickly. "I don't fear them anymore." She waited for his reply. In the silence, she heard Signar's bedroom door open and close. "And him?" she asked.

"He'll come with me to Xia," Tzarik said. "We cannot leave him here alone."

Sybal nodded. She scooted back down and snuggled close to Tzarik. He wrapped his arms around her and held her tight. She rested her head on his chest and listened to his heart beat. He kissed the top of her head and sighed, content. They lay together like that until she heard him softly breathing. When she was sure he was asleep, she sat up and looked down at him. He looked so peaceful that she smiled. She gently pushed his hair out of his face and leaned down, taking his lips with hers. He didn't stir.

"I love you," she whispered.

Sharar looked down at the enormous map before them. He, Amir, Nefiri, and Rhaji stood in the sultana's war room inspecting the map, with Vicdan chained behind them. The admiral of the sultana's fleet stood with them as well, his dark eyes roaming over the seas.

"You wouldn't be alone," Sharar said to the admiral. "Bahratt's fleet will join you and together we will sail for Alika's shores." He pointed to the map. "We'd moor here in Gypsu, deploy the soldiers and take back the city. Once we have the base established, we move to Mysir and crush the Necro'Khan in his own halls."

The sultana nervously rubbed at her belly. "But the undead. How are we to stand up to them?"

"Tarkan has a blade," Amir said. "He sustains and commands them with this blade. Once we get to him, the rest will fall. The same goes for the Apostles. Fight your way through the risen and to the necromancers. They are no soldiers and will fall easily."

"Once we can actually get to them," the admiral reminded the Runer.

"So many will die," the sultana moaned.

"More will die if you don't stop him now," Sharar admonished. "And worse, the world will be covered in the malignation he has brought forth. We cannot wait for the God Deep to be released onto this world. We must fight Tarkan now, before that happens. Al'Myrah won't be immune to it. It will spread."

"But the time it will take," Rhaji said. He gestured to Bahratt on the map. "To sail to my home, then to sail to Gypsu. It will take a month at least."

"Faith, prince," Sharar said with a smile. "I am a sorcerer, after all. I will open a portal for the fleet and we will be there in a matter of minutes."

Rhaji's eyes rounded. "You can do that?"

Sharar nodded. "In fact, we can away to Bahratt now. We should tell Maharaja Saksham what we have discussed and what we intend to do."

"Now?" Rhaji asked, his face going pale. "Sabi?" He looked to the sultana. She avoided his gaze.

"Do as the sorcerer says," she mumbled. "He is right, I am sure."

"You trust this sorcerer?" Nefiri asked, speaking for the first time in a while. She glared at Sharar.

He didn't care that the magi was suspicious of him. He had no fear of almost anyone. He'd smite her down if he needed to. He relished the idea for a moment, imagining a bolt from the sky shooting down and striking her beautiful body. She'd make a pretty corpse.

"I do," the sultana said quickly. "His powers will protect Al'Myrah and he is our only hope against something like the Necro'Khan."

"Agreed," Rhaji said with a sigh. "Then I suppose your magic can take us there now?"

"Indeed," Sharar said almost jovially. "Shall we, then?"

"I will stay behind," the sultana said, shrinking away and clasping her hands over her belly.

"No," Sharar quipped. "You will come so the maharaja understands the severity of the situation and that you agree with the plan. After all, one ruler to another is better than me trying to convince him."

"He will see reason," Rhaji said to reassure them. "Have no fear of that. Allow me to go through first. Magic is not prohibited on Bahratt, and we do not fear it, but a sorcerer will make him wary."

"Of course," Sharar said with a giving grin. Unlike a real prince of Bahratt, Rhaji was simple to command. Sharar knew he'd have his hooks in the young man easily. Rhaji would convince the maharaja to do as he said.

Nefiri sighed and frowned. "I will come with you, prince. Saksham deserves the truth."

Sharar took several steps back from the others and raised his hands. Focusing his intent, he gathered his magic around him. He'd never been to Bahratt, so he hoped the magic understood his desire. He had perfect faith that it would, but still, a few nerves bunched under his skin as he opened the portal. He felt the magic pulled from him and a sudden wave of exhaustion washed over him, but was quickly doused.

Through the portal, he saw a gold and red throne room. A handsome older man dripping in gold and gems sat on a throne with an ornamental turban wrapped around his head. The man's face turned severe as he looked into the portal. He stood up, hand flying to a golden scimitar at his side.

"Rhaji, go," Sharar commanded as he held the portal open.

The prince leapt through the portal and stumbled. He vanished from sight for just a moment before appearing on the other side and falling to the ground. He stayed on all fours for a moment, sickened by his travel through the portal.

Nefiri followed the prince through, blinking out of sight for just a moment before appearing on the other side. She knelt next to the prince, helping him to his feet, and walked toward the maharaja on his throne.

"Go, sabi," Sharar said to the sultana.

She looked like she might weep, but stepped through anyway.

"Amir, with me," Sharar instructed.

Together, the sorcerer and the Runer stepped into the portal. Sharar's stomach flipped as he did. He suddenly felt sick and bile rose in his throat. His brain spun in his head and he found himself falling like the prince had. Eyes closed against the spinning, he gripped Amir to remain standing. He swallowed back the bile and felt instantly ill.

*I don't recall it being that unpleasant,* he thought as he clung to the Runer. Perhaps he had had so much adrenaline running through him at the time, he had not become as ill. Or he hadn't noticed. He decided then to only travel by portal if he had to.

Sharar straightened up and joined the trio facing the maharaja. Saksham was a handsome man with a short, manicured beard and piercing, dark brown eyes behind an intense layer of kohl. He glowered at them until he spotted Nefiri and Rhaji.

"What is this?" he asked when he spotted his adopted heir. "Rhaji?"

Around them, perhaps a dozen palace guards all pointed long, tasseled spears at them. They waited for their ruler's order. Sharar readied himself for them to attack. He almost felt the magic crackling between his fingertips.

"Hold, Saksham," Rhaji said, raising his hands high above his head. "I have returned with the magi, the sultana of Al'Myrah, and her sorcerer."

The maharaja stood rigid on his dais, eyes wide still. "I see that. What is the meaning of this, sabi?"

The sultana held herself high, one hand under her belly. "We have come to ask a boon of you as Al'Myrah finds itself on the brink of war."

"With who?" the maharaja asked. He pointed at Sharar. "Is it because of this man?"

Sharar stood by, letting the others speak in his stead. Him answering the questions would mean nothing to the maharaja. Someone else had to speak on his behalf, tell the maharaja that he was not the perpetrator of the war. He eyed Amir to order him to remain silent as well.

"No," Nefiri said, making her way to the dais where she no doubt felt more comfortable. "For once it is not Al'Myrah's dalliance with the magic they have outlawed that has caused the war."

"I've not heard of this," the maharaja said. He still had not given the order for his men to stand down. "Speak, sorcerer. Tell me who you are and what the sultana speaks of."

Sharar shifted and moved to stand before the others, facing the maharaja. "I am Abigor Sharar, and I am the sultana's sorcerer. I stand by her in this most needed time. Sira, a Necro'Khan has arisen and taken Alika hostage. I am not sure at this moment if Sokar'Xenoteph even lives. The Dynast Palace fell to this death fiend, and he now marches on the other countries, bringing a blight the likes of which we have never seen. Caerwren suffers already, and if my studies are correct, he will attack Xia next. It's only a matter of time before Al'Myrah is covered in this malignation, and Bahratt along with it."

The maharaja's face slowly changed as Sharar spoke. It fell into disbelief, then horror, and finally rested in a determined furrow. "A death fiend," he breathed. "You wish to attack Alika?"

"Not Alika itself," the sultana said, "but the one who took it. To free the people and stop the Necro'Khan."

"The Tashid temple will never sanction such an attack," Nefiri put in with determination.

"Then we will leave the kehann behind," Rhaji spat.

"Sira," Sharar said, "Alika has fallen, and the pharaoh is captured. If he is still alive, we can save him and his country. What of your treaty with Alika and your promise to defend it in times of need?"

The maharaja finally waved his hand and the guards stood down, going back to their positions on the sides of the great throne room. Saksham sat on his throne, almost falling into it as his face fell into contemplation. He eyed Rhaji and contemplated Sharar's words.

"A Necro'Khan," he breathed. "Never in my life did I think someone would find such power."

Sharar saw the opportunity and took it. "Sira, this is the very same death fiend who attacked Jarabu nearly five years ago and killed your son. This is the man who slew Prince Rahul."

The maharaja froze at this, eyes fixed on the floor. Sharar was sure he didn't so much as breathe. He watched as the man's hands gripped the arms of his throne. He knew in that moment that they had the maharaja. Several moments passed before Saksham looked up.

"You are certain?" he asked, his voice dangerously low.

Sharar nodded. "I have followed him for many years."

Saksham's eyes flitted to the sultana. "And you trust this sorcerer? His story is true?"

The sultana's sad eyes didn't waver. She pressed her lips together to stop the tears in her eyes and nodded.

"And I trust him," Rhaji said sternly. "Saksham, this could be the time to strike at the one who killed Rahul."

The maharaja took a slow, deep breath. His eyes never left the group before him. "What would you need from Bahratt?" he asked.

Sharar heard the sultana sigh in relief next to him. "Bahratt's fleet of ships and an army of several hundred."

"We only need them ready to sail," Sharar said. "I will use my magic to take them to the shores of Gypsu, where we will make our first stand. Then, once we have the city, we march to Mysir, where we will launch our attack on the Necro'Khan himself."

"How stands his army?" the maharaja asked.

"He has an army of undead," Sharar said. "But there is a way to stop them. Same as with the Apostles who command the risen."

"You can send the fleet anywhere?" the maharaja asked.

Sharar nodded.

"Then ignore Gypsu for now. Storming Gypsu's shores would weaken our army and take time. Let us go to the heart of the matter. Are you sure the death fiend has taken the Dynast Palace and that is the seat from which he rules?"

"Yes. I was there when he took the palace."

The maharaja nodded. "I will not suffer my men in two battles. Take them to the shores of Mysir and let us go for the Necro'Khan immediately. Once he falls, Gypsu will be more easily liberated. And he won't know we are coming."

"Of course, sira." Sharar bowed to the maharaja. "As you command."

"Then it is settled?" Rhaji asked. "We will gather our men right away."

Nefiri glowered at them from where she stood next to the maharaja. "We will lose hundreds of men, sira."

"For our alliance," the maharaja said in return. "It is our duty to protect one another. I wrote this treaty myself. We are to aid one another and come when one calls. If Sokar is alive, it is our duty to rescue him and save his country."

Nefiri rolled her eyes and scoffed. Her dark eyes bored into Sharar, like she hoped to read his mind and find his true intention. But she'd be disappointed. Sharar wanted what they did: the Necro'Khan dead and Alika saved.

"We will prepare," Rhaji said. "Give us three days to amass our fleet and army and then return to us."

"It will be done," the sultana agreed.

She turned to Sharar and motioned for him to open the portal again. He bowed and did as she instructed, satisfied, and for once feeling as if things were going in the right direction.

# Chapter 10
## Return to Xia

S ybal stood on the ramparts of her estate, overlooking the path
that led from the city to her land. This late at night, Hatal burned
brightest with the nightlife. Somewhere below her, Tzarik and Signar
were packing things for their journey to Xia. It would be a long one,
and they needed to be ready for whatever they found on those shores
once they arrived. They no longer had the medallion of passage Hiro
had given them, since Tzarik had given it to Yasuke, but she hoped
they would be welcomed back nonetheless.

A rider appeared on the road below her, racing toward her manor.
She dropped her crossed arms and looked over the ramparts, squinting
into the darkness. It took a moment, but soon she recognized the red
horse and the great crossbow on the rider's back.

"Amir," she whispered with a slight smile. He was brave for
constantly coming to her with information. He must have had something to say, else he wouldn't have come in the dead of night. "Open
the gate," she called down to the guard who stood watch. Then she ran
inside and down the stairs to greet him in the garden that doubled as a
grand foyer.

For once, Amir looked clean and not battle-beaten, though his eyes still looked tired. He greeted Sybal with a wave of his hand. They turned and marched into her home together.

"You bring news?" she asked before they were inside.

"I don't know if it's the worst news or something akin to that," Amir confessed.

They passed under the archway into her home and she spotted Tzarik and Signar coming down the steps in tandem. They joined them without asking questions and followed the pair into a library. Sybal poured them all a drink and handed them out before she spoke again.

"What has happened?" she asked.

Amir shot back the drink and swallowed it quickly. "Sharar has convinced not only the sultana but the maharaja of Bahratt to move on Alika in three days' time."

Tzarik exchanged a quick glance with Sybal. "Even with the combined might of two armies, they hardly stand a chance," he said.

"And they know that," Amir said, pouring himself more wine.

"How can they be so foolish, then?" Sybal asked.

"She's afraid of Sharar," he answered. "And the maharaja wants revenge. They told him Tarkan was the one who killed the prince all those years ago."

Sybal found herself instantly thrown back into the memory. She remembered the dragon, the blast, and the people crying out for their prince. "It's true," she whispered. Then rage washed over her. She clenched her fists and her teeth. "It took everything in me to forgive Tarkan for what he'd done. I wish now I hadn't found it in me to let it all go. I should have killed him there and then in that cave."

"We didn't know the monster he'd turn into," Tzarik reasoned. "All we knew then was that Sharar had Zeva, and that she was an innocent. We did the right thing rescuing her."

Sybal scoffed. "For all the good it did her." She dropped her face into her hands and let out a soft sigh. Then she looked up. "What else, Amir? What of Vicdan?"

"He's alive, but weak. He fights against Sharar in his own way. We're still not sure what Sharar has planned for him. I don't know if even Sharar knows what he wants with the necromancer." Amir rubbed his chin, thinking. "Sharar is wary of using his powers. Says power corrupts, and he wants to be in control."

Sybal hummed in thought at this. "I suppose that's good for us. But what about the attack on Alika? We cannot hope to stop that."

Tzarik shook his head. "We go on to Xia and the north, to the Frozen Nation. We know what Sharar is up to and where he is. Once the fate-binding is lifted, we can deal with him. With him dead, Tarkan won't be able to use his blood and become even more powerful."

"And what can we do against the Necro'Khan?" Amir asked.

"We'll cross that bridge when we come to it," Sybal answered. "For now, we need to get to Xia."

Amir suddenly perked up. "Why not strike when the battle is freshly over? Sharar and Tarkan will be weak after such a battle."

"Because of the fate-binding," Sybal said. "We must lift it first."

"What if Sharar dies in battle?" Signar piped up.

Sybal met Tzarik's eyes. Sadness quickly welled up in her. "We have to hurry."

"We cannot move in three days," Tzarik reminded her.

"Yes, you can," Signar said. "Kazamar. I can make another wish. He already knows he will not be free. What's another wish?"

Tzarik gave Signar a warning glare and opened his mouth. Before he could speak, Sybal said, "Did Sharar use portals?"

Amir nodded. "He can travel fast. That's how he's going to move the fleet to Mysir: magic."

"Gods," Sybal whispered. "They'll take Tarkan by surprise. That will give them some advantage. But what about us?" She looked to Tzarik. "Let him do it. We must travel as quickly as possible, and we have the means. Let's use Kazamar to get to Xia."

"Making wishes on a djinn is never a good idea," Tzarik replied. "What if this wish is all it takes and it breaks free and kills Signar?"

"We can take a chance," the Vaeson said. "I'm not afraid."

"You're never afraid," Tzarik grumbled. He looked away, crossing his arms and thinking.

"The north?" Amir asked into the silence, glancing at Tzarik. "The Frozen Nation you said?"

Sybal nodded. "To seek out the Dohkma."

"Why?" Amir gasped.

"He is the god of the djinn who bound Tzarik and Sharar," Sybal answered. "He can undo what has been done."

"A dangerous confrontation."

"Yes." Sybal fiddled with her leather gloves as she looked away from Amir's eyes. "But one I can brave. Even the Dohkma cannot take my life."

Amir frowned, confused. "Even if that's true, he could do other things to you. It's dangerous." He shifted his feet, then said, "I'll go with you."

"What?" Sybal cried.

"Tzarik and Signar will be on Xia for their mission," Amir reasoned. "You should not go alone. Let me come with you."

Amir looked to Tzarik for backup. Tzarik lowered his crossed arms. "Having someone with you might be a good idea," he said. "If you're sure, Amir."

The Runer nodded. "Sharar won't miss me if I'm gone while he runs his attack on Alika. I wouldn't be part of that even if I stayed."

Sybal smiled weakly at Amir, thanking him in her mind for volunteering to go with her. Company on that road would be most welcome.

"Then it's settled," Signar said, fingering the medallion around his neck. "I'll call upon Kazamar and make the wish."

"We're nearly done packing," Tzarik said. "I have fur-lined cloaks for you, Sybal. And the gold you gave me for horses once we reach Xia."

Sybal nodded. "Then we can leave in the morning?"

Signar smiled. "To Xia," he whispered in awe.

Kazamar floated before them in the garden foyer. Each one of them was dressed for their adventure and laden with a pack on their backs. The djinn studied them.

"Call upon my name when you are ready to come back," he instructed them, "and a portal will open. For your own protection, I will deposit you on the shores of Hikomi. That way no one sees the portal and accuses you of being a sorcerer."

"Perfect," Sybal said. "I can find a boat to take us to the Frozen Nation from there."

"No one will take us all the way," Amir said. "We'll have to purchase a small ship, something the two of us can handle, to take us the rest of the way."

"Do you know about sailing?" Sybal asked, knowing very little about it herself.

"I've been on many ships in my lifetime," Amir said.

Sybal nodded, knowing she could trust him.

Signar said, "Kazamar, open a portal and take us away."

"As you wish." The djinn waved his hand and a portal ringed in fire opened before them. Through it they could see the mountainous country of Xia. It was as beautiful as Sybal remembered. She was sad to not see more of it.

Signar leapt through then turned, smiling, to wait for them. Amir went through next. Sybal turned to Tzarik.

"I know you don't like portals. Signar told me."

Tzarik made a pained face, but walked toward the portal anyway. "It's the only way," he mumbled.

Sybal took his hand tight in hers and together they crossed through the portal. There was a moment of darkness, then in a flash of light, Sybal found herself taking in the scent of Xia's flowery trees. Tzarik doubled over, retching hard and clinging to her. She collected him in her arms and waited a moment for his mind to calm. She looked back and saw the djinn dissipate into white smoke and then the portal closed. She looked up.

Behind them, the ocean rolled softly, its pink waters glittering in the early morning sun. Before them, the mountain paths wound around the green hills and up. The familiar, humid air filled her lungs. She watched Signar turn around and around as he took in the new country. He looked up into the clouds and out into the roiling ocean. Her mind spun a little.

They'd really done it. They were on Xia, and it had taken a matter of seconds. She caught her breath before she passed out. She looked back at the shore to make sure she wasn't seeing things. No, Xia was there before them. Just like it had been before. She gasped.

"So many colors," Signar whispered. "Blue and purple mountains. Green hills. It's beautiful. If only Caerwren could boast so many colors."

Sybal smiled. She rubbed Tzarik's back and he nodded, letting her know he was able to stand. He straightened up, looking embarrassed, and joined them in taking in the country.

"It's divine," Amir added.

Sybal looked around for people and spotted a large boat out on the shore. Near the edge of the water, gathered in a clump, was a party of monks. The monks often went to the northern island and prayed to keep the monsters at bay.

"I think I've found our ride," she said. "Greetings," she called in Xian, waving her arm overhead in a wide arc. A few of the monks turned to look at her. It was a group of Masahk and humans alike, all wearing the orange robes of the monks. Their ship in the water was easily spotted among the others, small and covered in gold paint with the whitest sails Sybal had ever seen. They trekked up to the docks where the monks waited.

"Hello, traveler," one of the human monks said, waving back to her. He offered her a kind smile and immediately handed her his waterskin.

"No, thank you," Sybal said, walking closer. "I am actually more interested in your ship. We are looking for passage to the Frozen Nation."

The monk quickly drew a holy circled over his heart. "We do not travel so far. To the northern isle, yes, but farther than that? No. I am sorry, child."

She scanned the docks and found a small boat with a single sail. It was also gold. "What about your smaller vessel?" she asked. "We can buy it from you and sail ourselves. If you'll tow us to the northern isle, we'd be most grateful."

"Buy the boat?" the monk whispered, confused. He began to make excuses, so Sybal pulled out her pouch and dipped her fingers in to pull out a large gold nugget. The monk stopped his babbling immediately. He eyed it, then looked up at Sybal. "We have been needing new accommodations for the novices. But..." He rubbed his chin.

"Please," Sybal begged softly. "It's a matter of life or death."

"But the Frozen Nation is not a kind place, my lady," the monk said. He eyed the men behind her and frowned slightly. "Are you Runers?"

Sybal nodded. "We've been to Xia before. We—"

"Do you know TaoShin?" the monk interrupted. His eyes suddenly brightened.

"Yes," Sybal said quickly, a grin of relief relaxing her face. "He aided us the last time we were here."

"Ah," the monk said, a genuine smile spreading his wrinkly face. "So you are *that* lady Runer, come back to Xia once again on a dangerous mission."

"Yes!" Sybal said, excited to be recognized for something good they'd done. "Will you please help me as TaoShin did before?"

The monk nodded, his grin never fading. "The Runers who saved our Di-Huan and uncovered a dark plot within Wushito. I would be glad to offer you my services, as would the others. We were just about to set sail. We will rig up the boat and tow it behind us. I only wish there was more we could do for you."

"That will be enough." Sybal sighed in relief. She turned to her companions, who stood by in silence, not knowing the language. "They will take us to the northern isle and give us a small boat to travel the rest of the way."

She looked Tzarik in the eyes. This was it. They had to part ways.

"You two be careful," she ordered sternly. She reached for Signar and pulled him into a tight hug. "Don't do anything rash, listen to Tzarik's orders, and stay safe."

"I will," Signar promised, hugging her back.

Sybal stood on her toes and kissed his cheek before turning to Tzarik. She gazed at him lovingly, wanting to hug him so tight that they might meld together. She controlled herself and gently took him in her arms, embracing him hard.

"Please, be careful," she begged softly. "I need you to come back to me."

Tzarik lifted his chin and took her lips with his in a gentle kiss. He reached up and put his hands on both sides of her face, holding her there like he didn't want to let go. Sybal melted, her insides turning to liquid and pooling in her feet. She wrapped her arms around his neck and kissed him again and again.

Tzarik pulled away and looked up at her. "You be careful. We don't know what lies in wait on the Frozen Nation, let alone what the environment is like." He looked past her to Amir. "Take care of her. Watch out for one another."

"I will," Amir promised.

Sybal griped Tzarik's head in her hands and kissed him hard one last time. She held him to her for as long as she could before he broke the kiss.

"Go," he said. "They'll want to catch the tide."

Sybal watched Signar and Tzarik get smaller and smaller as the ship set out to sea. The northern isle wasn't far, but far enough to make the shores of Xia grow dim. Sybal didn't move from the railing, watching even though she couldn't see them anymore. Behind her, Amir waited quietly.

She took a deep, sad breath. "Thank you for coming with me. You didn't have to."

Amir shifted a little, coming abreast with her at the rail. "I wanted to know you'd be safe," he said. "And this is my fight, too. I've served Sharar for years without a second thought. In a way, I owe penitence."

Sybal hummed in absentminded thought, hardly hearing him. "How long?"

Amir leaned onto the rail, thinking. "Three, maybe four years."

"Hmm," Sybal said, thinking. "So you knew him when he had my body shipped from Xia in a box?"

Amir went rigid then and she felt it. She heard his heart change pace.

"That was you?" he whispered, as if he'd just solved an extremely hard puzzle. "That was you," he repeated with more finality.

"What was?" Sybal asked.

Amir dropped his head into his hands. "I have a confession to make."

She tilted her head to look at him.

"I've almost met you before."

"What?" she asked.

"When Sharar had your body sent from Xia to Al'Myrah, I was the one who was supposed to fetch you," Amir went on. "But I saw Tarkan found you first, so I sent word to Sharar. At the time, I didn't understand. I'm sorry."

Sybal shook her head. "You didn't know. I'm not angry about it. I was practically dead at the time. You didn't kill me. You were just doing your job." She looked up at him. "But thank you for telling me. I didn't realize we went that far back." She grinned.

"I never saw you, but I was curious," he admitted. "When he told me it was the body of a Runer, I was intrigued. But now I have so many more questions."

"Like what?" Sybal asked.

Amir shrugged, thinking. "How did the necromancer bring you back? He did, didn't he? That's how you're alive now."

"Oh," Sybal droned. "That's a long story, and part of the reason we're in the trouble we have now." She saw the monks taking down the sails. "I'll tell you once we're on the water alone. Like I said, it's a long story."

Amir smiled down at her. "I'd be glad to hear it."

As they gathered their things and prepared to disembark, Sybal replayed Amir's mannerisms in her mind. The way he'd leaned in toward her, what he'd said about this being his fight, too. With a heavy heart, she realized Nefiri was right. Amir quite possibly had feelings for her, and he'd embarked on a dangerous journey because of those feelings.

Pushing the intrusive thoughts to the side, Sybal helped the monks prepare the smaller boat and made ready to sail around the northern isle and out to sea once more.

# Chapter 11

## Siege and Rescue

Sharar stood at the prow of the Al'Myrahn war vessel and looked out into the sea. The fleet from Bahratt had reached them sooner than he'd imagined, and he was thrilled for it. Vicdan stood beside him, unshackled and unbridled. His eyes also took in the fleet they'd managed to procure, and the awe was visible on his face. Sharar appreciated that.

Overhead, Tanyin, his read dragon, flew. The monster was once again under Sharar's control; he'd summoned the dragon for himself. He had no intention of being on the ground when the siege broke out, and he needed to keep Vicdan at a safe distance so he could summon his own risen to help. It wouldn't be many, but some would be better than none.

"You will be safe on the back of the dragon," Sharar said when he caught Vicdan's frightened expression. "But I expect you to do as I say."

"Amir left," Vicdan said, gathering his courage.

"I knew he wouldn't march with the army," Sharar said. "I cannot blame him. I don't. He's wise to stay away. Besides, I need him alive." Sharar glared at Vicdan, repeating, "You will do as I say. Do you understand?"

Vicdan nodded. "This will be a slaughter. You know that, sorcerer."

"I am aware," Sharar replied curtly. "But we may also weaken Tarkan's defenses. He's not a military man, and the Dynast Palace is not a stronghold. It will be easy to penetrate. I will not leave Sokar to suffer in the Necro'Khan's prison if I can help it."

Vicdan glanced sidelong at Sharar, but said nothing.

Sharar heard his words. He'd almost sounded as if he cared what happened to the boy king. Such feelings were beneath him, and he didn't want Vicdan thinking he was soft.

"This will take Tarkan by surprise," he said. "We stand a good chance."

"Of course," Vicdan halfheartedly agreed.

"Admiral Sinan," Sharar called. "Are you ready?"

The admiral, a man with a scar over one eye and a thick beard over his chin, stood at the helm of his ship. "Yes, sira. The ships are ready to sail upon your command."

"How many men?"

"With Bahratt alongside us, we are three thousand strong," Admiral Sinan replied.

"Seems like so little," Vicdan murmured.

Sharar looked ahead, his head held high despite his words and the doubt he heard in Vicdan's tone. He reached up, imagining the huge portal he had to make. Closing one eye, he touched the watery horizon with one finger. Then he drew a massive arch over the ships he could see before him. As he did, the edges of the portal appeared. The fiery, snapping line glowed in the setting sun. Beside him, Vicdan gasped. Sharar smiled with pleasure. A small cry rose from the ships as the men witnessed the giant doorway appear in the sky.

"I see it," Vicdan said breathlessly. "I see Mysir, even the Cradle in the distance. It's right there."

Sharar's smile grew as he dropped his hands. He saw the golden waters of Alika begin to mingle with the bluer waters of Al'Myrah at the base of the portal. He opened his mouth to speak, but instead of words, a cry of sudden and sharp pain tore from his throat. He doubled over, hand to his side, where an unexpected pain lanced through him. The wound flared up and the pain spread. Sharar gripped the railing to steady himself, but it wasn't enough. The pain came worse than ever before, forcing him to his knees.

He pulled his hand back to look and saw dark red blood soaking the front of his robes.

Then he felt it.

The agony spread, but so did the tingling cold. It reached his chest and even touched his throat. He pulled aside his collar and saw the black veins had spread from the wound on his side to his chest and no doubt had crawled up his neck. Annoyance more than anything forced him to standing again as the pain subsided.

Had the magic upset the wound? Would it happen more often, the more he used magic?

"You're bleeding," Vicdan said, astonished.

"It will stop," Sharar quipped. He looked out and saw the first of the ships had passed through the portal.

As they did, a raucous roar of praise for him shot to the sky from the men on the decks. They whooped and shouted his name, punching their fists into the air.

Admiral Sinan called for half sail and the ship began to move again. They approached the portal once the rest had made it through. Above them, Tanyin shot through and then dived into a jungle on the shore. The Dynast Palace appeared several miles inland. Sharar had never seen it from this angle before and admired the fine facade from the waters. Somewhere, no doubt beneath the palace, Sokar waited. Hopefully alive.

Sharar was pleased to find that Tarkan had no fleet bobbing off shore, waiting for them or any other attacker. Behind them, Admiral Sinan approached his men and began to instruct them. He told them to kill only the necromancers and the undead, to not bother with the risen, as they could not be killed.

"How do we kill an undead?" one warrior asked.

Sinan looked to Sharar.

"Cut off their heads," Sharar instructed.

After this, Sinan instructed them to leave the people of Alika alone, unless they rose against them. "Those within the palace might turn when they see our army approach," he clarified. "If they do, our numbers grow and so do our odds. They can't all be as fiercely loyal as the Necro'Khan hopes they are."

The commanders then began to shout orders to their warriors on each ship. The ships weighed anchor and the army began to depart.

"And what are we doing?" Vicdan asked, sounding worried.

"We'll be on the back of the dragon, away from all the fighting. And you will raise as many as you can to help them fight." Sharar looked to where Tanyin had landed and reached out with his mind to the dragon, letting the portal fall. The red dragon waited, anticipating the action to come as if it understood.

"We will march on the Dynast Palace," Admiral Sinan said. "It will take us some time to get there, but we do have the element of surprise for now."

Vicdan smirked. "Unless someone goes to the palace and tells them an army marches through the streets of Mysir."

Sinan cocked his scarred brow at the necromancer. "Do you expect anyone to have that much love for the Necro'Khan?"

"No," Vicdan said simply. "I expect them to have that much fear. When we fail—and we will—what terror will Tarkan rain on the people of Alika for not warning him?"

"He can try," Sharar spat. "But we will cut a wound so deep in his army tonight that he will realize he is not untouchable."

The three of them watched the army depart and start its march up into the city.

"The battle will start before they reach the palace," Admiral Sinan said. "We will wait for the signal. What will you do, sorcerer?"

"I will break in and steal," he replied, distracted by a thought he'd just had. His hand went to his wound and gingerly touched the sensitive skin.

Necromancers had a spell that allowed them to take wounds onto themselves from another. He glanced sideways at Vicdan and wondered if this wound, magic and cursed as it was, could be taken from him. He shoved the thought away for now and focused on the siege. He'd have to look into it later.

"Will the army be able to penetrate the palace?" Sinan asked.

Sharar nodded. "As I said, it's not a stronghold. It's open to the world, made for grandeur and pomp. The only thing standing in their way are the risen and the undead."

Vicdan sighed and leaned onto the rail. "So now we wait?"

Sharar nodded. "We wait."

The sun had set long ago, but Sharar had not stopped his vigil. He scanned the shore over and over, waiting for the signal from their army that they had reached the palace and that the fighting had begun. He took out a brass glass and looked through it, scanning the dark sky. He was just starting to think they might have utterly failed when a single fiery arrow rose up from deep inland. He smiled.

Sharar kicked Vicdan, who had sat down and fallen asleep, leaning up against the ship's side. The necromancer woke with a jolt and stood.

"It's time," Sharar whispered. He looked toward the shore and called Tanyin with his mind. The great red dragon appeared over the tops of the jungle canopy and soared to them. It landed on the shore and waited, tied to Sharar's mind.

Sharar led Vicdan into a smaller boat. Sinan wished them good luck and together they made it to the shore. Sharar didn't waste any time and quickly scaled the dragon's leg to stand on the spot where his neck met his shoulders. Vicdan followed him, slightly unsteady.

"Dragon riding is not something I ever thought I'd do," the necromancer said jovially. "I shall write a ballad about this, perhaps. 'The Siege of Mysir.' No, not that. That's no good. 'The Dark Arrival'—no, that's worse."

"Shut up," Sharar commanded. He ordered Tanyin into the air and bent his knees to steady himself.

Vicdan gasped and lost his footing only once before he did the same. They gripped the smaller spines on the back of the dragon and held on as it rose into the air. The up and down motion gave Sharar a thrill as the trees and buildings became smaller the higher the dragon flew.

*Take me to the palace,* he commanded. The dragon lurched forward and began the short flight to the Dynast Palace. They hadn't quite reached it yet when Sharar saw smoke and heard the sound of battle. He wasn't sure how long they had been fighting, but knew it was a grand brawl. Once they were directly over the battle, he looked down and had Tanyin do a tight circle so he could inspect the fighting.

Many lay strewn across the courtyard and grounds already. "Raise them," Sharar ordered Vicdan as they flew over. "As many as you can."

Vicdan nodded and started his spell. He whispered, but his words were soon swept away in a dark wind. Sharar was used to this and didn't so much as bat an eye. He felt Vicdan start to shake behind him and turned to look. Bloody tears trickled down his cheeks from his eye. "Well done," he whispered, realizing Vicdan was pushing himself to raise as many as he could and the magic was taking its toll.

Looking below, Sharar decided he'd try his own magic, too. A line of risen and undead made ranks and prepared to march into a clump of Bahratt soldiers. He guided his mind carefully and willed a wall of fire to spring up beneath the risen and undead. Just as he thought about it, it happened. A great, towering wall of fire leapt to life from the ground, engulfing the risen and the undead alike. The undead screamed and dropped their weapons, fighting the flames.

He guided Tanyin to do another circled of the fight and looked for Tarkan.

But there was no sign that the Necro'Khan was in the battle at all.

Sharar spotted a single necromancer standing apart from the fray and hurled a small bolt of lightning at the black form. The necromancer fell and about two dozen risen fell with him. As he went down, an Al'Myrahn warrior sprang forward and stabbed him, killing him. Sharar looked for more opportunities to repeat the attack. Tanyin also belched a stream of fire down onto a horde of undead, igniting them. As they panicked in the flames, it gave their warriors a chance to lop their heads off.

"Do you see Tarkan?" Sharar asked Vicdan.

After a moment, he replied that he did not. "Perhaps he's hiding in the palace?" Vicdan added.

*Or he's not here,* Sharar thought. Could Tarkan be somewhere else on the map? Xia or Caerwren, perhaps, checking on the other large rifts of the God Deep?

Just as he decided to land his dragon and go into the palace, something shot past them on large, feathery wings. Sharar looked up to see the form of Acenoth outlined against the full moon. He held his scythe in one hand and glared down at them. Sharar forced Tanyin to reel back, flapping his wings. The giant leathery appendages came close to knocking the undead pharaoh out of the sky, but missed.

Acenoth dived at them again, preparing to slash at them with his sharp blade. Sharar maneuvered the dragon so that Acenoth missed them. Tanyin reared his head around, snapping his jaws. Acenoth flew in darting lines, avoiding the maw of the beast, but unable to get closer to them.

Sharar called upon the sky then, and lightning snapped down to him. He hurled a crackling web at the pharaoh and hit him once. With him stunned, he had Tanyin slash at him. The dragon's massive claws made contact and swatted at the Masahk as if he were a fly. Acenoth spiraled out of control and plummeted to the ground below. Sharar ordered his dragon to breathe a rain of fire down, hitting Acenoth. The Masahk screamed and dived out of the range of the fire, vanishing into part of the palace.

"Tarkan is not here," Sharar called over the noise to Vicdan. "We're going inside."

"Inside?" Vicdan cried. "Why?"

"Sokar," Sharar quipped while urging the dragon to make a wide, descending circle to the back part of the palace. "There are secret entrances to the dungeons all over this place. I know where they are. Trust me. And you, keep your risen close."

Vicdan looked apprehensive, but followed Sharar. Sharar looked for a place the fighting was light and landed there. When the dragon's feet hit the ground, the pair of them dismounted and quickly darted across the now smoldering courtyard into a back room of the palace. Sharar led the way, expertly keeping to the shadows and hiding behind corners. Vicdan had let his spell go, but there were plenty of dead around.

The fighting had not quite gotten into the palace, so it was empty.

No doubt the servants had run, and the guards had to have been outside fighting. Sharar wondered how many of them had turned on Tarkan and fought with their warriors now.

He came to a small alcove with a bust of a pharaoh in it. He moved the bust and pressed a large stone indented into the podium. When it sank in, the sound of stone grinding on stone filled the air. A small, narrow passageway opened up, a set of dark stairs spiraling down. Vicdan hummed, impressed. Sharar didn't have time to explain how the mechanism worked, though he greatly wanted to. Instead, he dashed down into the dungeon below the palace.

The dungeon was dark, save for a few oil lamps here and there. The guards were gone, and the cells were mostly empty. A slight shiver ran up Sharar's spine as he started down a row of cells. He didn't like not being able to see above. To know if someone would come down and follow them. But he didn't have a lot of time. They ran further into the prison, past doors that led to other chambers and through a maze of rooms and cells. Just when he began to wonder if there were any prisoners, he finally spotted something green and golden on the floor of a cell a few paces away.

Breaking into a run, he dashed to the cell to find Sokar lying prone within. The boy's back was red and bloody with crisscrossing scars, and the wound where his wing had been torn from his body had hardly healed. The boy looked dead. Something akin to worry strangled Sharar's heart as he hesitated in calling out to the boy. Sharar swallowed his emotion and whispered, "Sokar?"

The pharaoh flinched at the sound of his name and curled in on himself, trying to hide under his one good wing.

In the cell beside them, something else moved. Sharar took a step back, but saw it was only Nasor. The jackal looked beaten and weary.

"Scholar?" Nasor asked weakly.

At that, Sokar's long feathery ears perked up. He pushed himself up with a moan and turned. His gem-like eyes rounded and instantly filled with tears.

"Abigor!" he cried, throwing himself against the bars. "You came back. I knew you'd come back!" His voice cracked even as the tears began to fall.

Sharar put his hand through the bars and took Sokar's hands in his. "I can't believe you're alive," he whispered.

"Only just," Sokar replied. "I'm sure he'll kill me when he comes back."

So Tarkan was not in the palace. Sharar had been right to strike now. Tarkan would return to a devastated palace and hopefully realize Sharar was not afraid of him.

"Abigor, please," Sokar begged, a fresh wave of sobs shaking his body. "Get me out of here. Take me away."

Sharar swallowed hard and glanced around. There were no keys anywhere to be seen. Nasor looked at him expectantly. "Sokar," he began, and the boy instantly shook his head, hearing the tone of his voice. "You have to be brave," Sharar went on. "I see how he's punished you, that you must be suffering."

"Abigor, no, please!" Sokar begged. "Don't leave me again." He burst into a fit of sobs then, pressing his forehead to Sharar's hands, pleading.

Vicdan looked overcome with the boy's sorrow. "Do you have a small blade with you?" the necromancer asked.

"Yes," Sharar replied, confused.

"Give it to me." Vicdan held his hand out.

Sharar pried one of his hands away from Sokar and reached into his boot, where a small, thin knife waited. He pulled it out and handed it to Vicdan.

The necromancer knelt before the cell door and shoved the tiny blade into the lock. "I've picked many locks," he said, frowning in concentration, his lithe fingers getting to work. "This one doesn't look any more complicated than my father's study."

As Vicdan worked, the sound Sharar had been listening for came to him. The dungeon echoed and he heard footsteps above them.

"There isn't time," he hissed to Vicdan. "Sokar, we'll be back for you."

"No!" the boy wailed, gripping the front of Sharar's robes tight. "Please, Abigor, don't leave me. Take me out of here. *Save me.*"

Beside him, Vicdan continued to work, even after something clicked.

"Take the boy and go," Nasor said beside him. "You owe him that much, sorcerer."

"I won't leave you behind," Sokar said to Nasor, his voice thick.

"You have to," Nasor replied. "I'll be fine. Go with the sorcerer. He will keep you safe." He eyed Sharar then, almost glaring at him.

"Aha!" Vicdan crowed as he threw the door wide open.

Sokar ran out, leaping into Sharar's arms and hugging him tightly. Sharar awkwardly returned the gesture, his fingers grazing the tender scars on the boy's back. Feeling them, he realized he had done the right thing in saving Sokar. He didn't deserve any of this. The boy was innocent, trapped between Sharar and Tarkan and their war.

He squeezed Sokar once before letting go.

"Go!" Nasor shouted from his cell. "I hear the dead above us even now."

"But he'll kill you," Sokar said, gripping the bars of Nasor's cell.

"If he does, then so be it," the Masahk replied. "Just go, your eminence. Please."

"Come, Sokar," Sharar said, leading the way back to the stairs. His face twisting in sadness, Sokar followed.

When they reached the spiral stairs, Sharar stopped. Above them, the distinct sound of battle rang out.

"The back exit," Sokar said, turning and leading the way. "It's a secret way for the royal family to use in case of something just like this. It leads to the sewers and out into the river."

"I have a ride for us," Sharar said. "We'll be long gone within moments of exiting the dungeon."

The three of them slinked through the hidden tunnels and soon found themselves outside near a steadily running river. Sharar called his dragon with his mind.

Sokar faced Vicdan. "I think I remember you. Thank you for saving me."

Vicdan smiled weakly and gave Sokar a bow. "Happy to assist any and all who call upon me for aid."

Above them, Tanyin flapped his wings, coming in for a landing. They moved out of the way as the dragon touched down. Sokar's eyes widened and his mouth dropped open. Sharar smiled at his shock and moved toward the dragon. Sokar followed him, struck mute at the sight of it. Vicdan climbed up first and Sharar turned to help Sokar up.

"We're really going to ride it?" Sokar asked, taking Sharar's hand.

"We are indeed," Sharar said with a grin. "Have any pharaohs in your dynasty ever ridden a red dragon?"

Sokar shook his head, smiling wildly.

As they mounted, the smoke rose thicker and darker around them. The sound of battle still raged on.

"What's happening?" Sokar asked.

"I'll tell you when we're safe on the ground and behind closed doors," Sharar said.

Once they were all situated, Tanyin flapped his mighty wings and ascended into the starry night sky, carrying them to safety.

# Chapter 12
## Asami

Tarkan glared down at Xia from a terrace hanging off the royal palace. A few spires of smoke reached up to the sky as if begging the white dragon to come down and save them. The wars had started, and it had been three days of silent, distant battles. A few small skirmishes had happened outside the Royal City as some Xians had come to see what had happened, but they never left any alive. Tarkan wouldn't allow it. He'd wanted to sail back to Alika, but now saw he'd have to travel through the God Deep. With the battles raging over Xia, it was no longer safe to travel among the hills and valleys.

Ashkan joined him, looking out over Xia. They could see for miles from this height, but most of the view was covered in trees and rolling hills. Only the pyre of smoke told them that battles had broken out. Behind them in the throne room, Hiro stood lashed to a pillar along the side. He groaned often, his wounds festering.

"Why do we keep the prince?" Ashkan asked. "We should kill him, along with the others we've imprisoned."

"We might need his face," Tarkan replied. He spoke softly, wanting to hear the sounds of the battles. Not as many had broken out as he'd hoped, but it had only been a few days. "We cannot discard all of our valuable pieces." Tarkan turned to meet Ashkan's eyes, but his were trained on the sword at Tarkan's side. So Ashkan was still bitter about him using Elahel's bones? The Apostle had been loyal up till now, and he didn't want to think about Ashkan ever turning on him.

"We have the Hallow City under our command entirely?" Tarkan asked.

Ashkan nodded. "We killed a few of the higher ranking Wushito and part of the three hundred occupy the city now. They are ready to march on Wu-Tang whenever we give the word."

"I need some to remain behind," Tarkan said, leaning onto his elbows on the railing. "I need them to make Wushito hunt for us."

Ashkan frowned. "For what?"

Tarkan smiled half-heartedly. "A monster called a yokai. They are rare as djinns and almost as powerful. But they are flesh and blood. Corporeal monsters. They can be captured. Tortured."

"Ah," the Apostle said, understanding. "Will it satisfy you to take its blood, or do you still crave the blood of the sorcerer?"

Tarkan shot up at this. "I will hunt down Sharar until the end of days if I have to!" he snarled. "I want to spill the sorcerer's blood. I want him to suffer as he made me suffer. But I also want his power. There is power in everyone's blood, Ashkan. And I will have it."

Ashkan remained quiet for a moment before asking, "My Khan, what do you intend to do once the Crypt is open?"

"The scars of the God Deep are open," he said. "One on Alika where I ripped the souls of Acenoth and his One Thousand and One from the Deep. One on Caerwren, where I sacrificed everything I had and tore into the Deep, stealing from it. And then the one hidden behind the Crypt."

"And you're traveling through the Deep?" Ashkan asked. "How does that not leave a scar?"

"That is not strong magic. Not powerful. Not mighty enough to rip a rift into the Deep like the others." He took a slow breath, drinking in the beautiful scent of Xia. Closing his eyes, he exhaled and imagined the place covered in monsters, demons, spirits, and other horrors of the God Deep. "Soon the world will be covered in a malignation it cannot recover from."

Ashkan blinked, frowning. "And then?"

"I will have no fear, for I am master of the dead," he replied. "But everything else will be wiped out. All living things. The map will become lifeless. There will be no one left to lord power over a living thing ever again."

"An eternity of that?" the Apostle asked. "Of death and darkness?"

Tarkan blinked slowly, not seeing the scenery before him. His mind wandered far back into his memory. To his father's torture, and then to Sharar's. "I have been dead and living in darkness for eternity already. I see no difference."

Ashkan stood in silence.

"I will return to Alika," Tarkan said. "I will travel through the God Deep and await your message. Do as I have instructed and eternity will be yours as well."

Ashkan bowed. "Of course, my Khan."

Tzarik woke despondent on the third day of his and Signar's travels. They'd made it through Hikomi without being stopped or being able to converse much. Tzarik knew very little Xian, and Signar knew none. However, he proved to be a distraction for many Xians, who were taken in by his stature and bright hair. The people of the province didn't speak any Al'Myrahn, and neither did any of the Wushito they ran into on their way. Tzarik hoped to meet at least one familiar face in their three days up the mountainous paths, but didn't find even one.

They'd gone to temples to look for monks who might know what a yokai was or where to find one, but the language barrier proved too much. They even spotted a few Wushito outposts and approached the gates, eager to find someone who knew where to find this yokai. They had no success repeating the word and little else.

Tzarik noticed a sense of unease in the people as well. It was almost something he could smell in the air and see on their blank faces. Something was going on, but he didn't know what. They now waited on the border of the Shiuki province, and that was when Tzarik decided to head north. They'd go to the Royal City and find Hiro. Surely he'd grant them an audience when he knew they were on Xia. And there, at least, he knew they could communicate. Thunder rolled over the hills and mountains as he finally pulled himself from his bedroll and started the day.

He woke Signar and together they broke their camp. A small city he didn't know the name of could be seen above them within a few hours' march.

"We'll go to the city and find food," he told Signar when the boy was awake and packing things up on their horses. They'd at least been able to buy horses off a merchant in Hikomi before they'd started their climb. The man hadn't understood their words, but he'd understood the coins in their pouches. "Then I want to head to the Royal City. It might take us out of our way, but at least we can communicate there. Once we speak to Hiro, Wushito will be willing to help us locate this monster."

"Surely one of these Wushito scholars speaks Al'Myrahn," Signar said.

"Perhaps," Tzarik replied. "But I don't want to spend more time looking for one."

Signar pointed ahead as they started their early morning march. "I see the flag in the city. The blue and white. There is an outpost there."

Impressed, Tzarik focused on the city below in the valley. Terraced fields surrounded it and a small river cut through it. Atop a hill near the city entrance was a small castle-like structure with a blue and white flag waving above it. Signar was correct: it was indeed a Wushito outpost.

"Well spotted, Signar," he praised him. He squinted in the direction of the city and noticed a few pillars of smoke. The more he watched, the more he could smell the fire. "Let's go," he said cautiously. "Stay close."

They marched around a few hills and up toward the city that nestled between two hills. They passed a few farms and even a small wagon with a family in it. The wagon was full of things like trunks of clothing, barrels of water, and food. The man driving the wagon shouted at them and waved his arms. He babbled on, pointing back to the city and shaking his head.

"Something's wrong," Signar said. "Do you understand anything he said?"

"No," Tzarik confessed. "We need food, though. Stay wary."

When they didn't heed the man's words, he flung his arms up into the air and cursed at them. Those words Tzarik knew.

They traveled on and soon came to the city limits. One great manor blazed with fire, making one of the pillars of smoke they'd seen from a distance. No one moved to douse the home. In fact, a small crowd stood outside. Two factions faced one another, shouting and brandishing swords. Around them, other people of the city packed up their things and were leaving like the family they had seen before.

Tzarik looked around and realized the two arguing factions looked to be wealthy families. They wore silks and their blades were gilded with gems. A woman sobbed, gripping what must have been her husband. She pleaded with him in Xian and wept, motioning to the burning house. Behind her stood six young men that Tzarik realized must have been her sons. One had bright white hair.

"What are they angry about?" Signar asked, his face pinching in concern.

Tzarik took in the other family and noticed they had two sons, both with the white hair. His eyes flitted from one white-haired boy to the other quickly. He'd seen this the last time he'd been on Xia, but that was because the Di-Huan had had no heir. He'd left them with a white-haired child that he'd thought the entire country recognized as Di-Huan. Had he been wrong?

He glanced around and saw the city was in shambles. Other houses burned farther away, and he heard the sound of blades against blades.

Then he heard screaming.

This seemed to trigger the families before them. One of the men on the left side raised a bow and shouted. A man on the right screamed a warning, drawing his blade, and stood in front of one of the white-haired ones, defending him. Tzarik realized they had mere seconds before a small skirmish broke out.

"Go, Signar," he ordered. "To the Wushito outpost."

Signar turned his horse and started a quick trot up the muddy golden path. The rain started to fall just as the ruckus behind them reached its peak. Swords screamed, being drawn from their scabbards, and voices rose in battle cries. Tzarik turned back to watch as the two families met in battle, trying their best to kill off the other's white-haired sons. Some in the city joined one side or the other and the city square quickly fell into a bloody battle.

"What are they doing?" Signar asked as they retreated up the path.

Tzarik waited until they were a good distance away before he replied. "Xia believes the ones born with white hair are touched by their dragon god and destined to rule the country. As you saw, there were three there. More wealthy families with their ties to one another vie for the throne through civil war and bloodshed if simple diplomacy doesn't work."

"Any house could have a claim to the throne, then," Signar said. "What if the king has a child with white hair?"

"That's what happened last time I was here," Tzarik said, wondering what had occurred to undo all he'd done. "A child of the Di-Huan birthed a boy with white hair, and Hiro, the Di-Huan's eldest, took control and promised to raise the boy. I thought the country had agreed that an heir from the then-current Di-Huan was what the nation needed. Now, I'm not so sure."

"Has something happened to the child?" Signar asked.

*Gods, I hope not,* Tzarik thought. To Signar he said, "I don't know."

They galloped up the path in the rain until they came to the gate of the Wushito outpost. The gate lay open and no guards stood outside. Tzarik stopped his horse and looked around.

"Something has happened to them," he mused. "Stay on your guard." He wondered briefly if Wushito had left when the fighting had broken out, but that didn't seem likely. Wushito were tasked with not only slaying the monsters, but protecting the royalty as well, and the balance of Xia. They wouldn't have abandoned their post without cause.

Signar led the way into the outpost out of pure curiosity. Tzarik followed him, eyes flicking from shadow to corner, looking for anything that might show danger. Besides the civil unrest, Wushito trained Reavers who hunted Runers. Not every Wushito might be friendly, despite what he and Sybal did, so he was wary of them as well.

"Nothing," Signar said as they made their way around the open courtyard. "Unless they are holed up inside?"

Tzarik looked at the great double doors of the outpost. They were smashed open and hung on their hinges. "I doubt it. They must have fled. Or the city drove them out. Let's—" He stopped, perking his ears up. He'd heard something like a moan. He looked around.

"I heard it, too," Signar whispered, his keen green eyes flitting from one place to another. "Someone is here, and they're hurt."

"Signar," Tzarik barked when the boy leapt from his horse and dashed in the direction of the moan. "Stop!"

But he didn't. He prowled like a wolf on the scent, looking in the rubble for the source of the moan. Tzarik leapt from his horse then, too, knowing Signar wouldn't stop until he found the wounded sentient. His tender nature still got the better of him sometimes.

"Tzarik!" Signar shouted from a short distance away. "Come. He's hurt."

Tzarik made his way through the rubble and around a large chunk of stone that had fallen from higher up. Lying on the other side was a young Wushito warrior in Reaver's robes. He clutched his thigh, which bled profusely. An arrow stuck out of his shoulder as well.

"Get away from me!" the Wushito warrior cried, shuffling backwards and cowering into the stone.

"You speak Al'Myrahn?" Signar asked in the same language, startled.

The Wushito looked up, confused and pale. "I— I don't know," he stammered. "You look like them." His wide, yellow eyes pinned Tzarik where he stood.

"Who?" Tzarik asked. "Who attacked you? The people of the city?"

The Wushito shook his head rapidly. "No, someone else came and attacked the city first. They were looking for me, I heard them. So I ran."

Signar met Tzarik's eyes and saw the impatience growing there, and Tzarik didn't try to hide it. So the boy said, "Who was looking for you? What did they want?"

The young man moaned again and held his leg as a pained expression washed over him. His leg shook as he clutched it.

"Tzarik?" Signar asked, tilting his head down to the wounded Wushito.

Understanding, Tzarik gently touched the runes around his neck. "I suppose I could help a Reaver."

"Reaver?" the Wushito asked. "What's that?" He shrank away when Tzarik knelt beside him.

Tzarik knew then that something was wrong. The Wushito didn't know what a Reaver was and didn't know if he spoke Al'Myrahn? If Tzarik didn't know any better, he'd think this man had donned the robes of a Wushito without knowing what they were. But that didn't explain how he spoke Al'Myrahn and didn't know he had.

He gently touched the wounded leg and turned it so the wound faced up. The Wushito made a high, pained sound at that. "I'm going to help you," Tzarik said as gently as he could. "Stay still." He slowly began to draw the healing rune over the wound.

As he did, Signar asked, "What's your name?"

"Asami," the man replied with a gasp as the wound began to knit back together.

"Asami," Signar said gently. "Tell us what happened."

The Wushito watched in awe as Tzarik drew artiah one more time. A thick scar appeared where once a massive, bloody gash had been. "There are people who have come to Xia," he began. "They are killing as they move over the cities. They came here, looking for me. I was home, protecting my young, when I saw them come into the city's borders and begin to slaughter everyone. They asked where I was, but no one knew. I was hidden, you see, for many years."

Tzarik gently gripped the arrow in his shoulder next. "This will hurt, but I will heal you like I did your leg."

Asami nodded and clenched his fists. Tzarik pulled, and the narrow-tipped arrow came free easily. Asami gasped and moaned between clenched teeth, but didn't cry out. Tzarik tossed the arrow aside and started to draw the rune over the second wound. He let Signar continue to do the talking. The boy's gentle nature was far more effective than his brash questioning would be.

"You don't know who attacked the city?" Signar asked.

Asami shook his head. "They looked like him." He gestured to Tzarik. "Only they had an army of dead with them, walking as if they were alive."

Tzarik froze as he drew and looked up. "An army of dead? Risen soldiers?"

Asami shrugged with his good shoulder. "They wore black, had the bluest eyes I'd ever seen, and had words written on their skin."

Signar met Tzarik's gaze. "Necromancers?" Tzarik asked. "Are you sure?"

"Yes," Asami said with utmost conviction. "They were looking for me, hunting me down. So I hid. But they killed my mate. My sweet Yuki." At this, the Wushito gasped and dropped his face into his hands and began to sob softly.

"Tzarik, the way he speaks," Signar asked. "Mate. Protecting his young. It's almost like he's not human. Or am I misunderstanding his words?"

"No, you're right," Tzarik said, cautiously eyeing the Wushito. "I thought the same thing."

"And necromancers?" Signar went on. "Here?"

Tzarik sighed. "We may be too late. We have to hurry to the Royal City. Hiro and the young prince could be in danger."

"Wait," Asami said, dropping his hands. He took Tzarik's in his as he spoke. "I need help getting home. I must see that my young are safe. Please help me. It's not far."

Tzarik stood and looked down at the Wushito. No, not Wushito. A shapeshifter of some kind, perhaps? "Do you know what I am?" he asked. A Wushito, especially a Reaver, would answer easily.

Instead, Asami shook his head. "You've been kind to me," he said, as if bargaining. "Please, help me."

Tzarik adjusted his stance. "I'm a Runer, a monster hunter where I come from. Much like the Wushito here."

As he expected, Asami's yellow eyes widened even more. He swallowed. "I've not hurt anyone!" he pled, clasping his hands together. He tried to stand, but his leg gave out. "Please, don't kill me. I have a nest not far from here, up the mountain. I was protecting them!"

Tzarik saw Signar frown, confused.

"Stay still," Tzarik instructed Asami. Petrified, the Wushito did as he was told. Tzarik took out atan and slowly drew it over Asami. Confused but too frightened to move, the Wushito waited as Tzarik investigated.

As the light from atan washed over Asami, a shape appeared, ghostly and white inside him. It wasn't a monster like Tzarik had expected to find, but was instead a large, white egret. Signar gasped and stumbled back, looking at the revealed creature.

"I'm no monster," Asami said sadly, knowing his disguise had been torn away. "I'm called a yokai, and I am a peaceful spirit. Not all yokai are, but I am. I swear, I've never hurt anyone. Please, hunter, spare me."

Tzarik snuffed atan and met Asami's yellow, bird-like eyes. "I have to believe you. I need to know all you can tell me about the ones who attacked the city. Why are they looking for you?"

Asami shook his head, his face twisting in fear. "I don't know why they want me. But they asked the city where I was, knowing they pray to me. They offer me their worship, but that is only because they fear me. I love them, and would never hurt them. But the death fiends came with their risen horde once the child was found dead."

"The child?" Tzarik barked. His mind reeled as it concluded what child the yokai might be speaking of. He hoped he was wrong.

Asami nodded. "The young Di-Huan was killed. His body was found in the river. Some suspect the steward, Hiro. Others think it might be these death fiends. Xia is under attack, and I must find my young and make sure they are safe."

Tzarik took a few steadying breaths as his mind spun. The child was dead? No wonder the houses were fighting again. And after an attack from necromancers? Xia was a volatile country, and would no doubt explode into war once again. And now they had an outside force to reckon with.

"We may be too late," Tzarik said, hardly able to catch his breath. "Hiro could be dead. The Royal City could be taken."

"We can go and find out," Signar said. "And you can show us the way," he told Asami. "Your young are higher up the path, yes?"

"Yes," Asami said enthusiastically. "It's on the way."

"There will be more," Tzarik said, gripping Asami by his good shoulder. "We need you. Not in the way the necromancers do, but still. I helped you, and I need your aid in return."

Asami swallowed hard, but nodded. "We can talk on the way."

# Chapter 13
# Too Late

Tarkan stumbled out of the black mist that transported him through the Deep and onto solid ground once more. Smoke immediately filled his lungs, and the sounds of many voices shouting rang in his ears. The room he'd landed in was empty, but outside, something burned brightly. He ran from his rooms to a balcony overlooking the city. Fires burned here and there, and his Apostles ran frantically through the streets. His eyes darted from one place to the next, taking in the carnage and destruction. Below, on the garden path, an Apostle ran toward the gate.

"Stop!" Tarkan called. "What happened?"

"My Khan," the Apostle gasped. "You have returned. Too late, I am sorry to say. I will come to you."

Tarkan marched to the other side of the room and out onto the second balcony to look out over the other side of the palace. Far out in the ocean, one ship burned. He bent to the telescope near the edge of the balcony and looked through it to the burning ship. A Bahratt flag fluttered from it.

"The maharaja," Tarkan mused. "What was... How?" The questions raced through his mind as the Apostle rushed in.

The Apostle gasped and panted, hand pressed into his chest. "It is good to see you, my Khan," he began. "The sorcerer, he was here."

"Sharar was here?" Tarkan barked. "Where are the others? What happened?"

Swallowing, the Apostle began again. "We were taken by surprise. They appeared in the ocean, came through gates of fire. It was magic. We knew it the moment we saw it. We rallied Acenoth and the others to fight, but they overcame us."

Tarkan bit his tongue, but could not keep the rage off his face as he listened. The Apostle sounded more and more apologetic as he went on.

"He rode in on the back of a red dragon," he said. "His fire scorched us and ruined the risen. Acenoth tried to stop him, but was wounded. He cannot heal, my Khan, just as the other undead cannot. They are unable to so much as rise."

"I will give them blood," Tarkan promised. His temper flared and he marched a tight circle, thinking how to retaliate. "He brought an entire fleet through his portals?" he asked for clarification.

The Apostle nodded.

"He didn't know I was gone," he mused. "He thought he might face me. Bold of him. Luckily for him, I was still on Xia." He looked up at the Apostle. "Bring me the boy king. His blood will do to heal Acenoth." He unsheathed his sword.

"Oh, my Khan," the Apostle whispered now, his face going slack. "The sorcerer, he took the pharaoh. Sokar is gone."

Tarkan screamed wildly and swung his blood blade. He stabbed, shoving it up to the hilt into the Apostle's chest. He knew before the Apostle died that he'd severed the covenant scar on his heart with his blade. His eyes glowed and then smoldered, burning away before he was dead. The Apostle cried out, but died upon the blade. Tarkan used his blood then, filling his blade.

Marching from his rooms, Tarkan shouted for his Apostles. One warrior of the One Thousand and One came to find him and marched beside him.

"Where is Acenoth?" Tarkan asked as two more Apostle joined him.

"Just in here, my Khan," the warrior said. He pivoted off to the right and led Tarkan into a wing of the palace filled with wounded Apostles, undead, and near the head of the room, Acenoth.

The undead pharaoh lay prone, not moving, his chest barely rising and falling as he struggled to breathe. The two Apostles babbled, repeating what the first had told him. The warrior chimed in every now and then to add a detail about the fight and explain the bloody fray. Tarkan let them talk as he knelt by Acenoth.

"Can you hear me, Acenoth?" he whispered. The undead Masahk did not reply. "Bring me slaves," he called. "As many as you can find."

He looked around as the Apostles ran to fetch the slaves. The palace lay in ruins. At first, his mind raged at his followers for letting something like this happen. But then he realized they hadn't known. Sharar had struck quickly and had used his magic to surprise them. What would have happened if he'd been there? He tried to imagine it, wondering if the sorcerer's army, or somehow his magic, could have stopped him. Would he be dead now if he'd not been on Xia when Sharar attacked?

"The slaves, my Khan," the Apostle said, coming back, leading a small group of chained-together sentients.

Tarkan wasted no time. He drew his sword and cut and stabbed the trapped slaves. Their cries rose up in a sweet melody of pain and terror as he chopped through them, absorbing their blood into his blade. He hacked and slashed through them all before he was satisfied. Then he turned and merely willed the spell to raise the undead. The heart in the center pommel of his blade pulsed and glowed as the blood dissipated.

As the blood vanished from the blade into the air, the wounds upon Acenoth's body healed, as did those on the other undead lying near him. They began to stir. Satisfied, Tarkan turned and marched back out to take in the rest of the damage.

One Apostle ran after him. "My Khan, what shall we do? Give us orders."

Tarkan stepped over the body of an Apostle and kept on marching. "We will do nothing. Bahratt was brave to attack us, but I will not retaliate against them. I want searches done in Al'Myrah to find that damned Runer." It'd be easier to find and capture Tzarik than to capture Sharar. And once Sharar knew that Tarkan had Tzarik in his grasp, things might change. The scholar just might become more compliant. Or so Tarkan hoped.

Tzarik watched as Asami leapt easily over the rocks and dents in the path leading up into the more mountainous areas of Xia. He moved cautiously, not sure if the creature was leading them into a trap. The rain made the path slick and soon they were covered in mud. They passed a few travelers but couldn't speak to any of them. Signar marched ahead of Tzarik and kept pace with the yokai.

"How can you understand me?" Signar asked, this time in Caerwren.

Asami kept his yellow eyes trained on the path before them. "It is part of my magic. I speak in my own tongue, but I can understand any sentient creature. And if I allow it, they can understand me."

"That's why you were confused when we asked if you spoke Al'Myrahn," Signar clarified.

Asami nodded. "And thank you, again. For helping me."

"You don't seem dangerous," Signar said casually. "I can normally tell when someone is hostile. I don't sense that in you."

Tzarik let them chatter on while he turned his senses to the space around them. They entered a deep rut in the rocks, the stone rising up on either side of them, blocking off their view of the horizon. The stone made it hard to find footprints and signs of others around them.

A tingle ran down Tzarik's spine. His sulfates started to squirm, telling him there were eyes on them.

He looked around, wishing now they'd taken another path that wasn't surrounded by the rocks he could not see above. He scanned as much of the dark outcropping as he could, but didn't see anyone. Then he heard it: the strange shuffling steps of risen soldiers. He snapped his head up and looked around, unsheathing his blade.

"Signar!" he called just as a host of bodies appeared above them. The boy turned and snarled when he caught sight of them.

"More of them!" Asami gasped, pointing ahead. They were surrounded.

Two bodies appeared, one before them and one behind them. They were not risen. They looked too alive. But they were not Apostles, either.

"We've found the yokai!" one of them called. "And a Runer."

A voice called back, but Tzarik couldn't hear it over the rain or through the stone. Then the risen flung themselves off the rocky ledges above and into the pathway. Signar shouted and gripped his axe. The small horde immediately rushed them. Asami cried out as they laid hands on him and began to drag him away. The yokai kicked and screamed, but couldn't throw off the grip of the risen warriors. The two lifelike sentients leapt down into the path as well and charged. One came at Tzarik, the other at Signar. They wore Alikan armor and carried Alikan blades. Tzarik wondered at first if these were some of Tarkan's undead, but they looked too alive.

Tzarik swung and his blade hit the warrior's neck, but didn't stop it at all. Yes, these were some of the undead. He ripped it out and stumbled backward, wondering how to defeat the monsters. The undead lurched toward him, flinging his long blade. Tzarik ducked, ripping his runes from his neck, and drew buhkar to mist away. He turned and made sure Signar was all right. The boy was locked in combat with the other undead and had already landed two wounds to its side.

"It won't die!" Signar shouted.

Tzarik spun as he rematerialized and blocked a blow from one of the risen. The gulch they found themselves in was small and hard to navigate in the fight. Tzarik used his stature to his advantage and was able to outmaneuver the others. He cleaved off the heads of two risen and quickly drew halat as the undead swung down on him again. The warrior's blade bounced off the barrier and was flung backwards, giving Tzarik time to regain his footing.

He took the moment to once again check on Signar. As he did, the undead thrust and clipped his side. Tzarik grunted in pain and spun, whirling his blade to make the warrior back off. He shoved it hard into the stone wall and kicked it, winding it. He glanced around and couldn't see Asami anywhere. The risen must have taken him.

"Signar," he shouted. "Find the yokai."

Signar shoved hard against his foe and ran around a small bend in the rocky gulch.

Tzarik quickly loaded his small hand crossbow and fended off a few risen as he did so. The undead warrior came at him again. Tzarik cut the heads off two risen and kicked their corpses down before aiming the bow. The undead froze for just one second, but it was enough. Tzarik pulled the trigger and the orichalcum-tipped bolt landed with a thud in its chest, where its heart lay underneath. The thing screamed and reeled back, giving Tzarik enough time to cleave its head from its shoulders. The body staggered and fell dead. Tzarik panted, almost smiling in his victory.

Signar suddenly yelped piteously, like a wounded wolf. Tzarik spun on the spot and all the sulfates drained from his face. The other undead stood before the boy, smirking. The undead warrior's blade had stabbed Signar through the middle, the bloody blade protruding from his back. Signar took a blood-filled, rattling breath before dropping his blade, his arms going limp.

Tzarik's vision turned red.

The undead warrior ripped his sword from Signar's gut and smiled at Tzarik as the boy collapsed. Tzarik ran at the warrior. He leapt up onto the stone wall, took two steps along it, and slashed downward at the undead. Not expecting the speed of the smaller man, the warrior leaned sloppily away, tripping over his own feet. Tzarik took advantage of the stumble and rained a weave of blows onto the undead. The warrior tried to block them all, but Tzarik hit his mark three times.

With the undead on the run, the risen behind him chased after him. He thought perhaps he felt an arrow hit his shoulder, but he ignored it and hacked away at the undead. At last, he landed the blow he'd been aiming for. His scimitar blade sliced through the warrior's neck, severing his head. Tzarik swung with such force that the head spun, smattering his face with blood. It thudded into the rocky wall, then splattered into the mud.

He turned and faced the risen now. They shambled toward Signar's prone form. Tzarik leapt over the boy and shoved back at them. It was a useless fight. He couldn't see the necromancers that controlled them. Then his shoulder surged with pain. He had indeed been shot. He'd just not noticed it yet. He ripped the arrow out and shoved it through the eye socket of a risen that lurched at him.

"Asami!" he called, not sure where the yokai was now. He hoped he could hear him. "Find the necromancers."

A shrill trill rang out farther down the path. Tzarik recognized it as a bird call. A massive white egret buzzed past him and flew up and out of the rocky path. As he battled the risen away from Signar's body, lightning snapped above him. Thunder rolled and then two voices cried out.

The risen fell.

Tzarik panted, watching their corpses collapse to the ground for only a moment before he turned and ran to the fallen Vaeson.

"Signar?" he called, scooping the large boy's body up into his arms. Signar was limp and his eyes were closed. Tzarik gingerly touched the wound. Signar gave no indication that he'd felt the pain that should have accompanied the touch. "Please," Tzarik begged, finding the healing rune on his leather string. He gripped it hard and slowly drew it over Signar's wound.

Behind him, Asami ran up, returned to his human form.

The wound mended on the outside, but Tzarik didn't know what kind of damage had happened within. He gently pressed his palm against Signar's face, willing him to wake. Hot tears filled his eyes. He blinked them away and they mingled with the raindrops on his cheeks.

"Signar, please," he begged. He laid his hand over the wound again, slowly drawing artiah once more. Still, the boy didn't stir. Fear mounted in Tzarik the likes of which he'd never felt in his life. He wished he had the spells of a necromancer and could take Signar's wound onto himself, even if it killed him. Unsure what to do, he clutched the boy to his chest and hugged him tight as emotion and fear washed over him. Signar was limp and heavy in his arms.

"Let me," Asami said, kneeling next to Signar. "He's gravely hurt.

His spirit teeters on the edge of life and death. I feel him preparing to leave."

Rage, anger, and fear crashed in a thunderous maelstrom inside Tzarik. Signar was dying in his arms and he could do nothing to stop it.

"But my magic can save him," Asami said quickly, reaching his hand out in an offering.

Tzarik rarely trusted sentients, and monsters and creatures even less. But his heart hammered painfully in his chest and his gut told him to trust the yokai.

Asami gently placed his hands on Signar's front and back where the entry and exit wounds were. He closed his eyes and took a deep breath. As he let it out, a dim light shone from his palms. Signar moaned and squirmed, but didn't open his eyes yet.

Asami sat back on his heels and opened his own eyes. "There. He will wake in a moment. If he is strong—"

Signar blinked his eyes open. He looked up into Tzarik's eyes, still swimming in tears. "What..." Signar started, but stopped when Tzarik engulfed him in a tight embrace. Tzarik squeezed the boy around his shoulders hard, burying his face in Signar's wet hair. He wanted to kiss him, but didn't, satisfied just to have him breathing in his arms.

"I saved you," Asami beamed. He panted as he spoke, the magic having taken its toll on him.

"Thank you," Tzarik said. He shifted Signar and stood up, helping the boy to stand.

"I'm all right," Signar said with a grin. He untangled his long arms from Tzarik's grasp and stood on his own. "I feel marvelous, as a matter of fact."

Asami smiled. Signar leaned over and helped the yokai to his feet. The three of them looked around, taking in the carnage.

"I struck them down," Asami said. "There were only two this time. When they found me the first time, there was an army of them. I couldn't stand up to them."

Tzarik remembered the blood that had pulsed from Asami's thigh. "I think I know why they wanted you. Tarkan, the Necro'Khan, can consume the blood of sentients and gain any powers that sentient has. He wants your blood."

Asami cringed, fear twisting his face. "I won't let him have me."

Tzarik nodded to the risen around them. "They almost did. We need to get you home, quickly. Then we have to head to the Royal City."

# Chapter 14
## The Frozen Nation

The clouds were so thick above and around Sybal that no sun shone down. She didn't know if it was day or night or how much time had passed. Snow blinded her, filling the air around them. The wind cut her face and burned her cheeks, but she tried to ignore it. She shivered so hard she swore she rocked the little boat. She'd taken down the single sail some time ago, not wanting to run aground. They had to be close.

"I can't see more than a few feet in front of us," Amir called to her over the wind. "And there is a fog rolling in."

He was right. Before them, a strange kind of glowing green fog congealed in the air, undisturbed by the wind. To Sybal, it looked familiar.

It looked like the God Deep.

She swallowed hard and readied herself for whatever awaited on the Frozen Nation. Now, as they drifted closer, the green mist grew brighter. It had to be god-mist, or at least made from the presence of god-like creatures; it didn't dissipate in the wind.

"Be ready," she whispered to Amir. "We're close." She took her runes from around her neck and wrapped them around her left hand. Amir did the same.

As they drifted closer, she saw the green mist more clearly. It rose up around what she thought must be the peaks of mountains. The entire horizon was soon taken over by walls of white ice and green mist. Something scraped along the bottom of the boat. She took a paddle and gently dipped it into the water, moving closer to the shore. She didn't want to leap out in the cold to pull the boat onto land.

Amir joined her, paddling with long, strong strokes.

Soon the scraping sounded loud and harsh. The boat gently bobbed in the shallows and came to a stop. Sybal hopped out and landed on hard, cold, frozen ground. Snow piled up around her legs up to her knees. She sighed. It would be a hard walk.

Amir hopped out after her, bringing their packs. He handed hers to her and slung his own on his back. Then he looked around and took in the green, glowing peaks before them.

"There're walls of ice all over," he said, pointing into the darkness. "We'll have to find our way through."

"Get the torches," Sybal said, taking out her own. She used her flint and steel to spark a flame and then used her torch to light Amir's. "Stay close together. This place reminds me of the God Deep. There may be monsters everywhere."

On their voyage, Sybal had told Amir her story. She'd told him everything from the day she'd met Tzarik in the courthouse up to the moment she'd met Amir. He'd taken her death and resurrection story well, making little comment. She saw in his face, though, that he wanted to speak. Part of her wondered what he'd thought about it all, but the other part was glad he hadn't asked questions. Having heard her tale, he understood the danger they were in now.

Together, they entered the maze of icy walls. Pillars of snow and ice rose up around them like trees in a forest. They could see through it to the peaks beyond.

"I think we should head northeast," Sybal said, squinting into the darkness. "They say the Silent Tower is the home of the Dohkma and is not far inland. It used to act as a lighthouse before the Pale God took the north as his own."

Amir nodded and followed her. She noted how, with his long strides, he was able to keep up with her. It was odd not having to wait for Tzarik and his much shorter legs. Thinking of his smaller, lean body made her smile in the cold darkness and sent a flush of warmth through her. She missed him.

"What is it?" Amir asked.

Sybal looked up at him. "What?"

"Your heart rate just picked up," he replied. "I was listening and my sulfates rushed when yours did."

She flushed then. "Nothing. I was thinking of home."

Amir had been that in tune with her? A guilty feeling rose in her then. She loved Tzarik, even though she'd never told him. She should have said it before they parted ways on Xia. Her heart warming, she decided to tell him the moment they were reunited.

They marched on until they were exhausted. Stopping for several hours, they pitched a single tent and snuggled inside for warmth. Sybal dosed off a few times and noticed that no sun shone no matter how much time passed. Amir breathed softly and she was glad he'd found time to rest. The journey would be hard.

Wondering if anything had passed them while they rested, she untangled herself from the bearskin blanket before Amir rose and checked the snow around them. There were no prints. Even if there had been, they might have been blown away in the wind.

Satisfied, she returned to the safety of the tent's walls and Amir's warmth. She slept again and didn't wake until some time later when Amir gently shook her awake. Opening her eyes, her lashes cracked with ice and frost.

"I don't know what time it is," Amir said, gathering their things, "but we need to move. We cannot stay still much longer."

So they marched on.

A silence passed for some time then as they plowed through the snow together. The green mist grew thicker and the pyres of ice thinned out. From the glow and the bit of light that came through the sky, she could see the outline of a village down in a valley before them.

"There," Amir pointed. "I see a tower."

Sybal squinted, her sulfates suddenly rushing cold and fast. Amir drew his scimitar and spun on the spot, looking around, having felt the same thing. A strange smell filled Sybal's nose then. It was fleshy and dark, rank, almost. Then a loud bugling rose up on the howling wind.

"Stay close," Amir said. "That's a Mahar'nolreith. They are rare outside the northern continents and very dangerous."

Sybal looked around. "One of the monsters we must slay for the sulfates?" she asked, recalling what Amir had told her about the sulfates on their voyage.

"Yes, but we don't want to fight it if we don't have to." He glared deep into the darkness.

Sybal pressed her back into Amir's as they slowly turned, looking for the danger. Her sulfates didn't stop rushing. She heard them in her ears and felt them running like a river through the tight veins in her hands. "Something is wrong," she whispered.

Then she froze. She saw it outlined in the green mist before her. Something tall and many-limbed stood before her on six legs. Antlers made of human arms and fingers rose from its head, and tentacles swung lazily from its back. The thing's body was made of many sentient bodies. It rose up before her, massively tall. Its flaming eyes looked down at her. Her mouth popped open in a silent, horrified gasp.

Amir spun and faced the same direction as her. He took two steps back as the thing's eyes landed on him. The nolreith reared up, its four front hooves clawing at the sky. When it landed again, it bent its centaur-like body, pointed the frozen antlers at them, and charged.

Sybal steeled herself and leapt out of the way, falling hard into the deep snow. Amir, being larger, hadn't been as quick. The antlers caught him and the monster tossed him over its shoulders and onto the nest of tentacles and spines on its back. She heard him grunt in pain as he tumbled over the hunched back. Seeing him in distress, Sybal unsheathed her scimitar and ran at the monster.

She dived between its front legs and hacked at them. The beast lunged and bucked, aiming a kick at her. She drew halat quickly and the hoof cracked the barrier, destroying it. Drawing buhkar, she misted away and ran out behind the creature. Amir hadn't fallen from the thing's back, tangled in the tentacles. He hacked at them, but that only succeeded in angering the nolreith. It reared up again and charged at Sybal, head bent.

Sybal spun to the side as she rematerialized and hacked at its tines. A good chunk of the antlers fell away, leaking a thick, white substance. The monster bugled in pain and shook its great amalgamated head. Sybal watched as it reached its long arm back and gripped Amir. It pulled, yanking him forward and freeing him from the writhing tentacles. He dangled from his wrist as it held him high above the ground.

"Drop him," Sybal spat, picking up his large crossbow from where it had fallen. She aimed the massive weapon at the nolreith.

The monster stopped and trilled, going still as it contemplated the Runer before it. Then it threw its head back and bugled loudly into the darkness. A loud, yowling roar replied from behind Sybal. She spun around to find an enormous cat-like creature with long black fur crouching behind her. The thing had three tails that twitched in anticipation. A green mist hung around its body.

"Monsters and the supernatural are drawn to the nolreith," Amir grunted. "We must hurry away from here."

Sybal spun around, fired the bolt into the nolreith's hand that held Amir's wrist, and then drew halat as the hell cat pounced. The cat landed hard against the barrier and yowled again, clawing at her. Sybal swung her blade at the cat, dropping Amir's crossbow. When she did, the cat blinked from sight and reappeared several yards away.

"Shit," Sybal cursed. She checked over her shoulder and saw Amir dive for his scimitar. She looked back to see the hell cat prowling low to the ground, green eyes honed in on her. She readied herself for the jump.

But it never came. The cat stopped and stretched its neck up, looking around. Sybal felt it, too. Her sulfates rushed madly as they had before. Looking into the surrounding darkness, her heart skipped a beat. Behind her, she heard Amir battling the nolreith still. She heard it roar as he landed a good blow, but she didn't hear much beyond that.

Before her, in the green mist, marched an entire herd of nolreith. Their orange, glowing eyes looked in their direction. The hell cat gave a hissing growl and prowled away into the darkness. Sybal felt the earth shaking as the herd came closer.

"Amir!" she cried. "Enough. We have to run." She turned and

dashed away, scooping up his crossbow and running past him and the nolreith he battled. He faded to mist and dashed to run beside her.

"The village," she called, gasping for air.

They hurried up the mountain path and broke through the perimeter of the village. No one moved around the village streets. Ice covered every structure. Sybal turned and saw the nolreith still marched slowly into the mist, no longer interested in her. The one they had been fighting had vanished into the herd as well, joining them. It looked like they were on the move, but she didn't care. Gasping in relief, she looked around. Doors hung open on small homes, thin fabric flapping in the open windows. The thatched roofs were covered in thick snow.

"This place is old," she whispered. "I've only seen stone homes like this on Caerwren. But look." She walked to one of the house and touched a small scroll there. "The mihals. Al'Myrahns lived here."

"Or our ancestors," Amir suggested. He rubbed his wrist.

"Are you all right?" Sybal asked, gently taking his hand in hers to inspect him for damage.

He nodded, letting her touch his bare skin as she looked at the burn around his wrist. "Nothing our runes cannot heal."

She quickly let go of him then and stepped away. She turned to the east. "The tower is right there. The Dohkma must be close. Those nolreith must be drawn to his presence."

Leading the way, Sybal wound around the village and out behind it, closer to what the god-tales called the Silent Tower. She looked up at it, the details coming into focus the closer they got. It was attached to a small castle with cruel, pointed turrets made of some kind of black stone. Around it, a smooth, perfect stretch of snow spanned several yards. She guessed a moat or some kind of river surrounded the small castle. Carefully, she stepped out onto it, testing the strength of the ice.

She slipped almost immediately and Amir caught her.

"Frozen river," she panted, steadying herself. "I see the gate on the other side. We have to cross."

For the first time, something like concern flashed behind Amir's blue eyes. "Cross the water?"

Sybal smiled gently. "Afraid of the water?"

Amir narrowed his eyes at her and stepped defiantly out onto the frozen river, leading the way to the portcullis. "No bridge," he mused, looking up at the black palace. "As if the water never thaws."

"It probably doesn't," Sybal agreed. She stopped then and looked deep into the archway where the gate waited. She swore she saw the outline of a tall man outfitted in cruel-looking black armor. The harder she looked, the more the figure melded with the shadows, vanishing.

Behind her, something cracked. The sound rumbled through the river, snapping and popping as it raced toward her. Sybal gasped and turned around to see Amir fall into the water. The ice shattered underneath him and the water swallowed him up. His hands scrambled at the edge of the hole while a current pulled at his long legs.

"Hold on!" Sybal shouted, dashing back to him.

Amir grunted, slipping as the water splashed out, soaking the ice. "The current is strong," he managed to say. He slid a little farther off, his face barely staying above the water now.

"Don't let go," Sybal ordered him as she slid down next to him. She gripped his arm and tried to get a good hold of him. "Don't go under the ice."

Once she had one of his arms, he reached up with the other and grabbed onto her tight. Between his large frame and the current, she couldn't pull him out. She growled and grunted, pulling as hard as she could, but she couldn't lift him. The more she pulled, the more the ice cracked around her. The waves splashed out and soaked her pants, making her shiver more.

"I can't feel my hands," Amir gasped through a terrible shiver.

"Hold on!" Sybal shouted as she lost her grip. Amir slipped from her grasp and his head vanished under the water. She screamed and plunged her arms in after him, searching for him. She found nothing.

Panicking, she dusted the snow away from the ice and looked underneath. She spotted him being gently carried by the current, under the ice. His hands scrambled at it, hammering and clawing, trying to break it. Sybal stood up and called upon her god-touched strength. Her body frosted over quickly and her breath no longer rose in puffs of steam. With a savage yell, she stomped on the ice, breaking another hole a few feet from where Amir was. As she'd hoped, the current carried him to the new hole and she plunged her arms in, grabbing him.

She yanked him above the water with her cursed strength and pulled him out. Amir crashed onto his back and coughed up water, choking and sputtering. Sybal fell next to him, panting as well. She pried her fingers off him; they were half frozen closed. Her joints creaked and cracked as she moved them.

Beside her, Amir shivered uncontrollably. "I hate snow," he managed to say around his chattering teeth. "I hate the cold."

Sybal smiled, remembering all the times Tzarik had complained about the weather on Xia, and, no doubt, on Caerwren when they'd first arrived. But her smile quickly faded. They had to find heat, and quickly. She pushed herself up and looked toward the gate.

"Braziers," she whispered. "Thank the gods." She hauled Amir to his feet and helped him walk to the gate. The braziers had some wood inside them that looked as though they had not burned in years.

Sybal took out her flint and steel and struck them. It took many tries and her hands shook as well, but eventually she got a fire going. She guided Amir to the fire and had him stand close. There was another brazier on the other side of the archway. She went to it and took out the wood and coals, adding them to the one with the fire.

Once they were heating up, she faced the portcullis again, where she'd seen the figure standing. *He's been watching us,* she thought. *He knows we're here. What's he waiting for?*

# Chapter 15
## The Pale God

Sybal looked down at her frost-covered hand. The touch hadn't receded yet. "Hear me, Dohkma," she called into the gate. "I know you're near. Come out and speak to one who carries your blood."

Silence followed.

"How do we get in?" Amir asked, still shaking uncontrollably.

Sybal took out her sword and ran it along the portcullis's bars. The clanging rang in her ears, deafening her. "Come out and face me!" she shouted over the ruckus. "What are you afraid of?"

She took a breath to keep going, but a rumbling stopped her. The portcullis jerked once, then slowly started to rise with the clinking and clacking of chains. She squinted through the snow beyond the gate and spotted a black form. This time, it sat astride a great black horse of some kind. A single sharp horn rose from the horse's forehead. Something like blood covered the creature, gleaming in the dim green light.

The figure atop the horse was a massive man. Sybal saw his glowing blue eyes before anything else. His long white hair whipped gently about his face in the wind. His skin was white as the snow around them and his cruel-looking armor was black as the sky. A three-pronged spear sat across his back, looking freshly coated in blood.

The horse slowly approached them, carrying the rider. Sybal was shocked to see, despite the rider's massive height, how human he looked. Every other god was animal or Masahk-shaped. Never had she seen a human-like god. She took a step back as the creature drew nearer, gripping her sword harder. She made eye contact fearlessly and held her ground.

The Dohkma stopped his steed and glared down at Sybal, blinking slowly. Before he spoke, he swung one long, black-clad leg over his bloody horse and slid off. The snow puffed up around his feet when he landed. He stood almost as tall as his massive horse, easily head and shoulders taller than her. Sybal swallowed but kept her footing.

The Dohkma took two steps toward her, glaring with his glowing blue eyes. "You dare come to my gates and invoke me?" he asked. His voice was deep and steady, filled with a controlled rage.

Amir unsheathed his blade and stood with legs apart, ready to strike. The Dohkma's blue eyes snapped to him. The spear on his back vanished and rematerialized in his left hand. Sybal noticed, despite it being black, that it had an opalescent sheen to it. The spear was made of black orichalcum.

"Your blood is my blood, and I command it," the Dohkma said. He raised his right hand, flexed his fingers, then clenched his fist hard.

Amir grunted in pain and twisted, doubling over. The Dohkma turned his hand, pulling another cry from Amir.

Sybal advanced with her blade out. "Release him. I've come to bargain with you."

The Pale God dropped his right hand and Amir collapsed to the ground. "Bargain with me, lady Runer? I want for nothing. You cannot bargain with me."

He vanished in a swirl of dark smoke and snow, reappearing behind her. Sensing he was about to strike, Sybal whirled around, blade held high, and attacked. The Dohkma caught her blade in his bare hand and smiled. Sybal pulled, but couldn't dislodge it from his grip. With a twist of his hand, the god snapped her blade in two. Sybal gasped and stumbled back.

"I make others grovel in my presence, Runer," the god said, tossing her broken blade aside. "But *you* may kneel."

"I'll do no such thing." Sybal lunged forward and stabbed the god with the broken point of her scimitar. The blade sunk into the Dohkma's chest, white blood leaking profusely. She shoved the blade in up to the hilt, then let go, standing back.

Behind her, Amir stood, picking up his blade and looking in awe at her.

"Fool," the Dohkma said with a sigh. He gripped the sword and pulled it out of his chest, his white blood leaking down the center channel. In a flash of movement, the god swooped down on Sybal and reciprocated her attack, stabbing her through her chest and shoving the blade up to the hilt.

Amir cried out and ran forward, but Sybal held her hand up to stop him. She smiled at the Dohkma, gripped the handle, and pulled the sword out. The god's eyes widened and he took a step back.

"I've come to bargain," she repeated. She felt Amir's anxiety pulsing out from behind her. She looked at him and offered a small nod to let him know she was all right. To the god she said, "I am one who has died in the God Deep. I have been sacrificed to the white snake of Xia. I have been struck down by the Vorlamir. I will not taste death again."

"You are mine already," the Dohkma hissed back. "I know you, Sybal. You have defied me and not let your sword cut down others in my name. Even now you confess that you could, immortal. Why should I bargain with you?"

"I didn't know," Sybal confessed. "I thought the runes might try to take me if I killed."

"*I* would try to take you," the god said steadily. "But I cannot take what the Vorlamir holds fast. You are doomed to roam this side of the God Deep forever. Alas."

"And your claim on me?" she asked. She held her hand up and a thin layer of ice frosted over her fingers. "Will I become a djinn?"

"To become a demon is not death," the Dohkma said. He smirked in satisfaction. "You will. Undeath cannot stop my claim. Eternity as my slave. Is this what you've come to bargain for?"

Sybal shook her head. "I am not worried about myself."

"Because you are immortal." The god lowered his spear and considered the woman before him. "I should perhaps not take you as a djinn.

When one is struck down and shackled to the spiritual world as my slave, their body is destroyed. It seems I cannot do that with you. I would simply be bestowing the powers of a djinn on an immortal human." He shook his head. "No. That I will not do. I recant what I said before." A strange blue light of disappointment passed over his eyes.

Sybal frowned. "You won't turn me into a djinn?"

"I am no fool, Sybal."

"Then why keep your claim over me?" Genuine curiosity and confusion filled her.

The Dohkma smiled wickedly. Sybal felt his presence consume her then. He took over her body and made her turn to face Amir. Against her will, she moved.

"What are...you doing?" she grunted, fighting his control. The frost covered her skin. She heard it crackling all over her body as the Pale God took control of her. "Don't!" she begged.

"Relinquish control of you?" the Dohkma said, forcing her to walk forward. "Never."

Sybal thrashed against the god's control as she stepped toward Amir. The other Runer slowly backed away, sword held up, ready to defend himself.

"Sybal, stop," he said. "You can overcome him. Take your mind back."

Even as he spoke, his voice sounded far away. Sybal felt something dark pull her lips up into a hideous grin. "Come here, Amir," she heard herself say. She reached for him. *Stop!* she screamed to herself, unsure what the god was going to make her do.

He froze, watching her get closer. She reached up and touched his cheek gently. The touch sent a shiver through him. His chest rose and fell with deep breaths as she stroked his face.

*Don't!* Sybal ordered herself.

"You have feelings for the lady Runer," the Dohkma said, fascinated. "You won't strike her down even if she attacked."

"Let her go," Amir growled.

Sybal felt the Pale God's intention before he pushed her. She saw herself taking Amir in her arms, kissing him hard.

*No,* she raged at herself. *Don't make me do this!*

She thought of Tzarik and forced his face into her mind's eye. Her love for him swirled within her and warmed her. The frost on her skin crackled at the warmth. The Dohkma's presence in her mind waned. With another wave of thought, Sybal threw off his hold on her. She screamed in the effort and doubled over, falling to her knees. Amir gripped her and pulled her to her feet.

"Are you all right?" he asked.

She nodded, panting as her flesh warmed again. She looked up and glared at the Dohkma. "I don't want those powers. That's not why I'm here. I don't care what you do to me."

A small glint appeared in the Dohkma's eyes. Was it admiration? He smirked. "Then what do you want from me, lady Runer?"

The wind picked up and brought a shiver down her spine. "I've come to ask you to remove your curse from another. A fate-binding."

"The one who runed you." The god stood still as understanding came to him. "Your fate is worse than his, and yet you come to beg for him?"

"Hear me," Sybal said, setting herself into a strong stance. "There is a sorcerer on the map, but I don't even fear him. He is bound to Tzarik. If he dies, Tzarik dies. But this sorcerer is being hunted by a Necro'Khan for his blood. A Necro'Khan who defies the gods and blasphemes them. Does that not matter to you?"

The Dohkma's eyes turned down to the snow-covered ground as he thought. "Do you know what the lives of sentients look like to us gods?"

Sybal waited, knowing she wasn't meant to answer.

"Small," the Pale God went on. "Nothing. A smudge on a grand design. What one Necro'Khan does now is a trifle. He is one in the lifetime of existence. I see all existence from the beginning. He means nothing to me. Do you understand?"

"But..." Sybal stammered, trying to find some way to convince the god to care. "He defies Nephron. He is making his own magic—defiling the gift from the gods."

"The followers of Nephron do not concern me, lady Runer." The Dohkma spoke offhandedly, but she saw she had his attention. He was curious about what she'd offer. "You have nothing to bargain with. I could take you anytime I wish, forcing you into my service as a djinn, and yet I haven't. Perhaps I am a merciful god."

Sybal couldn't stop the scoff that snapped out from between her lips. "You are not merciful. I've heard the tales of the cruel god in the north. You said yourself you wouldn't give an immortal the powers of a djinn. Perhaps I have nothing to fear from you?"

"You would still be my slave. As you are now, but tenfold. Yes, you could not be bound, but a slave to my whims, you would still be. And powerful."

"But you won't," Sybal said. "You don't want a physical body to be endowed with the powers of a djinn."

The Dohkma's twisted smile returned. "So you shall spend eternity bound to me."

Sybal gasped as a thought struck her. "That's what I can offer you. I can give you myself."

"Sybal, no," Amir said behind her.

"A willing servant is not better than a forced slave," the Dohkma said. "But perhaps I can rescind my claim on your soul. Would that satisfy you?"

"No!" Sybal shouted. She almost fell to her knees then to beg. She fought the urge to clasp her hands before her and prostrate herself before the Pale God. "I'll give you whatever you want. You can have all of me, I won't fight you, if you only remove the fate-binding from Tzarik."

The Dohkma raised his white head and looked down at Sybal. He sneered in disgust. "Pathetic," he murmured. "Begging does not suit the first lady Runer, the first immortal, one who has tasted death in the God Deep. You cannot offer me anything I do not already have. It is I who must give for nothing. And I shall not."

Sybal took a shaking breath and fell to her knees. "Please," she begged. "There must be something you want."

The god shook his head. "You offer me nothing. You will not kill in my name. You defy me every chance you get, and still you ask a boon of me. Am I not merciful even now by not striking down this one you have brought into my presence?"

Sybal glanced back at Amir. He still held his blade, but she knew they didn't stand a chance if the Dohkma really did decide to kill them. In a way, he was right: he was showing mercy even now. She looked back up at the Pale God.

"What if I promise to..." She swallowed hard. "I promise to kill in your name? To send souls to you as you direct my blade."

"Sybal," Amir whispered behind her.

The Dohkma smiled. "You'd take lives to save Tzarik's? How would he feel about that?"

She knew the answer. He wouldn't allow it. He might even hate her for promising to take lives to save his. She'd have to live with his disgust. Would he even want to stay with her then?

Sybal hung her head and let out a soft sob. The damned god was right. "I couldn't do it," she confessed.

"I know," the Dohkma said, sounding bored now. "I have all I want. I have you. And to show you how merciful I can be, I promise not to make you my slave until you have slain this Necro'Khan." He looked down at where Sybal knelt. "You may thank me."

She didn't look up, tears filling her eyes. "Please," she tried again. "I'll do anything."

The Dohkma made eye contact with her and held her gaze. "You've already admitted that you would not do anything."

She fought the urge to fall to her knees and beg. The Pale God watched her. She thought for a moment that he might say yes, that he had thought of a bargain they could make.

He took a long, slow breath in and sighed. "No," he mumbled at length and turned away from them to walk back into the gate.

"Wait!" Amir called, running past Sybal.

The Dohkma whirled around and snatched Amir off the ground, his hand around the Runer's neck. He held him up so his legs kicked in mid air. "I will not wait," the god roared. "You have come and offered me nothing." He squeezed hard, cutting off Amir's air.

"Drop him," Sybal shouted, raising up the stump of her scimitar.

Amir swung his own sword, but the Dohkma caught it, wrenched it from his grasp, and tossed it aside. "You have angered me now, Runers. And my mercy runs thin."

"I'm sorry!" Sybal shouted, tears leaking down her face. "Let him go."

The Dohkma tossed Amir into Sybal, the two colliding hard. Winded, she held him as he gasped and coughed, rubbing his neck. The Pale God faced them again and raised his spear. Sybal shrank away, shielding Amir.

The blow never fell.

The Dohkma lowered his weapon and looked down at them. "I wanted to meet you, Sybal. To see the first woman to bear my blood. You have disappointed me. But you have spilled my blood, and for that, I commend you. I will bestow my blessing upon you for that."

"What does that mean?" Sybal snapped. Hot tears still streamed from her eyes.

"You will know in time," the Dohkma said softly.

Sybal gnashed her teeth. "I don't want your blessing. I want to save Tzarik."

"I have spoken," he said simply. He turned and walked under the gate. As he did, he vanished into a swirl of smoke and snow.

Sybal looked after him, scanning the darkness for any sign of the god. He was gone.

"Come back!" she shouted, standing up and running to the gate.

"Sybal," Amir said softly. He stood and took her hand, pulling her back. "He's gone. We should leave before he changes his mind."

"But," she stammered. "I couldn't... I didn't..." Sobs overtook her then and she turned and collapsed into Amir's arms. "I didn't save him."

Amir wrapped his arms around her, but she shoved him off and rounded on the Pale God's gate.

"Damn the gods!" she screamed into the darkness. "Would that I could give away my immortality."

Silence followed then. Only the howling of the wind whipped around them. The tower before them loomed as dark and lifeless as before. The Dohkma was really and truly gone.

Sybal took a shuddering breath. "We have to return to Xia. Maybe Tzarik and Signar found the yokai. Maybe there is still a wish that can be made."

# Chapter 16
## Healing

Sharar directed his red dragon through the portals as the ships slowly made their about-face and headed toward the portals too. He glanced back over Sokar's head to see many warriors still stranded on the Alikan shore. A few leapt into the water and paddled to the ships, but others stayed behind, calling out.

Behind him, Sokar gripped his middle and buried his face in Sharar's shoulder. The boy sobbed piteously and spoke between gasps of breath, but Sharar couldn't understand what he was saying. He was paying little attention anyway.

"We have to get back to Jarabu," he said once they were far enough away. "You'll be safe there."

"Don't ever leave me again," Sokar sobbed. "I didn't think you'd come back for me. Please, don't leave me again."

Part of Sharar felt guilt at the boy's words. He had run away and left Sokar that night he and Tarkan had clashed in the palace. But what else could he have done?

"You're safe now. That's what matters," he answered.

He directed Tanyin through the portal and into Bahratt's air over the docks near Jarabu. The ships slowly sailed through and he hovered, watching them, ready to close the portals. He looked through back to

Alika and saw no pursuit coming after them. They had soundly beaten a part of Tarkan's army, and a sense of accomplishment filled Sharar. He'd report to the maharaja and hopefully the successful rescue of the Dynast Pharaoh would spur on and encourage the sultana and the maharaja to follow his next orders. He needed another attack. One more would surely do it.

And this time, they needed to find Tarkan.

Sharar set Tanyin down in the massive courtyard just outside the maharaja's throne hall. Sokar's iron grip around his middle didn't let up until Sharar pried him off and helped him down off the dragon. Even then, Sokar hovered so close to Sharar that he could almost feel the boy's anxious breath on his neck. Vicdan followed them at a short distance.

Guards flooded the courtyard, spears out. They surrounded the dragon and the three that rode in on it. Sharar held his hands up and started to say he was there on the sultana's orders when the maharaja, Rahji, and the sultana appeared around the corner. The maharaja led the trio into the courtyard and up to Sharar.

"Well?" he asked. "I saw my fleets returning from the tower where my magi are prophesying even as we speak. Did you slay the death fiend?"

Sharar took his outer robe off and draped it over Sokar's bare shoulders, giving him some semblance of modesty in the presence of his fellow rulers. The pharaoh's white garments were shredded from the beatings he'd endured and hardly covered him. Sharar put his arm around Sokar's shoulders and led the way back into the palace.

"We went to save the Dynast Pharaoh, and, as you can see, we were successful," he quipped. "What mattered was Sokar's safety."

The maharaja glared at Sharar, jogging to walk abreast with him. "So you did not kill the death fiend? He walks the map still?"

Sharar didn't answer the question. "Your warriors fought valiantly, and we were triumphant," he began. "Yes, lives were lost, but we have sent a message to the Necro'Khan he will not soon forget. I have wounded his general, the undead Acenoth, and we slew dozens of his Apostles. This was a success, Your Majesty."

The sultana wrapped her hands around her belly and looked between Sharar and the maharaja. "And now?" she asked. "What is your grand plan, sorcerer? Surely the Necro'Khan will retaliate."

Sharar heard the insult in her tone, but chose to ignore it. "I need you to round up Runers."

"Runers?" she asked. "Why?"

"I am searching for one in particular. I need him found and locked away somewhere safe. Tarkan was not in Alika when we struck, and I fear he may be searching for that same Runer. If he finds him before I do, my life may well hang in the balance."

"Why?" Sokar asked.

"Not important right now, eminence," he replied, gently taking Sokar's shoulder in his grip. "We must also rouse the armies of the other cities, your majesty," he said to the sultana. "Send messengers if you can. We will need the overseers in Bagdula, Singad, Moshav, and Ala'nar on our side."

"You want to launch another attack?" Rahji asked. Sharar was happy to see the young man look eager.

"Soon enough," Sharar went on. "I see no other way to stand up to this Necro'Khan, and we know now that we can."

"Sounds dangerous," the sultana whispered. "But they will understand and do as I say. I promise you that."

"Good." Sharar looked to the maharaja now. "And can we count on Bahratt to aid us?"

The older man looked Sokar up and down and then silently nodded. "As long as our treaty stands. Yes, we will join you."

Once they took the portal back to Hatal—and Sharar had Vicdan shackled away once again—he led Sokar to a room set aside for visiting royals. The room was expansive, with a small veranda and an attached garden with a fountain in it. Gauzy curtains hung over the openings and blew gently in the night breeze. Sharar ushered the youth to the bed.

"Lie down," Sharar said, "and I will heal you."

"Can you do that?" Sokar asked, obeying and lying down on his belly on the bed. He slipped out of Sharar's robe and exposed his marred back to the sorcerer.

Sharar took in the boy's lashings with a grimace. Gently, he traced his fingers over the markings. Sokar gasped and cringed at the touch. "I'm sorry this happened to you," Sharar said softly. "And this." He lightly touched the bloody stump where once another beautiful feathered wing had been attached to Sokar's back.

The pharaoh didn't say anything, but Sharar knew he wanted to ask. Why had he run away that day? Why had he left him to Tarkan and his tortures? Sharar wasn't sure, but he regretted it now.

"Sokar," he said softly, not wanting to disturb the quiet night. "I am sorry I ran that night. But there was nothing I could do in the moment. I—"

"Abigor," Sokar interrupted and Sharar heard him smiling, if weakly. "I don't blame you. I am just glad to be alive. And free. One of the worst tortures was seeing inside his mind. I couldn't help it. But I'm safe now."

Sharar pressed his hand into Sokar's wound, making the boy gasp in pain. Then he called on his magic and started to heal the marks.

"You read Tarkan's mind?" he asked. "What did you see?" He lifted his hand to find fresh scars where once there had been open, bleeding wounds. Gently, he touched the scarred flesh again. Sokar didn't wince.

"I saw horrible things," Sokar whispered, burying his face in the silken pillows. "I saw things he wanted to do to me. To you. I saw his desires for the map. The horrors, Abigor. He will cover the map in a darkness the likes of which I've never seen."

Interested, Sharar asked, "Did you see where Tarkan was? What he was planning in that moment?" He pressed his hand into another spot, feeling Sokar shake under his fingers.

"He wanted to go to Xia," the pharaoh said. "He had me locked away before he left."

"Ah," Sharar mused. "He and I studied Xia some time ago. He knew about the Crypt there. I tried to open it once, but I failed." His hand went to his own side where the wound he'd received festered still. "I have no doubt that Tarkan will succeed."

"Why did you want to open the Crypt?" Sokar asked as Sharar continued to heal him.

"I thought the book might be there," he said simply. "I was wrong. But I have it now, so it matters little." Even as he spoke, his own wound began to twinge again. It didn't ignite like it had before, but it hurt. Hating once again that his magic did not work for himself, he concentrated on Sokar's wounds instead.

"Abigor," Sokar said softly with a sigh. Sharar felt him becoming more at ease as they spoke. The boy's anxiety and shaking had almost disappeared. "Why do you want that Runer? What about the one I have seen with you?"

"Amir," Sharar said. "The Runer I am looking for is special. Unlike other Runers, like Amir, this one is innocent. And yet the runes took to him. I need him. I need to understand why the runes chose to let him live." He swallowed and moved to another part of Sokar's back, almost finished healing. "I had a son once," he went on. "Just a few years older than you. He died during a runing, though he was innocent."

"Oh, Abigor," Sokar whispered. "I'm so sorry. And you think this Runer holds the answer?"

"Among other things." Sharar finished healing the last spot on Sokar's back and ran his hand over the scars now. "Do you know what a fate-binding is?"

Sokar sat up and looked Sharar in the eyes. "Yes." His face turned concerned, serious. "Abigor, no. Tell me you are not fate-bound."

Sharar looked away, a strange feeling of shame coming over him. "I am. My powers have come at great cost. More than I had imagined. There is nothing I can do about it now but find that Runer and keep him safe."

"I will help you in any way I can," Sokar promised. He slid to the edge of the bed and wrapped his arms around Sharar's neck, hugging him tightly. "We will find this Runer, I swear."

# Chapter 17
## Captured

Tzarik scrambled over the last rocky ledge and pulled himself up. He turned and offered a hand to Signar, who then helped Asami up. They were higher up now and deep within the mountains of the highlands of Xia. If it weren't for the rocky gulches and mountains, they would have been able to see the Royal City from there. The sun was just rising and Tzarik had lost count of how many days they'd been on Xia. They'd rested for a few hours, but Asami had insisted they march through the night. Being a spiritual sentient, he had little need for rest like they did.

Asami led the way now, hopping over crags and steep openings farther up into a maze of rocky dips and valleys.

"How are you feeling?" Tzarik asked Signar as they followed. His eyes went to the scar on Signar's stomach, where the undead had stabbed him.

"Just fine," Signar replied. "In the moment, I thought I'd leave this world forever. Everything went cold and dark. I heard you, though. I wanted to come back, but I couldn't. Then Asami pulled me back. I don't even feel it anymore."

Always wary of magic, Tzarik tried his best to trust Signar. Creatures like Asami hardly gave without taking, but maybe in this instance the yokai thought he owed them. He hoped he could still bargain something from him once he was safely back in his home.

"There!" Asami shouted from ahead of them. He ran around a bend and into a cave mouth that yawned open before them.

Tzarik galloped after him and caught sight of the yokai vanishing into the cave. Signar ran after him, leaving Tzarik behind. Cursing Signar's long legs, Tzarik trudged after the pair. He rounded the mouth of the cave and looked in. Just inside, a giant bird's nest waited. It was made of branches, leaves, and soft feathering. It was so large he could have lain down in it. Asami knelt by the nest and gently reached to a clutch of eggs inside. There were four of them, and they were the size of a human head. Asami gently ran his hands over the pale gray shells. His yellow eyes glowed with pride and relief as he ran his long fingers over their smooth surfaces.

"My family," he explained. "They killed my mate, not knowing she was a yokai. These are in my charge now." He picked up one of the huge eggs and held it to his chest, embracing it gently. "Each one is a miracle. Do you have children, Runer?"

Tzarik shook his head. "The offspring of Runers are not sentient kind." His eyes flitted a moment to Signar. No, he couldn't think of Signar like that. He was the Reks of Altevine, not his.

But he looked too long. Signar met his eyes and the tiniest smile flitted across his face.

Tzarik looked back at Asami. "We helped you and you saved Signar." How could he ask for another favor? One wish, even? He contemplated his next words as Asami gently placed his egg back down.

"And you want something from me," the yokai said, saving him the words. "Don't be shy, Runer. I owe you not only my life, but the lives of my children. Ask, and I will do what I can."

Tzarik shifted on his feet, thinking. "I don't know if you can help. It seems that one magic cannot undo another. But I have to try."

Asami nodded and stood. "I can offer you a wish, if nothing else. I'd gladly grant you one."

The offer struck Tzarik. A wish was a powerful thing, and one given freely, even more so. But he only had one thing on his mind. "I'm fate-bound to a sorcerer," he said. "I admit we came to Xia to find one of your kind and try to leverage that magic against that of a djinn."

"A sorcerer," Asami whispered in awe. "You have dealt with powerful magic, Runer." He frowned slightly. "You are correct, though. I am sorry. I cannot undo what has been done." His face fell in dismay. "Truly, I am sorry. But I can still grant you a wish."

Beside Tzarik, Signar lowered his head. "There is nothing that can be done?"

Asami sighed and nodded. "Nothing I can do. Perhaps the djinn that placed the fate-binding will undo it?"

"He's dead," Tzarik replied quickly. "The sorcerer that I am bound to consumed his essence." He looked up. "Could the sorcerer undo the fate-binding?"

"Alas," Asami said gently, "djinn magic does not work upon themselves. He cannot remove any curse from himself. A fate-binding is the most powerful magic. And the most cruel. It is to ensure servitude and fear."

"There is a Necro'Khan who wants his blood," Signar said, his tone hopeful. "The same one that hunts you. He will soon destroy Xia by opening the Crypt. Is there anyway you can aid us?"

"Yes," Tzarik said quickly. "How can we defeat Tarkan? I've been so focused on Sharar, I almost forgot. I unleashed this Necro'Khan onto the map and it's my duty to see him fall. But I cannot even fathom how to take him down."

Asami tilted his head in thought. "You could wish to know. My magic will give me the answer you seek."

Tzarik looked to Signar. "What are your thoughts?"

"You are asking for my advice?" Signar asked. Tzarik nodded. "Do we have to be in your presence for the wish to be granted?" Signar said to Asami.

The yokai nodded. "That is how it must be. For a wish to be granted, the one wishing must be near me."

Signar nodded to Tzarik. "Wish it. Wish to know how we can defeat him. If we hurry, we may stop him before the Crypt is open."

"What about the rifts on Caerwren?" Tzarik asked. "And Alika. How do we close them?"

Asami winced. "I can offer you one wish. I am sorry."

Tzarik understood. They could bind the yokai like they had the djinn and force him to give them as many wishes as they wanted. But turning on Asami like that disgusted Tzarik.

"Bringing down Tarkan will perhaps show us the way to heal the rifts," Signar suggested. "Perhaps once he is gone, his magic will die with him."

"Perhaps," Asami confirmed, a slight frown bending his brows. "But I think the God Deep has been wounded. The rifts need to be mended, and only a necromancer can do that. Perhaps even only a Necro'Khan."

Tzarik said slowly, "So tell me: how can we defeat the Necro'Khan?"

"Is that your wish?" the yokai asked.

Tzarik nodded mutely.

Asami raised his head and his yellow eyes glowed. His body went rigid as the magic coursed through him. Slowly, he rose off the ground until he was suspended in the air a few inches.

"The way to defeat the Necro'Khan is through blood," he said. "The Necro'Khan can control all red blood, calling upon it, manipulating it. The only blood he cannot control is the key to his downfall."

Tzarik growled. "Speak plainly."

"You, Runer," Asami said, his eyes still aglow. "You are the key to defeating your nemesis. And those who share your blood. The blood of the Pale God."

"Runers?" Tzarik asked.

Then he understood.

Runer blood was not the life-giving red blood Tarkan used in his magic. The white sulfates had their own magic and were protected from most other kinds.

"I don't understand, though. How can Runers kill Tarkan?"

Asami gasped and closed his eyes, falling to the ground. He panted, pressing his hands into his chest. "I don't know, my friend. But I have revealed the answer to you."

Annoyed, Tzarik reached out and steadied Asami, helping him to stand again. "Thank you," he mumbled anyway. "And thank you for saving Signar."

"A life saved is a life owed," Asami said. "We are even now."

"We must be going," Tzarik said. "We have to meet the others at the Royal City as planned. They should be back in a few days. Hiro will no doubt have news for us, and we need to warn him about the necromancers."

"Thank you once again, Runer," Asami said, giving Tzarik a slight bow. "I will remember you for the rest of my days, and will tell my children of the Runer who saved them."

Tzarik returned the bow, a familiar custom on Xia, and turned to leave. Signar followed him out of the mouth of the cave and back onto the road.

The sun was setting by the time Tzarik and Signar reached the Royal City. The gates were closed and only two Xian warriors stood guard outside. When one saw Tzarik, he stood, shaking. He leaned over to his comrade and whispered quickly to him. The second warrior ran toward the palace and vanished. The first warrior vanished into the guard tower and the gate began to slowly open. He appeared under the archway and babbled in Xian, but Tzarik couldn't understand. The man put his hands up as if stopping Tzarik, his words still spilling from his mouth.

"I don't understand," Tzarik barked over the man. "Where is Hiro?"

"Hiro?" the warrior asked, then went on again in quick Xian. Behind the man on the stone bridge that led to the palace, a host appeared on horseback.

Tzarik squinted into the dark and caught the gleam of Alikan armor on at least twelve of the approaching soldiers. His sulfates rushed madly and the hairs on his arm stood up.

"Signar, run!" he shouted.

The boy obeyed instantly, turning and dashing back to the gate. When Tzarik spun to gallop away, another host appeared in the gate, blocking their path out. A necromancer sat astride a horse and glared down at them.

"Tzarik, I presume?" the necromancer asked. "I am called Ashkan, first Apostle of the Necro'Khan. We have been looking for you."

Tzarik's hand had flown to his sword on instinct, but he released it and slowly lifted his hands to shoulder height. He looked around. They were perfectly trapped in the gate, twelve undead Alikans before them and eleven and the Apostle behind them. There was nowhere to run or hide. If he tried, he'd be dead before he got five paces away. Beside him, he heard Signar growl from behind bared wolven teeth.

"Don't," he warned the boy, not wanting him hurt again. "Very well, Ashkan, first Apostle of the Necro'Khan," he said mockingly. "What have you done with Hiro?"

"Come and see," Ashkan replied. "Walk."

Tzarik turned and grabbed Signar's arm, forcing him to walk with him. The horde made its way across the bridge and into the palace. Tzarik kept his eyes peeled for any opening they might have to escape. Once they were in the palace, there would be places to hide, but he wasn't sure how occupied it would be. But no opportunity presented itself and soon they were outside the throne room doors. Ashkan pushed them open and marched in, flanked by the undead.

Inside, a man with the blackest skin Tzarik had ever seen sat upon the throne. He wore the black of a necromancer and had the glowing blue eyes as well. He looked up, interested in the horde that had entered the throne room. Lashed to the pillar closest to the throne was Hiro. The prince raised his head when the doors opened. When his eyes caught sight of Tzarik, they widened.

"Tzarik, no!" Hiro shouted in Al'Myrahn. "Why did you come here?"

"Keep quiet," the man on the throne barked. He rose and eyed the pair of them. "So you are the Runer our Khan has tasked us with finding. You came right to us."

Tzarik glared, keeping one eye on Signar and the other looking for a way out. "What has Tarkan done?" he asked. "Xia is at war with itself again after only three years of peace."

"The little Di-Huan is dead," Ashkan answered. "Tarkan slew him. And we have the prince at our mercy."

Tzarik's blood ran cold. Tarkan had killed the child heir. His eyes went to Hiro and saw the necromancers spoke the truth. Hiro winced and his eyes filled with tears. He dropped his head.

"Why were you looking for me?" Tzarik asked. His sulfates hadn't stopped rushing since seeing the undead.

"We do not question our Khan," the man on the throne said.

"Faraji," Ashkan called to him. "Send word to Tarkan that we have the Runer and his boy in our prison. Use the blood to scry to him so he knows immediately."

They needed to move. Without the guards in the towers, they stood a better chance at getting away. The risen would fall if they could take down the Apostles. Then, they could sneak out of the palace. Tzarik waited until the other necromancer, Faraji, rose and departed before he sprung into action.

"Signar, run!" he shouted. He drew his blade and rushed at Ashkan. The necromancer cried out and stumbled backward, away from the Runer's swinging blade.

Signar leapt, transforming into a giant wolf and clearing the horde of undead. His claws clacked on the ground as he sped down the throne room and rounded a corner out of Tzarik's sight. He turned back to the undead and hacked into them. He knew he couldn't win the fight and so did they. They encircled him and watched as he cleaved heads from shoulders.

"Stop him!" Ashkan barked as he fled behind the wall of undead. One of the undead pulled out a small bow and aimed.

Tzarik grunted in pain as the bolt pierced his shoulder. He gripped it and tumbled backward, falling onto his back. He thought about ripping the bolt out, but knew that would do more damage than leaving it in.

Just as he made up his mind to stand, surrounded though he was, a sound erupted from down the hall that made his blood run cold: the yipping of a dog in pain. The sound didn't stop. The pained canine yowling turned to the cries of a boy in a matter of seconds.

"Signar!" Tzarik shouted. He stood, but his head spun. His arm started to go numb and he dropped his scimitar.

"Reaver poison," Ashkan said, coming out from behind his army of undead. "You'll go entirely numb within minutes."

Signar's cries didn't stop and Tzarik's slowly numbing mind could think of nothing but the boy. Suddenly Signar's cries were cut off. Tzarik pushed himself to his feet and ripped the bolt from his flesh. It stung and he hissed in pain, but at least it was gone. He reached for his scimitar, but one of the undead kicked it out of his reach. Then another came up behind him and grappled him. A third rained several blows onto him until his head spun. When the one who had grappled him let go, Tzarik fell to the ground, his mind whirling. The poison disoriented him. He tried to look up, but the world spun around him.

He spotted a few warriors coming back from the way Signar had run. They hauled his unconscious body between the two of them.

"What have you done to him?" Tzarik slurred. "Signar!"

They tossed his body onto the floor with a hard slap and stood back for orders. Tzarik crawled toward the Vaeson, but moving made his stomach knot in agony. Bile rose in his throat and he had to stop before he vomited. Ashkan stood before him.

"Take them to the prison below. Separate them. Have this one beaten until he wakes. We cannot risk his transforming. We need him weak and docile."

"Don't touch him," Tzarik growled, trying one last time to push himself up.

"You cannot stop us, Runer," Ashkan said simply.

Somewhere, a door opened and Tzarik heard footsteps.

Ashkan looked up. "Faraji, have you summoned Tarkan?"

"He comes," the deeper voice of the other necromancer said.

More words were spoken, but Tzarik couldn't hear them. He turned as his vision started to fade and crawled to Signar. He reached out for the boy's hand, but his entire body failed him just before he could take it.

Sybal glanced at Amir as they climbed the muddy path up the mountain to the highlands of Xia. His face was pale and sweat trickled down his brow. He breathed heavily, but kept up with her. She guessed he'd gotten ill from the cold in the Frozen Nation, but hadn't said anything to her. She slowed her steps to give him time to breathe. His breaths came in hard, rattling rasps. Though it pained her to slow, she knew he'd never admit to being ill and his pride would be wounded if she left him too far behind.

On the third day of their march, they happened upon a small village in the Shiuki province. Sybal was shocked to find it burned and bodies lying around the perimeter. She stopped cold in her tracks when they crested a hill outside the village and spotted three Xian crosses facing the north there. She gasped when she saw them and the marks on her back immediately twinged in familiarity. Upon the crosses were three young men with stark white hair. Rather than being tied to the X-shaped cross as she had been, they were nailed there.

"What is this?" Amir asked, shock at the gruesome sight obvious on his face.

"The Xians believe those with white hair are touched by their white dragon and are destined to rule," she began. "But any sentient can have the white hair, and thus the families feud with one another." She looked back into the village and the smoldering structures there. She frowned. "I've seen this before, but it should have ended."

"Why?" Amir asked.

Sybal looked up at the poor, dead men. She sighed sadly. "Something must have happened. We put an heir on the throne the last time we were here. And Hiro, the Di-Huan's eldest son who was not dragon-touched, should have been steward to the throne until the babe was old enough to claim it. I thought all of Xia had agreed to that. They support the white touch when it is passed down from one ruler to another. But..."

Her frown deepened.

"Something must have happened," she repeated. "This isn't how we left things." She glanced around, suddenly wary. "We need to get off the road and move through the thicket. We don't know what's wrong."

Amir didn't argue, merely nodded and followed her off the main road and into a less manicured area. They continued on and saw more evidence over the next day of more civil unrest. They witnessed an execution in the streets of Shiuki and had to hide from a small battle they encountered in the woods.

When they reached the road that led directly to the Royal City, Sybal stopped and moved to an outcropping that hung over a deep gulch. She pulled out her brass glass and pointed it in the direction of the Royal City. As she scanned the walls, she looked for anything out of the ordinary.

"I don't see any guards on the walls," she whispered to Amir. "That seems—" She gasped. Her lens picked up a black-clad figure on top of the gatehouse. She focused in on it and saw the markings on the pale skin before she noticed anything else. "Necromancer," she hissed.

She directed her lens around the Royal City, but didn't see any signs of damage. "There are Alikan warriors around the perimeter," she said. That was when it hit her.

They shouldn't be there. There was no reason for Alikan warriors to be guarding the Royal City. Her heart turned to ice and sank.

"We're too late," she whispered. "Tarkan is here. Or at least his army is."

Amir reached up and took the glass from her, looking to the palace for himself. "What does that mean? Where are the other two?"

*Where are Tzarik and Signar?* she wondered. "Perhaps they saw the necromancers and the undead as well," she said. She looked up into the darkening sky. "We cannot find them tonight, so let's camp. Far away from here. We'll look for them in the morning."

# Chapter 18
## Fate

Tarkan waited only one day before traveling through the God Deep back to Xia. He had to make sure Acenoth and the others were healed and that Alika was back under his control before he left. But the anticipation shot through him.

Faraji had said they had Tzarik.

He hoped it was true and that some other Runer had not wandered onto Xia, unlikely as that was. He could hardly contain his excitement as he rushed through the darkness of the Deep and finally burst back through a small opening into the throne room.

Faraji leapt up from the throne and greeted him. Beside him, Hiro hung from his wrists, half passed out. Faraji approached Tarkan and bowed deeply when they drew close.

"Where is he?" Tarkan asked eagerly.

"Below with his boy," the Apostle replied.

Tarkan frowned. "Boy? He's not with Sybal?"

"No. The lady Runer was not with him. He has a tall, pale boy. Perhaps from Caerwren." Faraji led the way out of the throne room and out into the palace's halls. He strode quickly, making his way to the dungeon door. The door creaked and ground on its hinges, telling Tarkan it had not seen use in some time.

Tarkan wondered who the boy Tzarik had with him was. Had he picked up an apprentice on Caerwren before he'd left? Did that mean something had happened to Sybal? Part of him hoped the lady Runer had been swallowed up by the mountain in Northica. His hand went to his chest where she had stabbed him over and over again, almost killing him.

But that time, like on Caerwren, Tzarik had saved his life.

Tzarik had stopped Sybal from finishing him off. He remembered lying there in the cave tunnels of the desert, thinking he'd never see Zeva again. That she'd die by Sharar's hand if he never came back. All he'd cared about in that moment was Zeva. And then Tzarik had appeared, drawing his healing rune over his chest, asking why he'd not killed him before. Even now Tarkan wasn't sure why he'd spared the Runer then. Perhaps it was because Tzarik had had nothing to do with his feud with Sharar. But it had been a good thing. Without Tzarik, Tarkan wouldn't be the Necro'Khan he was now.

Tarkan stopped outside the garrison. Despite Xia's beauty, the dungeon was dark, damp, and haunting. He spied a table with the unmistakable items of a Runer splayed out on it. He eyed the scimitar, recognizing Tzarik's blade.

"I want you to have them beaten until they are sufficiently ready to be seen by me," he said, taking no chances. "Do what you have to, but don't kill them. I want them weak."

"Of course, sira. It would be a pleasure." Faraji bowed and vanished inside the last thick, metal-reinforced door.

Tarkan turned to Tzarik's things and began to pick through them while he listened for sounds of the torture beyond the door. He heard nothing. Perhaps their cells were too far away.

He found the hip satchel Tzarik always carried with him. Inside was a bottle of sulfates and a few other things. Two packs with bedrolls and some rations waited on the floor beside the table. He wondered what would have made Tzarik take on an apprentice, if that indeed was the case. He looked through the other things, but didn't find a second set of Runer armor, nor another orichalcum blade. But he did find a strange medallion that had an Al'Myrahn family crest on it. Curious, he picked it up and examined it.

There was nothing special about the medallion. It looked like something a sheikh might wear during ceremonies or grand events. A small but delicate thing. Tarkan turned it over. On the back, etched into the soft gold metal, was a rune. Tarkan didn't recall the name of the rune, but knew it was the binding rune. Curious, he rubbed his thumb over the mark and thought. Could there be a djinn inside? Had Tzarik found himself a powerful demon? Was he using it?

Before he could think too deeply about what it meant that Tzarik had a djinn, the door opened again and Faraji appeared. Sweat beaded on his brow and he smiled.

"They are well beaten, my Khan, though still conscious. We put the Runer on a Xian cross and the boy is tethered to a whipping post in his own cell."

Curious to finally see this Caerwren boy, Tarkan followed Faraji into the garrison. They walked past a few cells and the few kehann standing guard to the cells that held their prisoners. The first cell, with the Xian cross inside, held Tzarik. Tarkan stopped and looked inside to take in his prisoner. Tzarik hung by his wrists from the X-shaped cross, his legs bound to the bottom. His black tunic was damp with white sulfates, showing that Faraji had indeed done his job. Tzarik's head hung low and he panted for breath.

"Signar?" the Runer called weakly.

Tarkan looked at the cell across from Tzarik. Inside, lashed to a whipping post by his wrists, was a tall, pale young man with long, wild yellow hair. Tarkan narrowed his eyes and came closer to the boy, inspecting him. His back was flayed, blood dribbling from strips of flesh that hung off his shoulders from a savage flogging. But beyond that, Tarkan recognized him.

"Sjörna's son?" he whispered, shocked.

When he spoke, Tzarik's head snapped up. "Tarkan," Tzarik shot, a peppering of desperation in his voice. "What are you doing?" He pulled on his restraints, but they held. "Let me go."

Tarkan shook his head, loving the sight of the Runer bleeding, tied, and desperate.

"Is Signar alive?" Tzarik asked. He looked up and his eyes widened when they took in the sight of the boy across from him. "Signar!" he shouted.

Tarkan turned to look. The boy hung from his wrists, his legs having given out. His head was tilted back and his mouth hung open. Tear stains tracked down his face. Tarkan saw his chest gently rising and falling with breath. "He's alive," he confirmed for Tzarik. "But I am curious, Runer. Why did you take the son of the Reks? I remember him. Chained outside Sjörna's thronehall. He was a wild beast."

"He's not anymore," Tzarik snapped back. "I took him to save him. They were...going to torment him for the rest of his days."

"And now look where he is." Tarkan had to force a smile away. Of course Tzarik had wanted to save the boy. Tzarik wanted to save everyone. He was brave like that. "You ruin all you touch, Runer. You cannot save him. You cannot save yourself."

Tzarik swallowed and looked up, meeting Tarkan's eyes. The Necro'Khan was glad to see something that resembled fear flit behind Tzarik's eyes. "Yes," Tarkan said simply. "I am going to kill you, I'm afraid."

Tzarik flexed his muscled arms and pulled on the restraints again, growling as he did so. They held strong. "Kill me here and now?" he asked. "Shackled like a monster? Coward."

"Coward?" Tarkan snarled, taking a step closer to Tzarik. "I have faced every fear I've ever had. I have gone on down the long road of loneliness without *her*. How did she die, Runer? Alone?"

Tzarik dropped his eyes then and looked away.

Tarkan restrained himself, wanting to strike the Runer, to kill him immediately. Instead, he struck like a viper, gripping Tzarik's throat in his long, thin fingers. Tzarik choked, but didn't fight. Tarkan squeezed.

"You killed her. You turned her against me. She didn't need to die on that frozen mountain." With a shout of disgust, he let go and turned away. His eyes landed on Signar and he froze as a thought came to him.

"No, Tarkan, don't. Please," Tzarik begged. "Leave the boy alone. He has nothing to do with what has happened between us."

"So selfless, Tzarik," Tarkan whispered. "Rest assured, I will not slay the boy. I promise you that. But I am no coward. I am giving up the blood of a sorcerer. I wanted it desperately. But I see now I cannot let Sharar live. And I know that killing you will kill him. I am sorry, Tzarik. We were almost friends once." He turned back to face the Runer.

Tzarik squirmed in his restraints once again, but to no avail. "I saved you," he tried. "More than once. In the tunnels of Ala'Nar. In the frozen waters of Caerwren."

Tarkan nodded. "You did. I remember that day. I was...terrified for my life. I remember sinking beneath the waves, drowning. I tried to swim, but the waves were too strong. I sank below and into the frigid dark. But I knew I wouldn't be lost."

Tzarik frowned, listening.

Tarkan went on. "I knew, beyond a shadow of a doubt, that you'd save me. I trusted you with my life, Tzarik. When the waves pulled me under and my lungs burned for air, I knew you'd come. I just had to wait."

Tzarik's eyes suddenly shone. Disbelief twisted his face.

"Yes," Tarkan sighed. "I knew you'd come. You want to save people, Tzarik. You always have. Including yourself. You think you craved death, but really you looked for a reason to live." He smiled sadly. "You knew no one would save you, so you had to save yourself. You found that reason in Sybal. Tell me, Tzarik, did you love her from the moment you set eyes on her? I have no doubt she loved you. You saved her life."

"Tarkan," Tzarik panted, his voice turning desperate. "We are not your enemy. We gave you all the power you have. And Zeva... We didn't kill her. She fought against you that day because she thought she'd lost you."

"I was a captive!" Tarkan snarled back. "I was a slave to Sjörna-Reks, bound and voiceless. I have been a captive all my life, Runer, and for once I will not yield!" His voice rose and he felt his emotions getting out of control. He stopped and took several deep breaths. "But you? You're a savior. A good man. You saved the boy. You saved Sybal. You saved Xia, even. Tzarik, you want someone to save you now, but that's not how the world works. No one will come and save you. All your valor was for nought."

He searched the Runer's face for fear now, but found only hardened resolve. Tzarik glared at him, despite his eyes filling with tears.

"Even now you prepare to weep," Tarkan said softly. "But not for yourself. You fear for the boy. I will tell you this: I will spare him. I promise. But I need you to know that no one is coming to save you, Tzarik. You spent a lifetime helping others, hunting monsters. And now, in your time of need, you are utterly alone. How cruel is the world?"

⌒

Tzarik pulled on his restraints once more, praying they pulled free. But they didn't. The shackles held his wrists and ankles tight. He glared at Tarkan as hard as he could, disguising the mounting fear inside himself. Tarkan was right; he didn't fear for himself. He was afraid for Signar.

He looked around, but there was nothing nearby he could grasp. No way to free himself. He blinked and the tears fell.

"This world is not half as cruel as you," he growled, balling his fists. "Don't do this, Tarkan. We can find a way."

The Necro'Khan raised his pale brows. "Begging does not suit you, Tzarik. But I suppose you have nothing left to try."

Rage filled Tzarik then. He gnashed his teeth, but knew Tarkan spoke the truth. He tried to steel himself but something inside him quelled in fear. He was trapped. He couldn't move. There was no escape. He began to shake as he saw the decision be made behind Tarkan's eyes.

"Please," he whispered once more. Would any god hear him? Did any god care? Or was he just one more mortal life to be snuffed out in the grand design?

He looked over and met Signar's half-awake eyes. The boy shook and gasped for air through a tight throat. He didn't want Signar to remember him this way.

Tzarik steeled himself and clenched his jaw. He turned his icy gaze back to Tarkan and glared steadily at him. No, he'd not cower in his last moments. He locked his eyes onto Tarkan's and was glad to see the Necro'Khan's brows twitch. Tarkan took a step back.

꒰꒱

Tarkan turned to Faraji.

"Bring me the Runer's sword," he commanded. Faraji bowed and left. Tarkan faced Tzarik again. "The time has come, I am afraid. Don't think I am taking any pleasure in this, Tzarik."

"I see it in your eyes," the Runer growled back. "When you slay me, you won't see me. You will imagine Sharar taking his last breaths. I mean nothing to you. You are not remorseful. You feel nothing."

Faraji reappeared and handed Tarkan the orichalcum blade. Behind them, Signar moaned and began to wake fully. He pulled on the chains on his wrist and struggled to stand. The beating had done its job and he couldn't find the strength to rise.

꒰꒱

Tzarik's heart twisted. He wanted to save Signar. To go to him. He saw the gleam of his own blade and yet all he could think about was Signar. And Sybal. His heart hammered for her. She was so impulsive. Would she be safe without him?

Yes, he had to have faith in her.

"Good," Tarkan said. "I want the boy to witness this."

"No, Tarkan," Tzarik said, almost pleading now. "Don't let him see this."

"Everyone must learn to suffer, Runer," Tarkan replied. He approached Tzarik, holding his own blade. "It is a blessing that he sees you die. I was denied my last moments with Zeva. Am I not merciful for letting him be with you? Unlike her, you will not die alone."

He raised the blade and set the tip against Tzarik's lower ribs. Tzarik gasped as the point broke the surface of his skin. He tried not to breathe as that just drove the point in harder.

"I promise to give Sybal a quick death as well," Tarkan whispered.

Then he pushed. He threw all his weight behind the sword and shoved it up to its hilt into Tzarik's middle. Tzarik immediately choked, white blood trickling out of the corner of his mouth. Behind them, Signar screamed. He heard the boy's shackles clinking and clanging madly as he thrashed against them.

Tzarik fought madly to breathe around the blade in his ribs. It hurt, every breath agony. He wanted to call out to Signar. To tell him it was going to be all right. A cold shiver overtook him and made his skin grow clammy. He couldn't stop the tears that leaked out of the corners of his eyes now. This was what he'd wanted all those years ago. An end. Death. Now that it was happening, he'd give anything to stop it. To have more time. To be with Sybal. To save Signar.

He fought to live as his blood choked him.

⁂

Tarkan ripped the blade out and looked into Tzarik's eyes. Too much life still shone there. Tzarik struggled to breathe, his gasps gurgling in his own blood. The Runer fought hard against the wound.

Signar screamed and pled as he yanked against the shackles. His large green eyes latched onto Tzarik.

"Signar," Tzarik whispered weakly, more blood dribbling from his lips. "It's all... It's all right."

Tarkan poised the sword again, this time pointing it into Tzarik's chest. But he hesitated. He could stop now. Maybe even save the Runer.

But Sharar...

"Please!" Signar screamed from behind. "Don't!"

Tarkan shoved the sword hard again, feeling it scrape along Tzarik's ribs this time. The Runer made a horrid groan as the blade went all the way through him once again. Blood spilled out from his lips and he threw his head back, trying to gasp for air. Tarkan watched as Tzarik's throat spasmed and his eyes closed. He fought for one more breath, but none came. His fingers unclenched and his head finally lolled to the side.

Silence followed.

Tarkan stepped back, gasping for air and wrenching the blade free. He'd been holding his breath while the Runer took his last ones.

"No!" Signar screamed behind him, thrashing once again in his bonds. "I'll kill you! I swear, I'll kill you!"

Tarkan had to turn and watch, making sure the wild boy's chains held him. "I am so sorry, child," he said weakly. He motioned Faraji forward and the Apostle entered Signar's cell. He laid several blows to Signar's head, silencing him. The boy hung his head and moaned, only half conscious now. Then Faraji went into Tzarik's cell and unbound him, letting his body fall to the ground in a heap. Tarkan stumbled back, not wanting to touch the corpse.

"Tzarik," Tarkan whispered, looking at the Runer's now peaceful face. "I am...so sorry." The more he looked down at Tzarik, the more he expected the Runer to leap up, take his sword, and stab him. Did part of him wish he would?

Tarkan turned and exited the cell. He took several steps back and motioned to Faraji once more. "Let the boy into his cell. I will afford him that mercy at the very least."

Signar was so weak from the beating that he didn't fight Faraji as the Apostle opened his cell and pulled him by his shackles into Tzarik's cell. The boy could hardly walk and he was still bleeding profusely. Faraji practically dragged him across to the other cell and tossed him inside. Tarkan watched, interested, as Signar threw himself over Tzarik's body and began to weep, howling like a wounded wolf.

Tarkan expected the sight before him to move him in some way, even just a little.

But no. The bloodletting had only ignited a lust in him he'd not felt before. A thrill shot through him as he looked at Tzarik's body and the big Caerwren boy who wept over him.

He smiled.

Somewhere, and it didn't matter where, Sharar was taking his last breaths as well. Tarkan only wished he could see it. At last, he was free of the scholar. Really and truly free.

᠑᠊᠋᠊

Sharar marched from one end of his room in the palace to the other to inspect himself in the mirror. He would meet soon with the sultana and Sokar and discuss their next move. He opened his robes and looked at the malignant wound on his ribs. He touched it gingerly and it twinged in pain. The black veins from it spidered out over his torso and up his neck now. He laid his hand over his heart and breathed in. He held the breath, taking in the slight pain that came with the deep inhale. His wound throbbed, but didn't ignite in pain.

"It's getting worse," Vicdan said from behind him where he was shackled to the wall, but for once without the bridle. "It's spreading, isn't it?"

"What do you know about it?" Sharar asked, closing his robes and tying a sash around his middle. He looked at Vicdan in the mirror's reflection.

"Nothing, honestly." Vicdan pulled a face. "I don't like not knowing things. Something we have in common, no doubt. But I can tell it's not good, sorcerer. I believe it will only get worse, eventually taking your life." Realizing what this meant for Tzarik, Vicdan's face fell. "Maybe there is a cure."

"No, necromancer," Sharar sighed. He ran his fingers through his long, glossy hair. "There is no cure for this fate. There is no cure for anyone's fate. We all meet the same end. Some things are just inevitable."

"Like Tarkan?" Vicdan asked. "Do you really think you can beat him with a larger army? Or is his demise unachievable? He's very powerful."

"He is," Sharar agreed. "But he doesn't have the one thing he craves: my blood. He will—"

A knock sounded on his door, interrupting their discussion. Sharar could tell from the shy rapping that it was Sokar.

"Come in, dear boy," he called.

Sokar opened the door and peeked inside. His long, feathery ears perked up when Sharar smiled at him. "The sultana is in the garden, waiting for us," he said. He pushed inside and came to stand behind Sharar, where he looked one last time at himself in the mirror.

Sharar smiled at the boy in the mirror and turned to face him. He was about to speak when a sudden pain cracked through his chest. Sharar cried out and pressed his hand against his flesh. He gasped as his breathing became labored. He felt blood well up in his lungs and into his throat. Coughing, he fell forward into Sokar's arms.

"What's happening?" Sokar cried, catching him even as blood splattered over his face. "Abigor? What's wrong?"

Sharar couldn't stand, the pain and sudden weakness taking him to the ground. Sokar knelt with him, cradling him in his arms. Sharar panted, trying to catch his breath, but couldn't. He clawed at his throat, gasping.

"Abigor," Sokar sobbed, pressing his palm to his cheek. "Tell me what to do. What's happening?"

Sharar tried to speak, but couldn't get any words out just yet. He coughed, sending a fresh geyser of blood onto Sokar's face.

"Scholar?" Vicdan called from where he was shackled. "What the bloody hell is wrong with you? Is it the wound?"

"No," Sharar managed to groan. He pressed his hands into his chest and moaned loudly. "Something is happening..."

"Help!" Sokar shouted toward the door. "Someone, please, help me!"

For just a moment, Sharar caught his breath and his throat cleared. That was when he felt it, though. A cold, icy hand gripped him. Suddenly he knew; this was the end.

What had happened? Had Tzarik died in battle, fighting some monster? Had he fallen to Tarkan?

"Sokar," Sharar mumbled.

"What is it?" the pharaoh asked, tears spilling down his face. "How can I help you?"

Sharar reached up and touched Sokar's chin. He had so much he wanted to say to the boy. He had more to do on the map, some things he'd not even realized yet. But he knew the sensation that rose in his gut now. His heart fluttered, understanding as well, but fighting to stay alive.

"Check the wound," Vicdan called to Sokar. "On his side."

Sokar gently laid Sharar down and opened his robes. He gasped upon seeing the black wound. "It's not bleeding," he said to Vicdan.

"Not...the wound," Sharar panted. His chest suddenly tightened and his guts roiled. A strange fear of something out of his control drove him wild.

Then the stabbing pain came back again, harder this time, and fiercer than before. Like someone had shoved a spear through his chest. He couldn't stop the moan it pulled from his lips as more blood leaked down his chin.

"Gods, help me!" Sokar shouted. He collected Sharar in his arms again, hugging him to his chest, and began to sob. "Abigor, don't leave me. Please. Stay."

Sharar took a shuddering inhale and tried to meet Sokar's eyes. In that moment, he regretted everything. He should have struck Tarkan harder, faster. He should have studied the book more and delved into his power rather than squandering it. He had been too afraid. He thought with this power, he would have more time.

"Sokar," he managed to murmur around the blood drowning him and the pain in his chest. "Listen to me."

"No, Abigor, don't. Please," the boy sobbed.

But he couldn't go on. His voice left him, too weak to even get simple words out. The world around him started to turn black. He didn't have time. He couldn't tell the boy what to do.

"Scholar?" Vicdan shouted. "Oh, gods, no!"

The necromancer understood.

Sharar gasped a final breath and his mind went blank.

Somewhere, Tzarik was dead.

# Chapter 19
## Release

Tarkan turned away from the bloody sight before him. He went to the table where the Runer's items lay and picked through them. He took up Tzarik's runes and the medallion with the djinn inside. Behind him, Signar's sobs had subsided. Now a low growl emanated from the boy's throat. It sounded like the deep growl of a wolf. He turned back and faced the cell.

Signar held Tzarik's body, but watched Tarkan with a dark gleam in his green eyes. The boy's nose wrinkled in a snarl and fangs were barred behind his lips. Tarkan paused, deciding whether or not to put his hand into the bars to hand the boy the medallion.

"What now, Necro'Khan?" Signar whispered. "Open this door and I will rip you to shreds."

"I know," Tarkan replied. "But I am going to let you go."

Signar tilted his head, still glaring.

"I need you to tell Sybal what has happened. She deserves to know. And I don't want you dead." He met Signar's eyes. "I remember you from Altevine. I saw you chained outside like a dog. Saw them beat you. You don't deserve to die by my hand."

Signar spat a scoff. "Your sympathy means nothing to me, death fiend."

"Perhaps not," Tarkan sighed. "Tell me. Why did Tzarik take you? How did he tame you?"

"Open this door and I'll show you how tame I am," Signar snarled.

"Don't make me hurt you more than I have to, boy." Tarkan held up the medallion. "I'm going to give this back to you. We will let you go. Find Sybal and inform her of her master's death."

"She'll hunt you down." Signar gently laid Tzarik's body onto the ground and stood up to face Tarkan. He was still bleeding and weak, his legs shaking. "She'll not rest until you're dead."

Tarkan raised his head. "I have been hunted my entire life, boy. This is not a threat to me. I expect her to. And I expect I will put her back from whence I pulled her soul. If you are wise, you will stay away." He turned and motioned to three kehann who stood guard behind him. "Take him outside the Royal City and let him go. I don't care how or where. Just remove him from my sight."

Signar planted his shaking legs apart and readied himself as the kehann unlocked the cell door. Signar leapt, trying to take them down, but he was too weak. The kehann easily parried his wild, swinging arms and grappled him. Signar snarled and tried to bite one of the kehann. One of the others went behind Signar, pulled out his sword, and knocked the boy in the back of his head with the pommel of his sword. The boy went limp in their arms.

"Wait," Tarkan called, now feeling safe enough to approach the wildling. He slipped the medallion over the boy's head along with Tzarik's runes. "Give him his axe and take him far away. Leave him somewhere he won't be found. His fate is in the hands of his god now. Then dispose of the Runer and his things. I want them gone."

The kehann nodded and hauled the tall boy out of the garrison. Tarkan watched them go before turning and marching back up above ground to the throne room. Faraji sat on the throne and Hiro still hung from the pillar beside him. They both looked up when Tarkan re-entered the room.

"What have you done?" Hiro asked.

"The Runer is dead," Tarkan said as easily as he could. Somehow, Tzarik's demise still affected him. He swallowed back the strange emotion and met Hiro's wide eyes.

"You killed him?" Hiro cried, pulling on his bonds.

"And thus I have killed the sorcerer." Tarkan looked into the middle distance, wishing he could have seen Sharar die. Wishing he could have watched as the life left his eyes. He regretted having to kill Tzarik, but the Runer had walked right into his hands. Perhaps he should have kept him alive, told Sharar he had captured him and faced Sharar himself. Had he really taken the coward's way out? Was Tzarik right?

"I will head back to Alika," he went on. "Faraji, open the Crypt when I send word. We will leave Xia to its fate."

"Why not open the Crypt now?" Faraji asked.

Tarkan's eyes unfocused as he thought. Sharar was dead. He had nothing left to fear. He didn't need to rush. "I want Xia to suffer at its own hands a little longer. Let it destroy itself. Only then will opening the Crypt finish the job."

"And the prince?" Faraji asked, gesturing to Hiro.

"You killed the sorcerer!" Hiro shouted. "What more can you want?"

"Nothing so complicated," Tarkan replied. "I want the world to suffer, to know pain. Loss. It's nothing compared to the pain I have endured, but it will do. The world needs to understand what it has done to me."

Hiro glowered. "You've lost sight of what you want. You've gone mad in your pursuit of power."

Tarkan rounded on him. "Mad? No, Prince, I am not mad. I have never thought more clearly in my life. Madness is for the weak. I know exactly what I am doing."

The prince kept his eyes steady. "You cannot hope to live in the kind of world you are creating. With the God Deep open, the world will be consumed by darkness and horror. People will die."

"If all goes well, everyone will die." Tarkan turned away and looked out into the royal gardens, taking in the beauty that was Xia. Even behind the thick blanket of rain clouds, the gray sunlight lit up the world just enough for him to see the purple mountains, the pink trees, the blue rivers. "I will be the last sentient standing on the map. And then I will bow to my fate."

"What fate is that?"

Tarkan smiled. "That's for me to know, prince." He motioned to Faraji. "Do what you want with the prince, but do not kill him yet. Ashkan..."

The other Apostle, who had remained quiet and hidden in the shadows until then, stepped forward.

"You will come with me back to Alika for now. I want you at my side for a time."

"I would be of better use here," Ashkan argued weakly.

Tarkan glared at the Apostle. The truth was he didn't trust Ashkan any more now than he did before. He needed Faraji to be on Xia alone, to use his ruthless disposition without hindrance. "You will return. Have no fear," Tarkan said.

Ashkan lowered his eyes. "Yes, my Khan."

Tarkan turned and walked back up the hall. As he marched through the palace and out toward the gate, he thought about Sharar. About all the years of torture he'd suffered at the hands of the scholar. He thought about Tzarik and how he'd fought for his life, even as he'd gasped with his own sword between his ribs.

Then he thought of Sybal. She would come for him, and he needed to be ready.

Thunder rolled over the thick, blackening clouds. A gentle, cold wind picked up and rushed over Signar's prone body. He shivered, feeling the cold droplets begin to fall. He couldn't open his eyes yet and only heard the muffled sound of the thunder above. He lay on his stomach on the hard, rocky ground. He clenched his fingers into the mud, gripping it. Moaning, he pushed himself up and opened his eyes. His head throbbed and his back stung, the wounds still open and fresh. With a pained cry, he pushed himself up onto his knees and looked around.

Rolling green hills and silver rocky cliffs surrounded him. A few trees with pink flowers grew out of the stone gulches, and a blue river flowed to his left. Above, the thunder rolled again. Lightning snapped suddenly, making him cower. He yelped at the harsh crackle and scrambled to duck under a small outcropping. Fear gripped his heart in an icy grasp and squeezed. Tears filled his eyes as the realization hit him that he had no idea where he was. He fought to suppress them, but failed as they trickled down his cheek.

Another snap of lightning crackled past, just outside the small cave-like structure. He shouted and covered his ears, pulling his knees into his chest. Closing his eyes, he willed the storm to settle. But the wind picked up, and the rain fell in torrents. Another thunder clap sent him over the edge and he cried out loudly. He let the sobs come then, wishing he were with Sybal. He tried to make himself smaller to hide from the rain, but he was too big for the small alcove.

He wept, his cries drowned out by the rain and thunder. When he closed his eyes, he saw Tzarik's body in his mind's eye. So he forced his eyes open. He watched the rain fall until his own tears ran dry. He didn't know how long he'd been weeping. His back stung and his legs were cramped now. He looked out and spotted his axe, watching the water run through the ornamental etchings like a river. The blade reminded him he was Reks of Altevine.

But right now, he was alone, lost, and frightened. He had to conquer himself and his fear. He had to stand.

Signar swallowed his final sob and stood. He looked down and realized he was nearly naked. His boots were gone. Everything but the soft leather pants around his hips had been taken. The medallion and Tzarik's runes were around his neck. His toes started to go numb in the cold. He pushed the discomfort aside and raised his hand, summoning his axe to him. The moment the haft thudded into his palm, he felt stronger. He gripped his axe and looked into the yellow gem between the axe heads. He couldn't see himself reflected back, but knew he must look weak. His arm shook from the weight of the weapon.

Facing the storm, Signar walked out from his shelter into the rain and lightning and started to look for a path that might take him to a village. He didn't know Xia at all. He didn't even know the names of the provinces. Looking up at the sky, he couldn't even find north. Fear once again tried to worm its way into his heart, but he kept it at bay. He touched Tzarik's runes and prayed for direction.

Something urged him to go to his right. Turning, Signar started a steady march down the hill. He walked for hours, pushing through the underbrush and looking for any signs of life. He sniffed at the air every now and then, trying to find a whiff of a campfire or something that would point to sentient activity. But he found nothing.

He continued to follow his instincts, turning this way and that as he marched. He found himself heading back uphill for several hours before finally the sun began to set behind the blanket of gray clouds. The night grew colder, and the rain didn't stop. He began to wonder if he'd wandered in circles. He checked the muddy ground, but didn't see any of his own footprints and couldn't catch his own scent.

Long into the night, he stopped and took a drink from a small stream. He was hungry, so he dropped his axe and transformed into his wolf to hunt for food. He caught a brace of rabbits and halted before eating them. There was no way to make fire in this rain without a flint and steel, so he ate them raw. The familiar taste reminded him of the time Tzarik had told him he'd not eat raw meat anymore. The emotion that rose in his throat almost made it impossible to swallow, but he forced himself to eat the animals.

In his wolf shape, he was much warmer. His thick yellow coat supplied a barrier between himself and the rain. He thought about bedding down and sleeping the rest of the night, but knew that even in his wolf form, sleep would evade him.

Signar hung his head as he remembered coming to Tzarik's room that first night they'd slept in Sybal's home. He'd told the boy to return to his own room, but Signar hadn't been able to. He couldn't sleep in the soft bed and couldn't sleep alone. It was all too foreign to him. So he'd slept on the floor in Tzarik's room. Signar had always waited until later at night, to give Sybal and Tzarik time alone. He liked hearing them breathe beside him. He liked knowing he wasn't alone.

The sadness filled him and he threw his wolven head back and howled up at the thunderous clouds above. He let a long, wild yowl out before starting his march once again, axe clutched in his maw. He'd not gone on five minutes before a tiny, faraway sound reached his pointed ears.

A voice.

Not just a voice, but someone shouting his name. He dropped his blade and perked up his ears, listening. His nose twitched, smelling for anything. The cold night air carried sound and smell far, so he knew anything he did pick up would be farther away than he thought. Curious, he howled again, as loudly as he could.

The voice replied, screaming his name, but was still very far away. That was when he recognized it.

"Sybal," he said, his heart leaping in his chest. "Sybal!" he shouted. He turned back to his human form, picked up his axe, and ran in the direction of the voice. Then he picked up her scent, recognizing her and someone not as familiar. It had to be Amir. Signar broke into a run, despite his weakness. He shouted her name, listening hard and smelling the air to find her.

She replied, calling his name, and her scent grew stronger. They called and replied to one another, moving through the night. Signar soon smelled fire, and Sybal's scent grew even stronger. He ran through the woods for several minutes before he saw fire through the trees.

"Sybal!" he screamed, his legs finally giving out. He'd lost too much blood and couldn't go on any longer. His back stung and his head throbbed. He fell onto all fours and panted.

"Signar!" Sybal's voice cried. "Where are you?"

"Here!" he shouted back. He tried to speak more, but he couldn't catch his breath. His heart thudded painfully hard in his chest.

Someone crashed through the underbrush, appearing before him. A tall man with long, dirty hair.

"Sybal, he's here," Amir called. He ran to Signar's side and gathered him in his arms, pulling him to his feet.

Signar held on tight to Amir so he would be standing when Sybal arrived. She burst through the foliage and ran to him, arms outstretched. She collided hard with him, hugging him tight.

"We couldn't find you two," she started to babble. "We looked, but the Royal City was taken over by the necromancers and we feared the worst. We tried to look for you, but weren't sure where you'd be." She kissed his forehead and squeezed him tight.

Signar cried out in pain as her arms pressed into his flayed back. He arched it, trying to relieve the pain. She let go and looked at him.

"Gods," she whispered. "What happened?" She looked around. "Where's Tzarik?"

Signar crumpled then, crying loudly again. Amir caught him before he fell and sank to his knees, supporting him. Together, they knelt in the mud.

"What happened?" Sybal repeated, her voice becoming more strained. "Signar. Where is Tzarik?"

Signar couldn't control himself. His wildling rose in him, making his sobbing an untamable sound. He wanted to lash out, to transform and run and hide. It would be so much easier than holding on to himself. Turning to his wolf was easy. Comforting.

Sybal's eyes went to the runes around his neck. She froze. "Where..." She choked. "Where is he, Signar?"

Signar pressed himself into Amir's arms, imagining they held the monster within him at bay. He wanted to say so many things at once, but his mind couldn't organize his thoughts. He wanted to howl. To tear. To hunt. Anything but feel the emotions that coursed through him right then. Being a human was so much harder than being a wild wolf.

"I-I," he stammered. "I couldn't save him. Tarkan—" The words were too hard. He growled instead, pulling against Amir now. "Let me go!" he screamed.

With that fit, Amir locked his arms around Signar harder and Sybal gripped his shoulders.

"Signar, please," she begged. "Tell me what happened. Where is he? Where's Tzarik?"

"What's wrong with him?" Amir asked.

"His wolf is taking over," Sybal said, still gripping him hard. "He could turn at any moment, but we cannot let him. Not here, not now. Signar!" She took his face in her hands and spoke more softly. "Listen to me, please. Tell me what happened. Where is Tzarik? You said Tarkan's name. Speak."

With her more soothing voice, the growling inside his head dissipated. The howl that rose in his throat receded. He caught his breath and moaned in pain.

"What happened?" Sybal asked again, her hand gently cradling his chin now.

Still unsure how to tell her, and with the wildling whispering in his ear, Signar grappled with himself. He finally got a small hold of his wolf and gripped it tight.

"Tarkan was there, in the city," he said breathlessly. "He'd captured the prince. The entire place was crawling with necromancers and the undead. Tarkan took us. Had us beaten." The memory was still too fresh, like the open scars on his back. He swallowed a sob. "Sybal." He looked up into her face. He could hardly get the words out. "He... Tarkan, he killed him." Saying it brought a long, loud wail from his throat. "I couldn't save him. I'm so sorry."

Sybal dropped her hand from his face and stumbled back, eyes wild and unblinking. Signar felt Amir let him go, and he collapsed all the way onto the ground. Sniffling, he looked up at Sybal. She didn't breathe, her lips gently parted. Her eyes were unseeing and yet they danced around the dark forest. She looked lost. Confused. Signar was keenly aware of Amir's presence. He smelled the worry seeping off him and felt his desire to hold Sybal.

"How?" Sybal breathed. "Why?" Her voice broke as she tried to understand. "Signar..."

She knelt next to him and reached for him. He let her take him in her arms and pull him close. He heard her shuddering breath as she tried to remain strong. A single, hot tear ran down her face and into his hair. Her heart hammered violently against her chest, belying her calm exterior.

"I understand," she whispered over and over again, each time her voice wavering more and more.

"We cannot stay here," Amir said after a moment. "We have to get back to Hatal. Sharar must be dead, and Vicdan will need to be rescued. He can tell us what has been happening."

Sybal nodded, but didn't speak. Signar didn't have the courage to look into her face.

Amir knelt behind Signar and pried Sybal's hands off him. He touched the bloody scars gently and then pulled out his runes. He drew the healing rune slowly over Signar's back while Sybal stood and walked a few paces away. Signar wanted to call her name, to have her turn and speak to him, but the way she held tension in her shoulders and turned her face from him told him to stay his words. Slowly, the pain subsided. Amir's hand was gentle and steady. Signar closed his eyes and leaned into the strange sensation of his flesh knitting back together.

When he was done, Amir helped him stand.

"Sybal," Signar whispered. "I couldn't... I tried. I'm so sorry."

Amir's hand appeared on his shoulder. "It's not your fault," he said softly. "She knows that."

Then why wouldn't she look at him? He wanted to burst into tears all over again, but knew he shouldn't. He had to be brave for her now. She wasn't reacting how he'd imagined. The quiet was worse than her weeping.

Amir took over then, leading them back to the campfire. He mumbled about taking a few days to ride back to the shore and finding a ship to take them home. Sybal didn't argue. She didn't speak at all. Her face was placid and expressionless.

"What about his body?" Signar asked when Sybal had walked into the woods. "We must bury him, or burn him on a pyre. For his soul."

Amir's blue eyes tracked Sybal's form as she wandered away from them. "We can't go back to the palace. It's too dangerous. I'm sorry."

Signar opened his mouth to argue, but stopped. Amir was right. But it hurt all the more. Tzarik was gone and they couldn't even honor him. Tarkan had taken even that away from them.

Sybal didn't speak the several days it took them to ride back to the shore. Signar wanted to use the djinn, but thought Sybal wouldn't want to use Kazamar. And she needed the time. The silence killed him, driving him mad. But he let her have her solitude, even though it hurt.

# Chapter 20
# The Star of Mourning

A mir climbed the ladder leading out of the lower decks and lifted his face into the sea air and rising sun. The wind tore playfully at his long hair as he glanced around the upper deck. He spotted Signar on the other side, near the railing. The boy had been quiet the last few days, and he understood why. But so had Sybal. Neither of them had spoken to the other, and he was caught in the middle. He saw the hurt and confusion in the boy's face every day, but didn't feel like it was his place to speak to him. But now that they were almost home, he decided he would. There was a lot about the boy he didn't understand, but he wasn't afraid of him or the monster Sybal had warned him he could turn into. Monsters were his job, after all.

He walked up behind Signar and joined him at the rail. The boy's face was hard and his eyes distant.

"She must grieve in her own way," Amir said after a moment. "Just as you do."

Signar glanced sidelong at Amir, glaring. Almost like he was annoyed that he'd spoken. But he didn't reply, so Amir went on.

"I'm sorry you had to witness that. Losing someone close to you is never easy."

"What do you want, Runer?" Signar snapped, and Amir could have sworn the boy snarled.

He brushed it aside. "I want you to know you're not alone. And that she's not abandoned you."

Signar's face softened then and he looked away. "I'm sorry," he whispered. "I have been alone most of my life, despite the people around me. I was a wildling in my home. Treated like an animal. I find it hard to leave that behind right now. I feel weak."

"You are not weak," Amir said. When he said those words, Signar finally looked over at him, eyes wide and shining with unshed tears. "I saw you in the coliseum. I know what you are capable of."

Signar looked away then, fiddling with his fingers. "I have to be strong. I'm Reks of Altevine. But I don't know how to be."

Amir almost stepped back at that. "I didn't know," he said. "I know so little of Caerwren."

"My mother was Reks," Signar said, and Amir was pleased to see a little of his barrier breaking down. "She was cruel to all. She used Tarkan's power to rip open the rift that now haunts my lands and has brought the malignation to it. Her desire to bring my father back to life drove Tarkan to the power he now possesses."

Amir waited, glad the boy was finally speaking.

"I worry for my people," he went on. "I need to go back. To defend them. To find a way to close that rift. But I don't know how."

"Neither do I," Amir confessed. "But we will find a way. I promise you that."

Signar looked over at Amir, his eyes almost pleading with him. "You will help us?"

Amir nodded. "I owe the map retribution for all the years I served Sharar. I thought I was a better man than that, but I suppose not. I have a lot to make up for."

Signar sighed, and it almost sounded like relief to Amir. He faced the west where Singad started to come into view. "I have to be brave. For Sybal," he said. "But I don't know how. I have only fear, anger, and rage."

"Rage is fine for you to feel," Amir said quickly. "You are a Reks of Caerwren. Rage and violence are in your nature. But you must control your rage. Use it to your advantage. That is what separates us from the monsters."

Signar made a sound that was somewhere between a laugh and a sob. "You talk like him, you know. Tzarik told me something similar once." Now he did sob softly. He turned away and squared his shoulders, trying to show his strength.

"Did Sybal ever sleep last night?" the boy asked after a moment.

"I'm not sure." Amir leaned onto his elbows on the railing. "She laid down late last night, but I doubt she slept. She wants time alone." He thought for a moment. "We need to give her that. When we reach Singad, we should use the djinn to take us back to Hatal. Any more time journeying might drive her mad."

"I thought about it," Signar said, his voice was strained. "But I thought she'd object. I thought she could use the time." He turned away from Amir and raised his hands to his eyes. Amir didn't say anything then, knowing the boy was fighting within himself. They both needed to grieve, but they couldn't or wouldn't do it now. They needed time.

To help, Amir changed the subject. "I have to go back to the palace and get Vicdan. He'll be able to tell us what Sharar was up to and what has happened since I left."

"And I must go home soon," Signar said.

This took Amir by surprise. He stood and faced Signar. "Go back to Caerwren? Now?" The boy was speaking out of emotion, he was sure of it. Surely he didn't want to leave Sybal. Not now. Signar was just confused and grieving—making a rash decision.

"My people need me," Signar reasoned. "Altevine needs me. I was to go back anyway. I left once and someone took my canton, enslaving the one who should have saved it."

"We need to plan our next steps," Amir said, trying to agree a little. "But let's not do anything rash. There's only so much we can do against the rifts."

"There are ways to contain them," Signar said. "But that will require constant vigilance. I must do what needs to be done."

Behind them, the captain of the ship shouted for the men to prepare to dock the ship. They'd arrived in Singad.

"We'll disembark and find a quiet alley to use the djinn," Amir said. "Go find Sybal."

Signar nodded and departed below deck. Amir looked out at the city and took in the beauty of it from the sea. He was glad to be back on Al'Myrah, but they could not stop. Tarkan was surely on the move, and Amir didn't know what that meant yet. All he knew was that he'd do anything for Sybal.

᷍

Signar trotted down the steps into the lower decks. Sybal stood near a horse tethered to a beam. She was braiding its mane, but her eyes were a million realms away. Signar quietly approached her.

"We're going to use the djinn to return to Hatal," he said. As he expected, she stiffened a little.

"We shouldn't," she mumbled. "Using the djinn only makes it stronger. There's no telling what it might do to you if it breaks free. Especially after you tricked it."

"We can't waste any more time," Signar tried. "The journey to Hatal will take days."

"He wouldn't want you to use it," she whispered and Signar heard her trying to control a sob that rose in her throat. "We could have..." She stopped and took a gasping breath. "No. Never mind."

"This is my decision," Signar said firmly. "We're using Kazamar to go home." They should have done it in the first place, but he'd known she'd object. And he wanted to give her time.

Sybal's hands stopped their work for just a moment as she considered his words. She hummed as his authority resonated with her. "Fine. I leave it up to you."

᷍

Signar leapt through the portal and landed with sure, strong footing on the desert sands just outside the white walls that surrounded Sybal's estate in Hatal. He turned and watched Amir step through and then turn to offer Sybal a hand as she did. The three of them faced the open gates of the land. Sybal walked wordlessly through them into the manor. Signar watched her go, wishing she would speak.

"I didn't see her eat the entire voyage home," he said, leading Amir to the stables. "I don't know what to do."

"Nor do I," Amir confessed, following Signar. "She needs privacy to mourn, so perhaps give her that."

Signar thought about it. Did Sybal not want to break down in front of him? He'd been unable to help himself when he'd met her. Did she think less of him for it? He furrowed his brow and set his jaw, vowing to never let her see him that weak again, no matter how loudly the wolf inside him howled.

When they opened the door to the stables, the horses inside perked up their heads. His own pale yellow horse walked to the stable door and nickered quietly, happy to see him. He'd never named his horse, but he thought now, since he was happy to see it, that he should.

Alvakar lightly hopped up onto his back hooves, neighing softly and inspecting the two who entered. Signar's heart fell for the steed. He walked up to Alvakar and gently stroked his face.

"I'm sorry, wild one," he whispered. "He's not coming back."

Alvakar snorted impatiently, his head swinging back and forth, looking for Tzarik. Signar pulled on the bridle, steadying the beast.

"Why don't you take him?" he offered as easily as he could, though it hurt his heart. "Vicdan will need a horse, and I have a feeling they'd get along."

Amir had been petting his own horse and looked up at Alvakar and Signar. "Was that his horse?"

Signar nodded. "He's wild, but he behaved for Tzarik. Tzarik had a way with wild creatures." Signar smiled. "He tamed me. I didn't make it easy for him, either. I almost killed him once. But he still came into my cage."

"Signar," Amir said gently, saddling up his horse. "Don't forget to let yourself mourn. You need time as well."

"Thank you, Amir. But I will mourn in my own way when I am ready." He said it more stoically than he'd meant to. Amir meant well, but the Runer couldn't imagine the pain Signar felt. How hard he struggled to contain himself.

"I understand," Amir said gently. "I don't know you well, Reks, but I am an ally should you need one."

Signar met Amir's blue eyes and nodded his thanks. "I am angry we cannot properly honor Tzarik with a pyre or even a grave."

"You'll find a way to honor him," Amir said, tightening the girth around his horse's middle. He flipped the reins over the horse's head and began to lead him out of the stables.

Signar saddled up Alvakar and followed Amir out.

"Take care of Sybal," Amir said. "Don't leave her alone too long."

Signar narrowed his eyes slightly at Amir. The way the Runer spoke about Sybal and to her made Signar think he had feelings for her. But if Amir wanted to be any kind of friend, and not make an enemy of him, he had better take care with how he spoke to Sybal.

"I'll be back," Amir promised. "I'll have Vicdan with me, and we can decide how to proceed from there once we know what has happened."

"Be careful," Signar said, looking up at the Runer.

Amir nodded and then clicked his tongue, quickly galloping away to the gate, Alvakar in tow. Signar watched the horse go, knowing it was confused and curious as to where its master was. He turned and looked up at the tower that was Sybal's room. Amir had said to give her space, but Signar didn't want to. He watered his horse and ordered the stable hands to let them out into the pasture to stretch their legs, then strode into the manor.

At first he thought about calling her name, then decided he didn't want her to know he was coming. Barefoot and quiet, he ascended the many steps to her room and waited outside the door. It hung open only about an inch. Carefully, he pushed it open enough to look in. Sybal stood in the center of the room. She had tossed her armor and boots to the floor, standing in just her black shirt and pants. She faced the bed.

Signar pushed the door open quietly and approached her. She didn't move, didn't give any sign that she knew he was there. He came up just behind her and saw her tense, knowing he was there. Slowly, he reached around her and wrapped his arms around her shoulders. He pulled her close to him and buried his face in her hair, hugging her tight. She tilted her head back onto his shoulder and took a shuddering breath.

"I don't know what to do," she whispered in a broken voice. She slowly turned, holding his hands and placing them back around her. She set her face against his chest and squeezed him tight. He felt her tears sink through his shirt and touch his skin. "Signar," she said, a sob rising in her throat. "Help me, please. Please, help me!"

She suddenly wailed loudly and her knees gave out. Signar caught her and picked her up, walking to the bed. He sat down and draped her limp body over his legs. She clung to him, screaming her sorrows to the sky. He held her, not speaking. His mind went back to the cell in Xia. Even with his eyes open, he saw it clearly. Saw Tzarik hanging from the Xian cross, heard him fighting for breath even as his lungs filled with blood.

Signar held Sybal even tighter now. "We have to stop Tarkan," he whispered when Sybal's wailing turned to moderate sobs. "My people are in danger. So is Xia and Alika."

"I don't care about them anymore," Sybal said, her voice thick. "I just... I just want Tzarik back. I didn't get to say goodbye, Signar. I never told him—" She sobbed loudly, unable to control herself.

Signar let her have her moment, not pressing her.

She sniffled. "I never told him I loved him."

"He knew, Sybal," Signar said gently. "You didn't have to tell him."

"But I should have," she argued, eyes red and tears staining her face. "I loved him from the moment I saw him in that courthouse. I did. I know I did. He came to save me and I loved him for it."

"He saved us both."

She nodded and looked up at him. She took his face in her hands, eyes almost pleading with him. "I love you. Do you understand? I love you so much." She wrapped her arms around his neck and embraced him like she'd never let go. "Don't leave me, not yet. I can't be alone. Not now."

He pet her hair, stroking it fervently. "I'm not. I won't. Sybal, I'm not going anywhere."

They sat together for a long time, Sybal weeping and sometimes babbling. Signar just held her and let her cry until she fell asleep in his arms. Then he laid her on the bed and covered her with a blanket that had Tzarik's scent all over it. Signar almost wept again, smelling it, but fought the urge. He tucked Sybal in and then went outside to build a pyre. He moved out into the vineyard of the land and ordered a few of the servants to help him.

Together, they constructed a pyre like the ones he had seen on Caerwren. He had nothing to burn, and knew the stones of the runes around his neck wouldn't burn, so the wood had to suffice. The sun had set long ago and the moon was out. A great white star glowed next to the moon. Signar stood by the pyre, torch in hand.

He was about to light it when the soft sound of bare feet in the sand halted him. He turned to see Sybal walking toward him, arms crossed against the cool desert night. Her hair was down, long and white. She had no blonde hair left since coming back from the Frozen Nation. When she approached, he stepped back and handed her the torch.

Sybal took it and walked to the pyre. "I don't know my ancestor's ways," she confessed. "My mother was from Northica, but I know nothing about them."

Signar wordlessly took her wrist in his hands and guided the torch to the pyre. "It's simple," he whispered. "We burn the bodies and let their spirits rise to Rahrgalah if they have had a good death."

The wood caught and the fire ignited with a deep whooshing sound. The pyre immediately crackled. Sybal stepped back, holding the torch aloft. "He had a good death," she said, not asking. "Would Raudnir take his soul for safekeeping?"

"Raudnir knew Tzarik," Signar said with a tiny half smile. "Tzarik stood up to him on my behalf. Raudnir was not pleased. So, yes, I believe he would welcome him into Rahrgalah."

A single tear trickled down Sybal's face. "I'll never see him again. Even if I could go to Janna. He wouldn't be there. I'll never know where he is."

Signar didn't reply, his heart suddenly growing heavy. "Tzarik had no faith. You could still pray for his soul to find its way to Janna. For your god to accept him. To show him mercy."

Sybal looked up at Signar, her blue eyes shining with tears. "Do you believe that?"

He nodded. In truth, he did. "I will miss him in Rahrgalah in my afterlife, but he belongs in yours."

"Then I will pray without ceasing," she whispered. She looked into the flames. "When you burn a pyre, do you say anything? On Al'Myrah, we offer speeches in honor of the one who has passed."

Signar looked up to the white star near the moon. "Iluthian," he said. He pointed the star out to Sybal as she looked up. "The star of mourning. That's what we call it on Caerwren."

"We do as well," Sybal said. "Though we call it Adahar." She stopped and frowned. "The legend says that Adahar and Mirzam were at war with one another. They were brothers in war, the best of friends. But Mirzam betrayed Adahar and so Adahar was forced to slay his brother. Thus, he mourns." She looked over at Signar. "Tarkan's family name is Mirzam. We will slay him just as Adahar did."

Signar met her eyes. "Let us not speak of him now." He motioned to the pyre. "I remember my father's pyre," he whispered. "I was perhaps twelve or thirteen. Mother wept for weeks after his death. She loved him, in her way."

"I forgot you witnessed that." Sybal took his hand in hers. "You have suffered much, Signar. I wish this had never happened, for your sake as well as mine."

"We have both suffered," he reminded her. "But our suffering is not who we are, and we cannot let it define us." He looked back into her eyes. "Tell me instead how you loved Tzarik."

Sybal blushed, her cheeks going pale. She looked away. "I followed him. I did as he said. I trusted him. That's how I loved him. I wondered if he loved me for as long as I loved him. I remember the first time I tried to kiss him. We were on Xia together. He'd taken me there to run away from Sharar, Tarkan, and the people who hated me on Al'Myrah. He froze, though, when I leaned in to kiss him. I knew he was afraid. So I ran away." She sighed and smiled. "Then on Caerwren, when he brought me back..."

"I understand," Signar said with a grin. He reached over and took the torch from her hand. He faced the pyre and tossed the torch onto it. "He saved me that night when Skarde brought the cursed totems to Altevine. I was so scared that night. I was often afraid. But not when he was near. I want to be like him one day. To be as brave. To save people as he did. Maybe even tame monsters."

Sybal smiled. "You want to be cynical, hard, and brutish?"

Signar nodded. "And selfless and brave. He saw the potential in me when no one else did. He saw it in you, too. He took two damaged monsters and tamed them. Gave us a second chance at life."

Sybal let out a tiny sob and nodded. She slipped her arms around Signar's middle and hugged him tight. He reciprocated the hug and leaned his cheek against the top of her head. He looked into the fire and whispered, "Goodbye, Tzarik."

"I love you," Sybal added in a tiny voice. "And I'll see you again. I promise."

# Chapter 21
## Retrieval

A mir galloped through the streets of Hatal to the gates of the sultana's palace. The guards recognized him as Sharar's Runer and let him in. He asked them where the sultana was and was directed to the war room. As he marched through the halls of the opulent palace, he wondered where Sharar had died. What had they done with his body? Part of him hoped the young pharaoh hadn't witnessed the scholar's death. He didn't know Sokar well, but knew he didn't deserve to watch a man he loved die.

Amir reached the war room and saw the door slightly ajar. He waited a moment outside, listening. He heard the sultana's low and soft voice, then Sokar's much louder voice arguing with her. No other voices came from within, so he guessed they must be alone. Carefully, he pushed the door open and entered. Both sets of sharp eyes turned to him.

"You," the sultana growled at the same time Sokar cried, "Runer!" The young pharaoh ran to Amir, hands out, and grasped his.

"Where have you been?" the sultana asked, planting her fist onto her hip. "I have been looking for you since the scholar's death."

"Busy," Amir replied, letting the pharaoh take his hands. "I have come to fetch the necromancer. And I see Sharar was successful in rescuing Sokar."

The sultana narrowed her eyes.

"Have you come to take me home?" Sokar asked. "Oh, Runer, do you know how Abigor died? It was so mysterious. I..." He stopped, swallowing a sudden lump in his throat.

So the boy had been there when Sharar passed. "Tell me what happened?" he asked, coming to the great table the sultana had been poring over when he entered. He looked down at it and saw a map of the known lands. Small brass pieces were placed over it and he didn't know what they meant.

"We were in his chambers," Sokar said. "I came to fetch him, for we were to discuss our next steps in taking down the Necro'Khan. He acted as though he'd been stabbed. There was blood." The boy's eyes went vacant as he relived what must have been a terrible sight that night. "He died in my arms. I don't know what happened. Some sort of magic."

"It was," Amir confessed. There was no use in keeping it a secret now. "Sharar was fate-bound, and the man he was bound to was killed by Tarkan."

"The Necro'Khan?" Sokar gasped. "He killed Abigor?" He spun around to glare at the sultana. "We have to do something, sabi."

The sultana looked almost at ease. Of course Sharar's death didn't disturb her in the least. "I have done my part," she began. "I am free of the sorcerer, and that is all I wanted."

"But the Necro'Khan," Sokar begged. "Alika. I must free my country from this death fiend. I cannot do it without you and Bahratt behind me."

The sultana raised her head in defiance, but didn't reply. She examined the young pharaoh before her, her hand absentmindedly stroking her round belly. "Sokar, my boy, I have my own troubles to deal with. I am sorry Alika has fallen."

"But our treaty!" Sokar pled. "Al'Myrah swore to aid Alika should we call for aid. I am here now. I am begging you." He looked to Amir, eyes pleading. "We must wrest control of my country from this

Necro'Khan at all costs. We must see him fall. The map is in danger, sabi."

"That is what I have heard," Amir offered. "There are rifts torn in the God Deep that will allow spirits and dead monsters to pass into our realm. Along with it is coming a black curse that is blighting the land and drawing the living monsters and creatures on this side to it. It is spreading. Soon the map will be covered in death and a malignation we cannot control."

"I already attacked Alika once," the sultana replied. "We were able to save Sokar, but that is all. We don't know if we weakened his army."

Amir looked around. "Where is the necromancer? He'll know."

"The slave of the sorcerer?" the sultana asked. "I had him chained up in my dungeon."

Amir fixed his eyes on the sultana. "You can trust him. And you can trust me."

She scoffed and rolled her eyes. "Servants of the sorcerer who held me captive in my own palace?"

Sokar opened his mouth to argue, but Amir put his hand on his shoulder to stop him. "I was spying on Sharar for two Runers who were trying to stand against Tarkan and Sharar."

"Why?" Sokar asked, jerking out of Amir's grasp. "You're a traitor?"

"Sharar's quest for power was almost unmatched," Amir said. "He and Tarkan would have plunged the map into a war it wouldn't soon recover from. Now that he's gone, we only have the Necro'Khan to deal with."

Sokar blinked and his face twisted in sadness. "Abigor wasn't as evil as all that."

"You are a blind child," the sultana spat at Sokar.

Amir didn't argue. He didn't have time to try to get the boy to see Sharar's darker secrets. All Sokar knew was that Sharar had been there for him in a time of need. That he had been good to him. "It doesn't matter now," he tried. "The Sharar you knew is gone. What we are left with is a foe we cannot hope to overtake without working together."

"I will not risk my people," the sultana reiterated.

"Please, sabi!" Sokar begged, clasping his hands before his face. "I am alone without you. I can do nothing without your aid."

Amir saw a light he didn't like appear behind the sultana's eyes at that. She almost quirked her mouth in a small grin. "If you don't help him, I will," Amir said quickly.

The sultana raised her elegant brows. "You, Runer? What can a Runer do?"

"Maybe not just me," he said as stoutly as he could. "But there are others. Runers are the only ones who can fight the demons and monsters coming from the rifts. You will need us before the year is out. But there are others who will fight for the map if you won't."

"I will help you," Sokar said enthusiastically. "Take me with you, Runer."

Amir shook his head. "You are brave, Sokar. Braver than most, perhaps. But, if you can, you should stay in the palace. Here, you will be safe." He looked at the sultana.

She pressed her lips together, stopping some comment she swallowed, and nodded. "He may stay. I will protect him as I would myself."

"That is all you will do," Amir said, seeing that light behind her eyes again. "Protect him only. He will not stay on Al'Myrah."

She gently narrowed her eyes. "Of course, Runer."

"No, please," Sokar begged, taking Amir's hands in his again. "Don't leave me behind. I can help if you let me."

Amir shook his head, gently prying his hands free. "I am sorry, your eminence. But we must keep you safe. You must stay here. The road and life of a Runer are no place for an ordinary pharaoh, let alone the Dynast Pharaoh. But I promise, I will come back for you and take you to Alika when it's safe."

"Swear to me," Sokar said, his brows knitting in worry.

Amir nodded and gave the pharaoh a small bow. "I swear I will come back for you and take you home when it is safe."

Sokar looked wary, but satisfied.

"Now," Amir said to the sultana. "Where is Vicdan? The necromancer."

The sultana pursed her lips and looked away, waving her hand. "Below. In the dungeon." She motioned to a guard by the door and he opened it. "You may go below and fetch him. But I want you gone after you have him."

Amir bowed to the sultana. "You will protect Sokar. Is that understood? We cannot risk losing the Dynast Pharaoh at a time like this."

The sultana sighed and her eyes finally went dim. "I will protect him with my life, Runer, I swear."

Satisfied, Amir nodded and followed the guard out and down into the dungeon. It looked like every other dungeon he'd been in: dark, slightly dank, and cold. They passed a few cells and went to one farther down the line. Inside, Amir spotted Vicdan. The necromancer lay on the hard ground, curled up for warmth. When the keys jangled in the lock, Vicdan looked up. He was shackled by his wrists to the wall behind him. He spotted the guard and looked curious. Then his eyes went to Amir.

"Runer!" Vicdan cried, scrambling to his feet. "I prayed to the gods you'd not forgotten me. I thought to myself, 'Vicdan, you're done for now.' But here you are."

The guard opened the door and knelt, unlocking the shackles around his wrist.

"I need you," Amir said. "Sybal needs to know what's happened since I last left you."

"Sybal's alive?" Vicdan asked, his pale face showing relief. "When Sharar died..." His face fell and he swallowed. "I feared the worst. I really did."

"We'll catch up later," Amir promised. "For now, we need to get back to her."

The guard unleashed Vicdan and stood back. The necromancer stood and rubbed his raw wrists. The guard exited the cell and stood back so Vicdan could leave.

"My personal savior," Vicdan crowed, throwing his arms around Amir. "This isn't the first time you've saved my neck, and it won't be the last. I'd follow you to the ends of the earth and back. Especially after how brave you were during the battle on Alika. You could have left me to die, but you didn't."

Amir pried Vicdan off him without acknowledgment. "When we get to Sybal, tell us everything."

"I have much to tell. But before we leave..." Vicdan turned and quickly walked down the line of cells and out, leaving the palace guard behind. "I need to speak with the sultana and implore her to part with something she took from the sorcerer upon his death."

"How will you do that?" Amir asked.

Vicdan smiled and cocked a dark brow. "Trust me, Runer, I could talk a forge into putting itself out."

Sybal woke the next morning with her eyes red and puffy and her face stinging from all the weeping she'd done the night before. Somewhere, the pyre still smoldered and she could smell it. Behind her on her bed, Signar snored softly, buried deep in the bedclothes. She'd not slept much and had let him take the bed while she wandered her grounds and slept here and there on lounges throughout the manor. Now she looked out the window and watched the road, wondering if Amir would be on his way back.

No sooner had she thought of him than two small black dots appeared on the horizon galloping toward her. She squinted into the rising sun and smiled. She recognized Amir and even Vicdan at that distance. So Vicdan was alive and well. Her smile broadened.

Running inside, she threw on her black shirt and pants and then charged down the stairs to greet them in the foyer. Signar woke and followed her, slightly blurry-eyed. Sybal threw open the grand doors and rushed out. Amir was helping Vicdan walk when she spotted them.

"Vicdan!" she cried, throwing her arms around his neck. "Are you all right?"

The young man nodded, his wild smile wrinkling his face. "Better now that I see you are in good health. I'm just hungry and weak. Sharar was not the kindest of wardens. Gods damn his soul."

Sybal held Vicdan for one more moment after that and nodded into his neck. "So he's gone." She pulled back and looked at him.

"Yes," Vicdan said, his face turning serious. "I suppose we have a lot to talk about."

"Signar, call for food to be brought," Sybal instructed. She looked to Amir. His eyes were surrounded by dark circles and his back was bent. "Take any room you want, Amir. Sleep."

"I will once we are all informed," he said, and his voice was strong despite his exhaustion.

Sybal thanked him with a gentle squeeze to his arm and led them into the dining hall. The servants moved about quickly, setting up wine, water, and bringing up food as quickly as they could. Sybal helped Vicdan into the dining hall and then sat next to him once the others had taken seats.

"Whenever you are ready," she said gently.

Vicdan tore into the roasted lamb the servants brought up and nearly drowned himself in fresh water before he spoke even a single word. "Sharar starved me," he explained. "Wanted me to only consume sentient flesh so I could cast the spells and do his bidding. I refused as much as I could."

"You were brave," Sybal said, making sure to look Vicdan in his emerald eyes. "You've been brave since he caught you the first time and turned you."

Vicdan's old charm ignited behind his eyes and his mouth quirked up into a smirk. "I am quite the hero, aren't I? Speaking of which, I am not sure what we can do with it, but..." He stood and went to his pack, which he'd dropped near the entrance, and rifled through it quickly. "I did bring us back something." He pulled out a thick, old tome.

Sybal's jaw dropped open. "Is that...?"

"The Mahit'Onomicon?" Vicdan said. "Yes." He flopped the book onto the table and sat back down, taking a large bite of lamb. "I can't read it, though. Sharar thought the part we necromancers could read, the part we write upon our flesh and bones, was gone."

Sybal frowned and flipped open the book. She gripped a large handful of pages and flipped further. "These are the Xian sigils," she whispered, overcome by awe. Her hand tingled as she touched the pages penned by the gods themselves. "I recognize them. But other parts are written in other languages." She flipped to another section. "I cannot read it, but I can see that there are sections written in various tongues. Ancient, perhaps." She looked up at Vicdan. "Your scriptures are not in the book?"

Vicdan shook his head. "Our theory was that the gods removed the necrotic scriptures. That way one man, a sorcerer in this case, wouldn't have all the power. There had to be one and the other. A balance. A sorcerer would be master of this world and a Necro'Khan would be master of the God Deep and the afterlife. Or perhaps the necrotic scriptures were never written in the book. Maybe they were given directly to Ishmael all those centuries ago. We don't know. What we do know is that the necrotic scriptures are not in the Mahit'O-nomicon."

Curious, Sybal asked, "What do the scriptures say? The ones on Tarkan's flesh."

Vicdan raised his brows and puffed out his cheeks with an exhale. "It's been a while since I've read them, but they are the five spells of necromancy and the covenant we take upon our hearts. Last, of course, are the instructions for how any may become Necro'Khan. But the trials and the sacrifice are too much for most."

"Not Tarkan," Sybal sighed. "But perhaps he was desperate." She closed the book and looked up. "Thank you, Vicdan."

The singer nodded and took another long drink of wine before wiping his hand across his mouth and asking, "I am sorry to bring it up, but...what happened?"

Sybal looked to Signar, bracing herself for the conversation. Beside her, Amir shifted like he might take her hand, but stopped himself.

"Tarkan killed him," Signar said softly, looking down into a candle flame. "He captured us on Xia, had me beaten and released after."

"So it's true," Vicdan said, his voice going soft and low. "You saw it."

Signar nodded mutely.

"Gods," Vicdan whispered, tears making his eyes shine in the dim light. "I had hoped it wasn't true. That something else had taken Sharar."

"You saw him die?" Sybal asked.

Vicdan nodded. "Poor Sokar. Sharar died in his arms."

Sybal felt bad for Sokar. The young pharaoh didn't deserve that, but she was glad the man who had slaughtered her family was at last dead.

"But," Amir cut in, "why would Tarkan give up the blood of the sorcerer? That was what he wanted, after all. He could have been the most powerful sentient on the map."

"Perhaps the risk was too great," Signar offered.

"Yes," Vicdan confirmed. "The sultana, under Sharar's control, got Bahratt to lend their fleet and army to Al'Myrah and they launched an attack on Mysir."

Sybal snapped her head up at this. "War?" she asked. "Al'Myrah has entered war with Alika?"

Vicdan tilted his head and hummed in thought. "Not like you might think. It was quick and devastating. We went in, attacked, weakened them, stole Sokar from the dungeon, and fled. Tarkan wasn't there."

"He was on Xia," Signar put in. "That must be when you attacked."

Vicdan frowned gently, understanding. "So it would seem. When he returned, he no doubt feared the power Sharar had pulled together. He had united two of the three in the eastern triangle against Alika. Tarkan knew then that the maharaja and the sultana were aware of him and not afraid to strike. He had to have known it was Sharar behind it so he had to remove him. He was afraid."

Sybal tapped her fingers against the table, thinking. "It was a small dent in his undead army, no doubt. At least we know they can be taken down. But does the map have enough sentients willing to stand up to Tarkan? How many will it take to defeat him?"

Signar shifted in his seat. "And the rifts. My people are in danger from the opening in the Deep. I worry about them every day."

"We will find a way to heal them," Amir said.

Sybal nodded, eyeing the Mahit'Onomicon where it lay forgotten on the table near Vicdan. "There is a way," she mumbled, more to herself than the others. "And we'll find it. Wushito contained the rift on their continent for years. The sigils must be the answer."

"Containment isn't a permanent solution," Signar fought back. "And it has spread on Caerwren. It moves even now."

Sybal heard the desperation in his voice. "Tarkan tore the God

Deep open," she said. "Maybe he can close it. Could another necromancer close it somehow?"

Vicdan blanched at this. "I doubt it. Magic of that magnitude is wielded only by a Necro'Khan."

Amir pointed to the book. "I bet anything it's written in that book."

All eyes landed on the Mahit'Onomicon then.

Sybal sighed in frustration and leaned back in to her seat. Amir was probably right. But none of them could read the book. It was useless to them. She glared into the middle distance. She had to think of something. Tarkan was more than deserving of death now.

# Chapter 22
## White Army

Sybal pressed her lips to Tzarik's neck and kissed him, sucking hard. A white bruise formed under his dark skin. She trailed kisses up his neck, over his sharp jaw, until she found his lips. Then she ran her hand down his hard chest and muscled stomach. She slipped her hand beneath the bedclothes and he moaned.

Then, in a flash, he was gone.

Sybal rolled over in her bed and listened. She couldn't hear Tzarik's breathing. Didn't feel his weight on the other side of the bed. His warmth was gone. She reached over to feel the cotton sheets and only felt the coldness of an empty bed. She withdrew her hand like she'd been burned. She expected tears to well up in her eyes and for her chest to tighten with emotion, but no sensation came. She was numb.

She slid to the edge of the bed and slipped off, wrapping herself in her silken robe. It was left over from before her Runing and felt like a frivolous, silly thing now. But it was all she had.

*We should leave,* she suddenly thought. *I need to hunt. I miss the road. Hiding makes me feel trapped.* And what use was there in hiding any more? Tzarik was gone. Surely Tarkan didn't care about her. But he'd let Signar go. What was his plan? What had he been thinking?

*He's not afraid of us,* she realized.

Silently, she slipped through the halls and went to Signar's room. The door hung open a crack and she peeked in. The moonlight spilled over the room, lighting it up. The bed was empty. She drew in a breath and looked around the room. Then she spotted him.

Signar stood on the other side of the room, looking into a full-length mirror that hung from brass legs. He wore soft cotton pants and was barefoot. His long hair hung down his back to his hips. He studied his own eyes in the mirror. Sybal thought every day that he looked more and more like his father. He had the same angled face, the same sharp jaw and straight nose. But his eyes were his mother's: still, calculating—the eyes of a hunter. The only thing missing was the cruelty that had radiated from Sjörna's eyes.

Curious, and not wanting to scare him, she pushed the door open and walked in, making sure she appeared in the mirror image. Signar didn't look up to meet her eyes, but examined his naked torso instead. From where she stood, she could clearly see the marks Tarkan had left on him. The crisscrossing scars on his back sent a flare of rage through her. Already Signar had wounds of that nature, but these new ones were thicker, more painful looking. She walked up behind him and stood to his right.

"They don't have mirrors like this on Caerwren," Signar said. "I don't like looking at myself."

She offered a kind look without smiling. "I see a great and powerful Reks. And that's what you are."

"I see a weak boy," he countered. He didn't go on.

Sybal took his hand in hers and stroked his muscled arm. "You can tell me anything. You told him everything, didn't you? Tell me what's on your mind."

She ran her hand up his back, touching the scars. Signar inhaled softly and straightened his back. "There is nothing to tell," he said flatly.

"Signar," she tried, reaching up to embrace him.

He raised his hand, gently pushing her away. "I'm tired," he said. "I want to sleep."

Hurt, Sybal backed away. Signar walked to his bed, but did not lie down. She watched him for just a moment longer before deciding she didn't want to upset him. So she turned and left. A single tear tracked down her cheek. She wished more than ever that Tzarik were there. She was afraid of what his death might do to Signar if he held in his feelings like he was doing now. She didn't want her sweet and kind boy to turn into a rage-stifled Reks.

She walked down the steps to the library. Yes, Signar was a kind and gentle giant. She wanted him to stay that way. No good would come from hiding the pain that had come with Tzarik's death. She didn't want revenge to manifest inside him.

The library was dark except for one candle on the wall near the door. She picked it up and went to the hearth, where she lit a fire, then lit a few more candles around a large table in the center. Looking around the shelves, she spotted a rolled-up map. She took it and spread it out on the table, looking down at it. She traced Alika and then drew a line to Bahratt, then to Al'Myrah. Porsh hovered in the center, dead and useless. Looking back at Al'Myrah, she realized she missed Ala'-Nar. She missed her old life less and less, but she still loved the city.

"There must be a way to stop him," she whispered to herself. "We need an army, but bringing him ten thousand blood bags doesn't seem like the wise thing to do."

The floor squeaked to her left. Her head shot up, her hand instinctively going to where her scimitar should have hung.

But she didn't have one. The Dohkma had broken it. She made a quick note to buy a new orichalcum blade.

Someone moved in the shadows by the door. Someone tall. She waited, her hand now going to the runes around her neck.

"Calm down, Sybal," Amir's voice said. He stepped into the dim candlelight, hands raised. He smiled at her.

Her eyes immediately went to his exposed forearms and bare feet. He was wearing silken night garments, unlaced to show his chiseled chest. She swallowed and looked away. Amir was taller than her. And he was strong. She couldn't help but suddenly imagine those arms wrapped around her, giving her comfort.

Guilt flooded her and she pushed her needs away. It was the dream that had brought on those emotions. She was still hot from the scenes her mind had conjured up. She wanted to douse herself in cold water, but there was none around.

"What are you doing up?" she asked breathlessly, looking back down at the map.

"Checking on Vicdan," he said easily, sauntering over to join her. "I don't think he's slept through the night since he was turned. Tonight, he snores loudly."

Sybal smiled genuinely at this. "Good. He deserves a good night's rest."

"We all do," Amir said, and she saw that he still looked tired. The dark circles around his eyes were not gone. His face was wan and lined.

"You should be sleeping," she said. "I need to find a hunt soon, and I need you at your best."

"Can't sleep," he said, leaning onto his palms on the table. "Too many thoughts in my head."

She almost asked him what the thoughts were, but something in her rushed, warning her against it. She wouldn't like the answer.

"What are you doing?" he asked innocently, motioning to the map.

Sybal sighed. "Trying to find our next move. I feel like we need to split up. Find allies wherever we can. Maybe I should try to see the sultana."

"She won't be happy to see you," a voice said from the doorway. Vicdan appeared, wreathed in soft candlelight. His green eyes glowed in the darkness. He entered the library and joined them at the table. "She doesn't want to fight Tarkan."

"She may have to," Sybal said. She waved her hand over the map. "Tarkan is waiting now. He won't strike; he's waiting on the rifts to do their work. This is our time to gather allies and strike. Tell me, how did it work out last time?"

Vicdan blew a long breath out. "It was terrifying, of course, but we did take down Acenoth. At least, we wounded him. It seems severing the heads of the undead stops them, at least for a time. Tarkan can heal them."

"How?" Sybal asked.

Amir glanced at Vicdan. "We saw during the initial fall of the Dynast Palace that Tarkan had a blade—a blade made of what looked like blood. He's using it as some sort of artifact to keep the undead alive and standing."

"He's channeling the magic through it," Vicdan added. "It must be made of some sort of magical material to do that. But if we can get close enough to him and his blade, destroying it, the undead will fall eventually. But getting close to Tarkan might be the hardest task."

Sybal frowned slightly. "I don't know enough about magical artifacts. Is that something that can be done?"

Amir nodded. "Any material, even orichalcum—which I believe his blade to be—can be undone. There is some sort of gem in the hilt as well that pulses like a heart."

Sybal leaned back, crossing her arms, thinking.

"I wonder," Vicdan said, a thought striking him, "if it's not the heart of the last Necro'Khan. If so, it's simply red diamond. We could destroy it."

Sybal shrugged, confused. "Why would it be Ishmael's heart?"

"For the power," Vicdan said simply. "Who knows what kinds of magical properties the heart of a Necro'Khan holds? And Tarkan knew where it was. In fact, I would bet my voice that the entire blade is made with necrotic pieces. I'd be shocked if the bones of a Bone-Scriven were not the hilt and handle. They looked to be inscribed, but I haven't seen it close enough to know for sure. Yes, very clever, Tarkan. We often say there is power locked in our bones. The flesh may rot away, but the bones stay longer. Tarkan took the bones of a Bone-Scriven and used them. That's how he made the artifact." Vicdan smiled, pleased with himself. "Everything he made it with can be destroyed, but the true power is coming from the bones and the heart."

"We won't know until we are face to face with him," Amir cautioned. "And in that moment, we will have only seconds to act. But that still doesn't help us get close to him, unless an all-out war is what we want. Even then, an army will just be a pool of blood for him to take. He could slaughter hordes in a matter of seconds."

"Unless we don't use red blood," a soft, high voice said from behind Sybal.

She spun once again to see who had invaded her library. Signar stood there, swathed in the white sheet from his bed. He held it around his shoulders. His green eyes were wide and sorrow still lurked there.

Just happy to have him speaking to her, Sybal said, "What do you mean?"

Signar slowly entered the room looking tired and sad. "We made a wish with a yokai we found. He told us how to defeat Tarkan. White blood."

Amir and Vicdan frowned slightly.

Sybal held up her hand, palm facing up, so they could see the white veins in her wrist. "We could get an army of Runers. Tarkan wouldn't be able to use their blood against us." She almost smiled. "Runers are the answer."

Signar nodded.

Amir blanched. "It's difficult to get a Runer to do anything, even for pay. How could we convince them—let alone an army—to stand up to Tarkan in Alika?"

Sybal looked around, raising her arms to indicate the entire room. "Payment. I don't know how much money my father had, but I can find out. I can offer them gold, gems. I'll put out a patents. A necromancer is a great hunt. We don't need thousands. Just enough to get close to Tarkan. And I know with Signar's help, we can get many from Caerwren."

At the mention of his home, Signar's eyes filled with tears.

Amir perked up at this, smiling at Sybal. "I know a few. My old apprentice and his connections could get some to join us, I bet. Though he's on Bahratt at the moment."

"Yes," Vicdan said, stroking his chin in thought. "Offer the brutes gold. Runers would do anything for gold. And as you said, we don't need thousands. Just enough to get to Tarkan. But that still leaves us with needing to get the sultana and the maharaja to strike again."

"I'll think of something," Sybal said. "I'll get in touch with Nefiri if I have to. There has to be a way."

"This is it," Amir said wholeheartedly. "All it will take is one more attack. We'll be strategic about it, have the Runers sneak in while the army and fleet attack from the front. The smaller the horde, the better."

For the first time in a long time, Sybal felt a thrill gently jolt through her.

"Gods," Vicdan sighed. "I hope this works."

# Chapter 23
## Departures

Tarkan walked among the lines of his undead soldiers. Every last one had had their head severed. Ashkan walked close behind him, explaining how they'd tried to attach the heads again, but they had not come back.

"However, we are able to raise them," he added when Tarkan didn't say anything.

On Tarkan's other side, Acenoth walked with long, striding steps. He glared down at his fallen men. "I thought your power was stronger than that," he said to Tarkan. "I thought we were immortal. But it seems not."

Tarkan bristled at this. He had thought about dismissing Acenoth and his One Thousand and One some time ago, but had held on to them just in case. This last remark made him think about it again. After all, he didn't need Acenoth anymore. The threat to Alika was gone. The pharaoh had served his purpose.

"It matters not," Tarkan said. He stepped over the bodies and began to stride back to the palace. "I have accomplished what I wanted. Sharar is dead, and soon the world will be covered in a darkness it cannot fight. We are done here."

Ashkan and Acenoth followed him as he made his way through the rubble of the palace toward the throne room.

"What is your plan, then, my Khan?" Acenoth asked.

"It will be the season of the necromancer," he replied. "We will be the only ones who need not fear. The map will be devastated beyond repair and then I will be able to rest in peace. Perhaps once I am satisfied that the world has been properly punished, I will save it." He didn't really believe that himself. He wanted the world to rot. "Leave me, Acenoth. Ashkan, with me."

The undead pharaoh bowed and split off from them, leaving them alone.

Tarkan entered the throne room and climbed the stairs to sit on the ruby throne. Once he was seated, he looked down at Ashkan and studied his Apostle hard. Ashkan didn't flinch and remained standing tall as Tarkan's eyes roamed over him. He admired the Apostle's fortitude. He showed no fear, as if he had nothing to hide.

"Are you still loyal to me, Ashkan?" Tarkan asked, leaning back into the ruby throne. He pinned the Apostle with his gaze. "If I slipped into the slumber of the Necro'Khan, could I trust you to not sever my head and take my heart?"

Ashkan spread his fingers, showing empty hands. "I have nothing, Tarkan. You took everything from me."

"That's not loyalty."

"We all fear you," Ashkan tried again. "Wouldn't you rather be feared?"

"Fear can be overcome." Tarkan leaned forward now, one elbow on his knee.

"None of us have betrayal on our minds, my Khan," Ashkan said, raising his head and looking Tarkan in the eyes. "We would follow you into the heart of the Deep, if that's where you led us. Like your father before you, the other Apostles will bend to you without hesitation."

Satisfied, Tarkan leaned back into the throne. He glanced outside to the partially constructed facade of Sokar's tomb. He wished the boy king was still shackled by his side, available for torment and torture to keep his mind from wandering into darker thoughts. But it was too late. He thought back to the undead and how they had perished. He couldn't truly bring a soul and body back without sustaining them. That wasn't true life.

"What burden bends your shoulders?" Ashkan asked.

Tarkan clenched his fist and didn't look his Apostle in the eye this time. "There must be a way to bring back a life, truly. Completely. Lady Sybal is able to walk this world because of me. But she was not truly dead. Her body was still alive. I can make an undead, but not true life. There must be a way."

Ashkan shifted his feet and let his eyes fall to the ground. "You are thinking of Zeva."

The truth stung, but he didn't lash out. "She was a powerful necromancer and shouldn't have died. The Runers killed her."

"My Khan," Ashkan said steadily, "you speak of controlling life, not death. We are masters of death."

"I should have power over both," Tarkan snapped back. "Am I Necro'Khan or am I not? What is the point of being a master of death if I cannot reverse it?" He stopped and pounded his fist into the arm of the throne. "I want to find her body. I want to bring her home. Even the gods may try to stop me, but I will find a way to bring her back. To give her true life."

Ashkan didn't argue. His brow furrowed and he blinked in thought. "What if you tried to take her wounds upon yourself?"

Tarkan looked up, glaring and confused.

"Take her death as your own?" Ashkan clarified. "Use the blood magic to weave her body anew as you have done before, then take her death upon yourself."

"And die myself, to not even see her again?" Tarkan spat. He waved his hand, annoyed with Ashkan. "It's time for you to return to Xia, I think. Leave me."

When the Apostle had gone, he slumped into the throne, thinking about what Ashkan had suggested. Maybe it didn't have to be him. Perhaps he could force another to give up their life for her. Would it work? Would the magic understand? No, that didn't matter. He was the author of the blood and it would do as he commanded.

*Could I give up my life for her?* he wondered to himself. Unsure, he dropped his face into his hands and let his thoughts wander to Zeva, tormenting himself with images he'd almost forgotten.

࿐

Amir watched Sybal's troubled face as he loaded up his horse with all the supplies he might need. She crossed her arms and didn't look at him or Signar, who was also saddling up his own steed. Her face puckered in worry and despair. He checked his saddle bag one last time and noted that he had enough sulfates should something happen. He tightened the saddle's belt and then came around to speak with Sybal. Taking a chance, he touched her shoulder gently.

"We'll be back before you know it," he said. "And in one piece. You have to be careful, too."

She reached up and took his hand in hers, squeezing it hard. "I know. Just promise you won't take any chances. You'll always choose caution. Both of you. Don't do anything reckless. Don't travel alone."

Amir looked back at Signar. The tall boy glared at him over the backs of their horses. Amir quickly dropped Sybal's hand. "I promise," he told her.

"Kazamar," Signar called, touching the medallion. "Open a portal for Amir."

One second later, a bright, fiery ring erupted. The portal opened right there in the middle of the stables. On the other side, they could see Jarabu.

"Please," Sybal called over the whirring and snapping of the fiery opening. "Be careful."

Amir nodded to her. "I will. You as well. And Signar."

The boy nodded stiffly to him.

"Meet me at the base of the statue of the maharaja outside the city of Vishna near Jarabu," he instructed. "That's where we'll gather."

Sybal dipped her head once in understanding. "Seven days."

Amir took the reins of his horse and stepped through the portal. His stomach flipped just a moment after a flash of darkness, but then it settled. His horse jumped through with a gentle thud as it landed. It whined a little and pulled at the reins, but then settled. He turned to look at Sybal one last time, but the portal had shut. Before him, the city of Jarabu stretched out and around with a great, thick jungle to the east. The grass felt strange beneath his feet.

Slinging himself up onto his horse, he started the short walk to Jarabu and hoped to find Ashar as quickly as he could, and to gather at least a few Runers to bring back to Sybal.

Signar looked at Sybal, seeing her eyes glassing over, watching where Amir had vanished. She took a deep breath and turned to him. She walked two quick steps toward him but stopped herself. He could tell she wanted to embrace him, but didn't want to force him.

"Be safe," she repeated. "I wish I could go with you. I cannot bear the thought of you alone in that country. Please find allies soon. Don't be alone."

"I won't," Signar promised. "I will find Dain and Tage the moment I am in Altevine. We will gather Runers and return to you as soon as we can."

He turned and picked up a wrapped blade, fastening it to the side of his saddle.

"What is that?" Sybal asked, coming forward.

"The sigiled blade," Signar replied easily. "I am taking it with me. Just in case. I don't know how malignant Altevine is, and I'd rather have protection."

"Oh," Sybal said, and Signar could tell she had more to say. But he pushed past her and grabbed a bridle for his horse.

As he did this, he noted her hurt expression. Stopping, he turned and faced her. She looked up into his eyes, her face still pinched in worry. Giving in, he wrapped her in his arms and hugged her close. She slid her arms around his middle and embraced him back.

"Last time you left me," she started, but couldn't go on. She gasped a sob and squeezed him tight.

"Nothing will happen. I swear," he promised.

"Kazamar," she called, prying herself off Signar. "Watch over him. If he comes to any harm, I swear, when I'm a djinn, I will hunt you down and kill you."

Signar smiled and let her go. He set the bit into his horse's mouth and fastened the bridle around its head. Ready now, he called on Kazamar to open a portal to Altevine. The fiery ring appeared once more. On the other side, only darkness greeted them. A cold wind blew through the portal, chilling them both. Signar pulled a fur-lined cowl over his head and faced the portal.

"I'll be back," he promised. "Sybal, stay safe."

He took a torch from a sconce on a beam of the stable. Then he pushed it through the portal, but no light fell on anything around it.

Sybal nodded and backed away as he led his horse through the portal. As he stepped through, darkness engulfed him. The light from the torch didn't touch anything. He pulled his horse through and it hopped over the fiery ring, following him. Once he was on the other side, it vanished. The wind immediately chilled him and he looked around. He could hardly see. Everything was black.

Caerwren had been swallowed by utter darkness.

# Chapter 24

## The Mahit'Onomicon

Sybal sealed the last of her patents and went to the magnificent gilded cage where her courier hawks waited. She selected a few to travel to each of the major cities on Al'Myrah and fastened the patents to them. Then she went to the window and let them go one at a time. She was already prepared to leave and travel to Ala'Nar to her estate to get the payments in order.

"Do you think any Runer will reply to the call?" Vicdan asked, appearing behind her, a pack in his hands. He was lacing the top closed as he walked in.

"I can only hope," she replied, taking up her letter to Ala'Nar to let Dorsa, her family's estate manager, know she was on her way. The hawk would arrive well before her and Dorsa could prepare for her arrival. "The sum I am offering is substantial. I won't be surprised if it plunges my estate into destitution. But this is the price to pay for an army of Runers."

"And what if we don't get an army?"

She turned and looked at Vicdan, making sure her gaze was soft, but serious. "Then I'll go alone if I have to."

Vicdan didn't reply, but she saw the worry on his face. He wanted to argue. She knew she needed more of a plan than that, but didn't have one. She imagined herself running into the Dynast Palace alone and fighting Tarkan one on one. But of course, something like that could never happen. He was too well guarded. And they were running out of time.

"We should leave," Sybal said as the sun rose just over the horizon. "The sooner we can get on the road, the better."

Vicdan nodded and left her alone to go and prepare the horses. Sybal looked over at the desk in the center of the room where the Mahit'Onomicon lay. She considered it only a moment before grabbing it and tossing it into her own pack. She didn't know why she felt compelled to take it, but it seemed better than leaving it behind.

The two traveled in silence all day and stopped at night in the middle of the desert between two smaller villages. Vicdan wanted to go into the villages and rest at a public house, if they had one, but Sybal advised against it.

"I'll never understand your and Tzarik's aversion to people," Vicdan said as he prepared his bedroll. "Not everyone wants to spit on Runers and run them out of town."

"It's also me," she reminded him. "People on Al'Myrah know me. I'm the murderer of Ala'Nar. I'm the reason Tarkan attacked all those years ago, devastating the city. They've not forgotten."

Vicdan shrugged and lay down, his back to the small campfire they had made. Sybal sat up a moment longer, staring into the flames. Her mind wandered into utter numbness in the silence of the desert night. Vicdan was right: they rarely stayed inside the cities and towns, despite always going to them to find hunts.

No sooner had she thought about it than her left hand began to tingle. A gentle pain crawled up her arm and gripped her heart before spidering up her neck and into her brain.

*Give me time,* she begged her white blood. *I cannot hunt now.*

But the sulfates ignored her pleas. A sudden pain shot through her and her spine bent. Her body seized and she toppled over, almost touching the flames of the campfire. Her limbs cracked and went rigid while her muscles spasmed. Her body locked up and wanted to flop like a fish at the same time. Her brain seared in her skull. A cry rose in her throat, but she couldn't scream through the tightened muscles.

The pain didn't stop. The world darkened around her, her vision going black. Her chest throbbed as her lungs burned for air. She couldn't breathe.

*No*, she thought, *this isn't how it happens. I won't let it.*

Then her vision went black. As it did, every sensation vanished. The pain withered away and the cracking of her bones ceased. Sybal opened her eyes to find herself standing in utter darkness. Only a gentle light glowed from above, like a full moon had appeared. Soft white flakes drifted through the air. One landed on her cheek, but it didn't melt away. Her flesh was frosted and cold. She looked down at her hands to find her skin almost white, glittering with frost. She gasped and turned on the spot, looking for the Pale God.

He was near.

"I gave you a great gift and you are squandering it," the voice of the Dohkma said. It came from all around, as if the darkness itself spoke.

Sybal spun, looking for him. Her hand went to her scimitar, but she remembered it was broken. She was going to get a new one in Ala'Nar. Instead, she took up her small crossbow.

"Don't be so foolish, child of mine," the Pale God said. In a swirl of smoky tendrils, he appeared before her, tall and imposing. His white skin and pearlescent hair stood out in the darkness. "You cannot hope to battle me."

Sybal pointed the crossbow at the god all the same. "I've fought gods before."

"Enough of this, Sybal." The Dohkma waved his hand and her crossbow vanished. "Why have you not used the blessing I gave you?"

She frowned, taking a step back from the frost-covered god. "I don't understand. You've given me nothing. You've only taken from me."

The icy blue eyes in the Dohkma's face narrowed. "Lies you tell yourself. Read the book, lady Runer. Don't squander it like the sorcerer did." He raised his head, examining her. "I have been nothing but kind to you since the day you took up the runes. I spared you then, as I have spared you for over a year. Am I not a benevolent god? To have not taken you as a demonic slave already?"

"No!" Sybal shouted, clenching her fists. "You took Tzarik from me. He's gone, and it's your fault."

The Dohkma's face changed a little then. Was that pity in his icy orbs? He shook his head. "The Necro'Khan would have killed him, no matter the curse. He wants you dead. That's why he spared the boy and sent him back to you. So you'd come to him. Sybal, I am trying to protect you. And I have shown you mercy. When you defied me and did not kill in my name, I spared you."

"Because I could not die," she shot back. "You want me dead, don't you? Once I perish, you will take my soul from Janna and steal it from Laith'asad. You have laid claim to my soul. But why? What good is one soul to you?" She smiled. "But the Vorlamir has stopped you. I cannot die. So why ask me to kill?"

The Dohkma fixed his eyes with hers and a shiver ran down her spine. "Obedience," he said simply. "You denied me, so of course I did not save your master. But I have been generous. I gave you the power to stop the Necro'Khan."

"What?" Sybal shot back. The wind picked up and a flurry of snow drifted around them. "Speak plainly, god. If you want my obedience, I must understand."

"Read the book, Sybal," he said. "And to show my benevolence once more, I will stay the Runer's death. You may thank me in your own time."

Before she could blurt another question, the Pale God vanished just as he'd appeared. She stood alone in the snowy darkness for just a moment more before it all went black.

Sybal shot up, gasping as her chest loosened and she could finally breathe. She coughed a few times to get the air flowing and clenched her hands. The sensation had vanished. Her limbs were loose and free once again.

*Damn the Pale God,* she thought, knowing he had released her from the Runer's death. What would he ask in exchange once he had given her enough favors? What did he want?

Her eyes went to her pack, where the Mahit'Onomicon lay wrapped in a blanket inside. She stared hard at it, wondering. To her left, Vicdan snored softly. With a heavy sigh, she stood up and marched to her pack. She opened it and pulled the book out. Carefully, she unwrapped it and stared at the rune on the cover. Gently rubbing her thumb over it, she studied it. She realized it said "The Father of Monsters" on it. Curious how she hadn't noticed before, she opened it to a random page. This one had a drawing of what she knew to be a mori on it. The monster was depicted with a victim slung over its arm, and blood dribbled from its mouth.

On the opposite page, the book described a mori and how best to kill one. Sybal had read several lines before shock shot through her. She gasped and cried out.

She could read it.

Beside her, Vicdan woke. He shot up, appearing ready for a fight. "What is it?" he asked, blinking into the firelight. He looked around, no doubt feeling for corpses to raise in defense.

"I..." she stammered. "I can read it. Vicdan, I can read it." She jabbed her finger at the pages, pointing. "This is about a mori. It says they cannot cross flowing water since they are considered unholy by all the gods and flowing water is clean—holy. It says the water burns them."

She gasped, taking in the words as her eyes flitted over the page. She flipped a few pages to another picture. This one depicted a djinn in a black, smoky, fiery shape.

"You can kill a djinn," she whispered, reading the passage. "It says an orichalcum blade dipped in lamb's blood will kill it." She exhaled. "If you can get close enough," she added under her breath. Reading on, she found that certain verses from the mihals would banish the spirit for three days. The next few pages described how to kill the djinn and then consume its essence. It detailed how to prepare a ritual for a mortal to consume a djinn's heart and ascend to sorcerer.

"It's almost impossible to catch a djinn," she said out loud. She remembered her encounter. Tzarik had almost died, and she would have been were she not immortal. They both would have been dead if not for her when binding Kazamar.

"How?" Vicdan asked, coming up beside her and trying to look over her shoulder at the pages. "How are you reading this?"

She gritted her teeth, rage at the Dohkma rising in her. "The Pale God. He gave me this ability when I asked him to save Tzarik."

Vicdan raised his brows and stepped back to look at Sybal. "You went to the Frozen Nation? How brave."

"And useless," she quipped. "He wouldn't hear me. Instead, he gave me this. What am I supposed to do with this?" She shook the book, shouting to the sky.

Vicdan touched the uneven edges of the pages, almost in awe. "Read it, I suppose. It has necromancers in it, yes?"

Sybal shrugged and flipped through it, looking for familiar imagery. She stopped when she found a drawing of a man in a black cowl. He had familiar markings over his face, and his eyes were blue. She looked to the adjacent page and read it quickly. Her mind raced as she took in the information.

"Nothing about how to become one," she said after a moment, "but how to kill one. It says his heart must be cut out and his body and burned. That will stop him, but his heart is immortal. It says..." She trailed off, her eyes stopping on two words. "The sigiled blades," she whispered. "They can kill him. Tzarik told me they were made of orichalcum and had the mysterious sigils on them. They can take his soul into the blade."

Vicdan frowned. "Where did those sigils come from?"

Sybal shrugged. "A god, perhaps. Same as the runes. Same as all magic." She looked down at the Mahit'Onomicon. "I suppose it might say in here. But what does it matter right now? We have one. We have what we need to take Tarkan down. Tzarik was right to take that blade." Her heart thudded once in pain as she thought about him.

"Killing Tarkan won't close the rifts, though. What about the scrip-tures, Vicdan? Do they say anything about opening the God Deep?"

Vicdan shook his head. "I have all thirty-one verses memorized. They declare the spells, our laws, our oath to Nephron—things of that nature. But Tarkan is writing his own spells. This must anger Nephron. The scriptures say the path to Necro'Khan is to bring one closer to our god, not usurp him. What Tarkan has done is heresy. There are no writings on how to undo what he's done."

Sybal's heart fell a little.

"But," Vicdan went on, as if giving a lecture to a room of scholars, "I'll wager a Necro'Kahn could close them. I was there when he tore open the Deep on Caerwren. I know how to do it."

Guilt filled Sybal. "We ripped open the God Deep to save me."

Vicdan gently touched her shoulder. "Not just to save you. Tarkan used you and Tzarik to his own ends. He manipulated you. He wanted the mantle of Necro'Khan and saw a chance to take it. Tarkan tore into the Deep with abandon. The place he became Necro'Khan was weakened. I dare not think what horrors are filling Altevine now."

At this, Sybal pressed her palm into her lips to stop the sob that rose in her throat. Signar could be in untold danger.

And she'd sent him there alone.

"He's a Reks of Caerwren," Vicdan said, guessing at what had made her react that way. "He's a strong man, and a crafty one. He'll be fine."

She nodded and took a shuddering breath. "Tarkan will never close the rifts. There's no way to force him, even. But..." She ran her hand over the page in the Mahit'Onomicon, tracing the outline of the necromancer there. "But someone else who took up the mantle could."

"There can only be one Necro'Khan," Vicdan said. "We'd have to kill him first. And it would require the blood magic. So much blood to heal such a rift."

"But maybe that's the answer," she offered. "Or it will be like the Crypt on Xia: a place requiring constant vigilance and guarding."

Vicdan shrugged and yawned, stretching his arms overhead. "The Wushito have done it for a thousand or more years. Surely Alika can as well. Caerwren might need some convincing, but I'm sure we could find a way."

"They are trying," Sybal said. "Tzarik told me." She closed the book and sighed. "I'm tired. We need to sleep."

"Could not agree more," Vicdan said with a weary smile.

〜

The next few days of travel were quiet and tense. Vicdan graciously didn't speak much, but Sybal wished he would. She didn't open the Mahit'Onomicon again for fear of reading something she didn't want to know.

When they reached her estate, she was let through the front gates but didn't go up to the main house. She admired it from afar, noting how the builders had done so well on it that it looked like the fire had never happened.

"I almost killed Tzarik in that fire," she said to Vicdan as they rode around the outskirts of her property. She smiled, remembering the event. She'd almost killed him more than once. But she remembered this one fondly. He'd come back to find her, to save her family from the city's wrath. She hadn't deserved that.

"Where are we going?" Vicdan asked as she turned down a path that led to a cemetery several yards away.

"To see my family," she said. She hoped Dorsa had had her family buried in the ancestral cemetery. "I haven't spoken to them in some years."

Vicdan remained quiet as she slowed her horse's gait to a trot, then came to a stop. The cemetery was full of unique markers for graves. Statues, small pyramids, and other grave markers dotted the acres. Sybal scanned the headstones and spotted three that still had a marble gleam to them. She smiled and dismounted, jogging to the three headstones and the statue of Laith'asad that watched over them from a stone dais. Each stone was marked with a name.

Vicdan came up behind her and looked at the largest. "Sheikh Riyadh Rashidi," he read.

"My father," she sighed. "He was the best of men. Strong, powerful. Ruled our part of the city with a rod of iron and a gentle hand."

"Freja Rashidi?" he asked next. "Your mother was from Caerwren? No wonder you are so tall. And Abdul?"

"My brother." A tear welled up in her eye then and she reached out, touching his headstone. "He was younger than me. He was supposed to run the mines, but he was too..." She fought to find the right words. "He was too kind. So it fell to me."

"Unusual," Vicdan mused. "You've always been strange, haven't you?"

Sybal smiled, but kept her eyes on her family's graves. "Sharar killed them. Then he made Tarkan raise them and had them fight me." She swallowed. "Mother, Father, Abdul: he's dead now, the man who took your lives, and with him the man who saved me." She closed her eyes and let the tears fall.

Vicdan backed up a pace, but she reached back and grasped his wrist. "Stay," she said. "I don't want to be alone right now."

He nodded and came abreast with her.

They stayed there for several more minutes and Sybal let her mind wander. She tried to stay away from darker thoughts.

"To the house," she said at length with a heavy sigh. "I need Dorsa to prepare our vaults."

# Chapter 25

## Runers of Jarabu

Unlike other Runers, Ashar had purchased a home some years back. Amir decided that would be the best place to start looking for his former apprentice. He wound his way through the streets of Jarabu to the lower district, where the poorer citizens made their camps and homes out of the worst the golden city had to offer. The upper districts were clean and devoid of people lingering in the street. Here, a poor man with three children sat outside a temple, begging for any scrap of coin or food. As Amir passed him, he dropped in a few rupees. The man cried and thanked Amir, calling on Krishvu to bless him.

A few working women hung out of a doorless frame to a flophouse, smiling at him and waving. He ignored them and pushed on through the dirty streets. Awnings made of threadbare cotton spanned the streets, offering some shade, but not much. The sun was hot.

Amir carefully made his way around street urchins picking pockets and men in dark robes trying to sell him suspect items, until he came to a hovel in better repair than the others. This one had a door painted black and shutters on the windows. He recognized Ashar's home right away. His apprentice had grown up on the street, and when he'd been runed and started to make more coin than he'd ever had in his life, he had purchased the home to get off the road.

Picking his way around mud puddles, Amir approached the door and knocked. He didn't expect Ashar to be inside this time of day. He most likely was out hunting with his own apprentice, Vitaly.

So when the door opened, he stumbled back. A beautiful lizard-like Masahk woman stood in the door. She had ovate pink eyes and tiny, glittering green scales along her too-human jawline and shoulders. Behind her, a long scaly tail curled up in curiosity. She had long black hair that shimmered in the sun. Her pink eyes darted around the street before landing back on Amir.

"Can I help you, Runer?"

Struck mute by the woman's beauty, Amir stammered at first. "Ashar," he said after a moment. "I'm looking for Ashar. He lives here, or did."

The Masahk smiled. "My husband."

Shocked once again, Amir stared at the woman. So Ashar had taken a wife? That would surely make the life of a Runer more complicated.

The woman giggled at the look on Amir's face and stepped aside. "Come in, Runer. I know who you are. My name is Vashti."

Amir ducked to enter the low frame and stepped into the humblest home he'd ever seen. When just Ashar had lived here, there had been little more than a pot on the fire and a bed in the corner. Now there was a table, a chest at the foot of a larger bed, and other homely accents that he would have bet his last coin were the doings of Vashti.

"I hardly recognize the place," he said after a moment, taking a cup of tea handed to him.

"Yes," Vashti said with another pleasant smile. "Ashar seemed to think it was acceptable to sleep on the floor like a dog. I hear he has you to thank for that."

"Not entirely," Amir said in his defense. "Ashar lived on the streets when I found him. He was something of a vigilante vagabond."

Vashti smiled at this. "He does have a good heart. Sometimes too good. He follows it into danger." She sat at the table and motioned for Amir to join her. "So, what can I do for you, Amir?"

"How long have you been married to Ashar?" he asked out of pure curiosity.

"About six months," the Masahk replied. "Not long at all." Her cheeks glowed pink as she smiled.

Amir shifted. "How does this..." He cleared his throat. "It's very dangerous to sleep with a Runer."

Vashti giggled behind her hand and looked away. She was young, he saw now, and perhaps smitten to the point of foolhardiness. "We are careful," she said at length when his serious face didn't fall.

Amir let the subject rest there. Ashar was rash, and he knew it. But he'd never been able to talk his young apprentice out of anything before, and he wasn't about to try again now.

"I know I will never bear children," Vashti added. "But Vitaly is enough of a child for me right now. He's brash and brave and thinks he's a man now that he's seen nineteen summers. I am satisfied, Runer."

"I suppose that's all that matters," he sighed. Still befuddled by Ashar's life, he shook his head. "I need to speak with Ashar. Do you know where he is?"

Vashti nodded. "He's out hunting with Vitaly. They have been paid a handsome price to dispatch a camiri, a spawn of the god Hashna. Very dangerous I hear."

Amir looked up, worry filling him now for his old apprentice. "Very," he repeated. He calmed himself, reminding himself that Ashar had been trained well. He worried too often about the boy. He had to let go, but it was difficult. "Where did they go?"

"To the east," she replied. "Into the jungle. The thing supposedly has been making its nest in the caves near the waterfall. It even killed a pack of wolves. They've been gone for three days now." Her face suddenly fell and her pink eyes creased with worry. "Do you think they're all right?"

Amir nodded quickly, placating the woman before she started to worry. "I'll find them. Thank you, Vashti."

Amir set out immediately to follow Ashar's and Vitaly's tracks. The two had left on horseback and journeyed east, like Vashti had said. Knowing where they'd gone made tracking them easier. A rain had recently fallen and their tracks were prominent in the mud and grass. The grass was tall where they had ridden, and was pushed to the side on the trail where it had parted for the horses.

He followed it to the edge of the jungle, where it became a little harder to follow. The jungle floor was covered in leaves and debris from dying foliage, making the tracks fewer and less obvious. The jungles of Bahratt were beautiful and bursting with color. Orange and red flowers grew on creeping green vines over silver boulders and rock faces. The succulent plants grew thick and rubbery. This was how Amir spotted where Ashar and Vitaly had gone. They had dismounted due to the thick foliage and walked on foot, hacking their way through it.

The trail disappeared a few times, and he had to backtrack to find it again, careful not to follow his own steps. Soon the sun began to set and the animals' sounds increased. Snakes slithered past his feet in search of food and somewhere a tiger roared. A few monkeys watched him as he passed. He spotted the tracks of a panther once as well and decided he didn't want to traverse the jungle after the sun went down. A little distraught, he made camp in a clearing near a brown brook beside a thick bush of a flower called Hashna's bane.

He tossed a few more small logs onto the fire once he had it going and stared absentmindedly into the flames. The jungle came alive at night with all the sounds of nature. The howler monkeys screamed their cries in the canopy above, and a few things prowled in darkness just outside his campfire's ring of light. Amir kept his scimitar close, and his large crossbow lay across his lap as he dosed.

He thought about Sybal as his mind wandered. He imagined what it might be like to settle down like Ashar had. And then she entered his mind. What would it be like to live with someone as wild and strange as her? He smiled, remembering the first time he'd seen her. They'd been in the market in Gypsu, and he'd spotted her from across the way. He'd known immediately that she was a lady Runer and his heart had beat. But the feelings had been quickly dashed when Sharar had made it clear Sybal was a target.

But Sharar was gone now.

And so was Tzarik, Sybal's master and love.

Amir growled, admonishing himself for thinking of her that way. She was in grief. And as far as he knew, she'd never love again. And Signar knew his feelings as well. The boy had glared at him when he'd taken Sybal's hand. He wasn't foolish or as naïve as Amir had thought he might be.

Tired of tormenting himself with thoughts of a life that could never be, he rolled over and went to sleep as best he could, the night full of wild animal sounds.

The next day, he followed the tracks of the other two Runers to a rocky cliff face with a huge waterfall spilling over the edge. He looked up it and gauged it to be several yards high. The water fell into a cauldron at the base, made of silver rocks. A strange kind of orange fish flitted about beneath the surface. On the muddy shore of the cauldron, he spotted the prints he'd been looking for. Huge, cloven hooves had stepped on the shore just moments ago.

Amir bent his knees and looked up into the trees and the surrounding high ground. These were the bestial prints of the camiri. The thing would be tall, he knew that much. It was a satyr-like creature with eight arms, a tiger's head with ram's horns, and it breathed poisonous air. If Amir remembered correctly, the thing could also make illusions of itself to confuse hunters.

Carefully, Amir followed the hoof prints up to a small alcove that opened into a larger cave. Inside the cave, he heard the unmistakable sound of bones being gnawed on. A moment of panic rose in him as he prayed it wasn't Ashar's corpse the thing chewed on. Ducking down to hide behind a small wall of rocks, he gripped his crossbow and moved closer. Then he spotted it.

Inside the cave, the camiri stood hunched, goat legs bent, over a corpse. It pried the arm of the dead person off and tore at it with its fangs. Tilting his head over the rocky edge, Amir inspected the body.

It didn't wear Runer armor.

Relief flooded him and he sighed softly. As he looked, he spotted a shadow move on the other side of the cave, in an opening a few yards away. He ducked down, but not before his eyes registered the black cloaks of Runers. Smiling, he knew it was Vitaly and Ashar. Deciding to watch, he adjusted and peeked through a crack in the rock wall.

Ashar came over a boulder, crossbow in hand, and Vitaly came up along the cave floor. His huge, straight-bladed Rhostranan sword was clutched in both hands. Vitaly looked up to Ashar, but Ashar's eyes were honed in on the camiri. Ashar fired. The arrow flew in a ridged straight line and thudded hard into the back of the camiri. The thing reeled back and bellowed a strange roar to the sky.

Vitaly rushed in then and tried to hack at the monster, but the beast was quick. With one hand, it caught the straight blade and wrenched it out of Vitaly's hand. The Runer fell forward and tripped. As he did, the camiri belched a cloud of noxious gas into Vitaly's face. The young man instantly paled and stumbled backward, clutching his chest as his breath turned to rattles.

Seeing this, Amir leapt from his hiding place and ran at the camiri. It turned invisible for just a moment and then reappeared. But another one appeared behind him. Then a third to his left.

"It's an illusion!" Ashar cried, tossing his crossbow aside and clambering down the rocks. "Go for the first one."

Amir ducked a blow from the camiri and cut at its legs. As he did, he swore the blade would stop on the bone of the thick, bestial legs. But instead, it passed right through them. The weight and might of his swing carried him forward as his blade cut through the air. Amir ducked and rolled, coming up onto his feet as the first illusion fizzled and faded. The camiri gave a strange cackle and all the illusions mirrored it.

"That wasn't it," Amir growled. He raised his scimitar, ready to fight. One of the illusions lunged at him, coughing a cloud of putrid green smoke toward him. Amir held his breath and ducked out of the way. But the smell never hit him. It wasn't the real camiri.

Ducking down, he gripped Vitaly by the collar of his armor and pulled him out of the way. The boy coughed and gagged on the poison, his veins showing up vividly despite his pale skin.

Once he was safe, Amir jumped back into the fight.

"Is he all right?" Ashar asked as he ducked and wove through three of the illusions, avoiding the poisonous clouds and dangerous claws.

"He will be," Amir called back, circling one of the camiri. The thing waved its eight arms at him, sticking out its long, snake-like tongue. Then it pounced on him. Amir grunted, raising his hands and sword to meet the creature, but the blow never fell. He stumbled backward, losing his footing. As he fell, one of the other camiri ran at him, maw open wide to bite. Amir drew halat and the monster's face smashed into the barrier. Then he drew buhkar and misted away a few paces.

"This is the one!" he called to Ashar.

But no sooner had he said it than the other illusions vanished and reappeared in different places. The one before him wavered and disappeared entirely. He cursed as he rematerialized and looked around.

Behind him, Ashar grunted. The camiri came up behind the younger Runer and grappled him around the neck with one of its eight arms. Ashar threw his head back, bloodying the monster's nose, but it held him tight. Amir dropped his sword and picked up his great crossbow.

The camiri smirked and made a growling laugh. Its long tongue flicked out and licked at Ashar's face. Amir saw in its bestial eyes that it was challenging him. He closed one eye and raised the bow. The creature roared and belched a mist of green into Ashar's face. Ashar instantly coughed and began to froth at the mouth, his eyes rolling.

Opening both his eyes, Amir fired the bow. The bolt flew straight and true, thudding into the camiri's skull right between its eyes. Its head jerked back and it moaned, dropping Ashar. Its eight arms went limp and then its body crumpled to the ground. Ashar fell forward on to his hands and knees, coughing. His hand went to his throat as he struggled to breathe.

"Stay calm," Amir said soothingly, kneeling by his old apprentice. "I have to go into the jungle and find some Hashna's bane. I saw some not too far back. Keep your heart rate down."

"Vi-Vitaly?" Ashar gasped.

Amir looked over at the young Runer and saw him lying still on his back. His chest hardly moved, showing he still breathed. "He's all right," he promised Ashar. He stood and dashed into the jungle's undergrowth to look for the purple flower.

Hashna's bane, when made into a tincture, would stop the camiri's poison. Amir ran from one bush to another until he found some creeping over a rock and up the trunk of a tree. He ripped handfuls of the flowers off and ran back to Ashar.

"Do you have alcohol?" he asked quickly.

Ashar nodded. "Vitaly's pack. Vodka."

Amir ran down the path past where he had seen Ashar and Vitaly sneaking up before and found their horses there. He dug through both packs until he found a large, round bottle full of clear liquid. He wasn't sure what vodka was, but this was the only thing inside he couldn't identify, so he guessed it was the alcohol. Making sure, he pulled the stopper out and sniffed at it. The stinging smell hit him deep in his nostrils. He took a tiny black cauldron from the pack, too, and ran back. When he returned, Ashar had fallen to his back and panted.

"Hold on," Amir said, smacking his flint and steel together to make a fire.

Ashar nodded, his breath a rasp in his throat. Amir checked on Vitaly and saw the boy's lips had started to turn blue. Panicking a little, he put the black cauldron directly on the fire and poured the vodka into it, adding the flowers. He had to wait as it boiled. He kept checking on Ashar and Vitaly, worry piling up inside him.

Once it boiled, he poured it into a small tin cup he'd found among their things and blew on it till it cooled. He went to Vitaly first and dumped the tincture down his throat, praying it worked. He didn't wait to see. He went to Ashar and did the same. Since Ashar was awake, Amir saw the healing take place right away. Ashar's veins receded and his breathing stopped coming in harsh rasps.

Behind them, Vitaly groaned. The boy turned over onto all fours and vomited onto the ground.

"That means it's working," Amir said, relief flooding him. He helped Ashar up and sat him down near the fire, where he soon vomited up the poison as well.

Ashar shuddered and wiped at his mouth. "Thank you, Amir. What are you doing here?"

Amir pulled Vitaly to his feet and sat him near the fire as well.

With all three of them seated, and the camiri's corpse nearby, Amir told them about the Necro'Khan, Sharar, and why he'd come to Bahratt.

"An army of Runers," Ashar said, eyes distant. "I can't think of a single one who would follow you to invade Alika. Not for all the gold in the world."

Amir nodded, disheartened. "They'd have to be a fool to follow us to Alika. Or full of more hubris than a bard."

Ashar tilted his head in thought. "There is a flophouse in a nearby village, Vishna, that is frequented by Runers. You might be able to find a few there."

Vitaly looked up at this. "The Rose Song?"

Ashar nodded. "There's some trouble in Vishna, but that may be something we can handle and swing to our advantage."

The three Runers traveled back to the city so Ashar could check in with Vashti before they departed for the small village of Vishna on the outskirts of Jarabu. It took them several hours to get there, and by the time they reached the flophouse, it was late morning. The house was quiet at that time as most patrons had left for the day, and the new set wouldn't be in until later that evening. The owner of the flophouse was a woman of Bahratt descent who dressed like a magi. When they asked about Runers, she directed them to a table near the back.

"Ishaan and Rishvi are here," she said, looking annoyed. "I told them if they fight, they pay for anything they break."

"Fight?" Amir asked.

She nodded. "They have warring tribes of Runers. Ask them; they'll tell you."

Amir led the other two back toward the table the woman had indicated. On their way, a girl with golden eyes grabbed Amir's front laces and pulled him aside.

"Five gold for a quick one," she whispered in his ear, smiling.

He shoved her off and continued to the back. He spotted the Runers easily in the sunlit main room. There were three of them. One was a brown-haired cat-like half-Masahk with the blackest eyes Amir had ever seen. He looked young, but strong. The others sat across from him. One was older, with a white and black beard, and the other was a young man with a snide eye.

"Vishna is ours, Ishaan," the older man spat, his eyes going wild. "It's in our territory."

The Masahk's cat-like ears pressed down into his long hair and his sharp teeth showed under his lips. "Vishna is the dividing line," he said. "Whoever gets there first can dispatch the jagumars. Neither of us has a claim to it."

"False, cat," the younger Runer said with a currish grin. "Everyone knows Vishna is more on the eastern side than the west."

"Brothers," Amir said, coming up to them, flanked by Ashar and Vitaly. "A pride of jagumar is worth enough for both of you, surely."

"That's not the point, foreigner," the older Runer spat.

"The protection of our city is the point," Ishaan put in.

The younger Runer smirked again. "Who cares about the city, cat? Just stay out of our territory!" He slammed his fist onto the table.

"Wait," Amir said, pulling up a chair and sitting at the table. The other two stood behind him, arms crossed. "This division is unwise. Are you two the only factions that claim the city?"

Ishaan nodded. "We each run a tribe of Runers, dozens strong. The west of Jarabu is my tribe's territory, and the east is his. But Vishna sits on the dividing line and it is currently overrun with jagumar."

Amir knew the creature: a huge, panther-like monster with spines down its back. The spines were often used to make a powder that held magical properties. Jagumar moved in prides and were led by a single female. "If it's jagumar you have, you will need help," he said.

The older Runer crossed his arms. "What do you want, foreigner? I can smell your ulterior motive all over you."

The younger Runer mimicked crossing his arms like the older and parroted, "Yes, what do you want?"

"Dev, silence," the older Runer barked. To Amir he said, "Call me Rishvi. And you are?"

"Amir," he said with a small tilt of his head. "From Al'Myrah. And I come with a most urgent request."

"What is it?" Ishaan asked.

Amir licked his lips and leaned his elbows on the table. "In Alika, there has risen a necromancer," he began. He told them briefly about Tarkan and his dealings with Sharar. He spoke about the attack from Bahratt and how the sorcerer was now dead, but that the Necro'Khan planned on covering the map in a malignation so severe there might be no way to defend against it. "And white blood is immune to his control," he finished. "We don't need an army. We just need enough of us to get inside, find him, and end him."

Rishvi didn't hold back. The moment Amir finished talking, he burst out laughing. Dev, the younger, mimicked his master's guffaw. Confused, Amir waited for them to quit their charade.

"No amount of gold will entice me to leave Bahratt and join an army marching on a necromancer," Rishvi said, still smiling. "We are Runers, my friend. We can handle a little malignation." He faced Ishaan. "Now, cat. Stay out of Vishna. I intend to offer the alderman protection from all monsters and outside influences, like opposing tribes. For a price."

"That's not how Runers operate," Ishaan said.

Amir sighed inwardly, knowing he'd lost the men to their argument again. Rishvi must have thought his word final.

"You will recognize my authority over Vishna or you will perish," Rishvi said simply.

"Maybe we don't kill this one," Dev said, sneering. "Maybe we just put him in a collar with a bell and make him hunt mice."

Ishaan's jaw muscles flexed as he held himself back.

Rishvi eyed Ishaan before leaning back in contemplation. "We fight for it. What say you to that? Meet me tomorrow outside the gulch between here and Vishna and our tribes will battle for the territory."

"That's a waste of life and time," Amir butted in.

"I agree," Ishaan hissed through his feline teeth.

"There's no other way to settle this," Rishvi said with finality. He slapped his knees and stood. "Come, Dev."

The boy stood and ran around the table. Quick as lightning, he gripped and pulled on Ishaan's long, cat-like tale. Ishaan stood, hissing, his ears pressed down into his hair. Dev leapt back, smirking as he followed Rishvi out.

Amir watched them go, hating them more and more.

"Runer," Ishaan said, sitting back down. "I heard your words and will consider what you have said. But I need your help first."

Amir nodded, looking at the door the other two had just left through. "I might have an idea."

# Chapter 26

# Ambush

A mir stood in his stirrups as his horse cantered across the grassy plains, Ashar and Vitaly behind him. Vishna sat nestled between two great hills in a sandy valley. A small mountain range waited just behind it, where he knew the jagumars would be hiding. As they rode out from the village, Amir slowed his horse and sat back down in the saddle.

"What is your plan, old friend?" Ashar asked, dusting himself off. Beside him, Vitaly coughed, breathing in the dry air.

"I will hunt the jagumar myself," Amir answered. "With it dead, the tribes will have nothing to fight over—for now—and will hopefully listen to me. But first, I want to find the alderman and hear what kind of deal Rishvi has threatened him with."

They trotted into the village, many eyes turning to look up at them. Some whispered and pointed and others just watched them pass with stony faces. Of course Amir was used to this kind of reception, as were Ashar and Vitaly.

"Where is your alderman?" Amir asked once they found the center of the tiny village. A well stood not twelve feet from him, where a few people were drawing water.

"There," one woman said, pointing to a man at the well.

A man in a once colorful robe and a dirty turban looked up at Amir. His brown eyes pled for no trouble. "Yes?" he stammered. "What can I do for you, master Runer?"

Amir glared at the onlookers until they began to disperse. Then he slid off his horse and approached the alderman. "You have been speaking with a Runer named Rishvi?"

"Oh, no!" the man whispered, wringing his hands. "Tell him I'll have payment as soon as I can. It's just that—"

"You misunderstand," Amir said. "I am not part of his tribe. I came to find out what kind of deal you have with him. You owe him money?"

The alderman looked around nervously, as if he expected Rishvi's spies to leap out of the sand dunes. "Yes, for now. He promises us protection from the other tribes of Runers and from the monsters in the caves, and we pay him every month. I've missed the last two months, because, well..." He gestured around him. "We are a poor village. I do the best I can. But Rishvi always expects more and more." He held up his left hand where his ring finger was missing. "He takes what he wants when I cannot pay."

Amir blanched at this. Some Runers were bad men, but Rishvi had elevated that reputation to something far worse.

"He's taking advantage of you," Ashar said with disgust. "Amir, we have to stop him."

"Oh, no!" the alderman cried again. "Don't stop him. If you fail, he'll come for me, or my wife or child. Please, don't interfere."

"We won't let anything happen to you or your family. Right, Amir?" Ashar said stoutly.

"We'll do our best," Amir said. "For now, do you know where the jagumar have come from?"

The alderman wrung his remaining fingers, his face wrinkling in worry. "Oh, gods, this is not good," he whispered as if to himself. "Rishvi will kill us all." He blinked. "Up in the mountain. Well, if you can call it a mountain. They come down at night, sleep during the day. Usually."

"Thank you," Amir said with a slight bow. "Have everyone stay inside. Just in case."

"Oh, no," the alderman whispered again, his voice warbling with worry. "Not good. Not good at all."

"We'll take care of it," Ashar promised. "Nothing bad will happen to you or your village."

Amir wished Ashar would stop talking. His soft heart had often led them into trouble when they were master and apprentice, and now seemed to be no different. But for now, he had to focus on the jagumars.

The three of them turned and marched their horses out of the village toward the mountain path.

"There's going to be an entire pride of them," Amir warned the other two. "Five or more. They are matriarchal, so look for the largest female. If she falls, the others will scatter. Understand?"

"Yes, sira," Vitaly said. "Anything else we should know?"

"They're not poisonous like other beasts. No black ectoplasm, nothing surreal about them. Just flesh and blood."

He looked down at the ground and began to follow the soft, padded tracks he found there. They led up the mountain path over rocks and little valleys. Unlike other beasts, the jagumars didn't worry about being followed.

Amir looked up into the small mountain. They'd find the pride soon.

"There," Amir whispered, pointing down into a small cauldron of the mountain. Below, in an open area outside a small cave, the jagumars slept, basking in the sun.

They were dark-furred with white spines down their backs and long, protruding fangs. The beasts were about the size of a pony and had massive paws for running.

Amir inspected the area. The cauldron opened up onto a grassy plain. He eyed the paths and saw a way down and around. "We'll take the path," he whispered. "Around and behind the monsters. We'll come at them from that grassy plain. Stay on your horses. They can outrun a jagumar. Use your bows to shoot them. They have a soft spot between their eyes and at the base of their skulls. Aim for that and you'll kill it in one shot."

Vitaly's face fell a little. "I'm a terrible shot with a bow."

Amir inspected the long blade on his back. "You might be able to use your sword from the back of your horse. You'll have to get close, but if you feel you have a better chance that way, then do it."

"I do," Vitaly said. "Our swords were made to hew a man from the back of a horse." He smiled proudly.

"Please, be careful," Ashar said to his apprentice.

Vitaly nodded.

Amir signaled for them to remount and led the way down and around where the pride rested in the sun. They lost sight of them for a moment as they rounded a rocky corner, but then came nearly face to face with the entire pride. A single guard at the entrance to the open cauldron spotted them and stood, its spines raising.

"Shit," Amir whispered, his horse starting to snort in worry. He pulled on the reins, urging his steed to back up.

The jagumar roared, alerting the others. Amir raised his crossbow and fired a single bolt into the soft spot of the guard's skull, right between the eyes. The monster toppled over and the huge matriarch stood. She eyed Amir and roared to her pride, signaling them to give chase. Amir yanked on the reins, turning his horse and galloping away. The pride leapt up and chased after him.

Behind him, Ashar and Vitaly released two arrows into the backs of two more jagumars' skulls. They fell into the sand with pitiful mewls. Amir looked over his shoulder and spotted them running in a wide circle around the six remaining jagumars. He watched as Vitaly drew the fury rune and then chased down a set of the beasts. The matriarch continued its chase of him, though.

He clamped his thighs tight around his horse and reloaded his crossbow, turning sharply as the matriarch leapt at him. Amir ducked, drew halat, and watched as the matriarch rolled off the shield. The animal roared as she fell to the ground and shook herself, a puff of sand surrounding her. Amir watched as Vitaly charged down one of the beasts and hacked its head off with so mighty a blow that it flew like a ball for several yards.

Amir smiled at the youth and went back to reloading his crossbow. He glanced up, but lost sight of the matriarch. Concerned, he whirled on the spot, looking around. Just as he turned to his left, the thing leapt at him from its hiding place in the grass. It snapped its maw over his left arm and tackled him to the ground, dislodging him from his horse. He landed hard but didn't have time to try to rip his arm from the beast's mouth before it broke into a gallop, pulling him along.

The pain ripped through his arm and shoulder as he fought to grab the small orichalcum knife on his thigh. The thing dragged him through rough brambles, drawing more blood. Amir raised the knife and shoved it into the monster's right eye. It yowled and let go of him. Before it could turn and snap at him again, he drew buhkar and vanished into black mist. He ran back to where he'd fallen and scooped up his crossbow as he became solid once again.

Just as he turned, the matriarch pounced on him again, maw wide. He landed hard on his back, dropping his runes and his crossbow. The jagumar tried to bite down onto his neck, but he blocked it with his already mangled arm. The weight of the jagumar was too much. He couldn't dislodge the beast, no matter how hard he kicked or pushed.

Suddenly, something hissed through the air and thudded into the back of the beast's skull. The matriarch growled and went still, falling on him with her entire body. It crushed him underneath, but he was able to pull his arm out of its mouth. Panting, he fought to look around the beast to see who had shot it. Someone sauntered up to him, standing over him and looking down.

Rishvi.

"Cat got your tongue, Runer?" Rishvi asked, smirking. "Or more in this case." He looked down at Amir's mangled arm. Then he reached down and pulled the knife out of the jagumar's eye socket. "You almost had it," he said.

Amir grunted, trying to push up on the dead beast, but it wouldn't budge.

"This was a valiant effort, Runer. But you have failed. We're going to ambush Ishaan before our meeting," Rishvi said casually. "He'll be dead soon, just as you will be."

"Don't do this, Rishvi," Amir tried. "Runers are brothers in the white blood. You—"

"You really believe that, don't you?" Rishvi asked. He smirked down at Amir. "I sense you haven't always thought so sentimentally, but here you are." He suddenly looked up. "Here come the others. Well, then."

He reached down and grabbed a handful of Amir's long hair and pulled his head back.

"Don't!" Amir begged, suddenly understanding.

But Rishvi didn't stop. He pressed the blade hard into Amir's neck and slashed his flesh. Amir felt his warm blood instantly spurt down beneath his armor. He gasped as Rishvi dropped his head.

"Bleeding out is one of the worst ways to die," the Runer sighed, tossing the blade far away. "I'm going to kill the alderman, too, and then appoint my own. I have a man in the village who will do as I say." He smiled. "Maybe I'll see you in the afterlife." Rishvi raised his hand in a parting farewell and stepped out of sight.

Amir gasped for air and choked on his blood. The cut had gone deep. He quickly glanced around and spotted his runes several feet from him. He reached out, knowing he couldn't grasp them. He listened, hearing horse's hooves against the hard ground. He prayed it was Ashar and Vitaly. He opened his mouth to call out, but something in his throat stopped him.

His mind started to turn fuzzy as he lost more blood. His heart hammered in a panic in his chest. Was this the end for him? His mind wandered rapidly, thinking of all the things he'd done in his life, the bad things as well as the good. Ashar was the only good thing he'd ever done, really.

Sybal came to his mind then. He imagined her beautiful smile and her long, white hair. Would he ever get the chance to confess his feelings for her? Not now, surely. She'd never have the same feelings he did, anyway. She mourned for Tzarik, and he couldn't try to replace him. She'd hate him for that. Would she hate him if more time had passed? He winced. How could he even be thinking like this?

"Amir!" Ashar's voice rang out.

Weakly, Amir raised his hand.

"There!" Vitaly shouted.

Ashar appeared and together he and his apprentice shoved the jagumar off Amir. When Ashar saw the blood, he knelt quickly and began to draw artiah over the neck wound.

"My saddle. Get the sulfates," Ashar commanded Vitaly as he drew the rune once more over Amir's neck.

Amir looked up into Ashar's face and smiled weakly. "Thank you," he whispered, his mind still dull and his body growing cold.

"I won't let you leave me so easily," Ashar said, gently laying Amir's head on his lap. He took the bottles from Vitaly when he returned. "We have a village to save."

"Ishaan," Amir wheezed around the scar on his throat. "I saw Rishvi ride toward the gulch on the northern side of the village. He's going to ambush him. We have to hurry."

جهـ

The three Runers galloped to the gulch between two of the smaller mountains. A path ran through it that led directly to Vishna. Amir spotted the gulch before they were close enough to see anyone hiding above the road. He gathered his strength and shouted.

"It's a trap!" he cried when he spotted Ishaan in the center of the road.

The Masahk Runer stopped and squinted in Amir's direction.

Amir looked up and saw the tip of an arrow gleam as Dev, Rishvi's apprentice, nocked it to the string. "Behind you, above the road!"

Ishaan didn't even turn before he drew halat. The arrow zipped down and cracked against the barrier. With that, Ishaan called for his men to scatter and take cover. Amir spurred his horse on, coming to their aid. A few more arrows rained down on them, but the others in Ishaan's tribe dived for cover and drew the barrier around themselves. Amir leapt from his horse and fired once up at Dev. The apprentice shouted and ducked, the arrowing missing him.

"We can't stay," Amir said when he reached Ishaan. "They'll shoot us like fish in a barrel." He glanced up and saw the Runers of Rishvi's tribe moving. "They're getting a better vantage point," he said quickly. "Tell your men to get into cover and fire. Only one of us is making it out of this alive."

Ishaan called for his men to take cover and then to prepare to work their way up the pathways on the sides. "I see twelve, maybe," he called to Amir. He ducked as an arrow flew past him.

Amir slowly drew buhkar. "Follow me," he said before he evaporated into black mist.

Ishaan did the same, as did Ashar and Vitaly. The four of them moved up the rocky road of the gulch, reaching a large set of boulders to hide behind. They crouched down and prepared to fire. On Amir's count, they shot up and fired their arrows into a small pack of Runers. Their arrows all hit their marks.

"Again," Amir called, drawing buhkar. The four of them moved out, climbing higher until they came almost face to face with Rishvi. Around them, the other Runers continued their battle with one another. Some had come close enough to cross blades, and the valley rang with the clang of the magic metal.

"I cannot kill," Ishaan called over the din as they fought their way toward Rishvi.

"I can," Amir growled, eyeing the man who had just moments ago tried to murder him. He drew his scimitar and pounced on the older Runer.

Behind him, Vitaly, Ashar, and Ishaan kept the other Runers at bay. The rest of Ishaan's tribe occupied the last of Rishvi's tribe. Amir swung his curved blade in an arch overhead and Rishvi knelt to meet it, raising his own blade higher. The metal met and a few colorful sparks flew.

"I should have taken care of the other rats," Rishvi growled, spinning away from Amir's advancement. "I knew they'd find you."

"Your mistake," Amir snapped back, raining blow after blow in quick succession. He drove Rishvi back toward the edge of the pathway.

Rishvi parried a blow and spun, getting behind Amir. Amir sensed the shove coming and quickly drew buhkar. Rishvi's shove passed through him and Amir danced around, away from the edge. Rishvi ran a few steps away, drawing jiun as he did. Amir noted it and knew now that the older Runer would be moving faster and more recklessly.

Amir gave chase, climbing higher after Rishvi.

He lunged and clipped the man's leg. Rishvi grunted, but ran until he came to another precipice. He stopped and turned to face Amir.

"Looks like you have me, Runer," Rishvi said with a careful grin.

Amir hesitated. He'd not killed in so many years. That wasn't who he was anymore. He'd come a long way since he'd been that man.

"Don't kill him!" Ashar pled from below.

Rishvi smirked and chortled. "After I kill you, I'll have my way with that sweet boy of yours and then finish him off. Slowly."

Something in Amir snapped. Before he could stop himself, his arm flew through the air and he cut Rishvi's throat deep, so deep his head lulled backward, exposing his inner throat. The body crumpled right away and fell below. Amir panted, listening until he heard the thud. Amir's mind went numb and his ears rang. Below him, the fighting stopped and voices rose.

Behind him, Ashar came running up. "You didn't have to kill him," he panted, looking disappointed at Amir.

The sad look on Ashar's face crushed Amir's triumphant spirit. He let out a sigh and looked at the white blood on his blade. Perhaps he shouldn't have, but he had. Something in him had made him.

"I'm sorry, Ashar," he said softly. "Sometimes the man I was rises up in me before I can stop it."

Ashar sadly shook his head.

Ishaan came up over the rise, looking pleased. "I saw the body," he said. "Thank you, Runers, for saving us."

Amir shook his blade off before wiping it on a small tuft of grass. He sheathed it and faced Ishaan. "You owe me your lives."

"Indeed," Ishaan agreed. "I understand." He crossed his arms and looked down, contemplating. "You want me and my tribe to help you on Alika?"

"If not you, then I don't know where else I can find Runers." Amir wiped sweat from his brow. "I have to head back soon. I cannot be gone long. It's not just a little malignation like Rishvi thought. The entire map is at stake, Ishaan. Tell your men that."

Ishaan considered the Runer before him. He stared into Amir's eyes for a moment before nodding. "Yes. I will speak with my men. Give us time to put our affairs in order and we will meet you."

"Meet me by the great statue of the maharaja outside Vishna," Amir said. "In two days' time. Come at sunrise."

"And we are getting paid," Ishaan said.

Amir smiled weakly. "Yes. More gold and gems than you've probably ever seen in one place."

Ishaan grinned, showing his sharp, feline teeth. "I like the sound of this. Rid the world of a Necro'Khan. Retire afterward. Maybe hunt household spirits or something." He nodded. "You have a deal. I will bring all I can. I cannot promise many men, but I will bring all who are willing."

"That's all I can ask for," Amir said.

# Chapter 27

## The Malignant Land

Signar tumbled through the portal, the ground farther away than he'd thought. He fell down on to all fours and waited a moment for his head to stop spinning. His horse waited behind him, snorting at something in the darkness he could not see. The animal hopped in place, nervous. It threw its head back and whined.

"Peace," Signar whispered, standing. He grabbed the reins and pulled the horse steady, patting its nose, but the animal's eyes were wide. He looked around. The wind blew around them, chilling him and cutting through his cloak, but he couldn't see far. Looking down, he found the grass beneath his feet was black.

Around him, not only the wind howled. Something moved over the ground, making a heavy slithering sound. Something else moaned. Signar spun on the spot, wondering what danger his horse had picked up. The animal stood stiff, eyes wide. Something slithered close to him.

The horse suddenly whinnied and reared up. It jerked the reins out of Signar's hands. Something shot out of the darkness toward him. He raised his arms to defend against it, but it ran into him, knocking him prone and making him drop his torch. It made a strange cackling sort of moan as it did. His horse whined and bolted into the darkness. Signar didn't have time to call after it before the black thing reappeared. He could hardly see it in the darkness. It towered over him, moving like water but in the shape of a giant. It had white, hallow eyes and clawed hands.

The shadow being lunged at him, clawing him hard across his chest, drawing blood. Signar stumbled backward, retrieving his axe from his back and standing up to face the creature. The thing warbled and vanished into the dark, but he still heard the crackling moan. Panting, he spun, trying to look for movement in the shadows. He stood still for too long. Something cold slithered around his neck from behind. He spun, hacking at it, but his axe only passed through the shadow, not harming it at all.

The touch chilled him, though. It spread from his neck down his shoulders and into his chest. As it crawled up his neck and to his head, his mind began to spin. An unnatural panic creeped into his skull and he began to grow fearful. Knowing the touch was the reason for the unknown fear, he tried to shove against it. He reached out to his wolf and reined it in, calling on its might and power. It worked for a moment, until he felt the touch again, this time at the base of his skull.

Turning, he hacked again, but his axe simply passed through it like the last time. Real fear started to mount in him then until he remembered the sigiled blade. But he didn't have it. It was on his horse. Cursing, Signar ran in the direction the horse had bolted. He heard the thing behind him give chase. The shadow being reached out a long, shadowy arm and pulled when it grabbed a fistful of his long hair. Signar was jerked backward and fell. The thing descended on him. It gripped his neck and bent over, biting him hard with invisible teeth. As it did, the chill and fear lanced through him. He couldn't stop the scream that was forced out of his mouth by the power of the shadow being. It felt like being struck by lightning.

His cries rang out into the dark night. As his body started to go numb, he heard voices. Someone called and a few others answered. Then he heard the pounding of hoofbeats. He counted at least four different horses coming toward him. His blood thickened, cold in his veins.

"Here!" he cried, trying to shove the shadow being off. The monster didn't budge.

Four Runers appeared out of the shadows on the backs of tall horses. One stood up in his stirrups and aimed a long bow. The tip gleamed pale in the dark light. The bolt flew, thudding hard into the back of the shadow being. It reeled back, screaming its crackling moan to the sky. As it let go, Signar rolled out from under it and stood. His entire body quaked from the cold and his mind spun as his blood slowly started to defrost.

Another of the Runers charged the beast and hewed it in half with his long orichalcum blade. The thing vanished in an explosion of black ectoplasm. The other Runers joined him and trotted slowly in a circle around Signar, looking into the shadows.

"The possessed ones are near," one of the Runers said. "We need to move."

"I had a horse," Signar said, touching the bite on his neck.

One of the Runers nodded and clicked his tongue, trotting into the darkness to find it.

"You shouldn't be out in the dark alone," the first Runer said. "Especially without light." He motioned to one of his band, who carried a torch. The Runer came forward and handed it to Signar. "The light keeps them away. Mostly. Where did you come from?"

"I had a torch. I lost it." Signar held himself tall. "I am Signar-Reks, and I am looking for Altevine."

The Runers exchanged glances. "We heard you'd come back last year, but weren't sure. Tage told us."

"How is he?" Signar asked.

"See for yourself," the Runer said. "We'll take you to Altevine. We're close."

As he spoke, the Runer who had run into the darkness to find the horse came back, leading his yellow mare by the reins.

"What's happened here?" Signar asked, taking the proffered reins. "Why is it so dark?"

"Only near Altevine," the Runer said sadly. "Head to Northica and the sun still rises and sets. There is a breach in the God Deep near Altevine that let out the horrors you saw. The other cantons fear it and have forbidden all from coming to Altevine. Any who leave are...

stopped. They think we carry this darkness within us like a plague or a curse."

Signar understood.

"Come," the Runer said, turning his horse. "We will take you to the village."

⌇

Signar held the torch high as they trotted in a direction he could not guess. Without the sun and not being able to see landmarks in the distance, he wasn't sure where they were going. It wasn't until he spotted a warding pole that he realized they must be close.

"To ward against the malignation," the Runer said. "It helps only a little. Tage can tell you what we've done with the breach."

Suddenly, the village came up out of the darkness. The little wooden homes appeared around him in the orange torchlight. The path was suddenly familiar, and he knew exactly where he was.

"Thank you, Runers," he said. "I know where I am now."

The one who had been leading them bowed his head. "Of course, my Reks. We cannot stay. The wilds need us."

Signar nodded. He looked ahead and raised the torch. A strange green light lit up the sky behind the hill where the thronehall was perched. He guessed that was where the rift was. He knew vaguely where it lay, but would need the others to lead him there.

He kicked his horse in the side gently and trotted up the path to the thronehall. As he passed the homes, some inside peeked out to watch him pass. One gasped and whispered his name. He hoped his people understood he hadn't abandoned them. Had he?

Worried now, he dismounted and marched up the stone steps to the thronehall. To his right, piled high, was a length of chain near a wooden pillar. He knew that spot well. Every morning, his mother would shackle him there. Sometimes for days. He knew the stones beneath his feet all too well, having slept on them for most of his life. The memory almost consumed him. He turned away. Inside, he heard voices and braced himself. Taking a deep breath, he shoved the double oaken doors open. Everything inside fell into a sudden hush. He looked in.

A small fire burned in the center of the thronehall. The sides were empty of soldiers and thralls. Only a few men stood inside. Tage, with his one good eye, sat on the throne, and Aras and Dain stood before him. The Volra, Viggo, stood with them.

"Signar?" Tage gasped, standing. The other three turned.

That was when Signar saw Aras wore the black of a Runer and had a set of runes around his neck. "Aye, it's me," he said, coming forward. "I see I may have come too late."

"Altevine is overcome with this malignation," Tage said. He motioned for a thrall behind the throne to fetch food and drink. "But the rest of Caerwren has abandoned us. They fight to keep us within."

"What's been done about the rift?" Signar asked. He climbed the stairs to the dais and stood with the other four.

"We are trying warding stones," Dain said, quickly embracing Signar. "We've made a stone circle around it. Almost. We have a few stones left to erect before the circle is complete."

"And what will that do?" Signar asked Viggo.

The Volra pressed his black lips together in thought before answering. "We are hoping the wards keep the malignation inside. Stop the horrors from coming out. Like a seal. But there is no way of knowing until we try."

Signar nodded and looked at Aras. "What have you done to deserve the runes?"

The big man shook his head. "I did nothing more than that for which I am already guilty. I took the punishment as recompense for what I did in your absence."

"I'm looking out for him," Tage added with a small smile.

Fascinated, Signar nodded. It seemed a good punishment for the evils Aras had committed in the name of Altevine.

"But there's more," Dain said haltingly. "More than the possessed, the shadow creatures, and the monsters that walk the moors now."

"What is it?" Signar asked, sensing his hesitation.

The other three exchanged glances. Signar frowned.

"Your mother," Dain said steadily. "She's escaped through the breach and has been seen walking the moors."

Signar's gut dropped out from under him. "Mother?" he asked, his face going numb. "Are you sure?"

Aras nodded. "Some other Runers and I have seen her. She prowls the moors, howling and hunting. We think she's looking for something, but we're not sure what. She roams the area near the breach. She's slaughtered the Volra and others we have trying to erect the last stone. We cannot contain the darkness from the breech because of her."

"Is she..." Signar wasn't sure how to ask. "Is she alive?"

"A strange green light accompanies her," Aras said. "We've never gotten close enough to try to put a sword through her chest. She's killed dozens."

Signar's mind went blank for a moment. His mother was alive, and looking for him, no doubt. Or was she *alive*? What had the God Deep done to her? Was she a monster now?

*She's always been a monster,* he thought. A sudden cold washed over him, making him shiver. He heard the crack of a whip as the fire snapped and he flinched. He saw the chains that had been his constant companions. His own howls of pain filled his ears as he remembered the beatings from the warriors. He'd tried to run, but the chains on his ankles had held him fast. He'd yowled and wept. Her green eyes had watched, a dark smile playing on her red lips.

His eyes flew open and he looked around. Tzarik always comforted him when the memories became too much.

But Tzarik wasn't here now. No... He was alone.

"Signar-Reks," Viggo said. "What has brought you back in this time of need?"

Signar sighed, shoving aside his darker thoughts. "I am in need of Runers. They are needed in Alika to fight the Necro'Khan who opened this rift."

Tage's blue eye brightened. "I know there are men in the rathskeller right now. I'll fetch them and bring them back here to hear you speak."

He scampered down the dais steps and out the open oaken double doors into the darkness.

"Let me show you something," Viggo said, motioning for Signar to follow him.

Dain and Aras fell into step behind Signar as he followed Viggo out the back door. They walked past the garrison and out onto a rocky cliff that overlooked a part of Altevine below them. From this height, Signar saw it. Out beyond the borders of the village was something that moved and snapped like green lightning. He could also see the stones around the rift. There was one left to be erected. It looked to be several hours' worth of a journey away.

"We've not seen our gods in months," Viggo said seriously. "We are abandoned, Signar-Reks. It is up to us to save ourselves."

"Father wants me to leave," Dain said. "To return to Northica and leave Altevine to its fate."

"Thank you for staying," Signar said. He let the awe and terror of seeing the rift fill him. The thing glowed with an almost evil light. He couldn't see them, but he knew monsters and horrors lurked within the snapping light of the rift. "You didn't have to."

"I promised you I'd look after Altevine," Dain said with a smile. "I'm a man of my word."

As Signar looked out, he scanned the moors for the wolven shape the others had said was out there. Part of him still feared his mother. But another part, a part he could not explain, wanted to see her again. He couldn't spot any details from that distance, but knew she was out there somewhere.

"Signar-Reks!" Tage called from inside. "I have the Runers."

Signar faced the Runers in the hall. About a dozen stood waiting to hear him speak. His mouth went dry, and nerves bunched under his skin. He knew he belonged in the throne he occupied, but that didn't stop the fear of ruling from filling him. He made eye contact with the Runers one at a time before he spoke.

"You have all seen the malignation that is consuming our canton," he said as stoutly as he could. "I know we have lost much to its dark touch. But there is a way to stop it."

The Runers shifted on their feet, arching brows and frowning in curiosity.

Signar drew himself up, hands on the arms of the wolven throne. "In Alika sits a Necro'Khan, the one responsible for this darkness. He moves even now to bring more of this curse to the entire map. We have learned that it is Runers and your white blood that can stand up to him. So I ask you to please rise with me, declare war on this death fiend, and follow me to Alika where we will put a stop to this once and for all. Let us spill the black blood of the one who has cursed our land, who has taken the lives of the innocent. Come with me and avenge Altevine."

One Runer stepped forward, his face creased in determination. "You are our Reks," he began. "And you could command us to fight for you."

"I ask you," Signar said, his own face stony and serious. "I do not want to be the Reks who dictates to his subjects. I implore you to come with me and fight."

"And the rift?" another Runer asked. "Who will defend Altevine if we are all on Alika?"

Signar looked to Dain. The prince of Northica shook his head. Signar understood. Skarde-Reks wouldn't risk his people for Altevine. They fought to keep his people inside the black curse and he'd not send his own men, even Runers, into it.

"We are alone in this," Tage said. "The other cantons even attack our people on the road, afraid they will bring the malignation to them."

Signar's heart fell. He'd hoped his promise of blood would appeal to his people. The Runer was right though: he could force them to go. He was Reks, after all. He took a deep breath. No. He'd not be that kind of ruler. He was not his mother.

"I admire your desire to protect Altevine," he said at length. "I would never ask that we leave it vulnerable. But I do ask that you consider my words. Hear me. Will you fight with me on Alika?"

The Runer who spoke first frowned in thought. "You ask, we will consider."

Signar nodded, dismissing the Runers. They filed out slowly, murmuring amongst themselves.

Dain said softly, "I admire you, Signar. You could have ordered them to follow you."

A heavy weight settled in Signar's chest. "No, I couldn't. I will not make anyone do anything against their will."

"I disagree," the prince said. "You could force them. But you are choosing not to. That is strength, Signar-Reks."

"And if my so-called strength ruins us all?"

Dain clasped Signar's shoulder in his hand firmly. "You won't allow it. I trust you."

⬥

That night, Signar lay on his back in his mother's old room, the room where the Reks was to sleep. He stared up at the ceiling, wondering if the Runers he had spoken to had heard his plea. They'd promised to think on it, but something in their eyes told Signar they would refuse him. No man from Caerwren wanted to go to a foreign land to die, let alone a Runer. And they were right; someone had to defend Altevine. He understood that.

Signar rolled over and looked out the window. The sky was black and streaked with green. No stars showed. He thought about the shadow being he'd met and then about his mother. His arm wrapped around his middle and his fingers found the scars on his back. The scars were fresh from the beating he'd endured from Tarkan, but beneath those scars were older ones. Ones Sjörna had given him. He couldn't remember his first flogging by her hand, or the last. He'd never known at the time what he'd done wrong to deserve such a punishment. Perhaps nothing. Perhaps she'd simply taken her rage out on him.

He remembered a cruel muzzle she'd forced on his face once when he was in his wolf form. The thing had scratched and made him bleed.

At the time, he couldn't transform back. He didn't know how. So he'd howled and yelped as the thralls beat him.

Signar jumped, almost hearing the sounds clearly. His scars burned at the memories. He stood, shaking off the shiver that ran up his spine, and took up the sigiled blade and his axe and marched out into the night for some air. A few warriors and others traipsed back and forth in the circles of orange firelight, hurrying from one blessed torch to another. Signar avoided them and slinked out the back of the village, heading for the rift. He couldn't sleep, anyway.

He took a torch with him and started on the path in the grass that showed where the workers and no doubt the Volra had walked back and forth to the rift. He kept his eye on it as he drew closer. He looked around, hoping none of the shadows and monsters attacked him. If they did, this time, he was ready. He walked with the sigiled blade out and gripped tightly in his hand.

It took hours for him to reach the rift, galloping on his horse. When he did, he saw the massive stones covered in warding signs around the opening. The thing crackled and popped, spitting out what looked like green ectoplasm. The rift zigzagged up from the ground, towering over him. Every once in a while, he caught a glimpse beyond into the Deep. He dared not cross the line of the stones and get closer. The wards on the stones glowed blue in the darkness.

He turned from the rift and looked out into the moors around them. The marshy lands spanned miles before reaching toward the north and the mountains. He couldn't see the mountain of Northica from there, but knew it lay waiting in that direction. Slowly, Signar started a march around the perimeter of the stones. He wandered farther away, eyes scouring the land, looking for his mother.

He didn't have to wait long. He froze suddenly, catching a glimpse of something green and glowing in the distance. At first he couldn't make out the shape, but as it drew nearer, he saw the shape of a great wolf. The monster stood as tall as a horse and was thick with muscle. It prowled the earth, nose to the ground. He waited, wondering if it was her or perhaps some specter. The urge to call out to her rose in him, but he swallowed it back down.

Then the wolf stopped. Its head rose in a snap and it sniffed at the air.

She'd found his scent.

He remained where he stood, waiting.

The wolf put its nose to the earth again and started to trot in his direction. She would spot him soon.

And she did. The wolf froze and looked up. The black eyes honed in on him and he swore he saw it smile. In a flash, the wolf vanished and the tall, imposing form of Sjörna-Reks appeared. Her hair, washed out to a green by the magic of the God Deep, swirled around her face in a slow wind none but she could feel. Her skin was pale and glowed green, and her eyes were pure black.

Signar looked at her hands and remembered the pain they had brought him. His nightmares came back to him, filling his mind with terror and his heart with fear. He wanted to run. He used to run to Tzarik in the night when the horrors overtook him.

But he couldn't now. He was alone on the moors in the dark.

"My son?" she asked softly. She began a slow saunter toward him. "Signar? Is that you?" She held a hand out to him.

As she did, Signar put one foot behind himself, preparing to attack. He drew the sigiled blade. "Stay back," he warned her. "I saw you enter the Deep, body and soul. What part of you has come back to the material plane? What revenge warps your mind?"

Sjörna stopped, eyes wide, and her lips parted. "You speak." Her eyes went to the axe on his back. "And I see Raudnir has blessed you. What fortune is this? Please, my son, do not draw your blade against me."

A part of Signar's defenses dropped. He eased his stance and faced her. "You shouldn't be here. You shouldn't have come back. They say you've killed Volra who are trying to stop the malignation."

Sjörna laughed. She held her hand out to the side and summoned her own axe from within the God Deep. "The monsters do not bother me. I could come back. Rule Altevine as the malignant Reks. Can you see it now, my son?" She held her arms out to her sides as if praising the sky. "The Deep has blessed me. I can pass through. I will find your father and bring him back. I will guide a host of shadows to Altevine and take it back. And you." She smiled at him, her black eyes boring into him. "You can rule at my side. No more shackles. No more beatings."

Signar swallowed a sob that suddenly rose in his throat. "Why?" he asked, trying to keep his voice even. "Why did you do those things to me? What had I done?"

Sjörna dropped her arms, and with it, her smile. She glared at Signar. "You were my shame. A reminder of my lust, my power, and the fear I put into your father. I wanted to be conquered, but that was not his nature. So I conquered him. You remind me of him. My prophesied love. A gift from the gods. But not you. You were a curse."

Signar's heart broke. His eyes burned with unshed tears as he listened. Why did it hurt? He didn't love her and she didn't love him. But she should have.

"I don't need your love anymore!" he shouted at her. "I have others who love me. And what you've done is vile. You will not take Altevine, and I will stop the malignation."

Sjörna pursed her lips and clicked her tongue, shaking her head. "No, my son. You are simply in the way."

Before he could react, Sjörna leapt at him. Mid-leap, she transformed into a wolf and clamped her jaws down onto his arm. Signar screamed as her teeth tore into his flesh, making his blood flow. She jerked her head, tossing him to the earth.

"Have you mastered your wolf?" she asked with a sneer. "Or are you just a boy?"

Signar rolled over. With a growl, he transformed into his wolven form and faced her. She looked impressed. Then she leapt again. Their jaws met, teeth tangling together and claws swiping at their muzzles. They parted and circled one another before lurching forward once again. Sjörna bit his shoulder hard and drew blood, but he latched onto her throat and ripped her flesh. She yelped and galloped away to put space between them. She transformed back into her human form and took up her axe.

Signar transformed as well and held his hand out, summoning his axe to his palm. It thudded hard into his hand as he watched his mother walk a wide circle around him.

"Don't make me kill you," she whispered. "You are my son."

Signar snarled like a wolf. "I'm not your son. I am your shame." He raised his axe and charged her.

Sjörna smirked and raised her blade, blocking his blow. She shoved him hard and hooked her long leg behind his, tripping him. Signar hit the moist ground hard and had all the wind knocked out of him. He coughed just as Sjörna brought the haft of her axe down onto his throat, choking him. She pushed down hard and Signar gasped. He flailed his legs in a panic and shoved against the wood, but Sjörna didn't budge. He looked up into her smiling face as he fought for air.

"Oh, my boy," she cooed. "You could never overtake me."

The weight of Tzarik's runes around his neck drew his attention away from his suffocation. The stones were cold against his neck. He couldn't use them, but they reminded him of Tzarik. Of all he'd done for him. The Runer had been brave, strong, and patient. Signar owed him his life.

"I won't die here," he growled. He pushed up on the haft of the axe with all his might, his wolf howling inside him. Sjörna gasped and fell backward. Signar advanced on her quickly and kicked her axe out of her hand, then landed a hard kick to her jaw. She grunted and fell to the ground.

Before he could lift his own axe to stop her for good, she leapt up as a wolf and snapped at his throat. Signar quickly raised his hands and blocked her maw with his axe. He flipped her over his shoulder, using her own momentum against her. She splashed into the bog and rolled back, transforming into her human form. She snarled and summoned her axe to her.

Signar did the same, unsheathing the sigiled blade.

"Do not fight me with that foreign metal," Sjörna barked. "Use the gift of our god or surrender now."

Signar didn't wait. He charged at his mother again, his shoulder aching and blood spattering over his face. Sjörna gasped and ducked, rolling to avoid the slash. She swung her axe behind her and nicked his chest with the blade. Then she spun back around and charged, axe held high. Signar feinted to the left and brought the sigiled blade up hard. He felt it hit his target. The blade lodged itself in her gut and slashed with the momentum of both bodies. Black blood rained down on him.

Sjörna cried out and doubled over, falling when she landed. Her hands wrapped around her middle and she didn't move. Signar panted, gathering his wits as he watched her prone form. She still didn't move.

Carefully, he approached her, turning her over with his foot. Her black eyes were wild and her mouth gaped open, gasping for air.

"Can't...kill me," she sputtered.

Signar didn't reply. He turned the sigiled blade, point facing down, and pressed it to her chest. Tears fell from his eyes. "Mother," he whispered.

Sjörna sneered weakly. "Should have...killed you when I had the chance."

Shoving his emotion aside, he pressed down on the blade. The sigils along the red blade ignited green as he did. They blazed brightly for only a moment, then went dim again. As they did, the blackness left Sjörna's eyes and they turned pure white. Her hair turned red once again and the color came back to her flesh.

She was gone.

Signar pulled the blade out and sobbed softly. He fell to his knees by his mother's corpse and touched her hair. He hadn't wanted to kill her, but she was no longer his mother.

Perhaps she never had been.

# Chapter 28
## Northern Allies

Signar returned to the thronehall just as the sun should have been rising. The fires were lit and a horde of Runers packed the space by the time he arrived back. When Dain caught sight of him, he ran to him.

"What happened?" he gasped, taking Signar in his arms to help support him. The exhaustion and being deprived of sleep made his legs weak.

"I...took care of my mother," he managed to say.

Dain didn't reply, but helped him to a table. He called for a Volra healer and for food to be brought. Tage rushed to Signar and immediately asked what had happened, taking his mauled arm in his hand and drawing the healing rune over it. Signar had seen this before. The runes had very little effect on Vaeson bites, and the same went for him. His flesh knitted together, but only a little. The Volra had to do the rest, cleaning and binding the wound.

"What were you thinking?" Dain asked softly so the others in the hall wouldn't hear him.

"I was thinking of Altevine," Signar replied. "It had to be done."

He didn't look Dain in the face, instead looking out at the small crowd of Runers that filled the hall. There were maybe twelve of them.

"Is this all?" Signar asked.

Tage nodded. "And they've come to refuse you. They won't sail to Al'Myrah and fight, they said."

"That's right," one of the Runers called. The hall fell quiet then. The Runer stepped forward. "I am sorry, my Reks, but we will not risk our lives for a foreign land. We will not leave Altevine while the rift is open. If we leave, there will be no one here to protect your canton."

Signar didn't stand, still too tired. "I understand," he sighed. "And you are right: someone must protect our people from the monsters and spirits that are emerging from the rift."

He looked at Dain. "What about your father? Would he give us men, a fleet?"

Dain's face looked strained for a moment. "As I said, I doubt it. You know how he is. I am here in defiance of his orders."

"That may be our only option," Signar said. He didn't know the other cantons well. The War Path was weak from his mother's actions, and Skarde was the only one who might heed his call, let alone grant him an audience. "Dain," he said after a moment of contemplation, "the world will end if he does not hear us. It is more than Altevine that will succumb to the malignation if we do not stand up to the Necro'Khan."

Dain's face fell then, and a dark look clouded his blue eyes. Signar saw the realization hit him then. "He must listen to us, then. I will make him hear your request. Once he understands your own people must protect the canton from the rift and hears what is at stake, he will heed your plea."

"Don't travel alone," Tage said. "Let Aras and me go with you."

"I want more than just the four of us," Signar said. "I want Skarde to see Altevine is not afraid. We will take a host of warriors with us and travel over the lands to Northica as a small army."

Dain nodded. "He will be glad to see the strength of Altevine. It will be good to tell him you vanquished your mother as well. He will see that as a good thing and it will show your fortitude."

Signar stood, holding onto the table for support. He faced the Runers in the hall once more. "You will protect Altevine in my absence. Save our people from the malignation as long as you can. I will do my part and gather allies from Northica and we will go to Alika and crush the Necro'Khan."

The Runer bowed to Signar. "We will. You can trust us to protect our land."

Signar nodded to Dain. "Help me gather some warriors. We leave in an hour."

જજ

A little more than an hour later, Signar stood outside his thronehall with a host of warriors, Dain, Aras, and Tage. He turned and faced the north, looking into the darkness. He prayed for a safe journey, free of the horrors that lurked in its depths. Aras and Tage took the lead with him on their horses. The entire host carried torches that granted them sufficient light.

"Once we pass outside the canton, the light will be on us," Dain said. "We should try to make it out of the darkness before we make camp."

Signar nodded and led his host on. The march out of Altevine seemed to take a lifetime. Every sound made Signar jump; every moving shadow made his flesh crawl. The moaning in the darkness kept him on edge. Dain told him about how some spirits possessed wanderers and turned them into mindless thralls that attacked like wild animals. Aras and Tage had stories of fighting shadow beings and even the spirits of deceased monsters.

"It sucks the life out of the plants as well," Tage added, pointing at the black grass. "Everything is dying or fading."

Signar had noticed the grass when he'd first come through the portal. He wondered how much time his canton had left before it was utterly overrun.

Soon they came upon a warding pole. The thing was made out of animal hide, rocks inscribes with warding runes, and other trinkets of protection made of bone and feathers.

"These surround Altevine now," Dain explained. "Others put them up, trying to keep the malignation inside the canton. Once we pass them, the light should start to rise."

And he was right. They passed the warding poles and traveled on. As they did, the darkness began to drift away and an orange light from the setting sun filled the sky. They marched on for some time when suddenly they broke through the darkness and the sun nearly blinded Signar. He turned back to look and saw the blackness hovering like a mist over his home. He even spotted a green dot, flickering. The rift.

"Is it spreading?" he asked.

"Yes," Tage answered. "Despite the warding poles, it spreads. The Empty has no protection, and it spreads more quickly to the west. Soon it will reach Rom."

With this knowledge, they continued their march until the sun set. They set up camp and had an uneventful night, for which Signar was grateful. The next morning, they continued on until the white mountain of Northica came into view through the thick clouds of snow and rain that shrouded it.

"Not long now," Dain said, smiling up at his mountain. "It's been some time since I've visited Father."

Signar glanced sideways at Dain as they trotted on. "Thank you for staying with Altevine. It's not your home, and I owe you for guarding it with your life in my absence."

Dain smiled proudly. "We are war brothers, Signar. Comrades in the War Path. Of course I'd do anything you need."

"You were also kind to me," Signar said. "When I was a captive of Northica. You didn't beat me, starve me. You fed me and gave me water. You spoke kindly to me. Called me Skelmir. You treated me like a man."

"Signar." Dain's face turned serious as he met his eyes. "You do not owe me anything for not abusing you. I saw something in you in those days. I knew you had the potential to be Reks, if only someone would give you the chance."

A lump formed in Signar's throat. "Tzarik gave me that chance."

At the mention of the Runer, Dain grinned wildly. "How is the old Runer? I admired him greatly. He stood up to Father when even I wouldn't have. And he saved my life."

Signar swallowed the pain. "He's gone," he said shortly. "Died on Xia."

Dain faced Signar, his face twisted in sympathy. "I am sorry to hear that. He was a good man, Signar."

Signar nodded. He felt compelled to tell Dain about how Tzarik had trained him. Taught him. So he did. Speaking about Tzarik somehow made him hurt and feel relief at the same time. The more he spoke about what Tzarik had done, the more he smiled. The entire journey to Northica, Signar told Dain about the last year of his life. How they had traveled, the business with the sorcerer and Necro'Khan —everything. Dain's face turned serious the longer Signar spoke.

"I am glad you told me," Dain said. "Now that I know, I can help you sway my father. I hope he sees sense."

The last leg of the journey took place in mostly silence. The journey up the mountain in the thunderstorms and rain made Signar nervous, but Dain promised them the lightning wouldn't hit them.

"Strigganoct is simply pleased I have returned home," he said with a pompous grin.

Signar doubted that, but didn't argue with Dain. They traversed the mountain, taking the well-warn paths until they reached the bridge that spanned the river. The bridge was one of the few ways in and out of the city. They crossed it easily with Dain taking the lead and soon came to the city. The small wooden homes and rathskellers looked only slightly familiar to Signar. He remembered little of his time in Northica, and didn't like most of the memories. He'd spent most of it inside a cage made from the swords of his mother's warriors. The Northican warriors had poked at him with sticks and spears until he'd bled. That was when Dain had come and stopped them.

They journeyed up through the city and soon the great thronehall of Skarde-Reks came into view. Signar looked up into it, the sun setting behind them, splashing its red light over the facade of the hall. As they neared it, the doors opened and Skarde himself came out, arms crossed and a big smile on his face behind his yellow beard.

"My son!" he called down, raising his arms. "The gods have blessed me this day for certain. You have seen sense and come home. And who is this man who rides at your side?"

Skarde clearly didn't recognize him. His eyes squinted and his brow furrowed. Then his eyes went wide.

"Not the wildling," he breathed. "Is this Signar Wolf-tor, son of the red wolf, Reks of Altevine?"

Signar pulled up on his horse's reins and looked up at Skarde now that they were at the base of the stone steps leading up to the throne-hall. "Aye," he said as strongly as he could. "It is I. I have come to speak with you about a matter most urgent."

Skarde's face never lost its look of amazement and shock. "Yes. Of course, Reks. Come in, have a drink." He turned and entered his thronehall, shouting orders the moment he crossed through the double doors.

Signar found himself pleased at Skarde's reaction. Knowing that the big Reks was amazed at what he'd witnessed brought a certain power to Signar that he enjoyed.

"Father doubted you," Dain informed him as they climbed the steps. "He thought the wildling in you would persevere and that you would never amount to anything, let alone Reks of Altevine. He doubted Tzarik's determination."

"I am glad to have shocked him," Signar confessed as they crossed the threshold into Skarde's hall.

A huge fire blazed in the center and many thralls moved about, quickly making space at a long table on the right-hand side. Skarde walked to one side and gestured Signar over. "Come, my child. Sit beside me. We shall drink and feast in your honor, and in celebration of my son's return."

"It has only been a fortmonth since I've seen you," Dain said, sitting on Skarde's left.

"It has been too long," the big Reks replied, pouring a drink for Signar and sliding it over to him. "I did forbid you from entering Altevine, but you went anyway. Too much of your mother in you. I am glad you are home."

Signar sat and took the tankard. He sniffed it, remembering the drink Tzarik had once tried to get him to imbibe. He hadn't liked it then, and this one smelled all the worse. It seemed a lifetime ago now. He held the tankard but did not drink.

Skarde waited until each of them had a portion of meat and drink before he spoke to Signar. "I must admit, I never thought I'd sit across from Signar-Reks," he confessed.

With Skarde's eyes on him, Signar held himself higher and raised his chin just enough to almost look down his nose. He squared up his shoulders. "I never thought I'd see these halls outside the bars of a cage," he replied. "I am happy to do so now."

Skarde's face fell a little. "You were a wildling. Dangerous."

At these words, something happened in Signar's head. His thoughts split in two. He wanted to roar at Skarde, recount his suffering and make Skarde grovel for forgiveness. But the other side of his mind told him to let it go. It was the past, and Skarde had made his choices for his canton. The two sides battled inside Signar for some time before he chose one.

"My mother attacked you," he said as evenly as he could. He felt Dain holding his breath beside him. "You did what you thought best for your canton. And in the end, you let Tzarik take me."

Skarde looked around. "Where is the Runer? I expected him to be here to gloat."

Signar almost took a drink then, but stopped when the smell stung his nose. "He's no longer among us. We made a pyre for him on Al'Myrah."

"Oh, lad," Skarde said, his chest falling. "I am sorry. He was a brave man." Skarde raised his glass, said a quick prayer, and drank. "To the Runer. May his soul find its way to Rahrgalah. Or to whatever afterlife he put his faith in."

Signar nodded in thanks. He didn't want to drag up the past any more than he had to. And speaking about Tzarik would bring tears to his eyes. "I have come for a reason, Skarde," he said, quickly changing the subject. "I need your men."

He spared no details in recounting the situation for Skarde. Dain chimed in now and then, bringing up a piece of information he thought his father might want to know and also doing his best to sway Skarde in their favor. Skarde listened with a deeply furrowed brow and his hand went limp on his tankard. He didn't so much as nod as he listened, going almost perfectly still.

"I see," he said at length. "And all this began on our shores with that mad red Reks." He took a deep breath and let it out slowly, still thinking. "I see no reason to not gather as many warriors as I can and send them with you."

"We need Runers," Signar said.

Skarde-Reks shook his head. "I will not send Runers from my shores when a portal to the God Deep is open mere miles away. But you may have my army and my fleet. But I cannot do it without asking for something in return."

Signar planted one elbow on the table. "I expected nothing less. What can I do for the Reks of the mountain?"

A twinkle came back to Skarde's eyes as he looked at Signar. "I have a valiant war chief, one of my best. His name is Magnus. His daughter Ragna has been captured by a tribe of Vilderkin who wish to sacrifice her to their bear god, Roth."

Signar sat back. "And you want me to find her and bring her back?"

Skarde smiled. "Sharp lad. Aye, we want her home safe. Magnus was going to leave in the morning to hunt her down himself, but I'd rather not risk my greatest war chief. And I am eager to test your mettle."

At this, Signar glared at Skarde. He didn't need to prove anything to the Reks. He was the ruler of Altevine, and should have been treated with the same respect he had tried to show, but Skarde still saw him as a boy. A child. A wildling.

"I will go with him," Dain said quickly.

Before Skarde could interject, Signar said, "I accept. I have a small host with me as it is. Surely we can stand up to a pack of Vilderkin. Tell us where they are, and we will ride out at first light."

Skarde looked between his son and Signar. "Of course I cannot stop you, Dain. But Signar..."

Without any hesitation, Signar met Skarde's gaze.

"Should my son perish, I will hold you accountable."

Signar steeled himself and downed the contents of the tankard. His stomach rebelled against him, but he kept it down. He slammed the tankard down in the tradition of his people and nodded to Skarde. "I will protect Dain with my life, as he did me."

# Chapter 29
## On Rivers of Blood

The next morning, Signar rose early. The mountain air was cold and almost uninviting, unlike the warm, honey-scented air of Al'Myrah he'd grown accustomed to. The clouds had already rolled in and the sky was gray. After so long on Al'Myrah, he thought perhaps he missed the dry air, the sand, and the constant warmth.

Signar roused his host and met Tage and Dain on the outskirts of the city. They mounted their horses and departed just as the sun rose behind the gray clouds. Signar followed Skarde's directions north and down the mountain. Supposedly, the Vilderkin of Roth were roaming the marshland at the base of the mountain in the northwestern area of Northica. It didn't take long to find their destructive tracks. The Vilderkin were violent, lawless tribes, and didn't care for the land they inhabited. Signar found a place where they had made camp and had left behind carcasses of deer they'd hunted, scorch marks from fires they hadn't put out, and an area where the muddy land was torn up from their beasts fighting one another.

"This had to be last night," Dain said, inspecting some tracks. "We're closer than we thought. There's a river to the west of here. They may have gone that way to follow it to a place of sacrifice."

"Is there such a place this far north?" Signar asked.

"Aye," Dain said. "An old place. Used long ago by tribes before we settled down and built our cities. The Vilderkin still use it as a place of sacrifice. There are burrows in the hills there that are like caves the Volra would use to prepare sacrifices, washing them in the river before being burned or slaughtered on a stone table there."

Signar looked ahead at the tracks. They did head west. "We have to hurry, then. They're most likely going to sacrifice her this morning."

Kicking his horse, he spurred it on and galloped into the marshland. Mud splattered up all over him from his horse's hooves. It was cold and stuck to him, but he didn't care. They rode on in this manner until Signar smelled fire. He held his hand up and stopped, signaling the others to do the same. He turned his face up to the sky and sniffed again.

"Fire," he said softly. "Off the horses. We walk from here."

As he climbed down, he inhaled the air again to make sure he didn't smell the scent of human flesh burning as well. He didn't catch the smell and his spirit rested a little.

Crouching, he pulled his axe from his back and ran through the tall marshland grass. Thunder rolled and rain began to fall as Signar and his host sneaked toward the place of sacrifice. The closer they drew, the more he heard and smelled. He stopped a moment to take in the scents: wet horses, fire, sweat, and something like the jasmine that grew over the rocks in Northica.

Curious, he honed his eyes, looking through the grass. Then he spotted them: a circle of totems enshrined a large flat stone in the center. Fire burned atop the totems. He spotted another glow of fire in a deep, cave-like burrow in the hill behind the place of sacrifice. He also heard the river that would be just beyond. Having taken in all that, he slowly slinked closer, signaling his men to follow him and spread out.

They drew nearer and could see the horde now. There were perhaps fifteen Vilderkin and two Volra that he could see. Their horses and other mounts were a good distance away. The Vilderkin were waiting as one Volra started to chant a prayer to the sky. He wore a bearskin over his white leather and his lips were painted black. One of the Volra departed and vanished over a small hill toward the river.

"He's going to fetch her," Dain whispered to Signar. "We should move now."

Signar nodded. He gripped his axe hard and ran. He made no war cry, wanting to take them by surprise. When he stood up to run, the rest of his small host joined him, Tage and Dain at his side. Signar ran and thought they would have heard them by now, but the Vilderkin didn't turn. He got close and heaved his axe up. When he ran two more paces, he brought it down into the skull of the nearest Vilderkin, killing him instantly. This brought the attention of the others to him.

Sudden cries and shouts erupted. Lightning struck the ground and the rain began to pour. Signar heaved his axe, taking down another easily with the element of surprise. But that only lasted a minute. The Vilderkin were wild and fearsome. Merciless. They retaliated hard, slaughtering several of Signar's men in an instant. Seeing this, the young Reks cleared a quick path to the river and ran, looking for Ragna.

He galloped over to the Volra that had been chanting and seized his throat, squeezing hard. "The girl. Where is she?" he growled, his wolven fangs appearing in his rage.

The Volra cowered before him, sputtering. "Th-the river!" he managed to say. "Being washed for the ritual."

Signar threw the Volra, heaving him several feet away. Then he turned, cutting through one more man before seeing two forms in the river and one on the bank. Signar ran toward them.

In the river stood the second Volra. He was attacking a young woman, trying to rip the last of her clothes from her body. The woman had long brown hair and gray eyes as fierce as the mountain peaks during a thunderstorm. She shouted and pulled, fighting against the Volra. The man stood by, watching and laughing. The woman had to be Ragna. Signar had expected a younger girl, but this one looked to be about his age, if not a little older. She screamed for help, fighting against the priest.

Signar leapt up from his hiding place and advanced on the Vilderkin standing guard. The man heard his leap and turned, unsheathing a long, straight blade. He lifted it, stopping Signar's attack with a clang of metal.

Ragna looked up upon hearing the fight. "Help me!" she cried as the Volra grappled her and held a knife to her throat.

In the second Signar took to look at Ragna, the Vilderkin got the upper hand. He shoved his shoulder into Signar, hitting him hard. Signar slipped on the mud and splashed into the marshes. The bigger man fell on top of him, grabbing handfuls of his long hair. He flipped Signar over onto his belly and shoved his face into the marsh water.

Panic immediately shot through Signar's limbs as the air vanished. He tried to push against the ground, but his hands merely sank into the mud. He kicked and fought before he could control his mind. Then he stopped fighting and concentrated.

With a roar, he transformed into his wolf and bucked the man off. He heard the Vilderkin scream and this thrilled him, shooting more savage pride through his limbs. He turned and snapped at the man, just missing him. Then he glanced quickly into the river and saw the Volra had wrestled Ragna to the ground and was attempting to stab her through the heart with his small blade. He had little time.

Spinning back to face the Vilderkin, he raised his hackles and snarled. The man's face showed pure fear. He clearly wasn't one of the Vilderkin, who still had their wild shape. The man looked around for his sword. Signar spotted it behind him. He leapt at the man, clamping his jaws around his throat, and ripped. He threw his head back and forth until he heard the man's neck snap. Disgusted at the taste of blood in his mouth, he dropped the man and turned back to face the river.

Ragna stood upright, panting and soaking wet, her clothes hanging off her shoulders. She clutched the knife in her hand and the Volra lay dead at her feet. Blood rushed out from the priest's neck, turning the river blood red. Signar froze, staring at her.

Raudnir's prophecy came back to him. The god had said that the one he was to mate would come to him in such a fashion. *She will come on rivers of blood.*

He took her in then, admiring her strength. She shook, but her teeth were clenched in determination. Signar walked toward her, holding his hand out.

Ragna threw the blade away with a grunt and took his hand. "Thank you," she said, her voice trembling. "I wasn't sure what to do."

"It seems you did," Signar said, admiring the corpse of the Volra. He stared at her and realized she was almost naked. He reached down and pulled the Volra's cloak off, draping it over her shoulders.

Ragna smiled as Signar came close, looking into his eyes. "Thank you," she said again. "Who are you?"

Signar took her hand and helped her out of the shallow river. "I am Signar-Reks of Altevine. Your father sent me to fetch you."

Ragna looked up at him, confused. "Signar-Reks? The son of the red wolf? They told me you were a wildling."

"I am," he replied proudly. "I merely control my wild side. It is a constant battle. I have to be alert at all times, but I can do it. Someone taught me how to take charge of my wolf and call upon it when I need to."

"They say you were born a wolf," Ragna went on. "That you were wild and untamed. But here you are." She smiled and then threw her arms around his neck. She suddenly gasped, letting out a light sob. "They were going to kill me. You saved me."

Signar awkwardly patted her on the back before she let go. "We need to get you home," he said. "It's cold, and the rain doesn't look like it's going to stop."

On the way back, Ragna held on tight to Signar's middle. They had to share his horse since they hadn't brought a second for her. He liked the feeling of her soft arms around him, and his mind raced with the thought of Raudnir's prophecy. Was this her? Should he speak to Magnus? He wasn't sure what to do. And he was even less sure what to do if Magnus did agree to let him take his daughter as his Reks. His stomach suddenly knotted up and his heart raced. He wished in that moment that he could ask Tzarik what to do and the sorrow washed over him afresh.

They soon came upon the city. People ran out to greet them, and one ran up the city's main pathway to the thronehall to alert Magnus and Skarde. The war chief and the Reks stood at the top of the stone steps when they approached. Skarde beamed down at Signar and Dain, and Magnus ran down the steps to greet his daughter.

Signar gripped Ragna's wrist and helped her off the horse. She ran to her father, leaping into his great arms and hugging him tightly. They exchanged whispered words and showered one another in kisses and a tight embrace. Signar watched and a little joy lighted in his heart at the scene. Skarde approached him as he dismounted.

"Well done, Signar-Reks," he said. "We shall have a celebration in your honor and for the safe return of Ragna."

"And your promise?" Signar asked as Skarde led him into the thronehall. "Will you give me as many warriors as you can spare?"

"I have sent missives far and wide," he said earnestly. "And I have commanded all within my realm to heed the call. Give it a few days and we shall see what we can muster for you."

"Thank you," Signar said, taking the mead Skarde handed him.

The thronehall soon filled with minstrels, thralls cooking dripping meat over the open fire, and many citizens from the city dancing and celebrating the return of Ragna. Signar watched the thronehall fill quickly and was once again in awe of how fast the people of Caerwren could throw together a celebration. Several other war chiefs came by and praised Signar. They spoke about their own daughters and dropped hints that they'd be pleased to give them up to him, should he be looking for a wife.

But the chatter and music soon became too much for him. The bodies pressed in and his mind began to spin. His wolf inside howled at the madness and wanted to emerge. Signar pushed it down as he felt the wildling rising within him. His body tingled as the transformation urged him to let go.

"I'm sorry," Signar said to whoever had been speaking to him. He pushed past them and made his way to the door, focusing on it. He could step outside into the darkness of the night and find a moment of peace before the wolf raged out of him.

"Signar-Reks!" Magnus's booming voice called. "There you are."

A great arm snaked through the crowd and gripped Signar's shoulder, pulling him back. Magnus then threw his arm around Signar's neck, smiling broadly.

"Please," Signar whispered, "I must step outside. Just for a moment."

"Nonsense," Magnus shouted over the din. "The celebration is in here. And I have been wanting to speak some words with you."

His mind still spinning, Signar couldn't hear Magnus's words over the howling in his head. The close quarters drove a shiver down his spine; the wolf thought he was in danger because Signar was afraid of the crowd.

The noise. He had to calm his mind. He wasn't in any danger.

Forcing himself to look up into Magnus's gray eyes, he said, "What can I do for you, war chief?" Getting the words out steadily took all his strength. His heart still raced.

Magnus steered Signar to a table and planted him down on a bench, handing him another tankard of mead. This time, without hesitation, Signar downed the beverage. It warmed his chest and made his head light. A sort of bravery suddenly flooded his limbs. The wolf was drowning. A little more calm, Signar met Magnus's eyes.

"Ragna is pleased with you," Magnus started. "She has never spoken highly of a man before. She is strong-willed and stubborn." He eyed Signar. "How many summers are you, boy?"

Signar thought, counting back from when Tzarik had rescued him. "Eighteen summers, I believe. I lost much of my time in my mother's captivity."

"Of course." Magnus nodded, his brow bending in sympathy. "I wouldn't give my little warrior to just any man, however. But you have proven yourself a strong man and a loyal Reks to Altevine. A good man, I hear. Not one man here speaks badly of you. And Skarde, well, he admires you greatly."

Signar looked up at this. "Does he?" He glanced at where Skarde-Reks was regaling a pack of young girls with his war stories. He supposed there was some respect in the fact that Skarde had wanted to keep him chained and shackled like an animal. Maybe Skarde had been worried he would have come into his own mind sooner or later and taken Altevine back from him.

"Yes," Magnus said. "And I do as well. Which is why I offer you Ragna's hand in marriage. Take my daughter as your Reks, as your mate, and let her rule beside you."

As the strange fear mounted in him, Signar took another drink. He didn't know anything about marriage. His hand shook, so he placed the tankard down.

"This would be a great bond for the War Path," Magnus went on, "binding Northica and Altevine in marriage once more."

"A strong bond for you," Signar said boldly to hide his fear. "I am Reks of Altevine. I would elevate you and your daughter to the greatest status."

Magnus looked away, slightly ashamed. "Yes, that is true," he mumbled.

Signar looked across the room. He almost jumped when he spotted Ragna looking directly at him. She gave him a slight smile and her stormy gray eyes sparkled. She blushed a little and hung her head, biting her lip as a smile overcame her.

Signar didn't know how to say no. He also didn't know what to do if he said yes. But that seemed far less important. He needed Northica, and he needed allies beyond his and Dain's friendship. Marriage was a strong bond to the people of Caerwren. Tribe, even across cantons, was everything.

And he'd made a promise to Raudnir. The prophecy was vivid, and the rivers had indeed run red with blood.

His heart shaking in his chest, Signar squared up to Magnus. "I understand what this means for our cantons," he said. "But is this what Ragna wants?"

At this, Magnus laughed. "I am here at her behest, Reks. She was ready to take you to a private room already, but there is a way these things are done."

Signar's face burned hot. He forced himself to not look at Ragna again. Instead, he locked his eyes onto Magnus's face. "I accept," he said, and his mind reeled as he spoke the words. "I will take Ragna as my Reks and bind our cantons once again."

Magnus's face turned beet red behind his thick mustache and beard. He smiled broadly and held his hand out for Signar. The boy took it and shook the great war chief's hand firmly, trying to show his own strength.

"Thank you, Signar-Reks," Magnus beamed. "I must inform Skarde."

Magnus stood and departed into the crowd. With him gone, the wolf howled inside Signar again, afraid once more. Pushing past everyone and everything, Signar left the thronehall and found a room in a rathskeller. It was quiet inside since most in the close vicinity had gone to the thronehall. Signar flopped onto the bed and closed his eyes. With the sudden silence, his wolf's cries turned to low growls.

The room was cold, however. The only light came from a single candle on the bedside table.

He hadn't been lying there long when he heard the door open. He sat up quickly, leaning onto his elbows, and spotted Ragna in the doorway. She peeked in, her sheets of long brown hair making a perfect curtain over one side of her face.

"May I come in?" she asked. Something eager gleamed in her silver eyes.

Signar swallowed hard but nodded. Ragna entered and came to the bed, sitting on the edge. She looked into his eyes, then unabashedly let hers roam over his body.

"We are to be mated," she whispered. One of her hands pressed into his chest.

Signar suddenly couldn't breathe. Something like lightning rushed through his body. He instinctually grabbed her hand to stop her. She leaned away, tilting her head curiously. He sat up and let go of her hand. She smiled meekly, understanding.

"They say you were a wildling most of your life," she said, offering conversation. "But you seem..."

"Normal?" Signar asked. He sat up. "Every day is a fight to keep the wolf under control."

Ragna readjusted on the bed, planting her palms firmly into the covers. "How do you do it? Stop the wildling from coming out?"

Signar crossed his legs, getting more comfortable on the bed. "A man I loved taught me to harness my wild side, not banish it. He told me it was part of me, not something to be stifled. I tamed it the way he tamed me."

"The one who died," Ragna said sympathetically. "I overheard Skarde speak of him. I am sorry." She fiddled with a rogue string on the covers. "I lost my mother two years ago. I understand." She looked up at him through thick, black lashes. "You are brave to come to Northica and demand an army."

Signar scoffed lightly, hanging his head. He didn't feel brave.

"Yes," Ragna urged him. She gently touched his chin, raising his head. "Dain told me about the Runers. You are brave to leave Altevine behind and do what must be done. No good will come from staying here and fighting the darkness forever. Sometimes to save one's land, you must leave it. You cannot close the rifts, but you can stop this Necro'Khan. I believe in you."

Signar allowed himself to look up into Ragna's face. Her eyes shined with earnest determination. She nodded.

"You are doing the right thing, Signar-Reks. Though it is not the easy thing."

"You don't think I'm abandoning my people?" he asked.

She shook her head. "What can you do here?"

"I could force my people to leave, to follow me."

"You are not your mother." Ragna's brows dipped in a slight frown. "Don't think like that. Altevine must be protected. This is the way, my Reks."

Having someone trust him so implicitly made Signar's heart lighter. He looked Ragna over. She was lithe and strong with delicate fingers and soft features. He was drawn to her.

"You are brave," she whispered, leaning closer to him. "You are strong."

Ragna turned and sat on her knees, facing him. She leaned in close and her lips lightly touched the soft skin at the base of his neck. Petrified, Signar couldn't move. Ragna's lips moved up to his jaw, and then, before he was ready, found his lips. When she kissed him, something like a thunderclap sounded in Signar's ears and his face burned hotter than a fresh iron in the fire. He couldn't stop himself. His hands flew up and gripped her hair, holding her there as he kissed her back. Instinct took over and a new kind of wild wolf rose up in him.

Her hands found the bottom of his shirt and she threw it off him. Then she dived back onto him, kissing him madly. All fear gone, Signar's hands found the laces of her dress and went to work. His mind quieted except for the mad rush of blood and excitement that coursed through him.

Ragna was his. Raudnir had ordained it so. She would sit by his side and rule with him. She was fierce, and he liked it.

# Chapter 30

## Returns

Sybal walked around the dozen or so iron-clad wagons, chains and locks hanging off them. Dorsa, her family's estate manager, walked with her, quill and parchment in hand. The wagons were heavily laden with chests, gold and gems inside them. Each one was pulled by two horses. The twelve wagons had been brought to the front of the manor for her inspection. She tugged on the locks and banged on the back doors, admiring the make of the iron.

"You'll be a target," she sighed, crossing her arms and standing back. "You'll need to hire mercenaries to travel with you. For protection."

Dorsa nodded. "I have had a patents out for two days now and have hired several to accompany me. We will be safe. I will see to it that your wagons reach Hatal safely, sheikha."

Sybal smiled at the title. "You've done well, Dorsa, managing the house while we've been away." She looked up at her childhood home with longing. They'd spent a few days there getting everything ready. She didn't want to raid her family vaults for every last gold coin, but needed to.

"Sabi," Dorsa asked, cutting into her sad thoughts. "What if no

Runers show up like you think? What will you do?" He sounded genuinely worried. "Will you face this evil alone?"

Sybal dropped her arms and frowned. "I have to. This monster is my doing, in a way. And someone has to stop him before the map is swallowed up in shadows." She stopped there. No, this couldn't be about revenge, though part of it was.

"But how?" he asked. She finally met his eyes.

"I'll find a way." She thought back to the Mahit'Onomicon. She could read about the Necro'Khan. Everything she needed to know was within the pages of that book.

"Before I leave," she said, marching back into the manor, "I need to know if there is an orichalcum smith in town."

"Yes," Dorsa said, nodding. "Not far from here. He works the metal all the time for a few local Runers."

"Local Runers?" Sybal asked, raising a brow. "I never thought Ala'Nar would allow local Runers."

Dorsa tilted his head in agreement. "There are more haunts than normal these days. Like something is open and letting them out."

Sybal clenched her fists. So it was starting all ready. "Thank you for everything, Dorsa. I will see you in Hatal."

She bid her faithful servant farewell and found her horse in the stable. She saddled it up and took one moment to look around. Then she sighed and petted her steed. "It's been so long since I've seen this house. I want to stay. To spend more time within its walls. But we have to keep moving. I'm sorry," she added when the horse snorted.

Behind her, Alvakar whinnied softly, but she didn't turn around to look at him. Even seeing the horse with Vicdan on it had been too much for her. She wished she'd never seen the beast again.

Closing her eyes against sudden tears, she mounted and rode into the city. It wasn't hard to find the smith, with its black smoke billowing up to the sky. The blacksmith was more than happy to sell her a sword in exchange for a bag of gold.

"I have a few orichalcum blades ready made," he said, motioning to a table in front of her. "Take your pick."

Sybal inspected the swords before her. None were like her first blade, and each one felt heavy and foreign in her hands. She picked up one that resembled Tzarik's old blade and inspected it. Her heart suddenly squeezed and her eyes stung. She'd never see his blade again. Everything but his runes were gone. She made a mental note to ask Signar for the runes back, if he'd let her take them.

"This one," she sighed, picking up the matching scabbard. She swapped hers out for the new one and sheathed the blade.

The smith expectantly held his hand out for the bag and she tossed it to him. Then she turned and left, mounting her horse again. She took her time, walking lazily through Ala'Nar to take in the city she'd grown up in.

The city that had abandoned her.

"It was a fair trial," she whispered to herself, remembering that horrid night. She shook her head. If she allowed herself to wallow in misery too much, she'd be a mess and unable to think. She sniffed hard and shook her head. "Enough. We need to leave."

The sun was setting by the time she reached the manor. Vicdan greeted her outside.

"We leave at sunrise," she said to him, hopping off her horse.

"How long until you think Amir and Signar return?" he asked, falling in step with her.

"We cannot bring Amir home until Signar returns," she said, thinking. "He should be in the Hatal harbor soon enough. Then we'll use Kazamar to make a portal to where we said we'd meet Amir, and any Runers he has gathered." In her heart, she hoped Signar had already arrived. That would mean he was safe and everything had gone according to plan. She closed her eyes and said a quick prayer, hoping he was all right.

"He's a man now," Vicdan said offhandedly, guessing her thoughts. "Give the boy some credit. He's a Reks, you know. I've met some in my time. They are fearsome, terrifying beasts. And your boy has a wild side to him. I'm sure he's fine."

Sybal nodded and quickly wiped at her eyes. "Let's get some rest. I want to leave early."

The journey from Ala'Nar to Hatal would take a few days. Sybal let Vicdan chatter on and sing to his heart's content as they trotted quickly over the desert sands. She didn't mind his voice and was glad for the company. She noticed the more he was allowed to go on, the happier he looked. Vicdan had been haggard, thin, and weak when she'd met him before leaving Alika, and hadn't started to look any better in the following months when he'd returned from being Sharar's captive. Something of his spark had gone out. But now, the more he sang, the more she saw that light come back.

When they stopped at night, she pulled out the Mahit'Onomicon and perused it once again. Her mind reeled every time she read it, taking in the information. She hated that she could read the book now. It was a curse. A reminder that the Dohkma had denied her the one thing she'd begged him for. Why he had done this, she couldn't imagine. But she didn't want it.

"What does it say?" Vicdan asked after humming softly to himself for some time.

Sybal flipped one more page and pulled herself away from the dark thoughts that had been intruding. "It talks about necromancers," she started. "They were to be comrades of the sorcerers. Two halves of the same coin. The power was split, so no mortal would have both." She stopped and hummed in thought. "Until Tarkan. So that's why the scriptures are not in the book. They were written directly onto flesh."

She sighed, re-reading the part about how to kill a Necro'Khan.

"How can we stab his heart?" she asked.

"You'd have to rip his heart out," Vicdan said, grimacing.

Sybal looked up.

"His heart is red diamond," Vicdan supplied. "A Necro'Khan's heart does not beat like ours. If it is surrounded by the scriptures, it will harden to diamond and be unkillable. But I imagine ripping his heart out will be simple when he's not got a head."

Sybal imagined it. She stared into the campfire, thinking about approaching Tarkan. Once she got close enough, he wouldn't be able to stop her. In her mind, she watched as she severed his head with a mighty swing, then cut open his chest. She ripped his heart out and it thudded in her hand as she removed it from the protection of the scriptures. Then she stabbed it.

"Sybal," Vicdan said softly, seeing her lost in her reverie. "You can't kill. What will happen when you take Tarkan's life?"

Sybal blinked, washing away the bloody image. "I may turn into a djinn then. Maybe that's what he's waiting for."

"He?"

"The Dohkma. He hasn't changed me yet." She smiled wryly. "Maybe he's giving me a chance. Perhaps that was his gift to me. Or his plan. Maybe he's plotted this whole time to have me kill so he can take me then."

Vicdan reached up and gently took a few strands of her white hair in his hands. He let them run through his fingers like white silk. "He hasn't relinquished his claim to your soul. Not yet."

"He won't," she sighed. "But I don't know what he wants with me. I sense he has a purpose for me. I know he'll never tell me, though."

"I hope you find what it is," Vicdan said gently with a kind smile. "Maybe he will spare you then."

Sybal nodded, eyes unfocused as she gazed into the fire once again. Her heart fell as a thought sank deeper into her.

"I can't kill him. I really can't." Her eyes watered. "After all this time, it can't be me. If I do, the Dohkma will use the runes to destroy my body and take my soul. I know it. That's what he's waiting for. Damn him."

Vicdan gripped her shoulder. "Then you can't. I'm sorry, Sybal, but it's not worth the risk. But." His lips quirked up in a shy smile. "If it makes you feel better, you can sever his head. Then we'll have someone else stab his heart."

Sybal exhaled a light laugh to cover a sob rising in her throat. "You always know what to say, Vicdan."

"I do, don't I?" He grinned fully now before his face fell serious once more. "But in truth, we cannot risk your life. Or eternity."

She looked into the fire, eyes glassing over again. She wanted to risk it. She wanted to be the one to kill Tarkan. "Very well," she whispered. "We should sleep. We have a few more days' travel."

She lay on her bedroll and dozed, thinking of Signar and Amir, praying they were safe. If all had gone well, Signar would be at the palace before her, ready to retrieve Amir the next morning. She closed her eyes and willed herself into a dreamless sleep.

ॐ

A little less than two days later, Sybal and Vicdan arrived at the palace's gate in Hatal. It took several hours for them to gain access to the inside, but once the sultana was informed that the dead sorcerer's necromancer had come back, they were let in. A host of guards led them to the throne room, where the sultana now sat, waiting for them. She looked tired and thin. She glared at Vicdan.

"I wanted to make sure it was you," she said, her voice monotone and stoney. "Before I had you locked away in my dungeon."

"You've had your child," Vicdan mused, clasping his hands together in excitement. "Congratulations, I assume."

The sultana's face remained impassive, and she nodded. "A boy. He will rule after me, as is our way. He will make a fine sultan one day. I am very proud. Now." She stood and pushed her long skirts behind her to descend the steps toward them. "What do you want, servant of the sorcerer?"

"I would very much like not to be thrown into your dungeon, if it's all the same to you. I've brought the lady Runer to speak with you."

"Where is the other Runer? Where is Amir?"

"Not yet back from a mission," Sybal said.

The sultana frowned. "And you are?"

Sybal held herself high. "Sheikha Sybal El'Freja of Ala'Nar, and a Runer. You knew my master, Tzarik, I believe."

Recognition sparked behind the sultana's eyes. "You are no friend of the sorcerer, then?"

"No."

"Then welcome and well met." The sultana tilted her head. "I've never seen a woman Runer before."

"As far as I know, I am the first," Sybal said with as much humility as she could muster. "But I am afraid we must finish with pleasantries.

289

I have an army due any moment. I came to ask for use of the royal barracks."

The sultana's brows went up. "Explain."

Sybal took a deep breath to calm her nerves. If the sultana had not seen a massive fleet of Caerwren ships in her harbor yet, that meant Signar wasn't back. "You know of the Necro'Khan in Alika?"

The sultana nodded.

"I believe that with an army of white blood, we can stand up to him," she started. "So I have sent Amir to Jarabu to gather as many Runers as he can. And I sent my ally Signar-Reks to Caerwren to collect his army. Both are bringing them to you in a matter of days, if not hours. We thought with our combined strengths we could launch a war on the Necro'Khan and take him down once and for all."

The sultana spread her arms, fingers flexed. "We tried once, and all that got me was the boy king of Alika."

"Yes," Vicdan piped up. "But we did some serious damage."

"Sabi," Sybal tried, stepping forward. "You don't understand. The map is at stake. Not just Alika. Tarkan will cover the world in a darkness the likes of which we cannot recover from. We must stop him now."

"And we know more now," Vicdan added. "We have a way to kill the Necro'Khan. All we need is a small party of Runers to get close to him and then we can strike."

"You can kill him?" a small voice asked from the left.

Sybal looked over to see Sokar peeking around a great golden pillar. She bowed to him and smiled as gently as she could. She remembered how shy and afraid the young pharaoh had been even among his own people. "Yes, your eminence," she said with assurance. "I just need a way to get close to him. And with a large enough attack on the front, I believe his forces will be distracted enough to let me slip in and confront him."

"You can do that," Sokar said brightly. He came out from behind the pillar now and faced Sybal. "There are secret passages all throughout the palace. I can show you."

Sybal shook her head. "I won't put you in danger."

"I will draw them for you, then," Sokar suggested. "To show you the way. And Nasor..." His face fell. "You can rescue him as well?"

"Thank you, your eminence," Sybal said. "We will do what we can to find him. Should he still live. We will have armies coming in from Bahratt and Caerwren. Or so I hope. Sabi," she said to the sultana. "Can we house them in the barracks?"

The sultana looked at a loss. Her brows pinched and for a moment it looked like she might weep. Sybal's heart softened.

"I know you fear for Al'Myrah. I do as well. It's my home. But we have to strike and we need your aid. We cannot do this alone. Tarkan is targeting the entire map and the map must answer."

"Of course," the sultana said in a hoarse whisper. She looked defeated. "Whatever I can do to help."

Sybal was about to thank the sultana when a bright flash ignited through the opening to the right. She flinched and shaded her eyes, running to the open balcony with the others. Something bright and fiery had appeared miles away in the Hatal harbor. Sybal squinted and looked harder.

"Portals," the sultana said and Vicdan agreed. "Just like the ones the sorcerer used to transport my fleet."

Sybal's heart leapt into her mouth. "Signar," she whispered. "I'll be back."

"What?" Vicdan called as she cantered down the throne room.

"Stay," she called. "I'll be back."

She ran out of the palace to her horse and leapt up on it. Kicking it hard in the side, she held on tight as it galloped down the road and out of the city toward the harbor village on the water's edge. It took over an hour for her to reach the port village, even pushing her horse as she did. The poor beast's lungs were heaving by the time she slowed to a trot and entered the village.

The people were frantic, knowing sorcery when they saw it. A crowd near the docks cried out and panic ensued. Sybal, being taller than most, was able to hold her ground. She looked over the heads of the crowd and noticed a fleet of dragon-headed longboats drifting to the shore.

"Are we under attack?" someone cried.

"They come in peace!" Sybal shouted. "They are here on behalf of the sultana."

A few people gave her quizzical looks, but a small part of the terrified crowd calmed and watched curiously as the ships came closer. A few of them dropped anchors and smaller boats were placed into the water. Sybal ran to the docks and looked out, desperately searching for Signar. She scanned a few of the boats and then spotted one with three men in it. She recognized Dain and Tage in front. Then, behind them, stood Signar.

"Signar!" Sybal shouted, waving her arms wide.

The boy looked up and spotted her, waving back. He didn't wait until they were closer and leapt overboard, splashing into the water. He ran to her and they collided hard, wrapping one another in their arms. Sybal kissed his forehead and hugged him once more as the boat finally drifted closer to shore.

"You're alive," she cried, her eyes stinging.

"And I have so much to tell you," Signar replied, out of breath.

Sybal nodded, but couldn't let go of him. She pressed herself into his chest and squeezed him tight again.

"You remember Dain," Signar said, gently prying Sybal off him. "And Tage."

Sybal nodded, giving a small bow to Dain. "I'm glad you came," she said. "It was brave of you."

"Someone has to command my father's army," Dain said with a wide grin.

"Northica's army?" Sybal asked.

"I'll explain," Signar promised. "And this is Aras. He was steward while I was away and is now a Runer, apprenticed to Tage."

Sybal looked at the large man. He was clearly older than Tage, but she guessed when it came to Runers, that didn't matter. "I thought Altevine was to be under Dain's protection?" she said.

"Like I said," Signar sighed. "I have a lot to tell you. I never told you about my and Tzarik's journey there last year."

Sybal shook her head. "Dain, have the army march to the palace. We will be using the royal barracks to house all those we can gather."

Dain nodded. "Aras, with me. Let's get these men moving."

Sybal took Signar's hand and Tage followed behind them. As they walked back to the palace over the next few hours and the sun began to set, Signar told Sybal everything, about what happened when he and Tzarik went to Caerwren and how they'd rescued Dain. Then he told her about this journey, and saving Ragna and Skarde's promise of an army.

"And she is to be my Reks, my mate," Signar ended.

Sybal's heart leapt once again into her mouth. "Your...mate. Your wife?" Her brain spun in her skull. She guessed Signar was old enough. He was close to eighteen, if not already. But she couldn't imagine it. She still saw him as the scared boy in the cage. "I don't know what to say," she confessed at length.

"You'd like Ragna," Signar promised with a little grin. "She's strong and brave, like you."

Sybal offered him a forced smile. "I guess I keep forgetting that I have to let you go one day. That you have to go home. To your canton. To rule. I just don't want to lose you."

"You won't," Signar said, wrapping his long arm around her shoulders and pulling her close.

Sybal didn't have any words. She remained quiet for some time before saying, "We will inform the sultana that an army from Caerwren is here. Did you find any Runers?"

Signar dropped his arm and looked down. "None would come, no matter the temptation of gold. And they argued that they needed to protect Altevine since my canton stands alone. They were right. But I have Aras and Tage, and they are worth a dozen warriors. We have the fleet and the army, though."

Tage smiled proudly. "We will do what we can."

Sybal nodded. "Maybe it's better that way. A small host will have a better chance of sneaking in and ambushing Tarkan, like Amir said."

"You won't go alone," Signar said sternly. "I will go with you."

"I'd have it no other way," Sybal replied. She looked ahead to the palace on the horizon in the darkness. "We need to use Kazamar to retrieve Amir and any he has with him. We promised to meet at the statue outside Jarabu tomorrow morning."

Signar nodded. "We will go at first light. He will be waiting for us."

Sybal hoped Signar was right.

# Chapter 31

## A Threat

Tarkan walked to the edge of the steps that led out into the back garden. Beyond the garden was the open desert that faced Zhigo and Yenka, the two provinces he had yet to conquer. But he couldn't see them. The darkness from The Cradle had finally reached Mysir. The shadows did not penetrate the palace, which was lined with light-giving torches and braziers. The light tended to keep the shadows and the monsters inside it away. He didn't fear them, but didn't want to take any chances, either.

Out in the city, during the quiet of the night, he could hear screams. Not all the time, but every now and then, a terrified cry rose up from Mysir. He knew the people were learning quickly to keep fire with them at all times. The darkness had surrounded them for three days now. Some people had fled the city, and reports came back that the darkness did not extend to Zhigo and Yenka yet. Tarkan didn't care how many fled Mysir. Soon the continent would be a land of shadow, and none of them would be able to stop it. Then he'd return to Porsh and follow in his father's footsteps, resting for centuries if he needed to. He would let the undead army fall and then make his way there, alone and out of sight. The world would burn while he rested.

"My Khan," an Apostle called, jogging up to where Tarkan looked out over the city. "On the horizon." He handed Tarkan a long brass glass.

Tarkan took the tool and held it to his eye, looking through it. On the many dunes, perhaps a mile away, came a line of bobbing torches. They spanned yards and lit up a massive host, armed to the teeth. The light splashed over two banners, one green and one red. He recognized them both: the pharaohs of Yenka and Zhigo.

"The pharaohs have come to my doorstep," Tarkan mused. "Do they seek death or surrender?"

The Apostle gulped and followed Tarkan's gaze. "I believe they come to fight."

Tarkan smirked. "We will ride out to meet them. Fetch Acenoth and a few of his men."

A moment later, Tarkan, two Apostles, their small horde of risen, Acenoth, and a few of his undead trotted out into the darkness, torches held high. They could not see far around them, only the sandy dunes right in front of them. The line that greeted them was massive. Armed warriors on horseback held spears and bows, girded for battle. Each one held a torch to ward off the darkness and monsters, making a wall of fire before Tarkan. Unafraid, he approached them. Overhead, Rakthar made tight circles, waiting for Tarkan's command, should he give it.

Two men in golden armor stood in front of the wall of warriors. One was a half-Masahk with the features of a panther, his skin black and smooth. Tarkan knew this to be Hamit, the pharaoh of Yenka. The other was a tall man, his armor gilded in gems and gold. This was Masour, the pharaoh of Zhigo. He guessed then that the army behind them was a mix of the two provinces, come to threaten him. He sized them up and immediately prepared to flee should anything go awry.

"Necro'Khan," Hamit said in a stern and steady tone. "We have come to give you a chance to flee, to leave Mysir and turn the Dynast Pharaoh over to us." The Masahk's eyes glowed in the firelight, the slit pupils shooting bolts of fire into Tarkan.

*They do not know Sokar was taken from me,* he thought. The news must not have left Mysir yet. At least he had a bargaining chip, though he didn't think he needed one.

"You expect to drive fear into me with your horde, majesties?" he asked, sneering at the mass of warriors. "This darkness is my doing. You may be eaten alive before you even leave my sands. I have no fear."

"We do not fear the darkness," Masour said. He glanced sideways at Hamit. "We do not fear you. Gypsu may have fallen, but we will not be so easily conquered."

"I took Septeph's head as easily as I can take yours," Tarkan hissed back. He laid his hand on the hilt of his blood blade.

"Is that the blade?" Hamit asked, narrowing his yellow eyes. "The blade that summoned the dead Acenoth." His eyes then flitted to the undead pharaoh. "So it is true. Acenoth IV walks among us again. What heresy is this?"

"This is true power," Tarkan said. "This is what you should fear. You bring an army to my door, one we can slaughter and raise up again to fight against the next fool who comes to my city."

"You speak of no fear," Masour said, his golden adornments clinking. "*We* have no fear, Necro'Khan. You cannot hope to stand up to the entire map. We are but one people; the others will not suffer you long."

Hamit added, "Strike us down now, and the rest of the map will turn on you soon enough."

"Threats, threats!" Tarkan jeered. "Show me why I should fear you." He looked between them, waiting. "I see. You are no real danger to me. You will turn and leave now and never return. You will cower in your golden halls while the darkness spreads, sacrificing your people to it. Because of your cowardice."

Hamit held his head high, his feline ears twitching, listening to something Tarkan couldn't hear. "So shall it be," he said solemnly. "We have tried to warn you. To give you a chance to surrender."

Tarkan glowered, grinding his teeth. "I will never surrender. To bend a knee is weakness. You will find no such weakness in me, majesties."

Masour nodded. "So shall it be," he repeated. He raised his left arm into the air and the army started to stir, turning and heading back the way they had come.

"We will do you a service and not cut you down now," Hamit said, "nor will we fell your servants who stand beside you. But be warned, Necro'Khan: we will return if you do not change your mind. You have a fortnight to think on our threat."

Tarkan smirked darkly as the pharaohs turned and followed their horde to the south. They wouldn't come back. They were two cities. They wouldn't dare stand up to him now. Not in the darkness. He had nothing to fear.

Amir woke early and left the flophouse before the sun rose. He wasn't sure where Ishaan and the others were, but he'd told them to meet him by the ancient statue of the maharaja outside Vishna. He took his horse and traveled there while the air was still cool from the night. He met a few traveling Masahk and a wary farmer on his way, but other than that, no one stirred until the sun rose.

He trudged up the grassy hill, noticing that the dirt was dry, and some sand blew in the light wind. He gripped the reins of his horse, hoping at least a few Runers would appear on the horizon. He squinted up into the sky and watched the orange orb slowly rise over the horizon. Somewhere, Sybal was preparing to bring him back to Hatal. Or at least, he hoped she was. That was their deal. If she didn't show up, then something must have happened. What would he tell the Runers if she didn't arrive? Grunting in discouragement, Amir decided he didn't want to think about it. First, he had to make sure the Runers arrived.

Soon, the sun peeked over the mountains and hills. In the distance, he could see the city of Jarabu waking up. The golden light splashed over the blue and white buildings, making them glow. Amir leaned up against the base of the great statue and crossed his arms, watching.

"I haven't seen you look that sullen in some years," Ashar's voice said from behind him.

Amir didn't stand, just turned his head to see Ashar and Vitaly walking toward him, horses in tow. Ashar gave his kind, boyish smile.

"You didn't have to come," Amir said.

"Is that why you sneaked out before we woke?" Ashar asked, joining Amir in leaning against the base of the statue.

Amir nodded. "It's not your fight."

"And it's yours?" Ashar shot back gently.

Amir frowned into the rising sun, forcing himself to look at it. "Yes. I have a lot to atone for. You know this."

The younger Runer crossed his arms in thought, nodding. "I remember. I was reminded yesterday when you slaughtered that man."

Amir looked away in shame, turning his face away from his once-apprentice. "You know I left that life behind."

"It's right behind you," Ashar replied gently. "Amir, no amount of good works will ever make up for the lives you've taken."

At this, Amir snapped his head back around and glared at Ashar. "Why are you saying this? You know what I've been through. You know I have tried."

Ashar licked his lips in thought before he answered. "I don't want you to throw your life away on a suicide mission because of your guilt. I want you to live and to continue to try to do good. Like you promised me."

Amir dropped his arms in defeat. "I have to do this. For her."

Ashar's face suddenly changed, his brows shooting up in amusement. "Her?" he asked with a wicked grin.

"It's not like that," Amir said quickly. No matter how much he wished it, Sybal would never look at him that way. But she didn't have to. He had to atone for his sins, and this was a way to do that. "This is for me. And the map. The entire world is at stake, Ashar."

"I know. And I won't let you do it alone," Ashar said. "We're coming with you."

"I cannot put you in that kind of danger," Amir retorted. He took Ashar's shoulder in his grip. "We may not come out of this alive."

"We've been in situations like that before." Ashar smiled, taking Amir's hand in his. "At least we'll be together. Side by side."

"Master," Vitaly called, interrupting them. He pointed east. "On the horizon."

Ashar and Amir turned to look. A single man trudged up the hills to them on the back of a black horse. Amir recognized Ishaan before he got much nearer. He was alone.

The Runers waited until Ishaan was close before speaking. The Masahk spoke first.

"I am sorry, Amir," he said. "I spoke with my tribe for two days. None would come. I almost had a few that would follow me, but no amount of gold would sway their minds to travel to Alika and fight a monster like that."

Amir's heart fell. What would he tell Sybal? He had failed her. "This concerns the entire map, my friend. We are dead if we do not fight."

"I understand," Ishaan said. "But they do not. They cannot. They do not see the threat. It's thousands of miles away to them. They cannot comprehend what you have seen. To them, it is all words. Just talk."

"But," Ishaan said with a feline grin, "if you will have me, I will come with you."

Amir nodded in thanks. "And you understand?"

Ishaan's smile didn't fade. "I understand gold. But..." His slitted green eyes slowly turned away from Amir. "I believe you. Though I cannot say why. Almost like I feel in my white blood that you speak the truth. Before I was a Runer, I was a man of faith. And I have faith now that what you say is true."

"I cannot guarantee your safe return."

"And I cannot guarantee that I will not run the moment I set eyes on this monster," Ishaan replied in good humor. "Now, are we traveling to New Gypsu for a boat?"

Amir shook his head. "We're using another means of travel. We have a djinn."

At this, Ishaan looked impressed. "Dangerous and useful," he said.

Ishaan dismounted and joined the other three on the ground as they waited. Five minutes later Amir's sulfates rushed madly. The others must have felt it, too, because all four Runers stood to attention at once. Just as they did, a fiery ring appeared a few feet before them. The portal snapped and crackled with energy as it burst open.

Amir winced against the sudden brightness, but looked into the center of the portal. Inside, Sybal stood waiting. She smiled when she saw him, relief relaxing her face. Amir led the way through the portal, hopping into it. He glanced back and watched as Ashar and Vitaly cautiously followed him. Ishaan's face showed amused amazement. The Masahk coaxed his horse through after a moment, and soon they were all inside some kind of barracks.

Sybal rushed to Amir and quickly hugged him before stepping back. Amir's heart thudded in his chest as she did. He watched her face, looking for signs of disappointment. Her blue eyes scanned the three other Runers.

"That's more than what I've gathered," she sighed. "No one has replied to the patents. I should have known. Runers are a selfish lot."

"I don't blame them," Amir said. "They are trained in self-preservation and don't understand what is at stake. Or they don't want to believe it. And Signar?"

"Here," Sybal said, leading them out of the training yard they had appeared in. "He has a small host of Caerwren warriors with him. Only two Runers."

Amir motioned to Ashar and Vitaly. "My former apprentice and his, Vitaly."

"We've met," Sybal said with a smile. "On a hunt on Alika."

Amir nodded. "And this is Ishaan."

"Pleased to meet the fabled lady Runer," the Masahk said with a grin. "We've heard of you on Bahratt. Some think you are a myth."

Amir watched Sybal blush and shake her head.

"I didn't know I was that famous," she said.

They marched through the halls of the barracks and out onto a sunny path that led back up to the palace. Amir looked around, realizing exactly where they were.

"The sultana is cooperating?" he asked.

"For now," Sybal replied. "She's worried about the threat of Tarkan retaliating the attack and regrets it. And Sokar is keeping her mind on Alika for now."

"And do we have a plan?" he asked. "We don't have the army of Runers you wanted."

Sybal's brows knitted in gentle thought. "We have enough of us. We'll think of something." She looked up at him as they marched into the palace. "We're a bigger threat than Tarkan realizes, too."

# Chapter 32

## Plans and Sigils

Sybal led the small pack of Runers to the royal stables, where they stowed their horses before proceeding into the palace. They were informed that the sultana and the pharaoh would meet them in the war room. Sybal tried to breathe evenly to settle her nerves, but her sulfates would not stop pumping. This wasn't what she had envisioned. She'd wanted an army, and she didn't even have a dozen.

Amir strode up beside her and fell in step with her. She tried to make her face passive, to be strong, when she felt his eyes land on her.

"This may be the better option," Amir said softly as they marched through the halls. "A smaller group will be harder to track. We could do this with stealth."

She wasn't so sure. She didn't reply, swallowing hard instead and locking her eyes on the huge double doors ahead. "We'll see," she sighed. He was trying to comfort her, and it made her feel weak. And strange. She sensed he wanted something from her, but she couldn't place what it was. She pushed the thought to the back of her mind and focused instead on the present.

The guards opened the big doors and ushered them in. Inside, a huge table waited in the center of a room. The sun spilled through some open windows and through an open wall where a balcony overlooked the city below. Maps spread over the table and the sultana and Sokar stood over it with Vicdan behind them. Signar and his two Runers stood with them, bent over the table, talking in hushed voices. When they entered, the others looked up.

The sultana put her hand on her hip and raised one brow. "These had better simply be the men who speak for the army you promised me, sheikha," she said, eyeing Ishaan, Ashar, and Vitaly. "And the sorcerer's Runer is back, I see."

Sybal felt Amir bristle, but admired that he kept his mouth shut. Sokar smiled at Amir, but she noted he looked wary. Ill, almost. Sympathy for him rose in her chest as she looked at him across the table. He had lost his dearest friend and didn't understand why the others despised him. He would never understand, and she had to leave it at that. He was too young and fragile to comprehend what had really happened. She moved to stand by him and Amir stood on his other side. This seemed to relax him a little.

"Change of plan," Sybal sighed. She pressed her palms into the table and looked over the maps they had spread out. One was a detailed map of Alika, another was a very clean drawing of what looked like the floor plans to the Dynast Palace, and the last was a map of their known world. "There will be no Runer army," she went on. "They have decided to not join our cause. We will be going in alone."

Signar caught her eyes then and winced in concern. "What do you mean?" he asked. "We have the warriors from Northica. We have the Al'Myrahn army."

The sultana tilted her head in mock curiosity at this. "Yes, tell me, sheikha, how do you plan on using my warriors? I have generals who may lead their men, but they will not do so blindly."

Sybal turned the drawing of the Dynast Palace to face her right side up. "What is this?" she asked. "Who drew this?"

Sokar beamed. "I did. I know every secret passageway in and out of the palace. I thought it might help."

Sybal smiled at the young pharaoh. "It will. Immensely. This is exactly what I need." She leaned over it, taking in the lines and curves. "This is accurate?"

"Very," Sokar promised. "Before he died, father made sure I was trained a little in architecture. I sketched my palace a dozen times." He pointed to a large room in the upper center of the map. "This is the throne room. Tarkan was there when not traveling. He kept me chained to the throne. He never used this passageway here." He pointed to the left of the throne to what looked like a wall. "I don't think he knew it existed. But this tunnel leads to every important room in the palace. There are stairs in the walls as well. This one," he pointed to a wall of pillars, "leads to the dungeons."

At this, Amir grunted and nodded in agreement. "He held me there and tortured me. So he knows there are secret passages, just not all of them, perhaps."

Sybal smiled weakly. "This is perfect, Sokar. Just what we need." She scanned the front of the palace, looking at the walls. "We'd need siege equipment," she said, pointing to the walls. "Battering ram, ladders—everything. He'll see us coming from a mile away."

"And his undead?" Signar asked.

"He has a blade," Vicdan said. "It acts as a magical artifact, sustaining them. When I saw it, I thought it must be made of orichalcum. If we destroy it, we might be able to topple his undead army. Maybe even slay them."

"Nothing cutting off the head might not handle," Tage said. "There were some creatures of that sort coming from the rift. Cutting off their heads usually does the trick with most undead."

Sybal nodded, tapping her bottom lip in thought. "The people of Alika won't stop us," she said. "In fact, they may join our ranks. We should be able to get through the city easily." She pointed to the coast near Mysir. "If we dock here, it could take us a day or so to get to the palace. Tarkan will know we're coming, but the Dynast Palace is not a stronghold."

Sokar shook his head. "There are many open ways in. Once you are past the walls, it will be a slaughter."

"The men will be told to go after the Apostles," Sybal went on. "They will no doubt have risen at their sides, and the sooner we kill the Apostles, the sooner we can thin out the army."

"Tarkan has men on Xia," Sokar added. "Three hundred of his

undead are there. He commanded them there in my presence and I..." He swallowed nervously. "I read his mind."

Sybal raised her brows. "You can read minds?"

Sokar nodded. "In a way. Nothing is whole, just fractions of thoughts, feelings." His eyes flitted to Amir, then back to her. "I won't read your mind if you don't want me to. At least, I will try."

She shook her head. "I can't care right now. Tell me what else Tarkan was planning."

Sokar took a deep, shuddering breath, nervous as all the eyes were on him. "By now the malignation will have taken over Mysir," he said, shifting the map to uncover the map of Alika. "The rift is in The Cradle to the west of Mysir. It's not far."

The sultana looked up at this. "What do you intend to do about that, Runer?"

Sybal met her eyes over the table. "We will think of something. The Wushito on Xia have contained their rift for thousands of years, so there must be a way." And she had the Mahit'Onomicon. There might be a way outlined in the book that she had not found yet.

"The wards help keep it inside," Signar offered, "but it may become too strong and break them. There has to be a way to close them."

Sybal heard the worry for Altevine in his voice. It broke her heart to hear him in so much despair. "We'll find a way, I swear." She turned back to Sokar. "What else can you tell us?"

Sokar nervously licked his lips. "I saw it in his mind. He plans on going into a long sleep, like his father before him, he said. Until the map is covered in the darkness. He wanted to use my tomb or to return to Porsh. He hadn't made up his mind yet."

Sybal squinted, thinking. "All he wants to do is destroy the world? Cover it in this malignation? Why?"

Sokar shivered at this. "I saw his mind. He is in pain. And he hates. I've never felt someone who hates like him. I never could find why. Just those feelings."

"Does it matter?" Signar asked with something of a snarl in his voice. "He killed Tzarik for it. He deserves death."

"He does," Sybal agreed. A lump rose in her throat at the mention of Tzarik. She swallowed it down, nearly choking. She took a deep breath and looked back down at the maps. "We'll lose the most men as we try to penetrate the walls." She tapped the drawing. "But once we're inside, we can make our way to Tarkan."

Amir leaned over her and looked at the drawing. "Or we sneak in," he suggested. He tapped a hidden door in the garden. "We're a small troop. There are seven of us Runers all together. Once the siege starts, we can sneak in any way we desire. All eyes will be on the front where the battle is. We can fight our way through if we have to. Tarkan cannot control our blood nor take it. The only way we die is on the edge of a blade. If we come up from behind, we'll have a better chance."

Sybal smiled. "I was thinking the same thing."

"I'm going with you," Signar protested.

Sybal opened her mouth to argue, but Signar cut her off with a look. "All right," she said in defeat. "There is one way to kill a Necro'Khan," she went on, looking the Runers in the eye. "We have one sigiled blade, and that's how it will be done."

"I can wield it," Signar interrupted.

"No," Sybal said, the word cutting from her lips. "I will not have you going near him."

"Runers cannot handle the spirits within," Signar protested. "It makes your blood boil and drives you mad."

"I will have to stand it," Sybal said. "Besides, I'm used to reclaiming my mad mind."

"Sybal," Signar tried again.

"No," she snapped. "I can do it." She pushed off the table and began to circle in thought. "We have to cut off his head and remove his heart."

The other Runers exchanged glances.

Vicdan said, "Once a Necro'Khan's heart is removed from the protection of the scriptures on the outside of his skin, it will turn to flesh again. We'll be able to stab it."

"And when we do, we claim his soul within the blade," Sybal finished. "Locking him away within. He won't even see the afterlife." A bitterness drove her words.

"And your oath?" Signar snapped. "Are you willing to die to kill him?"

A thought hit her. She froze, lips slightly parted. "I can do it. The sigiled blades don't kill. They merely trap a soul inside. He won't be killed." Something like a dark, twisted joy filled her at the thought. She could be the one to slay Tarkan after all.

"You don't know that for sure," Signar argued back. "A blade to the heart will kill most things. He'll still be dead. His soul simply won't move on to his afterlife."

She didn't meet his eyes, glaring down at the maps instead. She'd have to risk it. She had to be the one to slay him.

"And what then?" Amir asked after a few moments of silence. "If he's dead and his spirit is locked away?"

"There is an entity within the God Deep that would love to have his soul," she replied. "Before we close the rift on Caerwren, we will toss the blade into the Deep, ridding us forever of it. Tarkan will be dead and his spirit trapped forever. We'll let the gods sort out his soul."

Saying the words cut her deep. She had once thought of Tarkan as an ally, a friend, even. But he'd used them. Had used Tzarik in his desperation to save her. She expected the thought of killing him to make a droplet of sorrow trickle down inside her heart. But it didn't. He'd killed Tzarik. Any sympathy or thoughts of old friendships were overshadowed by that.

A gentle hand rested at the base of her spine. She looked up to see Amir looking at her with concern. She waved him off.

"So that's it, then?" the sultana asked. "Do you plan to sail there?"

Sybal's head shot up at this. "Kazamar," she blurted. "No, majesty. We have ways of getting there. That's what we'll do." She smiled. "We'll use the djinn to make portals right outside the walls. No need to march."

"And endanger Al'Myrah?" the sultana burst. "What if a horde of undead come through, back to us?"

"We'll move quickly," Sybal offered. "We'll be far enough back that we'll have the element of surprise."

"And us?" Ishaan asked, speaking for the first time. "Djinn magic?" he added, looking skeptical. "That seems dangerous."

"It is," Sybal agreed. "But we have to. It's our best shot." She scanned the room before her. The Runers looked apprehensive, but willing. Sokar's drawn face had a little life come back to it. Signar's brow furrowed in determination. Finally, she glanced at Amir.

He nodded to her. "I trust you," he whispered.

The sultana dropped her arms and looked defeated. "I suppose I have to trust you."

Sybal smiled. "We're Runers, majesty. Let us do our job."

"And when will you march?"

"How soon can the warriors be ready?"

The sultana blinked in thought. "Give me two days."

Sybal sat in her library in her home in Hatal, flipping through the Mahit'Onomicon with Vicdan at her side. She examined the pages slowly now.

"See here," she said, pointing to a page. "It's like it's written in a different hand." She flipped farther back. "This one is jagged, sharp. And the last, where it talks about the sigils, is clean and clear writing. It almost looks Xian. Then there's the scriptures on the flesh of necromancers. Those look like a different hand penned them as well."

Vicdan nodded. "I cannot read it, but I see what you mean. Do you think three gods wrote the words of magic?"

"Perhaps," Sybal mumbled, flipping back to the section about the sigils. "Maybe the Dohkma, Nephron, and the White Dragon. They have their own word for the Mahit'Onomicon on Xia. That would make sense. The White Dragon is the god of light and life. Nephron, darkness and death."

"And the Dohkma, they say, was the first god," Vicdan added. "The maker of the light and the dark, of life and death."

She shrugged. "I suppose it doesn't matter who penned the words. Just what they say."

Sybal flipped back to a page written in the Xian hand. "Gods," she whispered, her eyes flicking up and down the page. "It's about the sigils. It describes plans for the Crypt. How to use the twelve sigils to protect a rift. This is what they did on Xia, and it worked for thousands of years." She stood up straight. "It's not ideal, but it's something."

Vicdan pressed his lips together, his face wrinkling in worry. "What if it's too late for Caerwren and Alika? What if the darkness has spread too far? The only choice may be to close the rifts."

Hopelessness overcame Sybal. She shut the book slowly and didn't reply. Yes, she'd feared the same thing. It had been too long; the malignation had spread too far. And now they had to kill the only person on the map who could close them. Overcome, she rubbed her temples and grimaced. "I don't know what to do about the rifts. We have to focus on Tarkan for now. Then we'll come to them."

Vicdan looked away and Sybal saw his brow bend in worried thought. Something ticked behind his eyes, like he had an idea, but wasn't going to share it with her. Before she could ask, a soft knock on the door announced the arrival of Signar and Amir. She looked up and smiled at Signar. "Did you bring it?" she asked.

Signar entered, Amir behind him. The Vaeson held a long, straight blade wrapped in black. "I don't think it's a good idea," he began. "I've seen what these swords do to Runers."

Sybal held her hand out nonetheless. Reluctantly, Signar handed the blade over.

"I've felt them before," Sybal said. "Tzarik told me about his battle with ShanBao. He stabbed Tzarik, and yet the sigils did not harm him because of the sulfates. They protected him. The same with me. When Wu-Zhiang stabbed me with her sigiled blade, my soul wasn't taken."

Signar frowned. "It's not just that. I saw what the blade did to Tzarik when it was close to him. The Xian Masahk said it makes your blood boil, makes your mind go mad."

Sybal couldn't stop the light smirk that played around her lips. "And I told you, I'm used to wrangling my mad mind. I should be able to stand it long enough to kill Tarkan."

Slowly, she grasped the black wrapping and unwound the red blade. When she saw the first sigil, memories of Wu-Zhiang and her death on Xia came back to her. The scars on her back tingled and the visions filled her mind. She remembered her torture, the way they'd hung her on the cross and the viper's bite. She madly shoved the memories behind her and focused on the blade.

The moment it was free of the wrappings, her blood rushed through her veins. Amir grunted and stepped back. She gave him a quick apologetic glance and stepped further away from him. Her vision blurred a little and an ache spread through her temples. Her mind started to spin as the sulfates in her veins began to panic so much that she couldn't think straight. Her muscles ached and a strange kind of fatigue overcame her. She sensed the souls inside the red blade. So many cried out. Hate for the dead Wushito master rose up in her at this. No doubt some of the souls within were innocent.

She looked up from the blade and caught Amir's eyes across the room. She focused on them, willing herself to feel beyond the rushing fear. It felt similar to when the Dohkma had taken over her body. She rose above it, reaching for a higher sense of feeling. She focused on Amir's eyes. The way his long hair fell into his eyes reminded her of Tzarik.

Tzarik.

Her heart filled to bursting with love for him. She let her mind reel into her memories, pulling up every single one she could remember of him, the good and the bad. The times she'd hated him and the times she'd loved him.

*I never really hated you,* she thought, a small sob rising in her throat as she gazed into Amir's eyes. *I think I always loved you. You saved me. So many times.*

Before she knew it, she realized she no longer felt the panic from the blade. The moment she thought about it, though, it came back tenfold. The fear surged through her and she dropped the blade, stumbling backward into Signar. Amir dived onto the thing, taking up the black wrapping and swaddling the sword again behind the protective fabric. Sybal saw the veins on his neck throb as he did this.

"I told you," Signar whispered, helping her to her feet. "Let me use the blade."

Sybal shook her head, clearing her throat. "I can do it. I'll try again. Amir, draw your blade."

A little confusion creased the other Runer's brow, but he did as she said, unsheathing his scimitar. Sybal took the sigiled blade and unwrapped it again. This time, she was ready. She brought her mind above the fear and pain and thought of Tzarik.

"Come at me, Amir," she said through gritted teeth. "You can't hurt me."

Obeying, Amir lunged forward, swinging his blade. Sybal brought the sigiled blade up and blocked it, spinning the straight blade to dislodge Amir's scimitar and advanced on him. They danced back and forth, fighting with all their might, until Sybal couldn't handle it any longer. Her mind slipped, distracted by her thoughts, and the pain came back. She cried out as her blood boiled and she dropped the blade. Her vision went dark and she fell. But she didn't want to stop.

Diving for the blade, she scooped it up again and spun, bringing a deadly strike down on Amir. Just before the blade cut his flesh, she held it still. Amir moaned and fell to his knees, his mind reeling from being near the blade.

Sybal turned and picked up the black cloth, wrapping it away again. "I'm sorry," she whispered. "But I had to know I could strike a deadly blow."

Amir panted, pushing himself up to his feet. "Tarkan won't be affected by it like I was. But nonetheless, that was impressive. You held the blade for some time."

A small, proud smile creased Sybal's lips. "I can do it. I have to. Signar, I'll need you to destroy his blade when I remove it from his grasp. Do you understand?"

The boy smiled, glad to have gotten a part in her plan. "Of course," he said stoutly.

Sybal turned to Amir. "I think we're ready."

A small lingering fear nagged at the back of her mind, though.

She couldn't kill. Not without the runes punishing her in some way.

But right now, she was willing to risk it. Would she have the strength in the moment to try?

She caught Amir watching her and quickly wiped the worried look off her face. But he'd seen it.

# Chapter 33
## The Battle

Sybal looked over the plans one more time. Outside the war room and the palace, she heard the Caerwren warriors shouting, rousing themselves for the upcoming battle. Signar was with them, and Dain, and she could hear his voice call to them before they replied in tumultuous unison. The warriors were hungry for blood. The Northicans were a wild and deadly lot. Being part Northican, she knew this firsthand. It had been a point of contention for Tzarik—her wild nature had often annoyed him.

She flipped the drawing of the map over and studied the facade of the Dynast Palace once again. Dain would soon be leading his army through those gates and into sure danger. She and the other Runers would wait until the fighting was in full swing, then sneak into the palace. She tilted the drawing, looking at the windows they would ascend in to. It was a long hall outside the throne room. She tapped the image with her forefinger, thinking.

"We've prepared as best we can."

She turned and saw Amir approaching her. He'd removed his armor and stood before her in a loose, unlaced, black cotton shirt.

"We march in a few hours," she said, turning back to the table. "Why aren't you dressed?"

"Why aren't you sleeping?" he challenged, standing close to her. "You need your rest."

Sybal became highly aware of Amir's body close to hers. She could feel the slight heat coming off him and heard his heart thudding. It didn't race, but it pounded hard. Almost like he was afraid. Confused, she glanced around, but didn't find anything. Her sulfates remained calm.

"I couldn't sleep," she confessed. "And neither could Signar. He's rallying the men now."

Amir nodded. "I could hear them from your estate. Which is how I knew you'd be here." He leaned his head down, closer to her face.

She looked up into his blue eyes and her breath caught. Something shone in his eyes that she did not expect to find there: desire. Her heart skipped a beat then. Her knees locked up and held her still as he raised his hand to her face, gently caressing it with the back of his fingers. A shiver flitted down her spine at the tender touch.

He leaned his head down to her.

"Don't, please," she whispered, stopping him. "I...can't. Not now." *Never again,* she added to herself. She didn't think she'd ever love again. Not after Tzarik. Yes, he'd taken her heart with him.

She reached up and pressed her fingers into Amir's chest, gently pushing him back.

"I'm sorry," he murmured, letting her disengage. His cheeks flushed pale with embarrassment.

To put him at ease, Sybal wrapped her arms around his middle and hugged him, tilting her head against his chest. "I'm glad you are here, at my side, going into battle with me. But that's all."

His hand went to the back of her head and pressed her closer. He embraced her and sighed.

A moment of silence filled the war room before Sybal pulled away. "We need to get ready. We're marching on the Necro'Khan in a few hours."

Amir nodded. "I'll wake the others."

୬ଡ଼

"Light your torches!" Signar shouted from the back of his horse. He watched as the army before him ignited in flames. "The darkness will test you, should it be there," he said. "Do not fear the monsters of the malignation. They will not harm you so long as you stay within the light." He nodded to Dain, who ran down the line of warriors, repeating the instructions to the other faction of warriors. Tage did the same in the other direction.

Signar watched them ride down the line. He hoped the malignant darkness had not swallowed up Mysir like it had Altevine, but he doubted it had not. It was best they were prepared.

Amidst the warriors were the siege weapons. Ladders, the battering ram, and other machines they might need were dotted here and there among their army. The Al'Myrahn generals stood at the head of their factions, listening to every word Signar said. He appreciated their obedience.

He turned his horse to see Sybal and the other Runers off to the side. Her face was drawn and pale, her eyes distant and empty. He clicked his tongue and trotted over to her. Behind him, Tage made his way there as well to join his fellow Runers.

"The warriors are ready," Signar said to Sybal. "Are you?"

Sybal didn't answer with words. She nodded and looked to the other Runers. Amir answered with his own nod.

"We are ready," Aras said for them. "We will cleave this Necro'Khan's head from his body and end his life swiftly."

"Dain will lead the warriors and I will join you," Signar said. He gave Sybal a quick, sharp glance, telling her not to argue with him. "But we have to wait until the battle is in full swing before we advance. We will wait on the dunes apart from the palace until Dain gives the signal."

The Runers nodded, mumbling acquiescence. Signar appreciated how everyone was doing as he said. It made everything much easier with no one challenging him and his orders.

He touched the amulet around his neck. "Kazamar," he said, "we're ready. Open the portals."

Without so much as showing himself, the djinn obeyed. Several yards in front of the army of warriors and their siege equipment, the portals opened. Signar gasped as a cool wind blew up from inside the portals. As he suspected, it was dark within. He could see the palace from there. They'd have a small march across some dunes, but then they'd be at the palace's gates.

He kicked his horse and rode to the front of the army to catch up with Dain. Then he took a torch from the other Vaeson and faced the portals.

"Onward!" he called, galloping into the fiery rings. Behind him, the men cheered and roared their battle cries to the sky.

The thunder that was the army on horseback rattled Signar's chest. He'd never heard so many warriors moving all at once. Leading the charge, a thrill shot through him. He suddenly couldn't wait to bloody his axe on an Apostle, to hew a man down from the back of his horse.

He got his chance sooner than he'd thought. A small band of kehann outside the walls turned to face the army emerging from the portals. The kehann unsheathed their weapons, but Signar and his warriors were on them before they could attack. He slung his axe from his back and cut a wide arch with it, slicing one of the kehann in two with a mighty stroke.

Signar jerked on the reins, turning his horse, and galloped back behind the line of warriors as the battering ram moved forward. They could see the gate by the torches on either side of it. Above, on the walls, a few lights bobbed into view as the palace warriors and no doubt some Apostles rushed to see the onslaught.

"Shoot them!" Signar ordered as he galloped.

A row of archers stepped up, firing onto the top of the walls. The men atop them cried out and some fell, the arrows finding their marks. The battering ram was pulled back and released, slamming into the stone and wood gate.

"Again," Signar ordered.

The motion was repeated until the gate cracked and collapsed in on itself. Sand kicked up, blinding them temporarily. Once the gate was down, the generals of the Al'Myrahn soldiers took over.

"Go," Dain ordered Signar. "I'll take it from here. Wait for my signal."

A little reluctant to let the adrenaline of the siege go, Signar nodded and galloped around the army as the ladders were brought forward. The battle was almost well underway. It had happened faster than he'd imagined.

"Remember, kill the Apostles!" he cried as he cantered back to Sybal and the other Runers. "Don't waste time on the risen. Kill the Apostles."

A cry of excitement went up from the Northican warriors at this as they rushed forward to climb the ladders. Signar didn't want to leave the front line, but knew he had to meet Sybal. In his heart, he wondered if she could wield the sigiled blade well enough to kill Tarkan. He knew he needed to be there in case she couldn't. Or if she fell.

*No,* he growled to himself. *That won't happen. I can't lose them both.* He had to protect her at all costs.

Signar ran down the line of warriors and behind them to the dunes, just as the portals closed. He thanked Kazamar in his mind and finally rejoined Sybal and the Runers.

"What now?" Tage asked, eager to get into battle himself.

"We wait," Signar panted. "The siege is done. The men are inside. Now all we have to do is wait for Dain's signal. We'll move to the east side of the palace and ascend into the hall."

"Well done," Sybal said with a gentle smile.

Signar glowed inwardly at her praise. He turned back to face the palace, eagerly awaiting Dain's signal. Tarkan had killed Tzarik and was soon going to pay.

Signar's wolf rose in him, snarling, snapping, and howling. He let it.

*He'll wish he'd never been born when we're done with him,* Signar thought savagely.

⌇

Tarkan stood on the back veranda of the Dynast Palace, looking into the darkness. He'd had braziers lit and torches brought up so the others could see. He could see to a certain extent into the darkness, but his mortal followers could not. As he gazed into the dark, he thought he heard the low growling of some beast. The rifts had been attracting other monsters of the continent recently. Not only were the haunts and spirits coming out of the rift, but living beasts from this side were drawn to it.

He studied Sokar's tomb. The outside of it was grand and beautiful, he had to admit. It would be a suitable place for him to wait out the malignation if he didn't return to Porsh. The young pharaoh had had the thing commissioned when his father had been killed.

Tarkan scoffed, remembering when Sharar had gone to Alika and killed the old pharaoh. Sokar had no idea. And now he never would. Sharar had never taken Tarkan into the palace, but they had explored other old sights and relics together, looking for clues to the Mahit'O-nomicon. Sharar had been right in the end; the book had been on Alika.

A deep sigh took Tarkan then as he thought back over his years spent with Sharar. It hadn't all been torturous. But the scholar had deserved death in the end. He wished he could see him now, his corpse cold and stiff. It really was a shame he'd had to kill Tzarik to get his revenge, but he couldn't change that.

A sudden loud cry rose up from far away. Tarkan stiffened and listened, turning back toward the palace. It had sounded like the cry of a thousand men, calling out in shock. Then another cry rose over that.

A war cry. One voice shouted above the others, "To the gate!"

A chill ran down Tarkan's back and settled in his gut. He turned and ran back into the palace, into the throne room. He didn't get far before the doors burst open and an Apostle came in, panting and clutching his chest.

"We're under attack again," the Apostle gasped. "White men and Al'Myrah." He looked confused and frightened.

"White men?" Tarkan repeated. "Caerwren?" He stopped then and understood. "The boy. And Sybal." He looked around, almost expecting them to materialize then. "Bar the doors to the throne room," he ordered. "Have Acenoth meet me here. He will lead this charge."

The Apostle bowed and scampered back out through the doors, slamming them on his way out.

Tarkan looked around again. The palace was not defensible, but he had an undead army. He drew his blade and moved to the ruby throne, where he sat and glared at the doors. Sybal was bullheaded and Signar was just a wild boy. They'd no doubt try to force their way through the front and to him. But they'd never get that far. He would be sorry to see Sybal perish as well, but if she was foolish enough to come after him now, she deserved her fate.

He laid his sword across his knees and waited.

Sybal's spirit grew restless the longer they waited. She watched as the army slowly filtered into the palace. The sounds of battle rose up to her, making her wish more than ever that she had been among them.

But this was her place. She watched the palace, wondering if Tarkan had barricaded himself inside somewhere. No matter where he hid, they'd find him. Beside her, Vicdan's breathing came in harsh rasps. He was just as nervous as her.

Her eyes roamed over the dark sight, taking in the fire billowing up here and there from the battle. A sudden roar made her jump in her saddle. She looked up to see a black dragon spring up from the darkness and soar over the battle. It threw its head back and spewed a burst of energy, blowing down one of the ladders. Men screamed as they fell.

"We need to move," she said urgently. Signar told her to wait when suddenly a fiery arrow zipped up into the sky.

"There!" Signar shouted, pointing. "Let's go."

Sybal and Vicdan kicked their horses in the sides and galloped around the outside walls of the Dynast Palace. The other Runers followed close behind her. Signar stayed abreast with her. They rode for several minutes, past swarms of glowing spirits and a few monsters drawn there by the rift. The light kept them at bay. She spotted one monster's glowing eyes watching them. If they weren't careful, some of them might venture into the battle.

"Here," Signar said, stopping the troop of Runers. "This is where Sokar said the library was."

They quickly dismounted and tethered the horses to a wall of ornate bushes growing on the parameter. The animals set their ears back and whinnied softly, but they didn't protest or bolt.

Sybal looked up and saw an open window above them. "Hooks," she ordered.

Aras and Amir took out grappling hooks and began to spin them. Each man released their hook, one after the other. The ropes shot up into the night and they heard the sound of metal on sandstone. Amir pulled on his, testing the hook.

"It's good," he said, stepping aside.

Aras did the same.

Ishaan, being the lithest and quietest, slinked up first. Sybal watched the Masahk almost vanish into the night air above them. He slipped into the open window and vanished. She held her breath while he looked around. Once his head popped back over the sill and he waved them up, she breathed again.

Tage went next, with Signar climbing in tandem on the second rope. Sybal's heart thudded as Signar vanished into the palace. Vitaly and Ashar went next, with Aras close behind. Amir looked sideways at Sybal, waiting for her.

"We'll help you up," she said, turning to Vicdan.

She nodded to Amir and gripped the rope. Using her legs and hands, she shimmied up the rope slowly. Amir reached the top before her and reached out to grab her hand and pull her through. When she landed on the floor of the library, she heard the sounds of battle.

She turned back around to see Vicdan scurrying up the rope in a sloppy manner. She looked to Amir and tilted her head, signaling for him to help the necromancer up. Amir went to the rope, gripped it, and pulled. Vicdan spilled through the window, landing hard on his knees. Amir hauled him to his feet.

"The secret passage is behind this shelf of books," Signar said, running to the shelf. He gripped the side and pulled, forcing the door open.

Sybal trotted down into the dark hallway that ran under the palace.

According to Sokar's drawing, they needed to run several yards down and then turn right through the third doorway. That would lead them to the next corridor that would eventually let them out in the antechamber outside the throne room. She counted each step as the troop ran down the corridor. They passed one door, then another. The third one had a lock on it.

"Let me," Tage whispered, pushing his way to the front. He knelt in front of the lock and pulled out two slim metal tools. He inserted them and went to work picking the lock.

"Impressive," Vicdan said with a smile.

A few seconds later, he stood. Sybal gently pushed the door open and looked through to the other side. It wasn't quiet. They could hear the battle overhead. The sounds echoed all down the stone corridor.

*Fifty yards down and then a left,* she reminded herself. She counted as she ran, the others behind her. They came to the door, also locked, and let Tage open it.

"Stay back and be quiet," Sybal whispered. She cracked the secret door open a little, knowing it was a blank wall on the other side. Anyone who saw it would know someone lurked behind it. She pressed her face to the slit and looked through.

On the other side, she heard the battle closer than ever before. She also spotted two Apostles and a dozen or so undead. She sighed and pulled back.

"We have to fight. They're outside the throne room door," she said softly.

"Let us spill their blood with glory," Aras said, unsheathing his long orichalcum blade.

"Take no risks," Sybal warned them, looking Signar in the eye. "Watch one another's backs."

She faced the door and raised her leg, kicking it open with a shout. The sudden noise startled the Apostles just as she hoped it would.

"Runers!" one shouted, turning to run.

Amir shoved past Sybal, putting himself between the danger and the others, and aimed his large crossbow. He let the bolt fly, hitting the Apostle square in the back of the head. The man fell to the ground dead. The others burst out and rushed the undead.

"Cleave their heads from their corpses!" Signar cried.

The Runers ran at the undead, entering a deadly dance of swords and spears.

"Keep them away from Vicdan!" Sybal called as she quickly shot an Apostle.

"I'll raise their corpses," Vicdan said with a gentle snarl as the bodies began to fall by the Runer's blades.

Sybal turned to catch the last Apostle. He ran a good distance away and began to chant. A dark wind rose up, signaling to her that he was about to summon some risen. She rushed him and he dropped his hands, turning to flee. She caught up to him and pulled him back by his black robes. Then she tossed him to the ground. The Apostle raised his hands and begged for mercy.

"Don't!" Signar shouted, stopping Sybal before she killed the man. He ran forward and slashed at him with his axe, severing his head from his shoulders, cutting off his pleas.

"Thank you," Sybal panted. "I lost myself. I..."

Signar slapped her shoulder bracingly, understanding.

Sybal turned to see Amir defending himself from two undead. She rushed to his side and took the attention of one of them. Back to back they dueled, fighting to get the upper hand. They moved flawlessly around one another, fighting in perfect rhythm. Together, they cut the heads and arms off their undead opponents.

Sybal gave Amir a quick grin before turning back to the others. She turned just in time to see Ashar take a glancing blow to his middle. The spear struck deep and hard, puncturing his armor easily. Ashar groaned and dropped his sword as the undead shoved hard, knocking him off balance. Amir saw and she felt him fly into a rage. He'd not be focusing, so she ran with him.

Sure enough, the moment he ran to Ashar's aid, another undead came at him from the side that he did not see. The undead raised his spear and would have killed Amir had Sybal not intervened. She swung her sword up with all her strength, knocking the spear into the air. Amir ignored her and ran to Ashar's side, hacking at the undead that had wounded him.

Sybal spun and kicked, knocking the undead back. As she did, she felt another come at her from behind. She drew her shield and blocked the attack, stabbing at the foe in front of her. As the one behind her advanced again, she drew buhkar, turning to mist and dodging the attack, also putting some distance between her and her foes. When she rematerialized, she was able to take up her crossbow and fire a bolt right between the eyes of the undead. As it reeled from the shot, she charged and lopped off its head. She struck so hard the thing spun, splattering her face with blood. The corpse fell, dead once again.

Spinning, she drew halat once more and blocked a jab from the second undead. As she fought this one, she spared a glance to take in the others. Signar was standing and fighting. Amir defended a fallen Ashar with Vitaly at his side. Ishaan ran to the antechamber's door and threw himself against it as it began to open. Aras joined him.

"They're coming through!" Ishaan cried, desperately shoving against the door.

Sybal quickly drew jiun and went into a fury. With the power of the rune spurring her on, she was able to hack down the remaining three undead. When she finished, panting, she looked around. Signar and Tage joined Aras and Ishaan at the door. Together, the four of them were able to shove it closed and lock it. On the other side, the undead hammered against it.

"To the tunnels," Sybal ordered. "Sokar said the one leading into the throne room was inside a pillar." She turned and looked. He'd said it was against the eastern wall. "There," she cried, pointing. She ran to the pillar and ran her fingers over it, looking for the indentation. She found it quickly and was able to push it open from the outside. "Leave it," she shouted to the men holding the door. "We'll be gone by the time they're through."

The others quickly joined her in the tunnel. Once they were all through, she closed it. Ashar groaned, holding his side as Vitaly supported him.

Amir quickly unlaced his armor and moved it aside to draw artiah.

"Can you fight?" she asked Ashar.

The younger Runer nodded, sweat beading on his brow.

"Ashar," Amir began, helping him replace his armor.

"Don't, Amir," Ashar cut in. "I can still fight. Some of us have to stay. We have to guard the doors."

Sybal frowned. "You don't have to."

Aras said, "There were more outside that door. They will go to the throne room. We can stall them."

Sybal looked up between them. "All right," she sighed, knowing she didn't have time to argue. "Signar, Amir, with me. Vicdan, wait for us in the tunnel."

"I can help. Let me raise the dead," he insisted.

"Stay," Sybal snapped. "The rest of you... May Laith'asad watch over you."

Tage led Ashar, Vitaly, Aras, and Ishaan back into the antechamber, closing the door behind them. Sybal watched Amir's face wrinkle with concern as Ashar left them.

"He'll be fine," she promised. "We're all getting out of here alive. I swear."

She turned and dashed down the short hallway hidden inside the walls. There was only one way to go: to the throne room. A door at the end of the hall appeared. She waited a moment to catch her breath, then pushed it open.

Inside, the familiar throne room came into view. The door opened on the side of the room. Sybal's eyes immediately went to the front.

There, in the ruby throne, seated with a large red blade across his lap, was Tarkan. Beside him stood Acenoth, scythe in hand.

Tarkan's blue eyes snapped from the back of the room, where the commotion rang out, to her.

He smiled.

# Chapter 34
## Fallen

Sybal locked eyes with the Necro'Khan and unsheathed her scimitar. Tarkan stood, mimicking the gesture. His blade was long and straight, blood red, and pulsing with life. Sybal stopped several feet before the ruby throne and looked up at him, then took in the blade more closely. The hilt was partially made from bones, with scriptures etched into them. She guessed that was what Scriven bone looked like. The center of the blade was a pulsing red diamond heart.

"Admiring my work, Sybal?" Tarkan asked with a dark grin. "Made from the bones of a necromancer and the heart of a Necro'Khan. Through it I sustain my armies."

Sybal ignored his gloating. Her body shook with fear and anticipation. She clenched her fists to hide it. "Tarkan, I give you this chance," she began, "to drop your weapon and come down from that throne without harm. We will find a way to spare you." Her heart screamed in rage at her. Spare him? How could she utter such a thing?

Her eyes went to his hands. She imagined them covered in blood. Tzarik's blood. No. She could not spare him.

"I am no fool, Sybal," Tarkan said, taking a few steps down from the golden platform where the ruby throne rested. "I know you will do no such thing. I killed him, the man you loved. I raised your family from their graves to fight you." He smiled darkly, his blue eyes twinkling. "I killed Rahul, too. I've taken everything from you. No, you will not spare me."

Something in Sybal snapped. She wanted to scream and charge Tarkan, but knew that would be foolish. Behind him, Acenoth stood, a long-handled scythe planted firmly on the ground. The undead Masahk eyed her, waiting for her movement.

"I am rather offended," Tarkan said easily. "You come to defeat me with only a handful of Runers and this traitor to the scriptures." He gestured at Vicdan, who stood behind them all.

Sybal growled inwardly. Vicdan had not obeyed her.

Outside the great double doors, Sybal heard what had to be Ashar shout something to Vitaly. The sound of blades against blades rang out. They were running out of time.

"Enough of this, Tarkan!" she shouted. She gripped her scimitar. "Will you surrender or not?"

Tarkan scoffed, offended and finding something slightly amusing. "You cannot defeat my undead army, no matter how many men from Caerwren you bring." His eyes went to Signar. "I spared you and yet you've come back. Do you long for death, boy?"

Sybal snarled and ran up the steps. Signar roared and leapt at Acenoth. The wolf flew over Sybal's head in a great leap, shocking both the undead Masahk and the Necro'Khan. This allowed Sybal to slash at Tarkan and force him to stumble back, losing his footing. Sybal advanced with a whirlwind of attacks, knowing Tarkan was not good in close combat. To her surprise, Tarkan answered her advances with a series of blocks and quick footwork. Seeing this, she took a few steps back as Tarkan ran down the golden dais. She followed at a leisurely pace, watching him like a hawk.

Tarkan turned to face her as Amir and Signar entered combat with Acenoth. Sybal kept one eye on Signar and the other on Tarkan. The Necro'Khan smiled and raised his blade.

"Come on, Sybal. I know you have more in you," he jeered.

Sybal reached up to her neck and took the runes into her left hand, readying them. *Please*, she prayed to the Dohkma. *Give me your strength once again. I need it.*

No answer came. Unsure if she had the fury still, she drew jiun and then leapt at Tarkan. He raised his blade and blocked her blow as she advanced. She had him easily on the run when he suddenly wavered from sight and vanished. Gasping, she quickly drew buhkar and turned to mist to avoid any sudden attacks. She heard Tarkan laugh behind her.

Whirling around, she slashed at the air. She hit nothing. She spotted Vicdan scurrying away as the fight with Acenoth brought Amir and Signar closer to him.

"Stay safe!" she shouted at Vicdan.

She rematerialized and prepared to be on defense again. A snapping sound preemptively told her where Tarkan was going to reappear. She spun, blade raised, and slashed as the black form of the Necro'Khan reappeared. Tarkan quickly raised his blade and blocked the blow. He shoved against her hard and vanished again.

Tarkan watched Sybal spin on the spot, looking for him. She was only a white ghost inside the God Deep. Glee filled him as he reached out for her blood. He'd only ever swallowed Runer blood once and it had given him some strength, though it had been vile.

He flexed his hand, reaching for her white blood. It would be so easy to kill the Runer if he could pull the blood from her very veins. He tried to grasp it, to pull it from her body, but it slipped between his fingers. Frustrated, he tried again. But the sulfates couldn't be grasped. He couldn't suck the white blood from her pores like he'd done with red blood.

Cursing, he felt his spell waning. He'd be visible again. But before he spoke the words to remain invisible inside the God Deep, he felt something else.

The eyes of his god, Nephron, were upon him, and the god laughed.

Nephron watched as he tried to pull the white blood from the Runer and failed. Before, Tarkan had been glad that they eyes of his god were upon him. Not now. He was a heretic and had spat in the face of his god.

A slight shiver of fear frosted over his spine at the god's joyful condemnation.

ॐ

*Coward,* Sybal thought, misting once again for protection. She spun on the spot, listening for the light crackling. When she heard it, she whirled around and frantically sliced at the air. She hit Tarkan once, but he parried the next blow.

Tarkan stumbled back, black blood dribbling from his shoulder where she'd clipped him. He glared at her, teeth gnashed. She took the opportunity to advance on him again. She'd been on the offensive the entire time, not giving Tarkan even a moment to swing his blade at her. Behind her, she heard Amir shout something to Signar. Sybal couldn't turn and look. She had Tarkan on the run.

She clashed blades with him once more and then shoved hard. Tarkan's light body was easy for her to push. She threw all her strength into the maneuver, making him stumble and flail. Then she lunged forward, slicing down at the fallen Necro'Khan. He rolled to the side and picked up his sword. He waved his arm frantically and called up for some risen. Sybal shrieked and misted toward him, stopping his incantation.

"Fight me, Tarkan," she hissed. Their swords entangled one another and she leaned down close to his face. She could see his black veins under his pale skin. His blue eyes snapped with electric rage. "Just you and me."

Tarkan roared and shoved her back, but she didn't stumble far. She drew halat and deflected a blow from his long-reaching sword before spinning and getting behind him. As she did, she kicked out, hitting him square in the back. He fell forward and stumbled, his sword spinning out of his grip. Sybal ran forward and Tarkan turned to watch her advance. Eyes on her, he gripped his blood blade once again. Then he stood and faced her.

Signar roared once more and leapt at Tarkan while he was distracted by Sybal. The Vaeson wolf landed on the Necro'Khan's back with such force that it knocked the blood blade from his hands. Sybal spun to the right to avoid the collision, panting. She'd not been able to catch her breath in some time now. Tarkan cried out as the huge wolf's body crushed him. But Signar didn't go for Tarkan. He leapt off him and dived for the blood blade.

"Destroy it!" Sybal called, rushing back to Tarkan's fallen body. She held her blade out, stopping Tarkan from running, pinning him down. She looked down into his blue eyes, and for once, she saw the slightest tinge of fear there.

She glanced back and watched Signar scoop up the blade in his maw. With a snarl, he clamped his jaws shut over the bone handle. Sybal was reminded of the axe above Sjörna-Reks' throne when he bit the blade. The axe had had a Vaeson bite taken out of one of the axe heads. She guessed the Vaeson magic gave them the power to destroy such metals.

Signar rended the blade with his teeth. The bones in the hilt snapped, releasing the red gem in the center. It fell to the ground with a wet plop, a soft, fleshy human heart once again.

"What have you done?" Tarkan screamed. His eyes went wide in horror at the sight before him.

Then he felt it again. Nephron watched him. Laughed at him. Though he wasn't inside the God Deep, the single great eye of Nephron watched him now, waiting.

Like the god knew Tarkan's fall was imminent.

Panic lanced through Tarkan, wondering what the god knew that he did not.

He wouldn't fall, not now. He had done what he'd set out to do. The malignation was spreading. He was so close to achieving his goal. All he needed was for the Runer to fall. But how?

His eyes snapped to Sybal.

⁓

"Sybal," Signar said, getting her attention.

She turned and saw Amir backing away from Acenoth, holding a wound on his side. White blood leaked from between his fingers. Acenoth stumbled back, his legs going weak. He fell to his knees and blood dribbled from his eyes, ears, and nose.

"My Khan," Acenoth whispered. His arms lost their strength and he dropped his scythe. The great undead Masahk tilted backward and fell in a heap, dead once again. His body quickly decayed, turning to rotten flesh and bone. Outside the palace, a loud cheer went up. The undead army must have fallen.

Amir collapsed onto his knees, fighting for breath. Signar ran to him.

Sybal heard Tarkan move fast as a scared cat. She spun around, scimitar held high. In the blink of an eye, she saw him bring his hands together to cast a spell. With a savage cry, she brought her curved blade down onto his wrists. Jiun still rushed through her blood and she felt the Dohkma's presence in her at last as she summoned all her strength into that one blow.

Tarkan screamed and fell backwards. A wet smacking sound drew Sybal's attention down. Tarkan's hands lay on the golden floor, severed from his body.

"You filthy bitch!" Tarkan yowled. His blood flowed from the wounds, pooling in a black puddle beneath him. He reeled backward and fell onto his knees, panting and screaming. "This won't stop me," he started again, gasping for air as he spoke. "The blood bends to my will alone."

Sybal raised her blade again. She locked in on his neck and prepared to swing.

"Wait!" Tarkan said, raising his bloody arms to her in a begging motion. "Sybal, listen to me. I can bring him back. You know I can."

Sybal froze, arm up, ready to strike.

Tarkan smiled in relief, coming to his knees before her. "Yes, I can.

I'll bring him back for you. I only killed him to get Sharar. You know this."

Sybal closed her eyes against his words and shook her head. "Silence, Tarkan. Your words are poison laced in pretty promises. I'd not sacrifice anyone to bring him back."

"You wouldn't?" Tarkan gave her a dark, gentle grin. "He killed for you, Sybal. He ripped open the God Deep on Caerwren for you. Plundered from the gods themselves to save you. Let me help you bring him back. Don't you love him?"

A cold hand gripped her heart, stopping it from beating. Her chest tightened and her eyes stung.

"That's right," Tarkan whispered. "Think about it. Think about what he did for you."

"Sybal!" Signar called. "What are you waiting for?"

She locked eyes with Tarkan. No. Whatever he'd bring back wouldn't be Tzarik. Unlike her, Tzarik was truly dead. He was gone. There was no reversal of fate. Tarkan was a master of the dead, but he could not create life.

He must have seen the change in her eyes because he sprang up and turned to run. Just a few feet before him, a small green strike of lightning shot up from the ground, opening.

"He's running!" Amir shouted.

Sybal leapt after him, sword held high. She shoved her sadness down and focused on the fury. Tarkan had weakened her with his words and she had to fight to bring herself back to the moment. She grabbed the back of his black robes and pulled him away from the jagged opening. She spun, flinging him to the ground hard. Rounding on him, she drew the sigiled blade from her side and tossed her scimitar away. With the blade in hand, she bore down on him.

"Sybal, don't," Tarkan begged, crawling backward away from her. "We were allies once. Wait!"

She was done waiting. Raising the blade in both hands, she screamed a war cry and brought it down with all her might. The blade easily cut through Tarkan's neck, severing his head from his body. His head spun, flying away several feet before smacking grotesquely against the throne room floor. His lips moved in silence, still trying to speak as life still coursed through his body.

Signar leapt onto his body then, transforming back into his wolf. He ripped at Tarkan's chest until he exposed his ribs and his hard heart underneath. Face bloody, Signar stepped aside for Sybal. She walked forward, going completely numb. Reaching into Tarkan's destroyed chest, she ripped out the red diamond that was his heart. As soon as it left his body, it turned into soft flesh again. It didn't beat, but it felt slightly warm. Sybal tossed it to the ground. Re-gripping the sigiled blade, she faced it.

"Wait!" Signar called, running to Sybal in his human form. "Don't do it. Don't kill him. We don't know what will happen."

It took all her strength, hands shaking, to not stab the heart then. Tears filled her eyes and anger roiled in her veins. She looked down at the heart.

"I... I have to," she said. Her teeth clenched so hard her jaw hurt. "Let me do this."

"No," Signar insisted. He came up behind her, reaching for the blade. "Back away."

"Stay back, Signar," she snarled. "Even if I die—"

"Sybal!" Signar shouted, hand reaching toward her.

Without another moment's hesitation, she brought the red blade down, stabbing Tarkan's heart as Signar screamed for her to stop. She thought she heard the Necro'Khan scream again as a flash of red light ignited from within the blade. The sigils glowed for a moment, then went dark again.

Her sulfates pulsed and her head spun. Her body began to quake and pain lanced through her. Her every vein ran cold, shards of ice cutting her from the inside. She screamed and fell, dropping the blade. Her sulfates rushed madly, drowning out all other sounds.

Everything in Sybal's body was on fire. Her mind was a wildfire of emotions as she looked at Tarkan's corpse, headless and bloody. His last words still rang in her ears. His promises. She shook as a cold sweat overtook her. She quaked madly, unable to stop the shaking.

Signar wrapped his arms around her and held her close as tears streamed down her face. She gripped his arms and let herself go, safe in his embrace. A sob choked her and was quickly followed by a loud wail. Everything hit her at once. Every memory of the past five years, every loss, every victory. Her life as a wealthy heiress had been a golden one, one she'd never thought she'd leave. But in a single day, everything had changed. She'd traveled the map, had seen things she'd never thought she could face, and had lived to tell the tale.

In a final throe of agony, everything went suddenly numb and quiet.

She saw only darkness and snow as the Dohkma appeared to her. He didn't speak, just looked down on her. His face was impassive. Not angry. No judgment. He almost looked on her with pity.

"What's happening?" Sybal asked. "Am I dying?"

"I tried," the Dohkma said softly, "but it seems you have found a cure for your fate. Eternal life through death. I could punish you by forcing this pain upon you for eternity. But I am a merciful god. Remember whose blood runs in your veins, Sybal. Do not forget me."

"I am not dying?" she asked.

The Dohkma smiled now and shook his head. "You shall never taste death again. And should you kill in my name—now that we know the runes cannot take you—I would consider freeing you from your chains."

"Never," Sybal shot back.

For a moment, the Pale God didn't say anything. He looked on her and his face changed from anger to consideration. "You will work for me one day, Sybal. I promise you that. I have foreseen it."

"No," she said with just as much determination as before.

At this, the Dohkma smiled. "You cannot change your fate. You will protect my blood. It has been planned since the beginning. It is your destiny. Stop defying me and let me aid you." His smile widened. "Do you never wonder why I haven't enslaved you yet? I have bigger plans for you.

"Now." He crossed his arms and raised his head to look down his nose at her. "I will take your pain and spare you, my lady Runer. But remember my words."

The Pale God vanished. Light came back to her eyes and the smell of battle filled her nose. Sybal looked around and saw the thronehall again. The god was gone.

She threw herself into Signar's arms and sobbed into his shoulder, all the pain finally washing away. Amir came up behind her and gently gripped her shoulders. Signar pried Sybal off him and turned her toward Amir. She let him, falling into Amir's arms and burying her face in his chest as the weeping took her again. Amir gently stroked her hair, holding her close.

Behind her, Signar went to Tarkan's severed head and picked it up. She watched him march out onto the balcony with it. He disappeared from sight, but she could still hear him.

"Your Khan is dead," he shouted. "Surrender now or—"

The rest was drowned in the uproarious shouting from the Al'Myrahn and Caerwren warriors.

Sybal took a deep breath and motioned to Amir to help her up. He wrapped his arm around her middle and stood, letting her lean on him. She wasn't wounded, but the exhaustion weakened her very bones.

Sybal looked around the throne room. Everything was still dark and the torches danced in a light breeze.

"What now?" Amir asked.

She met his eyes, the last of her tears dripping down her cheeks. "We deal with the Apostles," she said stoically. "Most will run even as we speak. Then…" She took a deep breath. She wasn't sure about the next step. "Then the rifts. I'm not sure what to do about those, but we have to close them."

"There is a way?" Amir asked.

Sybal nodded. Her sad, tired eyes went to Vicdan. "We need a Necro'Khan to perform the rite. And we need blood to heal it. Not an easy task."

Amir frowned, confusion and worry creasing his brow. "How can we do that?"

Sybal wrapped her arms around herself, eyes looking into nothingness as she thought. "We might have a way. But it will require sacrifice. We cannot do this bloodlessly, and that is what I fear most right now."

Apprehension filled her. She didn't want any more death, but it was inevitable at this point. If they wanted the rifts closed, they had to spill more blood, take more lives.

The realization brought a fresh wave of tears to her eyes. She gasped, swallowing a sob. "I don't want to spill more blood."

Amir gently wrapped her in his arms once again. She gave in, leaning against him and letting him embrace her fully.

"It must be done," Amir whispered. "The rifts must be closed."

"I know." Sybal sniffled and nodded. "I know."

"There might be a way," Vicdan said softly. "We could use any Apostles we capture. It's still gruesome and a terrible way to die, but it will open the God Deep if we use them for the Blood Path."

"But we don't have a Necro'Khan," Amir said.

"Yes, well..." Vicdan sighed and wrung his hands nervously. "We might be able to make one, though I won't be happy about it."

"You?" Amir asked, still holding Sybal.

Vicdan sadly tilted his head. "Me. I don't have anything to sacrifice, though."

Sybal asked, "What does that mean, then? We can't make you Khan?"

The necromancer's green eyes looked sad. "I'll think of something I have that I can give up to the gods. We have no choice, really."

# Chapter 35
## The Rifts

Sybal drew the healing rune over Amir's side twice as Signar went to the doors at the end of the throne room. He threw them open, posing with his axe for a fight. But the room lay silent. Sybal looked out the doors to find Ishaan, Tage, Aras, Ashar, and Vitaly all still standing. Decaying corpses lay around them as well some slain Apostles.

"What happened?" Sybal asked.

Signar walked into the room and quickly embraced Tage. "Tell us what happened."

The young Runer almost beamed. "We kept them at bay. We killed the Apostles and the undead wouldn't fall. We couldn't get close enough to sever their heads. But then, suddenly, they fell. They turned to ash and dust, as you see here."

Sybal watched Tage poke at one of the fallen undead, now ashes and rot like Acenoth in the throne room.

"It was thrilling," Ishaan said as he drew the healing rune over several wounds.

Sybal's heart felt lighter. "I am pleased everyone made it out."

"So far," Aras reminded her. "We no doubt lost good Northican warriors outside."

Sybal nodded. "Of course. We will build them pyres and send them to Rahrgalah in fire. Or would it be better to bring them home and let their families do that?"

"Let us take our dead," Aras said, "and burn them upon our shores so their spirits do not get lost on the way."

"I understand," Sybal said. She looked around. "Let's finish what we've started, then. Tage, Aras, take the other Runers and ride to the battlefield. Tell them the Necro'Khan is dead. And..." She gulped. "Bring two Apostles to the Cradle. We will start there at once."

"What are you doing?" Ishaan asked.

Sybal held her head high. "Finishing this once and for all. At least on Alika. Vicdan, Amir, with me."

"Me as well," Signar said. When Sybal gave him a questioning look, he said, "You need red blood."

She wanted to argue, but he was right. Vicdan would need at least a little for what he was about to do. "Very well," she mumbled.

Some hours later, the Cradle came into view, huge and golden in the darkness. They'd run into only a few spirits and one mysterious beast they'd had to dispatch on their ride to The Cradle. Sybal was exhausted now and wondered if somewhere the sun was rising or setting. She hoped it had risen and they'd see the light once the rift was closed.

"The Deep is already open to us," Vicdan said as they marched up the steps of The Cradle and closer to its insides where the spring flowed. "I hope that helps when it comes to ascension."

"What are you going to sacrifice?" she asked. "Tzarik told me it has to be significant. That's why Tarkan chose Zeva in the end."

"I have one thing of value," Vicdan said, his face going slack. "I'm not sure how it will work."

"What is it?" Sybal asked. She didn't know what the necromancer was referring to. She couldn't imagine having to think of something to give up to the gods—especially a dark god like Nephron—though she had been willing to give up just about anything when she'd been speaking to the Dohkma. Maybe it felt similar for necromancers who sought the mantle of Necro'Khan. The desperation drove them. But Vicdan was giving up his mortality for them.

"Vicdan," she said softly. "I understand what this means, and I can't thank you enough. I can't thank you for the whole world for what you're about to do. I..." She didn't know how to go on.

"Sybal," Vicdan said with a smile reminiscent of his old self, "I'm not just doing this for you. I live on this map, too. I have the power to make this right, so I am."

She detected a sort of finality in his words, like a man being led to his execution. She stopped, grabbing his arm, and turned him to face her. "What are you giving to the gods, Vicdan?"

The young man sighed sadly. "The only thing I have and, frankly, the only thing I've loved all my life." He winked at her. "Myself."

She opened her mouth in shock, about to protest, when a snapping and hissing drew their attention to the rift. A sort of dark wind howled around this one, pulling at their cloaks and hair. The rift shot up from the ground in green and gray light. Sybal could almost see through it as it danced and flickered. She didn't miss the God Deep. Moans and roars came from the inside. It felt like the rift might burst open at any point, showing them monsters and haunts. Strings of gray and green lightning flashed from the rift, striking the ground near them.

"What does that mean, Vicdan?" Sybal called over the sound of the rift. "How can you give yourself to the gods and be Necro'Khan."

Vicdan smiled weakly. "I don't know. But it's all I have. Unless..." He reached into his robes and pulled out the two dead hearts. "Unless they'll take the hearts of other Necro'Khans."

Sybal looked on in disgust at the sight. "Please, offer them instead. I can't bear to lose another friend."

"And if it doesn't work?" Vicdan asked.

Sybal pressed her lips together, fighting the urge to weep. "It has to," she said.

Behind them came the other Runers and a few burly Caerwren warriors. Cries went up from the Apostles they had captured when they beheld the rift. They fought to get away, but the Runers held them in place.

"Kill them," Sybal instructed. "Then place their bodies, one half across from the other, to create the Blood Path."

The Apostles begged and cried for their lives, but Sybal ignored them, tears leaking down her face. She had to harden her heart against their weeping and pleading. Aras and the Caerwren warriors made quick work of the Apostles and then prepared their bodies by slowly cutting them in half. Once they were ready, they laid them out as instructed.

Sybal backed away as Signar approached Vicdan. The young Reks cut his wrist and offered it to Vicdan. Vicdan held it to his mouth, slowly drinking the trickling blood. He didn't take much, then motioned Signar away. Sybal watched with bated breath as Vicdan walked to the head of the Blood Path. At the other end, he faced the rift to the Deep. The necromancer looked frightened, his face wrinkling in fear. Sybal admired him in that moment. He was about to come face to face with his god. He was about to lose the last of himself. She almost ran to him, crying for him to stop. But there was no other way. Not if they wanted the rifts closed. She gripped her own hands while she watched.

Vicdan held up his hands, a heart in each one. He mumbled some verses before even more wind picked up and blew his robes around him, the ends snapping. Sybal gripped Signar next to her.

*Please,* she prayed to any god that would hear her. *Let this work. Hear him, Nephron. Take this sacrifice. Accept what he has brought you.*

Vicdan's green eyes were large as he finally shouted, "I have nothing to sacrifice, but I bring you the heart of the heretic who betrayed your power. The one who took the blood and made it his own. The traitor to your laws."

Sybal watched as Vicdan gasped and stumbled back. He clearly heard something she couldn't. His eyes widened in fear, never blinking. Tears streamed from them. She wished she could take his place, to protect him from that fear. To see what he saw. But still he held the hearts aloft, offering them to the gods above and below.

In a sudden flash, one of the hearts went up in black flames. Vicdan cried out, but held his ground. Sybal saw his hands shaking as the fire consumed the first heart. Then it happened again, taking the second.

As they burned, Vicdan cried out and dropped them, flaming, to the ground. The fire destroyed them, leaving behind only ashes.

Then Vicdan shouted in pain. He clutched at his chest and breathed hard, panting. He doubled over, moaning, more tears streaming from his eyes. Sybal stepped forward, hating the pain and agony he was obviously in. She wanted to take it from him. Witnessing the suffering was worse than taking it upon herself.

"Vicdan!" she called. But he didn't answer. He groaned and fell to his knees. He stayed down for some time. She took one step toward him, but Signar reached out and stopped her. "Speak to me," she begged him.

"Stay back!" the necromancer cried through a pained moan. On his knees, he sat up. He hovered his hands close together and started to chant verses she could not hear.

The blood around him on the ground began to float up in thin rivulets of red. Sybal stumbled back, taking Signar with her. She looked up as the blood hovered higher and higher. Soon it reached the top of the rift. Then it moved, knitting itself around the opening, pulling it together. Slowly, the gap closed as the blood flowed into it. Sybal found herself gaping at the sight.

As the blood healed the rift, spirits and other haunts rushed past them, being sucked back into it. They screamed and moaned as they were summoned back. One passed through Sybal, making her shiver.

Vicdan stood then, looking stronger now that whatever mysterious pain he'd felt had gone. He threw his arms wide like he was seizing a pair of double doors and then slammed his arms together, clapping his hands. With a thunderous boom, the rift shattered. A flash of green light blinded Sybal and she turned away, wincing. A cold gust of wind, like a chilled explosion, pushed her hair and cloak back. When she looked again, the rift was gone. Vicdan gasped and fell to the ground in a heap.

With the rift gone and the wind dying down, Sybal ran to him. She threw her arms around him and supported him as he collapsed into her. He was thin and pale, his face gaunt. He shook in her arms and black blood dribbled from his eyes. She looked up. The rift was truly gone.

Even in that very moment, the blackness began to dissolve. A hint of the sun shone through the dark. She looked back down at Vicdan in her arms.

"What happened?" she said, panting.

Vicdan swallowed and shook his head, closing his eyes as more bloody tears streamed from them. "I can't tell you."

She took a moment to catch her own breath, deciding to leave it be. "You did it," she whispered. "It worked?"

Vicdan nodded, sniffling. "I am... I never thought I'd be..." He laughed darkly. "Father never thought I'd amount to anything. Well, father, who is Necro'Khan now?"

Sybal smiled, seeing he still retained his jovial attitude. She hugged him tight, pressing her hand into the back of his head. "Thank you, Vicdan."

He nodded. "How about that kiss now? We never did get around to it. It's several years late, and I feel I've earned it."

She giggled brokenly behind her tears and pressed her lips to his forehead, kissing him. "Are you ready to move on?"

"Yes," he sighed. "The darkness here is lifting. Now, I just have to consume and do it all over again." He blanched at the thought.

"I am sorry," she whispered. She squeezed him tighter.

"Such is the life of the Necro'Khan," Vicdan said, sighing again. "Where to next?"

Sybal stiffened. "To Xia," she said.

They waited until the next night, gathering up the men and imprisoning the Apostles they could find during the day. The darkness lifted throughout the second day and vanished in time for them to see the sunset. Tired and bloody, Sybal stood with the Al'Myrahn and Caerwren warriors outside the palace walls at the end of the second day, ready to march.

She was about to call for Signar when an army of torches appeared on the southern horizon. They didn't advance, but two gilded warriors stood ahead of them, facing her.

"Stay here," she commanded the others. She mounted her horse and rode out to the army, curious and cautious. The closer she got, the more she recognized the royal army of the south of Alika. The two in the front were clearly pharaohs.

She trotted up to them and stopped several feet away. "The Necro'Khan is dead," she said stoically, seeing their army and gleaming weapons.

The pharaoh with the black skin of Yenka narrowed his eyes at her. "How can this be? Who are you?"

"I am no one," she said solemnly, "but you can see for yourself. Go into the city and you will find him dead. His body hangs in the square. The undead are gone as well."

The second pharaoh seemed to deflate with relief. "Thank the gods," he whispered. "We will see for ourselves. If what you say is true, we will depart."

Sybal nodded and cantered back to her small posse that waited for her outside the palace walls. She quickly explained before turning back to Signar.

"They won't attack?" he asked.

Sybal watched the men move into Mysir slowly, the heads of the pharaohs turning this way and that, taking in the sights of the devastation the battle had left behind. "I don't think they will once they see and understand. But I cannot stay and make them see.

"The sun will be rising over Xia soon. I don't know what kind of state we will find the place in. According to one of the Apostles, Tarkan left two of his most trusted in command before he left. One called Faraji has been there the whole time. Another called Ashkan has gone back and forth, bringing news. I searched for him among the Apostles but haven't found him, which means he must be on Xia."

"I know of him," Amir said. "He was not fond of Tarkan, as far as I could tell."

"That may give us an advantage," Sybal said, desperate for anything that might help them. "Perhaps he will submit willingly to us."

"But the undead will have fallen," Signar said with a satisfied grin.

"All that remains are the Apostles and any mortal warriors Tarkan may have left behind. They might be hiding in the Royal City. Surely Wushito has cornered them by now."

"The fact that the undead have fallen just means they know we're coming," Tage said.

"Which could mean many things," Amir said. "They could flee or they could fortify themselves inside the Royal City."

Sybal's heart skipped a beat at this. Would Hiro still be alive? Or would they have killed him once they saw the undead fall? She suddenly wanted to hurry.

"Signar," she said sternly. "Have Kazamar open a portal outside the palace, within the gates of the Royal City. We cannot wait for another siege. We must arrive ready to fight."

The Vaeson nodded and touched the amulet, communicating silently with the djinn inside. Sybal waited, knowing wishing on the djinn was dangerous. They'd have to deal with him later as well. They'd have to uphold their end of the promise and set him free. Remembering how destructive the monster was before they bound him gave her pause. But she didn't have time to think about it.

Massive, fiery portals burst open suddenly before their army. Sybal was shocked to look through and see the Royal City just as the sun rose. Had the Crypt not been opened? Darkness had not taken Xia, but her heart still thudded in her chest with worry for Hiro.

They pushed through the portals and landed on the other side. She marched toward the palace, up a muddy road. She kept her eyes peeled for anything that moved. Behind her, the men came in three by three. Amir, Signar, and the other Runers marched at her side. The pink trees of Xia moved in a slight pre-storm breeze and clouds moved in. It was going to rain. The palace jutted up before them, the many-layered roofs cutting up into the sky. Each tower, red and jade, looked like a spear. It looked just how Sybal remembered it.

"Once we're inside, we kill the Apostles and take a few prisoners," she ordered, then repeated the order in Caerwren.

As they marched closer to the palace, Sybal spotted a few Alikan kehann standing inside the gates. She watched as they noticed the army. They backed away, then dropped their weapons, immediately raising their hands above their heads. One, a commander by the looks of the ornaments on his armor, approached her. He drew his scimitar and dropped it onto the ground. Sybal drew hers and faced the kehann commander.

"Spare us," the commander said when they drew close enough. "The undead fell two days ago, but we have not been able to leave the palace. We don't know where to go. Sabi, we are loyal to Alika. We had no choice. Let my men and me go. Only the Apostles wait within. We ask that you show mercy."

"And Prince Hiro?" Sybal asked. "Is he alive?"

The commander nodded. "Last I saw him. We took him below into the dungeon."

"And the Hallow City?" Sybal asked as strongly as she could. "What of Wushito?"

"Tarkan killed their leader long ago," the commander said, his face full of trepidation. "But they stood up to us. A messenger came from the Hallow City last night: they have taken it back and even now they march to the palace."

"Killed their leader?" Sybal asked. Her heart froze. She hoped she was wrong in her thoughts.

The commander nodded. "A fox Masahk. They called him Yasuke."

She gasped. So the brave Masahk was dead. He'd helped them more than once when she and Tzarik first visited Xia. But he had been loyal to Wushito and ShanBao. Still, he wasn't an evil man. He didn't deserve death, as far as she knew. He had probably fought and died trying to save his country. Wushito was loyal to Xia if nothing else.

"You may live," she said stoically. "But you will answer for your traitorous ways in an Alikan court. The Dynast Pharaoh will deal with you as he sees fit." She signaled to her men and they descended upon the commander and the other kehann, taking them and binding them. She faced her army. "Scour the place. Kill any Apostles you find. Any man who surrenders will be taken back to Alika. Do you understand?"

Signar repeated the orders in Caerwren and Sybal noticed the Northicans looked disappointed. They wanted another battle, more bloodshed.

She turned back to the palace and motioned for the Runers to follow her. "Signar, stay with the men," she commanded. He didn't argue, nodding and leading them around and to the left of the palace.

"Spread out," he commanded. "Find the Apostles."

She watched him march away before heading to the golden throne room. When she reached it, she shoved the doors open and looked inside. She wasn't shocked to find two Apostles within, talking hurriedly. One was a tall, black Alikan man with the scriptures on his flesh and startling blue eyes. The other was pale, his flesh unmarked. His eyes were green.

"Ashkan," Vicdan said, almost shocked. "A Bone Scriven."

"So you live," the one called Ashkan said to Vicdan. "I wondered what had happened to you. And you bring with you an army."

Sybal stopped and let Vicdan speak. She glared at the Apostles.

"Not just an army," Vicdan said pompously. "I am Khan now, and you will show me loyalty or it is death for you."

The Scriven Apostle guffawed loudly. "You have taken Tarkan's place? I don't believe it."

"Can you not feel it in your blood, Faraji?" Ashkan asked, and Sybal noted his complacency. Ashkan bowed his head to Vicdan. "You will get no fight from me. I was no lover of Tarkan and was loyal out of necessity." Ashkan knelt before Vicdan and lowered his head. "I submit to your judgment, my Khan."

Vicdan looked to Sybal.

"Where is Hiro?" she asked.

"Don't tell them anything," the one called Faraji hissed to his fellow necromancer.

Sybal drew her blade and faced Faraji. "Comply or die," she said simply. "We've taken back Alika. Tarkan is dead, and the undead have fallen. Do you really want to be loyal to a dead man?"

Faraji eyed Sybal, looking like he might fight. Then his eyes softened and he lowered them. He faced Vicdan and nodded. "My Khan," he growled.

"Kneel," Vicdan ordered. When Faraji didn't move, Vicdan raised his hand and pointed to the ground.

Glaring, Faraji knelt before the Necro'Khan.

"Hiro," Sybal repeated. "Where is he?"

"Below," Ashkan answered. "He is alive. I protected him as best I could. I wouldn't let them kill him. Even Tarkan didn't want the prince dead."

"Traitor," Faraji snarled. "I should have killed you when I had the chance."

Sybal nodded, ignoring the bickering between the two Apostles. "Ishaan, Vitaly, Ashar, take them into custody. Bring them to the men and have them bound. We will take them back to Alika."

"Please," Ashkan said, not looking Vicdan in the eye. "I did what I could. I delayed the opening of the Crypt. I fought against our brethren. Remember this of me when you bring me before the pharaoh."

Vicdan grimaced at the begging. "I leave it up to the Dynast Pharaoh, I am afraid."

Ashkan lowered his head in submission.

The Runers moved and Sybal strode to the side door, Amir and Vicdan behind her. She looked around as she marched to the garrison, remembering her time there. The place was in disarray and damaged compared to the last time she had been there. She guessed, after Signar had told her what had happened, that Xia had been fighting amongst themselves, desperate to put a new Di-Huan on the throne.

She trotted down the steps into the small prison. There was a single row of cells.

"Hiro?" she called. "Where are you?" She spoke in Al'Myrahn so he'd understand it was her.

"Sybal?" the prince's voice called up from a few cells down. "Is that you?"

She ran and found him. Hiro sat up when he saw her and crawled to the bars, gripping them desperately.

"How— What?" he started, too shocked to get a sentence out. His face was bruised badly and his garments were bloody, especially the back of them. He'd been beaten and flogged, but he was alive.

She reached through the bars and took his shaking hands in hers.

Hiro babbled a string of praises and prayers to the White Dragon before saying, "I thought you were dead. They told me about Tzarik. I'm so sorry. I thought the worst after Yasuke."

"It's all right," Sybal said gently, taking his quaking shoulders in her hands. "You're safe now, and so is Xia."

"So much has happened," Hiro said, his eyes streaming. "I failed Yoshi. I couldn't protect him. I couldn't stop them."

"Quiet," Sybal whispered. "Don't blame yourself." She glanced up at Vicdan.

"Do you have a small knife?" Vicdan asked.

Sybal nodded and took her right hand from Hiro, unsheathing a small blade from her thigh. She handed it to Vicdan, who went to work on the lock right away.

As he worked, Hiro told them everything. He wept as he recounted how Tarkan had come, taken over the Royal City, then marched on Wushito. How he'd killed Yoshi, then Yasuke. "Once he was gone," Hiro said, "the Apostles were ruthless. They had the undead attack the cities even as they fought among themselves. I prayed for them to unite against the undead, but they would not. I feared the worst for my country. How did you overtake them?"

"It's a long story." Sybal sighed as the lock fell away. She flung the door open and reached in, supporting Hiro as he stood. He was thin and weak. "But we killed Tarkan. It's over."

"Not so long as Wu-Tang and Shiuki fight," Hiro said. "Before they locked me down here, they were the last cities standing."

"Are you in danger?" Sybal asked as she helped him limp up the steps. "Will the people come for you to take the throne?"

Hiro shook his head. "I will step aside for whoever comes for the throne. It's never been mine to have."

Sybal nodded. "I will stay a few days, help you regain control of Xia, but I must go to Caerwren. It appears the Crypt was never broken open here."

"No," Hiro said with the first slight smile Sybal had seen on his face. "Wushito fought like dragons to keep it safe. Many perished in the fight. But the undead never reached the Crypt."

"I'm glad to hear it," Sybal said. She thought back to what Ashkan had said. Perhaps the Apostle deserved some mercy for his part in not pushing the undead army on the Crypt. She guessed that without his interference, they might have overtaken Wushito and opened the Crypt.

"That's good." She sighed inwardly with relief. Xia was safe, for now, from everything except itself.

Before they left, Sybal went back down to the garrison, searching for any sign of Tzarik. She went alone and slowly walked through the prison's halls. There wasn't much down there so when she found a wooden table near a row of cells, she stopped. A set of keys lay there, but nothing else.

She looked up into the cells nearby. One held a whipping post inside and dark, old red blood stained it and the flagstones around it. She blinked looking into the cell and turned. The one opposite had a stream of sunlight coming through a single window. It shined onto a cruel-looking Xian cross. It was made of thin poles of black wood. Her breath caught in her throat.

White, glittering blood splashed over the cross and the stoney floor she stood on. It was old and dried, but the opalescent ingredients to the sulfates made it shine. The white contrasted sharply with the black wood. Sybal stumbled into the cell and reached her hand out. Her fingers traveled through the air for what felt like an eternity before they touched the hard black wood. She gripped it, feeling the dried white blood beneath her fingers. His blood.

She tried to swallow but couldn't. Closing her eyes, she wondered what his last moments were like. Was he in pain? Was he scared? Panting, tears ran down her face and she fell to her knees before the cross. A sob echoed out from her, trailing down the stoney row of cells. She wrapped her arms around herself and hugged herself hard. Glancing over her shoulder, she saw the cell with the whipping post was just across from her. That must have been where Signar was held. They made him watch. Tarkan had been that cruel.

Sybal looked up into the sunlight, letting it bathe her tear-stained face. "So you're gone," she whispered. "He took you and everything you had. Stole you from me." She raised her hand and gently touched the blood once again. "We made a pyre for you. But please: go to Janna. See my family. Be with them. They have watched over me and know who you are. Please, Tzarik..." She couldn't go on, choked on another sob.

Sybal wept in the garrison alone. She let the tears fall again until she was convinced she'd never see him again. He was truly and completely gone.

# Chapter 36
## The Mother of Runers

They used the portals to return to Al'Myrah and Sybal had messengers sent to the sultana. The Al'Myrahn soldiers went on their way once they reached the palace, but the rest marched to the shores over the next couple of days to where the ships of Northica waited. Once they were ready to sail, Sybal paid Ishaan, Ashar, and Vitaly. Out of a courtesy to them, she also offered them a portal back to Bahratt.

"I won't forget you, sabi," Ishaan said as he stood next to his loaded horse. "And should you ever have need of me, call on me. I don't travel far outside Jarabu."

Amir and Ashar embraced, holding one another like they might not ever let go. Sybal watched them, former master and apprentice. As they said their goodbyes, she wondered if that would ever be her. The thought shook her. Would she ever be a Runer master, responsible for the life of another sentient being? She suddenly didn't think she could do it, and certainly not with the affection that Amir held for Ashar. No, she could never love again, she was sure of it.

Once the three Runers from Bahratt were gone, she turned to face Amir, Vicdan, and Signar with his two Runers.

"We will return to Caerwren," she told them. "We'll fight our way to the rift, throw the blade within, and close it." She looked at Vicdan. "Are you ready?"

The Necro'Khan sighed in resignation. "I will be once we get some blood in me, though it gives me no pleasure."

He was right, after all. The things they had to do to close the rifts were gruesome and dark. But it had to be done.

"We have prisoners in Altevine," Tage offered. "Some who have done terrible things. We can use them. A guiltless sacrifice."

Sybal nodded, but inwardly her stomach still turned. She hated the magic of the necromancers and wished they didn't have to use it. It was dark, vile, and bloody. The loss of sentient life was atrocious to her. There was very little she thought a sentient could do that deserved to be punished by death, much less warranting cutting them in half and using them in a bloody ritual.

"Protect Vicdan from anything that comes out of that darkness," she ordered the Runers. "Amir..." She locked eyes with him. She wanted him to stay, something in her calling out to him. "You are free to go as well. You don't have to follow us any longer."

Amir cocked a gentle smile. "I'm staying, Sybal. I'm coming with you. Don't try to argue."

Relief flooded her and a warmth spread through her body. "Are you sure? This could be dangerous."

Amir nodded. "I won't leave your side. Not now."

She swallowed the strange feeling rising in her gut. "Thank you," she whispered.

Kazamar let the Northican fleet through the portals first. Dain raised his hand from the flagship and waved to them as the sails dropped and caught the wind. They watched the fleet vanish into the whiteness of Northica.

Moments later, the fiery ring showed only darkness within. Sybal looked into it and heard a long, wolven howl. Signar stood next to her, his face set in fierce determination. He removed his axe from his back and stepped into the portal ahead of her. Tage and Aras followed their Reks quickly, weapons also in hand. A few flakes of snow blew through the portal, melting onto the desert shore. Sybal squared up to the portal and stepped through, Amir and Vicdan at her sides.

The sudden change from warm, sunny weather to the biting, black, cold wind of Altevine made Sybal shiver. Darkness engulfed them the moment they stepped through, and white snow whipped all around them. They sank into the mire a little and she stumbled, falling into Amir's arms.

"Raudnir is angry," Signar whispered, taking a torch from his horse's pack. "I feel his displeasure."

"Tell him I'm here for the good of Altevine," Vicdan said sardonically.

Signar smiled. "If I see him, I will let him know."

"I hope we don't," Sybal mumbled, lighting her torch as well. "I've come face to face with enough gods for my lifetime."

As they spoke, something rushed past them in the darkness. It ran on six hooves, whatever it was, and made a wet snorting sound.

"Watch for monsters," she whispered. "For anything that might possess you." She looked up at this. Vicdan was safe from possession because of the scriptures. She and the Runers were protected by the runes. That's when she noticed Signar still wore Tzarik's runes. Her heart twisted in her chest, but she smiled. "Never mind. We're all safe from that."

"But watch for skygge," Tage said, his blue eye almost glowing in the darkness as they flitted from one shadow to another. "They swarm the moors right now."

"Skygge?" Amir asked.

Sybal answered, remembering the creatures from her time in the God Deep. "Dead ones from the God Deep who have been dead for too long, or died too many times to be conscious any longer. They shamble about seeking flesh to gnaw on. Simply decapitate them."

No sooner had she said this than one wandered to the perimeter of their torchlight. When the firelight touched it, it hissed and recoiled. All the same, it reached out toward Signar, its teeth champing and biting. Signar easily swung his axe and removed the head. It plopped down into the mud with a sickening plunk.

"Something else is out there," Amir suddenly whispered. "My sulfates are screaming."

As he spoke, Sybal felt it, too. Her white blood ran cold in her veins and rushed madly. There were any number of monsters and haunts on Caerwren that might make their sulfates rush. Sybal held her torch high to spread the light out just a little more. She saw nothing but a black shadow cringe away from the circle of orange light.

"Stay close," she whispered.

They walked in tense silence until they spotted something in the distance. Sybal held up her hand to stop the march and squinted into the distance. Snow caught in her eyes, stinging her, but she forced her eyes open anyway. Farther to the north—or what she guessed to be north—was a giant ring of fire. Torchlight flickered around a circle of giant stones, and in the center she spotted the rift, green, glowing, and snapping angrily. Upon the stones glowed blue wards carved and painted into the stones.

"A warding circle," Signar told them. "To keep bad magic at bay. They were constructing it the last time I was here. It looks finished now, but is it working?"

They heard the chanting of Volra coming up from the glen as well. Sybal spotted the white-clad priests around the outside of the stone circle, arms raised as they prayed to their gods to protect them.

"To the village first," Signar said. "We will fetch sacrifices from the garrison and bring them back here."

Sybal blanched. "Will an animal sacrifice not work?"

Vicdan shook his head. "It was a sentient sacrifice that opened the rift. It must be one to close it. I am sure."

They turned east and started the march to the village. It took them half a day to reach the base of Altevine, but once Sybal spotted the thronehall and the familiar village, her heart lightened a little. A great fire outside the thronehall lit up most of the space between it and the village. Torches lined the pathways leading through the place, and very few people milled about outside. The ones that did, Sybal noticed, were thin and weary looking. When they spotted Signar, they whispered his name, begged for deliverance, and bowed. Some even reached out to him and touched his legs, whispering prayers.

They passed through the crowds unscathed and made it to the thronehall where a huge fire burned inside. Thralls attended the fire and groveled to Signar when he entered.

"Aras," Signar ordered, "go to the garrison and find two prisoners. Ask the jailor who the worst of them are." He glanced at Sybal, and she appreciated his attempt to ease her conscience. Nothing would, but at least he'd tried. After giving this order, Signar walked up the familiar stone dais and took his place on the wolf-shaped throne.

Sybal looked up at him and thought about how far he'd come. She watched as a few people of Altevine came in and waited to hear and see what their Reks would do. Some whispered to one another and others just watched, their eyes full of hope.

Vicdan sighed and moved by Sybal, following Aras out the back door.

"Where are you going?" she asked.

He looked up at her, eyes full of revulsion and sorrow. "I need blood. Flesh. Or I won't be able to cast and close the rift."

Understanding, Sybal nodded. Vicdan followed Aras out and a strange hush fell over the thronehall. Vicdan was brave for what he was doing. Soft whispers still went up from the people as their eyes bored into Signar. Sybal walked up to the dais and stood beside him.

"I wish there was another way," she whispered. "We're committing the same atrocities Tarkan did."

"We're nearly there," Signar replied. "I know we have prisoners that deserve death. Think on that instead. Know that their imminent death is serving a purpose."

Sybal didn't understand the barbaric outlook on death those from Caerwren had. They saw it as glorious and necessary. Something that could be used in celebration. Even Signar saw it that way.

Out behind them, the pained scream of a man broke the air. The people inside the thronehall gasped and looked around. Signar kept his face stoic and determined, showing no fear. The man outside gurgled in his own blood and soon went silent. Sybal imagined poor Vicdan consuming, preparing to cast the spell to close the rift. She covered her face and turned away only to run into Amir. He gently took her in his arms and held her for a moment while she regained her composure. She took a deep breath and then gently pushed him away.

Aras reappeared with three other warriors pulling along two pris-oners in chains. They had the dark hair and eyes, but the pale skin of men from Rom. Sybal reminded herself that the people of Caerwren sacrificed others to their gods all the time. This was only terrible to her, no one else.

"To the rift, then," Signar said loudly to the hall at large. "We will close it now."

⌇

The journey back to the rift made Sybal anxious. Her sulfates still rushed once they were back out in the darkness and she felt eyes on her. She wondered at last if the god Mjordir, the prime god and abomination of Caerwren, watched them. He might be close. She remembered what Kjarton had said about no one ever seeing Mjordir, but him often watching them.

"The hunt is almost upon us," Signar whispered to Sybal. "The people will come into the darkness if we don't stop it."

She stopped her first reply. She thought the Eldritch Hunt was barbaric and bloody. "Will you participate in the hunt?" she asked.

Signar nodded. "I must. I promised Raudnir that I would kill in his name if I had to. I tried to do away with sacrifice, but he wouldn't let me. It was either that or I promised my children to him."

Sybal teetered on her feet. Thinking of Signar having children made her dizzy. He was still so young. She still saw him as a boy. That scared boy in the cage. But he wasn't. No, he was Reks of Altevine now.

They reached the stone circle in the darkness. Sybal stood back while Signar gave the orders to his warriors, Tage, and Aras. They took the prisoners inside and killed them swiftly before hacking them in two. Beside her, Vicdan retched and turned away, but didn't vomit. Amir waited silently beside her. She felt his eyes on her and wasn't sure what he wanted from her.

"We are ready," Signar called.

Sybal and Amir followed Vicdan into the stone circle, where he stood at the head of the Blood Path. She winced at the grotesque image before her. Vicdan placed his palms close together before his chest and closed his eyes. He whispered the verses and the wind picked up, kicking up snow and blood alike. Sybal gasped and stumbled back into Amir as the blood rose in rivulets and swirled around the opening to the Deep. The blood moved like a knitting needle, stitching the rift back together. Finally, Vicdan pressed his palms together and the rift sealed, vanishing with a thunderous clap. Vicdan cried out and crumpled to the ground.

Amir ran to him and gathered the frail Necro'Khan in his arms. Bloody tears streamed down Vicdan's face and his cheeks were sunken. He lay in Amir's arms, panting and shaking.

Sybal looked around and saw the darkness already starting to wane. The sun glimmered through the shroud and began to light the stone circle. The blue wards on the stones dimmed as the malignation slowly vanished. The grass began to turn from a bleak black to a vibrant green again under the snow.

The more Sybal watched the darkness vanish, the more she saw it was sunset. A huge, orange orb slowly drifted down toward the horizon.

"We need to head back," she whispered. "Night is coming, and there are still monsters afoot."

She went back to Vicdan and helped him up with Amir's assistance. Together, they supported him and started their journey back.

"Thank you, Vicdan," Sybal whispered. "I know this wasn't easy for you."

Vicdan smiled weakly. "You inspired me, Sybal. I couldn't have done it without you."

They'd sleep once they returned to the village, Sybal knew. Then it would be time to say goodbye. She looked up from her march and watched Signar's long yellow hair move gently in the wind.

She had to leave him. She had to let him rule. Her heart twisted in pain and tears sprang to her eyes. She wasn't ready to be alone again, not when she had eternity to endure.

Sybal stalled for a few days, not wanting to leave Signar's side. The boy didn't know she'd been fighting for any reason to stay when he announced that he'd sent a messenger hawk to Northica the night they'd returned from the rift, asking for Ragna to be brought to Altevine now that it was safe. Happy to have this excuse, Sybal decided to stay and meet the woman who would be marrying the boy she loved.

"Before she comes," Signar said to Sybal one morning as they walked the moors around the village, "I have something else to do." He touched the medallion around his neck. "We promised Kazamar we'd free him. I want to do that."

"Here?" Sybal asked. "He could turn on you, destroy everything in Altevine."

"I made a promise," the deep, gravelly voice of the djinn said as he appeared in his spiritual form, arms crossed. "As did you, immortal. And you, boy, have gone back on your promise. One wish, you said, but you tricked me. I am your slave. I have granted your wishes, small though they have been."

"You have no reason to not rain destruction down on us once you are free," Sybal said. "But I cannot stand you being bound to Signar any longer."

"I promised you something long ago, lady Runer," Kazamar said. "That you should join me once you are taken by the touch." He narrowed his eyes. "Keep that promise and I will spare your village."

Sybal arched one brow in amusement. "So simple," she said. "I would no doubt appreciate company once I am made a slave to the Dohkma. Is that all you desire?"

"Companionship for eternity is no small ask," Kazamar retaliated. "And the wishes have only made me stronger. I have no malice held in my heart for you. I desire only my freedom."

Signar held the medallion in his hand. "Then I release you. Take your freedom and be gone."

Kazamar smiled darkly. "So it shall be."

A soft wind blew through the moors and Kazamar took a deep breath. His spiritual body wavered and started to fade. "I will find you again, sister," he whispered as he vanished.

Sybal expected something else, not the soft way in which the djinn vanished. "He almost killed me once," she mused. "I wonder what he has in mind for our eternity together."

"That is some time off, I pray," Signar said. His eyes unfocused on the spot where the djinn had vanished. "I was wondering..." He cleared his throat and turned, making his way back to Altevine. The cold wind picked up and blew their cloaks about, whipping through their long hair.

"What?" Sybal asked. Her heart had an idea that maybe he'd ask her to stay.

"Will you wait before you sail home?" Signar asked. "Until after the mating ceremony?"

Sybal smiled. "I thought you'd never ask." She reached for his hand and held it as they walked back to Altevine.

⤞

Ragna arrived several days later, and the ceremony was carried out one morning as the sun rose over the mountains. Sybal stood back and observed as the Volra tied the couple's hands together and proclaimed them bound to one another. Many from the village came to watch and the celebration after was grand. Ale flowed and fires burned brightly. Many from Northica came to join in the celebration as well. Caerwren was not only celebrating the mating of the lone wolf to Ragna, but also the lifting of the darkness. The revels were unbridled.

Sybal stood in the back of the great hall as the revelries went on into the night when Skarde approached her. The big man smiled at her from behind his ornate golden beard. His gleaming silver axes hung at his side.

"Sybal, our wondering Northican," he said in greeting. "You have done what none of us thought possible." He turned to face Signar and Ragna where they sat, hands bound, at the head of the table. "You have tamed the wildling and brought him back to us. And he has saved his canton from the darkness. You should be proud."

Sybal swallowed down her emotions. "It wasn't me. I was a hinderance, if anything. It was all Tzarik."

358

Skarde nodded and raised his tankard. "To the glorious dead. He was a strong man. Signar spoke of his death. I am sorry, lass. I wished to speak to him again. To thank him for proving me wrong. For standing up to me. Some would say no man survives that. I admired him."

"As did I. I regret many things when it comes to Tzarik." She hid her feelings behind a long drink of the sweet ale.

"What now?" Skarde asked, looking down at her.

She'd been thinking about it for the last few days. She had an idea. "In his memory, I want to lead other Runers like he led me. To teach them, train them. Let them know they are not alone. As many as I can."

At this, Skarde perked up. "I have an idea. The Runers of Caerwren need a shepherd, and they are many. Perhaps if they had some place to go..."

Sybal looked up at Skarde. "What do you suggest?"

"Caer Ragmor," he said, a small smile pulling at his lips. "The castle in the northern mountains of Altevine. It is old and long abandoned, but is still a fortress. You could make use of it. Take the land, lass. Build a haven for Runers to come to you. Train them, teach them well. Show them the ways of the Runer and how they do not have to embrace their degenerate nature. There are other ways, as you have said. You are proof of that, as was Tzarik."

Sybal almost smiled at the idea. "Like an academy. New Runers could come to me and be taught how to hone their abilities. How to live the life of a Runer without succumbing to the darker desires. And I'd have eternity to do it."

"Aye," Skarde mused, giving her a sidelong glance. "I have not forgotten that."

The idea thrilled Sybal the more she thought about it. It would give her purpose, a reason to go on living her eternity. There was no cure for her fate, but she could do something about it.

She suddenly stopped and scoffed, laughing as she shook her head. "This is what the Dohkma meant. He knew all along." Her smile fell. "This was my fate. My Destiny."

"It is not a bad fate," Skarde said.

"I'll do it," she said, a thrill shooting through her as she made her choice. "I will lead the next season of Runers. They will not be abandoned. I will protect them and teach them to live in this world that despises them."

"Spoken like a true mother," Skarde chuckled, wiping at his beard. His eyes fell on Signar. "You did well. I have no doubt you will again." He hummed in thought. "That's what they will call you."

Sybal arched a brow.

Skarde smiled. "The Mother of Runers."

The title shot a warm lance through Sybal. She'd desired nothing more at one time than to be a mother. And now she would be. In a way.

"Yes," she said. "That's what they'll call me. The Mother of Runers."

*The End*

# The Runes

Artiah: The rune of healing. Drawing artiah will mend minor abrasions and heal larger wounds enough to allow escape. Artiah will also take away a small amount of pain.

Atan: The rune of light. Drawing atan will create an orb of light for all eyes to see by. Atan also reveals hidden spirits and can show disguised monsters in their true form.

Buhkar: The rune of mist. When buhkar is drawn, the Runer dissolves into a black, smokey mist able to slip between tight spaces, evade a grip, and blend into shadows easily to be undetected.

Halat: The rune of protection. When halat is drawn, the caster is safe inside a circle of protection. Anything that wishes the caster harm cannot pass the boundaries of the protective circle.

Jiun: The fury rune. Jiun—the most dangerous of the runes—turns the Runer into a berserker. Cutting off all feeling to wounds and ailments, the rune pushes the caster beyond their inhibitions. Jiun also lends temporary strength and heightened senses.

For more information about the world of the Runers, please visit www.abigaillinhardt.com/sotr

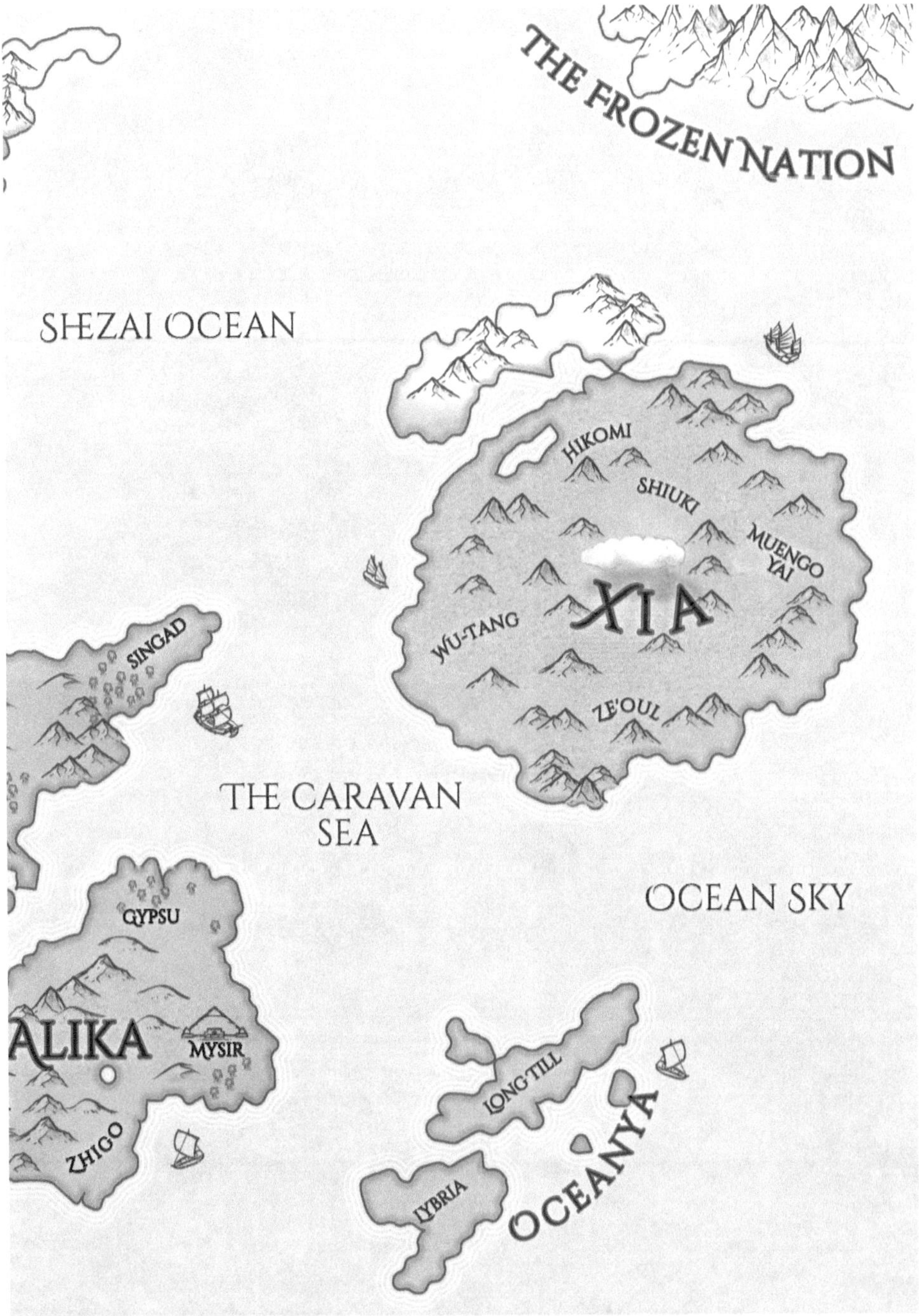

THE FROZEN NATION

SHEZAI OCEAN

HIKOMI

SHIUKI

MUENGO
YAI

XIA

WU-TANG

ZE'OUL

SINGAD

THE CARAVAN
SEA

OCEAN SKY

GYPSU

ALIKA    MYSIR

ZHIGO

LONG TILL

LYBRIA    OCEANYA

Abi works part-time as a freelance ghostwriter, editor, audiobook narrator, and is one half of the partnership that owns Altered Reality Magazine. She hopes to one day make these passions her full-time job while she hunts for the next bohemian adventure.

She has published works of fiction, poetry, academia, and even won awards for her short stories in science fiction and horror. Her novel, The Trial of Two, was named an Honorable Mention in the Writer's Digest 2021 self-publishing awards and won first place in the dark fantasy category in The BookFest Awards. Abi is also a proud mom of two ferrets. She currently resides in Kansas.

Abi is one of nine children--all who share the creative spark.

Find Abi online at: www.abigaillinhardt.com

## ALSO BY ABIGAIL LINHARDT

Season of the Runer Book I: The Trial of Two
Season of the Runer Book II: Sojourn
Season of the Runer Book III: The Eldritch Hunt
Season of the Runer IV: The Father of Monsters
Prince of MidWest
Why They Killed: A Waksha Virus Novelette
These Darker Streets

### Writing as A.J. Morgenstern
DarkFront Witness: Haunted
DarkFront Witness: Hunted
DarkFront Witness: Free

Coming Winter 2025

# SHADOW OF THE WINDSLAYER

A new, epic, grimdark fantasy series from Abigail Linhardt.